Rags to
RICHES
—— A DESIRE TO SERVE ——

Rags to
RICHES
COLLECTION

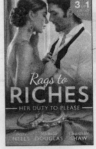

April 2017

May 2017

June 2017

July 2017

August 2017

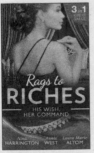

September 2017

Rags to RICHES

— A DESIRE TO SERVE —

Merline
LOVELACE

Teresa
CARPENTER

Janice
MAYNARD

MILLS & BOON

Published in Great Britain 2017
By Mills & Boon, an imprint of HarperCollins*Publishers*
1 London Bridge Street, London, SE1 9GF

RAGS TO RICHES: A DESIRE TO SERVE
© 2017 Harlequin Books S.A.

The Paternity Promise © 2012 Merline Lovelace
Stolen Kiss from a Prince © 2014 Teresa Carpenter
The Maid's Daughter © 2012 Janice Maynard

ISBN: 978-0-263-93092-4

09-0817

THE PATERNITY PROMISE

MERLINE LOVELACE

*To the Elite Eight, and the
wonderful times we've shared.*

*Thanks for giving me such
terrific fodder for my books!*

A career Air Force officer, **Merline Lovelace**
served at bases all over the world. When she
hung up her uniform for the last time, she decided
to try her hand at storytelling. Since then more
than twelve million copies of her books had been
published in over thirty countries. Check her
website at www.merlinelovelace.com or friend
Merline on Facebook for news and information
about her latest releases.

One

His fists balled inside the pockets of his tuxedo pants, Blake Dalton forced a smile as he stood amid the wedding guests jamming the black-and-white-tiled foyer of his mother's Oklahoma City mansion. The lavish reception was finally winding down. The newlyweds had just paused in their descent of the foyer's circular marble staircase so the bride could toss her bouquet. The couple were mere moments from departing for their honeymoon in Tuscany.

Blake was damned if he'd block their escape. His twin had waged a tumultuous battle to win the stubbornly independent pilot he'd finally finessed to the altar. Alex had earned these two weeks in Tuscany with his new bride, away from his heavy responsibilities as CEO of Dalton International.

Blake had no problem taking up the slack in his absence. An MBA, a law degree and almost a decade of handling the corporation's complex legal affairs had honed the leadership and managerial skills he'd developed as DI's CFO. He and Alex regularly took over sole control of the multibillion-dollar conglomerate during each other's frequent business trips.

No, the job wasn't the problem.

Nor was it their mother, who'd waged a fierce and unrelenting campaign to get her sons married and settled down for over a year now.

Blake's glance cut to the matriarch of the Dalton clan. Her hair was still jet-black, with only a hint of silver at the temples. She wore a melon-colored Dior lace dress and an expression of smug satisfaction as she surveyed the newly married couple. Blake knew exactly what she was thinking. One son down, one to go.

But it was the baby peering over his mother's shoulder that made his fist bunch even tighter and his heart squeeze inside his chest. In the weeks since person or persons unknown had left the six-month-old on his mother's doorstep, Molly had become as essential to Blake as breathing.

DNA testing had proved with 99.99 percent certainty that the bright-eyed infant girl was a Dalton. Unfortunately, the tests hadn't returned the same accuracy as to *which* of the Dalton brothers had fathered the baby. Although even identical twins carried distinctive DNA, there were enough similarities to fog the question of paternity. The report had indicated a seventy-seven percent probability that Alex was the father, but the issue couldn't be completely resolved until the lab matched the father's DNA with that of the mother.

As a result, the Dalton brothers had spent several uncomfortable weeks after Molly's arrival tracking down the women they'd connected with early last year. Alex's list had been considerably longer than Blake's, but none of the potential candidates—including the woman who'd just become Ms. Alex Dalton—had proved to be the baby's mother. Or so they'd thought.

A noisy round of farewells wrenched Blake's gaze from the baby. He looked up to find his brother searching the crowd. It was like looking in a mirror. Both he and Alex had their father's build. Like Big Jake Dalton, they carried six feet plus of solid muscle. They'd also inherited their father's electric blue eyes and tawny hair that the hot Oklahoma sun streaked to a dozen different shades of gold.

Blake caught Alex's eye and casually, so casually, shook his head. He had to forcibly blank both his face and his mind to block any more subtle signals. In the way of all twins, the Dalton brothers could pick up instantly on each other's vibes. Time enough for Alex and Julie to hear the news when they got back from Tuscany. By then Blake would have dealt with it. And with the shock and fury it had generated.

He rigidly suppressed both emotions until the newlyweds were on the way to the airport. Even then he did his duty and mingled until the last guests finally departed. His training as an attorney stood him in good stead. No one, not even his mother, suspected there was fury boiling in his gut.

"Whew!" Ebullient but drooping, Delilah Dalton kicked off her heels. "That was fun, but I'm glad it's over. Went off well, don't you think?"

"Very," Blake answered evenly.

"I'm going to check on Molly." She swooped up her shoes and padded on stockinged feet to the circular marble staircase. "Then I'm hitting the tub to soak for an hour. You staying here tonight?"

"No, I'll go back to my place." With a vicious exercise of will, he kept his voice calm. "Would you ask Grace to come down? I'd like to talk to her before I go."

His mother lifted a brow at his request to speak to the woman she'd hired to act as a temporary nanny. In the weeks since a baby had dropped into the lives of all three Daltons, Grace Templeton had proved indispensable. Become almost part of the family. So much so that she'd served as Julie's maid of honor while Blake stood up with Alex as best man.

She'd also started the wheels turning in Delilah's fertile mind. His mother had begun dropping unsubtle hints in recent days about how sweet Grace was. How well she interacted with Molly. And just tonight, how good Blake had looked standing beside her at the altar. The fact that he'd begun to think along those same lines only added to the fury simmering hot and heavy.

"Tell Grace I'll be in the library."

For once Delilah was too tired to pry. She merely waved her shoes and continued up the stairs. "Will do. Just don't keep her too long. She has to feel as whipped as I do."

She was about to feel a whole lot more whipped. Yanking on the ends of his black bow tie, Blake stalked down the hall to the oak-paneled library. The soft glow from the recessed lighting contrasted starkly with his black mood as he retrieved the report he'd stuffed into his pocket more than an hour ago. The facts were no less shattering now than they had been then. He was still trying to absorb their impact when Grace Templeton entered the library.

"Hey, Blake. Delilah said you wanted to talk to me."

His eyes narrowed on the slender blonde, seeing her in a wholly different light. She'd changed from the lilac, off-the-shoulder tea gown she'd worn for the wedding. She'd also released her pale, almost silvery hair from its sophisticated upsweep. The ends now brushed the shoulders of a sleeveless white blouse sporting several large splotches.

"'Scuze the wet spots," she said, brushing a hand down her front with a rueful laugh in her warm brown eyes. "Molly got a little lively during her bath."

Blake didn't respond. He merely stood with his shoulders rigid under his tux as she hitched a hip on the wide, rolled arm of the library's sofa.

"What did you want to talk about?"

Only then did she pick up on his silence. Or maybe it was his stance. Her head tilting, she gave him a puzzled half smile.

"Something wrong?"

He countered her question with one of his own. "Did you happen to notice the man who arrived at the reception just before Alex and Julie left?"

"The guy in the brown suit?" She nodded slowly, still trying to gauge his odd mood. "I saw him, and couldn't help wondering who he was. He looked so out of place among the other guests."

"His name's Del Jamison."

Her brow creased. Blake guessed she was mentally sorting through the host of people she'd met during her stint as Molly's temporary nanny. When she drew a blank, he supplied the details.

"Jamison's a private investigator. The one Alex and I hired to help search for Molly's mother."

She was good, he thought savagely. Very good. Her cinnamon eyes transmitted only a flicker of wariness, quickly suppressed, but she couldn't keep the color from leaching out of her cheeks. The sudden pallor gave him a vicious satisfaction.

"Oh, right." The shrug was an obvious attempt at nonchalance. "He was down in South America, wasn't he? Checking the places where Julie worked last year?"

"He was, but after Julie made it clear she wasn't Molly's mother, Jamison decided to check another lead. In California."

She couldn't hide her fear now. It was there in the quick hitch in her breath, the sudden stillness.

"California?"

"I'll summarize his report for you." Blake used his courtroom voice. The one he employed when he wanted to drive home a point. Cool, flat, utterly devoid of emotion. "Jamison discovered the woman I was told had died in a fiery bus crash was not, in fact, even on that bus. She didn't die until almost a year later."

The same woman he'd had a brief affair with. The woman who'd disappeared from his life with no goodbye, no note, no explanation of any kind. Aided and abetted, he now knew, by this brown-eyed, soft-spoken schemer who'd wormed her way into his mother's home.

And into Blake's consciousness, dammit. Every level of it. As disgusted by her duplicity as by the hunger she'd begun to stir in him, he stalked across the room. She sprang to her feet at his approach and tried to brazen it out.

"I don't see what that has to do with me."

Still he didn't lose control. But his muscles quivered with the effort of keeping his hands off her.

"According to Jamison, this woman gave birth to a baby girl just weeks before she died."

His baby! His Molly!

"She also had a friend who showed up at the hospital mere hours before her death." He planted his fists on the sofa arm, boxing her in, forcing her to lean back. "A *friend* with pale blond hair."

"Blake!" The gold-flecked brown eyes he'd begun to imagine turning liquid with desire widened in alarm. "Listen to me!"

"No, Grace—if that's really your name." His temper slipped through, adding a whiplash to his voice. "You listen, and listen good. I don't know how much you figured you could extort from our family, but the game ends now."

"It's not a game," she gasped, bent at an awkward angle.

"No?"

"No! I don't want your money!"

"What do you want?"

"Just… Just…!" She slapped her palms against his shirtfront. "Oh, for Pete's sake! Get off me."

He didn't budge. "Just what?"

"Dammit!" Goaded, she bunched a fist and pounded his chest. Her fear was gone. Fury now burned in her cheeks. "All I wanted, all I cared about, was making sure Molly had a good home!"

Slowly, Blake straightened. Just as slowly, he moved back a step and allowed her only enough space to push upright. Slapping a rigid lid on his anger, he folded his arms and locked his gaze on her face. Assessing. Considering. Evaluating.

"Let's start at the beginning. Who the hell are you?"

Grace balanced precariously on the sofa arm, her thoughts chaotic. After all she'd been through! So much fear and heartache. Now this? Just when she'd started to breathe easy for the first time in months. Just when she'd thought she and this man might...

"Who are you?"

He repeated the question in what she'd come to think of as his counselor's voice. She'd known Blake Dalton for almost two months now. In that time she'd learned to appreciate his even temperament. She admired even more his ability to smoothly, calmly arbitrate between his more outspoken twin and their equally strong-willed mother.

Oh, God! Delilah!

Grace cringed inside at the idea of divulging even part of the sordid truth to the woman who'd become as much of a friend as an employer. Sick at the thought, she lifted her chin and met Blake's cold, unwavering stare.

"I'm exactly who I claim to be. My name *is* Grace Templeton. I teach...I taught," she corrected, her throat tight, "junior high social studies in San Antonio until a few months ago."

She paused, trying not to think of the life she'd put on hold, forcing herself to blank out the image of the young teens she took such joy in teaching.

"Until a few months ago," Blake repeated in the heavy silence, "when you asked for an extended leave of absence to take care of a sick relative. That's the story you gave us, isn't it? And the principal of your school?"

She knew they'd checked her out. Neither Delilah nor her sons would allow a stranger near the baby unless they'd vetted her. But Grace had become so adept these past years at weaving just enough truth in with the lies that she'd passed their screening.

"It wasn't a story."

Dalton's breath hissed out. Those sexy blue eyes that

had begun to smile at her with something more than friendliness the past few weeks were now lethal.

"You and Anne Jordan were related?"

Anne Jordan. Emma Lang. Janet Blair. So many aliases. So many frantic phone calls and desperate escapes. Grace could hardly keep them straight anymore.

"Anne was my cousin."

That innocuous label didn't begin to describe Grace's relationship to the girl who'd grown up just a block away. They were far closer than cousins. They were best friends who'd played dolls and whispered secrets and shared every event in their young lives, big and small.

"Were you with her when she died?"

The question came at her as swiftly and mercilessly as a stiletto aimed for the heart. "Yes," she whispered, "I was with her."

"And the baby? Molly?"

"She's your daughter. Yours and…and Anne's."

Blake turned away, and Grace could only stare at the broad shoulders still encased in his tux. She ached to tell him she was sorry for all the lies and deception. Except the lies had been necessary, and the deception wasn't hers to tell.

"Anne called me," she said instead. "Told me she'd picked up a vicious infection. Begged me to come. I jumped a plane that same afternoon but when I got there, she was already slipping into a coma. She died that evening."

Blake angled back to face her. His eyes burned with an unspoken question. Grace answered this one as honestly as she could.

"Anne didn't name you as Molly's father. She was almost out of it from the drugs they'd pumped into her.

She was barely coherent… All I understood was the name Dalton. I knew she'd worked here, so…so…"

She broke off, her throat raw with the memory.

"So you brought Molly to Oklahoma City," Blake finished, spacing every word with frightening deliberation, "and left her on my mother's doorstep. Then you called Delilah and said you'd just happened to hear she needed a temporary nanny."

"Which she did!"

He gave that feeble response the disgust it deserved. "Did you enjoy watching my brother and me jump through hoops trying to determine which of us was Molly's father?"

"I told you! I didn't know which of you it was. Not until I'd spent some time with you."

Even then she hadn't been sure. The Dalton twins shared more than razor-sharp intelligence and devastating good looks. Grace could see how her cousin might have succumbed to Alex's charisma and self-confidence. She'd actually figured him for Molly's father until she'd come to appreciate the rock-solid strength in quiet, coolly competent Blake.

Unfortunately, Blake's self-contained personality had made her task so much more difficult. Although friendly and easygoing, he kept his thoughts to himself and his private life private. If he'd had a brief affair with a woman who'd worked for him, only he—and possibly his twin—had known about it.

Grace had hoped the DNA tests they'd run would settle the question of Molly's paternity. She'd been as frustrated as the Dalton brothers at the ambiguous results.

Then they'd launched a determined search for Molly's mother and thrown Grace in a state of near panic. She'd sworn to keep her cousin's secret. She had no choice but to do just that. Molly's future depended on it. Now Blake had unearthed at least a part of that secret. She couldn't tell him the rest, but she could offer a tentative solution.

"As I understand it, Molly's parentage can't be absolutely established unless the father's DNA is matched with the mother's. She…Anne…was cremated. I don't have anything of hers to give you that would provide a sample."

Not a hairbrush or a lipstick or even a postcard with a stamp on it for Molly to cling to as a keepsake. The baby's mother had lived in fear for so long. She'd died the same way, mustering only enough strength at the end to extract a promise from her cousin to keep Molly safe.

"You could test my DNA," Grace said, determined to hold to that promise. "I've read that mitochondria are inherited exclusively through the female line."

She'd done more than read. She'd hunched in front of the computer for hours when not tending to Molly. Her head had spun trying to decipher scientific articles laced with terms like hypervariable control regions and HVR1 base pairs. It had taken some serious slogging, but she'd finally come away with the knowledge that those four-hundred-and-forty-four base pairs determined maternal lineage. As such, they could theoretically be used to trace a human's lineage all the way back to the mitochondrial Eve. The Daltons didn't need to go that far back to confirm Molly's heritage. They just needed to hop over one branch on her family tree.

The same thought had obviously occurred to Blake. His eyes were chips of blue ice as he delivered an ultimatum.

"Damn straight you'll give me a DNA sample. And until the results come back, you'll stay away from Molly."

"What?"

"You heard me. I want you out of this house. Now."

"You're kidding!"

She discovered an instant later that he wasn't. In two strides he'd closed the distance between them and wrapped his fist around her upper arm. One swift tug had her off the sofa arm and marching toward the library's door.

"Blake, for God's sake!" As surprised as she was angry, she fought his grip. "I've been taking care of Molly for weeks now. You can't seriously think I would do anything to hurt her."

"What I think," he returned in a voice as icy as his eyes, "is that there are a helluva lot of holes in your story. Until they're filled in, I want you where I can watch you day *and* night."

Two

"Get in."

Blake held open the passenger door of his two-seater Mercedes convertible. The heat of the muggy July evening wrapped around them, almost as smothering as the worry and fear that clogged Grace's throat.

"Where are we going?"

"Downtown."

"I need to tell Delilah that I'm leaving," she protested. "Get some of my things."

"I'll let my mother know what's happening. Right now all you need to do is plant your behind in that seat."

If Grace hadn't been so stunned by this unexpected turn of events, the brusque command might have made her blink. This was Blake. The kind, polite, always solicitous Dalton twin. In the weeks since she'd insinuated herself into Delilah's home, she'd never known him to be anything but patient with his sometimes overbearing mother, considerate with the servants and incredibly, achingly gentle with Molly.

"Get in."

She got. Even this late in the evening, the pale gray leather was warm and sticky from the July heat. The seat belt cracked like a rifle shot when she clicked it into place.

As the convertible rolled down the curved driveway, Grace fought to untangle her nerves. God knew she should be used to having her life turned upside down without warning. It had happened often enough in the past few years. One call. That's all it usually took. One frantic call from Hope.

No, she corrected fiercely. Not Hope. *Anne.* Although her cousin was dead, Grace had to remember to think and remember and refer to her as Anne.

She made that her mantra as the Mercedes sliced through the night. She was still repeating it when Blake pulled into the underground parking for Dalton International's headquarters building in downtown Oklahoma City. Although the clicker attached to the Mercedes's visor raised the arm, the booth attendant leaned out with cheerful greeting.

"Evenin', Mr. Dalton."

"Hi, Roy."

"Guess your brother 'n his bride are off on their honeymoon."

"Yes, they are."

"Sure wish 'em well." He leaned farther down and tipped a finger to his brow. "How're you doin', Ms. Templeton?"

She dredged up a smile. "Fine, thanks."

Grace wasn't surprised at the friendly greeting. She'd made many a trip to Dalton International's headquarters with Molly and her grandmother. Delilah had turned over control of the manufacturing empire she and Big Jake had scratched out of bare dirt to her sons. That didn't mean she'd surrendered her right to meddle as she saw fit in either DI's corporate affairs or in her sons' lives. So Delilah, with Molly and her nanny in tow, had regularly breezed into boardrooms and conferences. Just as often, she'd zoomed up to the top floor of the DI building, where her bachelor sons maintained their separate penthouse apartments.

The penthouse also boasted a luxurious guest suite for DI's visiting dignitaries. That, apparently, was where Blake had decided to plant her. Grace guessed as much when he stopped at the security desk in the lower lobby to retrieve a key card. Moments later the glass-enclosed elevator whisked them upward.

Once past the street level, Oklahoma City zoomed into view. On previous visits Grace had gasped at the skyline that rose story by eye-popping story. Tonight she barely noticed the panorama of lights and skyscrapers. Her entire focus was on the man crowding her against the elevator's glass wall.

She hadn't been able to tell which Dalton twin was which at first. With their dark gold hair, chiseled chins and broad shoulders, one was a feast for the eyes. Two of them standing side by side could make any woman drool.

It hadn't taken Grace long to separate the men. Alex was more outgoing, with a wicked grin that jump-started female hormones without him half trying. Blake was quieter. Less obvious. With a smile that was all the more seductive for being slow and warm and...

The ping of the elevator wrenched her back to the tortuous present. When the doors slid open, Blake grasped her arm again and marched her down a plushly carpeted hall toward a set of polished oak doors.

Okay, enough! Grace didn't get angry often. When she did, her temper flashed hot and fierce enough to burn through the fear still gripping her by the throat.

"That's it!" She yanked her arm free of his hold and stopped dead in the center of the hall. "You hustle me out of your mother's house like a thief caught stealing the silver. You order me into your bright, shiny convertible. You drag me up here in the middle of the night. I'm not taking another step until you stop acting like you're the Gestapo or KGB."

He arched a brow at her rant, then coolly, deliberately shot back the cuff of his pleated tux shirt to check his gold Rolex.

"It's nine-twenty-two. Hardly the middle of the night."

She wanted to hit him. Slap that stony expression right off his too-handsome face. Might have actually attempted it if she wasn't sure she would crack a couple of finger bones on his hard, unyielding jaw.

Besides which, he deserved some answers. The detective's report had obviously delivered a body blow. He'd loved her cousin once.

The fire drained from Grace's heart, leaving only sadness tinged now with an infinite weariness. "All right. I'll tell you what I can."

With a curt nod, he strode the last few feet to the guest suite. A swipe of the key card clicked the lock on the wide oak doors. Grace had visited the lavish guest suite a number of times. Each time she stepped inside, though, the sheer magnificence of the view stopped her breath in her throat.

Angled floor-to-ceiling glass walls gave a stunning, hundred-and-eighty-degree panorama of Oklahoma City's skyline. The view was spectacular during the day, offering an eagle's-eye glimpse of the domed capitol building, the Oklahoma River and the colorful barges that carried tourists past Bricktown Ballpark to the larger-than-life-size bronze sculptures commemorating the 1889 land run. That momentous event had opened some two million acres of unassigned land to settlers and, oh, by the way, created a tent city with a population of more than fifty thousand almost overnight.

The view on a clear summer night like this one was even more dazzling. Skyscrapers glowed like beacons. White lights twinkled in the trees lining the river spur that meandered through the downtown area. But it was the colossal bronze statue atop the floodlit capitol that drew Grace to the windows. She'd been born and bred in Texas, but as a social studies teacher she knew enough of the history of the Southwest to appreciate the deep symbolism in the twenty-two-foot-tall bronze statue. She'd also been given a detailed history of the statue by Delilah, who'd served on the committee that raised funds for it.

Erected in 2002, *The Guardian,* with his tall spear, muscular body and unbowed head, represented not only the thousands of Native Americans who'd been forced from their homes in the East and settled in what was then Indian Territory. The statue also embodied Oklahomans who'd wrestled pipe into red dirt as hard as brick to suck out the oil that fueled the just-born automobile industry. The sons and daughters who lived through the devastating Dust Bowl of the '30s. The proud Americans who'd worked rotating shifts at the Army Air Corps' Douglas Aircraft Plant in the '40s to overhaul, repair and build fighters and bombers. And, most recently, the grimly determined Oklahomans who'd dug through nine stories of rubble to recover the bodies of friends and coworkers killed in the Murrah Building bombing.

Grace and Hope... No! Grace and *Anne* had driven up from Texas during their junior year in high school to visit Oklahoma City's National Memorial & Museum. Neither of them had been able to comprehend how the homegrown terrorist Timothy McVeigh could be so evil, so twisted in both mind and morals. Then, less than a year later, her cousin met Jack Petrie.

Frost coated Grace's lungs. Feeling its sick chill, she wrapped both arms around her waist and turned away from *The Guardian* to face Blake Dalton.

"I can't tell you about Anne's past," she said bleakly. "I promised I would bury it with her. What I *can* say is that you're the only man she got close to in more years than you want to know."

"You think I'm going to be satisfied with that?"

"You have no choice."

"Wrong."

He yanked on the dangling end of his bow tie and threw it aside before shrugging out of his tuxedo jacket. His black satin cummerbund circled a trim waist. The pleated white shirt was still crisp, as might be expected from a tailor who catered exclusively to millionaires and movie stars.

Yet under the sleek sophistication was an edge that didn't fool Grace for a moment. Delilah bragged constantly about the variety of sports Blake and his twin had excelled at during their school years. Both men still carried an athlete's build—lean in the hips and flanks, with the solid chest and muscled shoulders of a former collegiate wrestler.

That chest loomed far too large in Grace's view at the moment. It invaded her space, distracted her thoughts and made her distinctly nervous.

"How many cousins do you have?" he asked with silky menace. "And how long do you think it will take Jamison to check each of them out?"

"Not long," she fired back. "But he won't find anything beyond Anne's birth certificate, driver's license and a few high school yearbook photos. We made sure of that."

"A person can't just erase her entire life after high school."

"As a matter of fact, she can."

Grace moved to the buckskin leather sofa and dropped onto a cushion. Blake folded his tall frame onto a matching sofa separated by a half acre of glass-topped coffee table.

"It's not easy. Or cheap," she added, thinking of her empty savings account. "But you can pull it off with the help of a very smart friend of a friend of a friend. Especially if said friend can tap into just about any computer system."

Like the Texas Vital Statistics agency. It had taken some serious hacking but they'd managed to delete the digital entry recording Hope Patricia Templeton's marriage to Jack David Petrie. By doing so, they'd also deleted the record of the last time Grace had used her maiden name and SSN.

A familiar sadness settled like a lump in Grace's middle. Her naive, trusting cousin had believed Petrie's promise to love and cherish and provide for her every need. As the bastard had explained in the months that followed, his wife didn't require access to their bank account. Or a credit card. Or a job. Nor did she have to register to vote. There weren't any candidates worth going to that trouble for. And they sure as hell didn't need to talk to a marriage counselor, he'd added when she finally realized he'd made her a virtual prisoner.

Financially dependent and emotionally battered, she'd spent long, isolated years as a shadow person. Jack trotted her out when he wanted to display his pretty wife, then shuffled her back into her proper place in his bed. It hadn't taken him long to cut off her ties with her friends and family, either. All except Grace. She refused to be cut, even after Petrie became furious over her meddling. Grace wondered whether those horrific moments when her gas pedal locked on the interstate were, in fact, due to mechanical failure.

Grace and Hope had become more cautious after that. No more visits. No letters or emails that could be intercepted. No calls to the house. Only to a pay phone in the one grocery store where Jack allowed his wife to shop. Even then it had taken a solid year of pleading before Hope worked up the courage to escape.

Grace didn't want to remember the desperate years that followed. The mindless fear. The countless moves. The series of false identities and fake SSNs, each one more expensive to procure than the last. Until finally— *finally!*—a woman with the name of Anne Jordan had found anonymity and a tenuous, tentative security at Dalton International. She'd been just one of DI's thousands of employees worldwide. An entry-level clerk with only a high school GED. Certainly not a position that would bring her into contact with the multinational corporation's CFO.

Yet it had.

"Please, Blake. Please believe me when I tell you Anne wanted her past to be buried with her. All she cared about in her last, agonizing moments was making sure Molly would know her father, if not her mother."

Or more accurately, that her baby would have the name and protection of someone completely unknown to Jack Petrie.

Grace prayed she'd convinced Blake. She hadn't, of course. The lawyer in him wouldn't be satisfied until he'd dug up and turned over every bit of evidence. But maybe she could deflect his inquisition.

"Will you tell me something?"

"Quid pro quo?" His mouth twisted. "You haven't given me much of a trade."

"Please. I…I wasn't able to talk or visit with Anne much in her last year."

She hadn't dared. Jack Petrie was a Texas state trooper, with a cop's wide connections. Grace knew he'd had her under surveillance at various times, maybe even bugged her phone or planted a tracking device on her car, hoping she would lead him to his wife. Grace had imposed on every friend she had, borrowing their cars or using their phones, to maintain even minimal contact with her cousin.

Jack didn't know about Grace's last, frantic flight to California. She'd made sure of that. She'd emptied her savings account, had a friend drive her to the airport and paid cash for a ticket to Vegas. There she'd rented a car for a desperate drive across the desert to the San Diego hospital where her cousin had been admitted.

Five heart-wrenching days later, she'd retraced that route with Molly. Instead of flying back to San Antonio with the baby, though, she'd paid cash for a bus ticket to Oklahoma City.

She hadn't used her cell phone or any credit cards in the weeks since she'd wrangled a job as Molly's temporary nanny. Nor had she cashed the checks Delilah had written for her salary. She'd planned to go back to her teaching job once Molly was settled with her father. The longer she spent with the baby, though, the more painful the prospect of leaving her became.

The thought of leaving Blake Dalton was almost as wrenching. Lately her mind had drifted to him more than it should. Especially at night, after she'd put Molly to bed. The increasingly erotic direction of that drift spurred pinpricks of guilt, then and now.

"Tell me how you and Anne met," she pleaded, reminding herself yet again Blake was her cousin's love, the man she'd let into her life despite all she'd been through. "How... Well..."

"How Molly happened?" he supplied.

"Yes. Anne was so shy around men."

For shy, read insecure and cowed and generally scared *shitless*. Grace couldn't imagine how Blake had breached those formidable barriers.

"Please," she said softly. "Tell me. I'd like to know she found a little happiness before she died."

He stared at her for long moments, then his breath eased out on a sigh.

"I think she was happy for the few weeks we were together. I was never sure, though. Took me forever to pry more than a murmured hello from her. Even after I got her to agree to go out with me, she didn't want anyone at DI to know we were seeing each other. Said it would look bad, the big boss dating a lowly file clerk."

He hooked his wrists on his knees and contemplated his black dress shoes. He must not have liked what he saw. A note of unmistakable self-disgust colored his deep voice.

"She wouldn't let me take her to dinner or to the theater or anywhere we might be seen together. It was always her place. Or a hotel."

It had to be that, Grace knew. Her cousin couldn't take the chance some society reporter or gossip columnist would start fanning rumors about rich, handsome Blake Dalton's latest love interest. Or worse, the paparazzi might snap a photo of them together and post it on the internet.

Yet she risked going to a hotel with him. She'd come out of her defensive crouch enough for that. And when she discovered she was pregnant with his child, she'd had no choice but to run away. She wanted the baby desperately, but she couldn't tell Dalton about the pregnancy. He would have wanted to give the child his name, or at least establish his legal rights as the father. Hope's false IDs wouldn't have held up under legal scrutiny, and her real one would have led Petrie to her. So she'd run. Again.

"Did you love her?"

Damn! Grace hadn't meant to let that slip out. And she sure as heck hadn't intended to feel jealous of her cousin's relationship with this man.

Yet she knew he had to have been so tender with her. So sensitive to her needs. His mouth would have played a gentle song on her skin. His hands, those strong, tanned hands, must have stroked and soothed even as they aroused and...

"I don't know."

With a flush of guilt, Grace jerked her attention back to his face.

"I cared for her," he said quietly, as much to himself

as to her. "Enough to press her into going to bed with me. But when she left without a word, I was angry as well as hurt."

Regret and remorse chased each other across his face.

"Then, when I got the report of the bus accident…"

He stopped and directed a look of fierce accusation at Grace.

"I wasn't with her when it happened," she said in feeble self-defense. "She was by herself, in her car. The bus spun out right in front of her and hit a bridge abutment. She was terrified, but she got out to help."

"And left her purse at the scene."

"Yes."

"Deliberately?"

"Yes."

"Why?"

Grace shook her head. "I can't tell you why. I can't tell you any more than I have. I promised Anne her past would die with her."

"But it didn't," he countered swiftly. "Molly's living proof of that."

She slipped off the sofa and onto her knees, desperate for him to let it go. "She's your daughter, Blake. Please, just accept that and take joy in her."

He was silent for so long she didn't think he would respond. When he did, the ice was back in his voice.

"All I have right now is your word that Anne and I had a child together. I'll send in the DNA sample you offered to provide. Once we have the results, we'll discuss where we go from here."

"Where I need to go is back to your mother's house! She's exhausted from the wedding. She told me tonight she was feeling every one of her sixty-two years. She can't take care of Molly by herself for the next few days."

"I'll help her, and when I can't be there I'll make sure someone else is. In the meantime, you stay put."

He pushed out of the chair and strode to the wet bar built into the far wall. For a moment Grace thought he intended to pour them both a drink to wash down the hurt and bitterness of the past hour, but he lifted only one crystal tumbler from one of the mirrored shelves. He returned with it and issued a terse command.

"Spit."

Three

The melodic chimes of a doorbell pierced Grace's groggy haze. When the chimes gave way to the hammer of an impatient fist, she propped herself up on one elbow and blinked at the digital clock beside the bed.

Oh, God! Seven-twenty! She'd slept right through Molly's first feeding.

She threw the covers aside and was half out of bed before reality hit. One, this wasn't her room in Delilah's mansion. Two, she was wearing only the lavender lace bikini briefs she left on when she'd changed her maid of honor gown. And three, she was no longer Molly's temporary nanny.

Last night's agonizing events came crashing down on her as the fist hammered again. Scrambling, Grace snatched up her now hopelessly wrinkled khaki crops and white blouse. She got the pants zipped and buttoned the blouse on her way to the front door. She had a good idea whose fist was pounding away. She'd spent almost a month now with Blake Dalton's often autocratic, occasionally irascible, always kindhearted mother.

So she expected to see the raven-haired matriarch. She *didn't* expect to see the baby riding on Delilah's chest, nested contentedly in a giraffe sling. Grace gripped the brass door latch, swamped by an avalanche of love and worry and guilt as she dragged her gaze from the infant to her grandmother.

"Delilah, I…"

"Don't you Delilah me!" She stomped inside, the soles of her high-topped sneakers slapping the marble foyer. "Don't you dare Delilah me!"

Grace closed the door and followed her into the living room. She wished she'd taken a few seconds to brush her hair and slap some water on her face before this showdown. And coffee! She needed coffee. Desperately.

She'd tossed and turned most of the night. The few hours she'd drifted into a doze, she'd dreamed of Anne. And Blake. Grace had been there, too, stunned when his fury at her swirled without warning into a passion that jerked her awake, breathless and wanting. Remnants of that mindless hunger still drifted like a steamy haze through her mind as Delilah slung a diaper bag from her shoulder onto the sofa and released Molly from the sling.

Grace couldn't help but note that her employer had gone all jungle today. The diaper bag was zebra-striped. Grinning monkeys frolicked and swung from vines on the baby's seersucker dress. Delilah herself was in knee-length leopard tights topped by an oversize black T-shirt with a neon message urging folks to come out and be amazed by Oklahoma City's new gorilla habitat—a habitat she'd coaxed, cajoled and strong-armed her friends into funding.

"Don't just stand there," she snapped at Grace. "Get the blanket out of the diaper bag."

Even the blanket was a riot of green and yellow and jungle red. Grace spread it a safe distance away from the glass coffee table. Molly was just learning to crawl. She could push herself onto her hands and knees and hold her head up to survey the world with bright, inquisitive eyes.

Delilah deposited the baby on the blanket and made sure she was centered before pointing an imperious finger at Grace.

"You. Sit." The older woman plunked herself down in the opposite chair, keeping the baby between them. "Now talk."

"You sure you wouldn't like some coffee first?" Grace asked with a hopeful glance at the suite's fully equipped kitchen. "I could make a quick pot."

"Screw coffee. Talk."

Grace blew out a sigh and raked her fingers through her unbrushed hair. Obviously Delilah had no intention of making this easy.

"I don't know how much Blake told you…" She let that dangle for a moment. Got no response. "Okay, here's the condensed version. Molly's mother was my cousin. When Anne worked at Dalton International, she had a brief affair with your son. She died before she could tell me *which* son, so I brought Molly to you and finessed a job as her nanny while Alex and Blake sorted out the paternity issue."

Delilah pinned Grace with a look that could have etched steel. "If one of my sons got this cousin of yours pregnant, why didn't she have the guts or the decency to let him know about the baby?"

Grace stiffened. Shielding Hope—*Anne!*—had become as much a part of her as breathing. No one knew what her cousin had endured. And Grace was damned if she'd allow anyone, even the formidable Delilah Dalton, to put her down.

"I told Blake and I'll tell you. Anne had good reasons for what she did, but she wanted those reasons to die with her. She didn't, however, want her baby to grow up without knowing either of her parents."

Delilah fired back with both barrels. "Don't get uppity with me, girl!"

The fierce retort startled the baby. Molly swung her head toward her grandmother, wobbled and plopped down on one diapered hip. Both women instinctively bent toward her, but she was already pushing back onto her knees.

Delilah moderated her tone if not her message. "I'm the one who bought your out-of-work schoolteacher story, remember? I took you into my home. I trusted you, dammit."

Grace didn't see any use in pointing out that she hadn't lied about being a teacher or temporarily out of work. The trust part stung enough.

"I'm sorry I couldn't tell you about my connection to Molly."

"Ha!"

"I promised my cousin I would make sure her child was loved and cared for." Her glance went again to the baby, happily drooling and rocking on hands and knees. Slowly, she brought her gaze back to Delilah. "And she is," Grace said softly. "Well cared for and very much loved."

Delilah huffed out something close to a snort but

didn't comment for long moments. "I pride myself on being a good judge of character," she said at last. "Even that horny goat I married lived up to almost everything I'd expected of him."

Grace didn't touch that one. She'd heard Delilah say more than once she wished to hell Big Jake Dalton hadn't died before she'd found out about his little gal pal. His passing would've been a lot less peaceful.

"Is all this you've just told me true?" the Dalton matriarch demanded.

"Yes, ma'am."

"Molly's mother was really your cousin?"

"Yes."

"Well, I guess we'll have proof of that soon enough. Damned lab is making a fortune off all these rush DNA tests we've ordered lately."

She pooched her lips and moved them from side to side before coming to an abrupt decision.

"I've watched you with Molly. I don't believe you're some schemer looking to extort big bucks from us. You'll have to work to convince Blake of that, though."

"I can't tell him any more than I have."

"You don't know him like I do. He has his ways of getting what he wants. So do I," she added as she pushed out of the chair and adjusted the sling. "So do I. C'mon, Mol, let's go see your daddy."

Without thinking Grace moved to help. Swooping the baby up, she planted wet, sloppy kisses on her cheeks before slipping the infant's feet through the sling's leg openings. While Delilah tightened the straps, Grace folded the jungle blanket back into the diaper bag and handed it to the older woman.

"I'm sorry Blake doesn't want me to help with Molly."

"We'll manage until this mess gets sorted out."

* * *

If it got sorted out. Grace grew more antsy as one day stretched into two, then three.

Blake had her things packed and delivered along with her purse. She tried to take that as a good sign. Apparently he wasn't afraid she would pull a disappearing act like her cousin had.

He didn't contact her personally, though, and that worried Grace. It also caused an annoyingly persistent ache. Only now that she'd been banished from their lives did she realize how attached she'd become to the Daltons, mother and son. And to Molly! Grace missed cooing to the baby and watching her count her toes and shampooing her soft, downy blond hair.

She'd known the time would come when she would have to drop out of Molly's life. The longer she stayed here, the greater the risk Jack Petrie might trace her to Oklahoma City and wonder what she was doing here. Yet she felt a sharp pang of dismay when Blake finally condescended to call a little past 6:00 p.m. with a curt announcement.

"I need to talk to you."

"All right."

"I'm downstairs," he informed her. "I'll be up in a few minutes."

At least she was a little better prepared for this face-to-face than she'd been for their last. Her hair was caught up in a smooth knot and she'd swiped on some lip gloss earlier. She debated whether to change her jeans and faded San Antonio SeaWorld T-shirt but decided to use the time to take deep, calming breaths.

Not that they did much good. The Blake Dalton she opened the door to wasn't one she'd seen before. He'd always appeared at his mother's house in suits or neatly pressed shirts and slacks sporting creases sharp enough to shave fuzz from a peach. Then, of course, there was the tux he'd donned for the wedding. Armani should wish for male models with builds like either of the Dalton twins.

This Blake was considerably less refined. Faded jeans rode low on his hips. A black T-shirt stretched across his taut shoulders. Bristles the same shade of amber as his hair shadowed his cheeks and chin. He looked tough and uncompromising, but the expression in his laser blues wasn't as cold as the one he'd worn at their last meeting, thank God.

"We got the lab report back."

Wordlessly she led the way into the living room. Electric screens shielded the wall of windows from the sun that hadn't yet slipped down behind the skyscrapers. Without the endless view, the room seemed smaller, more intimate. *Too* intimate, she decided when she turned and found Blake had stopped mere inches away.

"Aren't you going to ask the results?"

"I don't need to," she said with a shrug. "Unless the lab screwed up the samples, their report confirms Molly and I descend from the same family tree."

"They didn't screw up the samples."

"Okay." She crossed her arms. "Now what?"

Surprise flickered across his face.

"What'd you expect?" Grace asked, her chin angling. "That I would throw myself into your arms for finally acknowledging the truth?"

The surprise was still there, but then his gaze dropped to her mouth and it took on a different quality. Darker. More intense. As though the idea of Grace throwing herself at him was less of a shock than something to be considered, evaluated, assessed.

Now that the idea was out there, it didn't particularly shock her, either. Just the opposite. In fact, the urge grew stronger with each second it floated around in the realm of possibility. All she had to do was step forward. Slide her palms over his shoulders. Lean into his strength.

As her cousin had.

Guilt sent Grace back a pace, not forward. He'd been Anne's lover, she reminded herself fiercely. The father of her baby. At best, Grace was a problem he was being forced to solve.

"Now you know," she said with a shrug that disguised her true feelings. "You're Molly's father. And *I* know you'll be good with her. So it's time for me to pack and head back to San Antonio. I'll stop by to say goodbye to her on my way out of town."

"That's it?" His frown deepened. "You're just going to drop out of her life?"

"I'll see her when I can."

After she was certain Jack Petrie hadn't learned about her stay in Oklahoma City.

"There are legalities that have to be attended to," Blake protested. "I'll need Molly's birth certificate. Her mother's death certificate."

Both contained the false name and SSN her cousin had used in California. Grace could only pray the documents would be sufficient for Blake's needs. They should. With his legal connections and his family's political clout here in Oklahoma, he ought to be able to push whatever he wanted through the courts.

"I'll send you copies," she promised.

"Right." He paused, his jaw working. "I hope you know that whatever trouble Anne was in, I would have helped her."

"Yes," she said softly. "I know."

His eyes searched hers. "Anne couldn't bring herself to trust me, but you can, Grace."

She wanted to. God, how she wanted to! Somehow she managed to swallow the hard lump in her throat.

"I trust you to cherish Molly."

Saying goodbye to the baby was every bit as hard as it had been to say goodbye to Blake. Molly broke into delighted coos when she saw her nanny and lifted both arms, demanding to be cuddled.

Grace refused to cry until her rental car was on I-35 and heading south. Tears blurred the rolling Oklahoma countryside for the next fifty miles. By the time she crossed the Red River into Texas, her throat was raw and her eyes so puffy that she had to stop at the welcome center to douse them with cold water. Six hours later she hit the outskirts of San Antonio, still mourning her severed ties to Molly and the woman who'd been both cousin and best friend to her since earliest childhood.

Her tiny condo in one of the city's older suburbs felt stale and stuffy when she let herself in. With a gulp, she glanced from the living room she'd painted a warm terra-cotta to the closet-size kitchen. She loved her place, but the entire two-bedroom unit could fit in the foyer of Delilah Dalton's palatial mansion.

As soon as she'd unpacked and powered up her computer, Grace scanned the certificates she'd promised to send Blake. That done, she skimmed through the hundreds of emails that had piled up in her absence and tried to pick up the pieces of her life.

The next two weeks dragged interminably. School didn't start until the end of month. Unfortunately, the open-ended leave of absence Grace had requested had forced her principal to shuffle teachers to cover the fall semester. The best he could promise was hopefully steady work as a substitute until after Christmas.

At loose ends until school started, Grace had to cut as many corners as possible to make up for her depleted bank account. Even worse, she missed Molly more than she would have believed possible. The baby had taken up permanent residence in her heart.

Only at odd moments would she admit she missed Molly's father almost as much as she did the baby. Like everyone else swept up in the Daltons' orbit, she'd been overwhelmed by Delilah's forceful personality and dazzled by Alex's wicked grin and audacious charm. Now that she viewed the Dalton clan from a distance, however, Grace recognized Blake as the brick and mortar keeping the family together. Always there when his mother needed him to pull together the financing on yet another of her charitable ventures. Holding the reins at Dalton International's corporate headquarters while Alex jetted halfway around the world to consult with suppliers or customers. Grace missed seeing his tall form across the table at his mother's house, missed hearing his delighted chuckle when he tickled Molly's tummy and got her giggling.

The only bright spot in those last, endless days of summer was that she heard nothing from Jack Petrie. She began to breathe easy again, convinced she'd covered her tracks. That false sense of security lasted right up until she answered the doorbell on a rainy afternoon.

When she peered though the peephole, the shock of seeing who stood on the other side dropped her jaw. A second later, fear exploded in her chest. Her fingers scrabbled for the dead bolt. She got it unlocked and threw the door almost back on its hinges.

"Blake!"

He had to step back to keep from getting slammed by the glass storm door. Grace barely registered the neat black slacks, the white button-down shirt with the open collar and sleeves rolled up, the hair burnished to dark, gleaming gold by rain.

"Is…?" Her heart hammered. Her voice shook. "Is Molly okay?"

"No."

"Oh, God!" A dozen horrific scenarios spun through her head. "What happened?"

"She misses you."

Grace gaped at him stupidly. "What?"

"She misses you. She's been fretting since you left. Mother says she's teething."

The disaster scenes faded. Molly wasn't injured. She hadn't been kidnapped. Almost reeling with relief, Grace sagged against the doorjamb.

"That's what you came down to San Antonio to tell me?" she asked incredulously. "Molly's teething?"

"That, and the fact that she said her first word."

And Grace had missed both events! The loss hit like a blow as Blake's glance went past her and swept the comfortable living room.

"May I come in?"

"Huh? Oh. Yes, of course."

She moved inside, all too conscious now of her bare feet and the T-shirt hacked off to her midriff. The shirt topped a pair of ragged cutoffs that skimmed her butt cheeks.

The cutoffs were comfortable in the cozy privacy of her home but nothing she would have ever considered wearing while she'd worked for Delilah—or around her son. She caught Blake's gaze tracking to her legs, moving upward. Disconcerted by the sudden heat that slow once-over generated, she gulped and snatched at his reason for being there.

"What did Molly say?"

"We thought it was just a ga-ga," he said with a small, almost reluctant smile. "Mother insisted she was trying to say ga-ma, but it came out on a hiss."

She sounded it out in her head, and felt her stomach go hard and tight.

"Gace? Molly said Gace?"

"Several times now."

"I…uh…"

He waited a beat, but she couldn't pull it together enough for coherence. She was too lost in the stinging regret of missing those first words.

"We want you to come back, Grace."

Startled, she looked up to find Blake regarding her intently.

"Who's *we?*" she stammered.

"All of us. Mother, me, Julie and Alex."

"They're back from their honeymoon?"

"They flew in last night."

"And you…" She had to stop and suck in a shaky breath. "And you want me to come back and pick up where I left off as Molly's nanny?"

"Not as her nanny. As my wife."

Four

Blake could certainly understand Grace's slack-jawed astonishment. He'd spent the entire flight to San Antonio telling himself it was insane to propose marriage to a woman who refused to trust him with the truth.

It was even more insane for him to miss her the way he had. She'd wormed her way into his mother's house and Molly's heart. She'd lied to him—to all of them—by omission if nothing else. Yet the hole she'd left behind had grown deeper with each hour she was gone.

Molly's unexpected arrival had already turned his calm, comfortable routine upside down. This doe-eyed blonde had kicked it all to hell. So he felt a savage satisfaction to see his own chaotic feelings mirrored in her face.

"You're crazy! I can't marry you!"

"Why not?"

She was sputtering, almost incoherent. "Because… Because…"

He thought she might break down and tell him then. Trust him with the truth. When she didn't, he swallowed a bitter pill of disappointment.

"Why don't we sit down?" he suggested with a calm he was far from feeling. "Talk this through."

"Talk it through?" She gave a bubble of hysterical laughter and swept a hand toward the living room. "My first marriage proposal, and he wants to *talk* it though. By all means, counselor, have a seat."

She regrouped during the few moments it took him to move to a sofa upholstered in a nubby plaid that complemented the earth-toned walls and framed prints of Roman antiquities. As she dropped into a chair facing him, Blake could see her astonishment giving way to anger. The first hints of it fired her eyes and stiffened her shoulders under her cottony T-shirt. He had to work to keep his gaze from drifting to the expanse of creamy skin exposed by the shirt's hem. And those legs. Christ!

He'd better remember what he'd come for. He had to approach this challenge the same way he did all others. Coolly and logically.

"I've had time to think since you left, Grace. You're good with Molly. So good both she and my mother have had difficulty adjusting to your absence."

So had he, dammit. It irritated Blake to no end that he hadn't been able to shut this woman out of his head. She'd lied to him and stubbornly refused to trust him. Yet he'd found himself making excuses for the lies and growing more determined by the hour to convince her to open up.

"You're also Molly's closest blood relative on her mother's side," he continued.

As far as he could determine at this point, anyway. He fully intended to keep digging. Whatever it took, however he got it, he wanted the truth.

"That's right," she confirmed with obvious reluctance. "Anne's parents are dead, and she was their only child."

He waited, willing her to share another scrap of information about her cousin. It hit Blake then that he could barely remember what Anne had looked like. They'd been together such a short time—if those few, furtive meetings outside their work environment could be termed togetherness.

Jaw locked, he tried to summon her image. She'd been an inch or two shorter than Grace. That much he remembered. And her eyes were several shades darker than her cousin's warm, caramel-brown. Beyond that, she was a faint memory when compared with the vibrant female now facing him.

Torn between guilt and regret, Blake presented his next argument. "I know you're facing monetary problems right now."

She bolted upright in her chair. "What'd you do? Have Jamison check my financials?"

"Yes." He offered no apology. "I'm guessing you drained your resources to help Anne and Molly. I owe you for that, Grace."

"Enough to marry me?" she bit out.

"That's part of the equation." He hesitated, aware he was about to enter treacherous territory. "There's another consideration, of course. Something frightened Anne enough to send her into hiding. It has to frighten you, too, or you wouldn't have gone to such lengths to protect her."

He'd struck a nerve. He could tell by the way she

wouldn't meet his eyes. Regret that he hadn't been able to shield Anne from whoever or whatever had threatened her knifed into him. With it came an implacable determination to protect Grace. Battling the fierce urge to shake the truth out of her, he offered her not just his name but every powerful resource at his disposal.

"I'll take care of you," he promised, his steady gaze holding hers. "You *and* Molly."

She wanted to yield. He could see it in her eyes. He congratulated himself, reveling in the potent mix of satisfaction at winning her confidence and a primal need to protect his chosen mate.

His fierce exultation didn't last long. Only until she shook her head.

"I appreciate the offer, Blake. You don't know how much. But I can take care of myself."

He hadn't realized until that moment how determined he was to put his ring on her finger. His expression hardening, he played his trump card.

"There's another aspect to consider. Right now, you can't—or won't—claim any degree of kinship to Molly. That could impact your access to her."

Her back went rigid. "What are you saying? That you wouldn't let me see her if I don't marry you?"

"No. I'm simply pointing out that you have no legal rights where she's concerned. Mother's not getting any younger," he reminded her coolly. "And if something should happen to me or Alex…"

He was too good an attorney to overstate his case. Shrugging, he let her mull over the possibilities.

Grace did, with ever increasing indignation. She couldn't believe it! He'd trapped her in her own web of lies and half-truths. If she wanted to see Molly—which she did, desperately!—she would have to play the game by his rules.

But marriage? Could she tie her future to his for the sake of the baby? The prospect dismayed her enough to produce a sharp round of questions.

"What about love, Blake? And sex? And everything else that goes into a marriage? Don't you want that?"

With a smooth move, he pushed off the sofa. Grace rose hastily as well and was almost prepared when he stopped mere inches away.

"Do you?" he asked.

"Of course I do!"

For the first time she saw a glint of humor in his eyes. "Then I don't see a problem. The sex is certainly doable. We can work on the love."

Dammit! She couldn't form a coherent thought with him standing so close. Between that and the blood pounding in her ears, she was forced to fight for every breath. It had to be oxygen deprivation that made her agree to his outrageous proposal.

"All right, counselor. You've made your case. I want to be part of Molly's life. I'll marry you."

She thought that would elicit a positive response. At least a nod. Wasn't that what he wanted? What he'd flown down here for? So why the hell did his brows snap together and he looked as though he seriously regretted his offer?

Let them snap! They'd both gone too far to back down now. But there was one final gauntlet she had to throw down.

"I just have one condition."

"And that is?"

"We play this marriage very low-key. No formal announcement. No fancy ceremony. No big, expensive reception with pictures splashed across the society page."

She paced the room, thinking furiously. She'd covered her tracks in Oklahoma City. She was sure of it. Still, it was best to stick as close to the truth as possible.

"If anyone asks, we met several months ago. Fell in love, but needed time to be sure. Decided it was for real when you flew down here to see me this weekend, so we found a justice of the peace and did the deed. Period. End of story."

She turned, hands on hips, and waited for his response. It was slow coming. *Extremely* slow.

"Well?" she demanded, refusing to let his stony silence unnerve her. "Do we have a deal or don't we?"

He held out a hand. To shake on their bargain, she realized as the full ramifications of what she'd just agreed to sank in. If her cousin's horrific experience hadn't killed most of Grace's girlish fantasies about marriage, this coolly negotiated business arrangement would have done the trick.

Except Blake didn't take the hand she extended. To her surprise, he elbowed her arm aside, hooked her waist and brought her up against his chest.

"If we're going to project a pretense of being in love, we'd better practice for the cameras."

"No! No cameras, remember? No splashy… Mmmmph!"

She ended on a strangled note as his mouth came down on hers. The kiss was harder than it needed to be. It was also everything that she'd imagined it might be! Her blood leaping, she gloried in the press of his body against hers for a moment or two or ten.

Then reality hit. This was payback for the secrets she still refused to reveal. A taste of the sex he'd so generously offered to provide. She bristled, fully intending to jerk out of his hold, but he moved first.

Dropping his arm, he put a few inches between them. He'd lost that granite look, but she wasn't sure she liked the self-disgust much better.

"I'm sorry."

"You should be," she threw back. "Manhandling me isn't part of our deal."

"You're right. That was uncalled for."

It certainly was. Yet for some perverse reason, the apology irritated her more than the kiss.

"Do we need to negotiate an addendum?" she asked acidly. "Something to the effect that physical contact must be mutually agreed to?"

Red singed his cheeks. "Amendment accepted. If you still want to go through with the contract, that is."

"Do you?"

"Yes."

"Then I do, too."

"Fine." His glance swept over her, lingering again momentarily on her legs. "You'd better get changed."

"Excuse me?"

"You scripted the scenario. I flew down to see you. We decided it was for real. We hunted down a justice of the peace. Period. End of story."

She threw an incredulous glance at the window. Rain still banged against the panes. Thunder rumbled in the distance.

"You want to get married *today*?"

"Why not?"

She could think of a hundred reasons, not least of which was the fact that she had yet to completely recover from that kiss.

"What about blood tests?" she protested. "The seventy-two-hour mandatory waiting period?"

"Texas doesn't require blood tests. I've checked."

Of course he had.

"And the seventy-two-hour waiting period can be waived if you know the right people."

Which he did. Grace should have known he would cover every contingency with his usual attention to detail.

"We'll get the marriage license at the Bexar County Courthouse. One of my father's old cronies is a circuit judge. I'll call and see if he's available to perform the ceremony." He pulled out his cell phone. "Pack what you need to take back to Oklahoma with you. We'll arrange for a moving company to take care of the rest."

The speed of it, the meticulous preplanning and swift execution, left her breathless.

"You were that sure of me?" she asked, feeling dazed and off balance.

He paused in the act of scrolling through the phone's address book. "I was that sure of how much you love Molly."

They left for the county courthouse a little more than three hours later. Blake was driving the Lincoln town car his efficient staff had arranged for him. As Grace stared through the Lincoln's rain-streaked window, she grappled with a growing sense of unreality.

Like all young girls, she and her cousin had spent hours with an old lace tablecloth wrapped around their shoulders, playing bride. During giggly sleepovers, they'd imagined numerous iterations of her wedding day. Grace's favorite consisted of a church fragrant with flowers and perfumed candles, a radiant bride in filmy white and friends packed into the pews.

After that came the smaller, more intimate version. Just her, her cousin as her attendant, a handsome groom and the pastor in a shingle-roofed gazebo while her family beamed from white plastic folding chairs. She'd even toyed occasionally with the idea of Elvis walking her down the aisle in one of Vegas's wedding chapels. This hurried, unromantic version had never figured in her imagination, however.

The reality of it hit home when they walked across a rain-washed plaza to the Bexar County Courthouse. The building was listed on the National Register of Historic Places. Unfortunately the recent storm and still ominous thunderclouds hanging low in an angry sky tinted its sandstone turrets to prison-gray. The edifice looked both drab and foreboding as Blake escorted Grace up its granite steps.

The frosted window on the door of the county clerk's office welcomed walk-ins, but the bored counter attendant showed little interest in their application. He cracked a jaw-popping yawn when the prospective bride and groom filled out the application. Five minutes and thirty-five dollars later, they entered the chambers of Judge Victor Honeywell. *His* clerk, at least, seemed to feel some sense of the occasion.

The beaming, well-endowed matron hurried around her desk to shake their hands. "I can't remember the last time we got to perform a spur-of-the-moment wedding. Brides today seem to take a year just to decide on their gown."

Unlike Grace, who had slithered out of her cutoffs and into the white linen sundress she'd picked up on sale a few weeks ago.

Blake, on the other hand, had come prepared for every eventuality, a wedding included. While she'd packed, he'd retrieved a suit bag from the Lincoln. Dark worsted wool now molded his wide shoulders. An Italian silk tie that probably cost more than Grace had earned in a week was tied in a neat Windsor. The clerk's admiring gaze lingered on both shoulders and tie for noticeable moments before she turned to the bride.

"These just came for you."

She ducked behind a side counter and popped up again with a cellophane-wrapped cascade of white roses. Silver lace and sprays of white baby's breath framed the bouquet. A two-inch-wide strip of blue was looped into a floppy bow around the stems.

"The ribbon—such as it is—is the belt from my rain-coat," she said, her eyes twinkling. "You know, some-thing borrowed, something blue."

A lump blocked Grace's throat. She had to push air past it as she folded back the cellophane and traced a finger over the petals. "Thank you."

"You're welcome. And this is for you." Still beaming, the clerk pinned a white rose to Blake's lapel. "There! Now I'll take you to Judge Honeywell."

She ushered them into a set of chambers groaning with oak panels and red damask drapes. The flags of the United States and the state of Texas flanked a desk the size of a soccer field. A set of steer horns stretched across an eight-foot swath of wall behind the desk.

"It's Ms. Templeton and Mr. Dalton, Your Honor."

The man ensconced on what Grace could only term a leather throne jumped up. His black robe flapped as he rounded his desk, displaying a pair of hand-tooled cowboy boots. He was at least six-three or four and as whiskery as he was tall. When he thrust out a thorny palm, Blake had to tilt back to keep from getting stabbed by the exaggerated point of his stiff-as-a-spear handle-bar mustache.

"Well, damn! So you're Big Jake Dalton's boy."

"One of them," Blake replied with a smile.

"He ever tell you 'bout the time the two of us busted up a saloon down to Nogales?"

"No, he didn't."

"Good. Some tales are best left untold." Honeywell shifted his squinty gaze to Grace. "I'd warn you against marrying up with any son of Big Jake if they didn't have the prettiest, smartest female in all fifty states for their mama." His nose twitched above the bushy mustache. "Speaking of Delilah, is she comin' to witness the ceremony?"

"No, but my brother is."

That was the first Grace had heard of it! She glanced at him in surprise while he confirmed the startling news.

"Alex should be here any moment. He was on final approach when we left the condo. In fact…"

He cocked his head. Grace followed suit and picked up the sound of footsteps in the tiled hallway. A moment later the judge's clerk reappeared with another couple in tow. The tall, tawny-haired male who entered the chambers was a mirror image of Blake. The copper-haired female with him elicited a joyous cry from Grace.

"Julie!"

She took an instinctive step toward the woman she'd grown so close to during her sojourn in Oklahoma. Guilt brought her to a dead stop. Grace hadn't lied to Julie or the Daltons, but she hadn't told the truth, either. Alex and his new wife had to be feeling the same anger Blake had when he'd first discovered her deception.

It wasn't anger she saw in her friend's distinctive green-brown eyes, however, but regret and exasperation.

"Grace, you idiot!" Brushing past Blake, Julie folded Grace into a fierce hug, roses and all. "You didn't need to go through what you did alone. You could have told me. I would've kept your secret."

Limp with relief, Grace gulped back a near sob. "The secret isn't mine to tell."

Her gaze slid to Blake's brother. Alex didn't appear quite as forgiving as his bride. She didn't blame him. She'd watched him interact with Molly these past months, knew he loved the baby every bit as much as Blake did. It had to hurt to transition so abruptly from possible father to uncle. Grace could offer only a soft apology.

"I'm sorry, Alex. I didn't know which of you was Molly's father. Honestly. Not until I'd been in Oklahoma City for a while, and by then you and Julie were, ah, working a separate set of issues."

The hard set to his jaw relaxed a fraction. "That's one way to describe the hell this stubborn woman put me through."

He stood for a moment, studying Grace's face. She braced herself, but his next words didn't carry either the condemnation or the sting she expected.

"Everyone, me included, will tell you that my brother is the better man. But once he sets his mind to something, he can be as ruthless as I am and as hardheaded as our mother. Blake's convinced us this marriage is what he wants. Is it what you want?"

Her fingers tightened on the stem of the roses. Their white velvet scent drifted upward as she turned to her groom. Blake stood tall and seemingly at ease, but his blue eyes were locked on hers.

"Yes," she said after only a minuscule hesitation. "I'm sure."

Was that satisfaction or relief or a brief flash of panic that rippled across his face? Grace was still trying to decide when the judge boomed out instructions.

"All right, folks. Y'all gather round so we can get these two hitched."

Blake held out a hand. Grace laid her palm in his, hoping he couldn't hear the violent thump of her heart against her ribs. As they faced the judge, she reminded herself she was doing this for Molly.

Mostly.

Five

It was actually happening. It was for real. Grace had to fight the urge to pinch herself as Blake slid a band of channel-cut diamonds onto her ring finger. Dazed, she heard the judge's prompt.

"With this ring…"

Her groom followed the cues in a deep, sure voice. "With this ring…"

"I thee wed."

"I thee wed."

The diamonds caught the light from the overhead lighting. Brilliant, multicolored sparks danced and dazzled. Grace couldn't begin to guess how many carats banded her finger. Four? Five? And she couldn't reciprocate with so much as a plain gold band.

"By the authority vested in me by the state of Texas," Judge Honeywell intoned, "I now pronounce you husband and wife."

He waited a beat before issuing another prompt. "Go ahead, Dalton. Kiss your bride."

For the second time that afternoon, Blake slipped an arm around her waist. Grace's pulse skittered. A shiver raced down her spine. Apprehension? Anticipation?

She knew which even before he bent toward her. Her whole body quivered in expectation. He was gentle this time, though. *Too* gentle! She ached to lean into him, but the deal they'd struck kept her rigid. Their marriage was first and foremost a business arrangement, a legal partnership with Molly as the focus. Grace might eventually accept Blake's oh-so-casual offer of sex, but she'd damned well better keep a close watch on her heart.

With that resolve firm in her mind, she accepted the hearty congratulations of Judge Honeywell, another fierce hug from Julie and a kiss on the cheek from her new brother-in-law. At that point Alex produced an envelope from his inside suit coat pocket.

"Mother wanted to be here, but Molly's cutting a tooth and was too fussy to fly. She sent this instead."

Grace took the envelope with some trepidation. Inside was a folded sheet of notepaper embossed with Delilah's raised monogram. Before unfolding the note, she looked a question at Blake. His small shrug told her this was as much a surprise to him as it was to her. Nervously, Grace skimmed the almost indecipherable scrawl.

I can't say I'm happy with the way you decided to do this. We'll discuss it when you get back from France. DI's corporate jet will fly you to Marseille. Contact Madame LeBlanc when you arrive. Blake has her number. Julie, Alex and I will take care of Molly.

For a wild moment Grace thought she was being hustled out of the country so Delilah could hammer some sense into Blake. Then the last line sank in. Julie, Alex and Delilah would care for Molly. She and her groom, apparently, were jetting off to France.

Wordlessly, she handed the note to Blake. After a quick read, he speared a glance at this twin. "Were you in on this?"

"I figured something was up when Mother had me ferry the Gulfstream V down to San Antonio. Where's she proposing it take you?"

"The south of France."

That produced a quick grin. "You get no sympathy from me, Bubba. She sent Julie and me to Tuscany on our wedding night. Good thing we're both pilots and know how to beat jet lag." He winked at his wife before addressing Grace. "Hope you have a passport."

"I do, but…"

But what? She'd decided in a scant few moments to turn her whole world upside down by accepting Blake's proposition. What possible objection could she have to capping an unreal marriage with a fake honeymoon?

"But Blake probably didn't bring his," she finished helplessly.

"He didn't," Julie interjected, fishing in her purse. "I did, however. Delilah had me race over and pick it up from your executive assistant," she explained as she slapped the passport into her brother-in-law's palm. "I forgot I had it until this moment."

He fingered the gold lettering for several moments, then shrugged. "Good thing you're packed," he said to Grace. "I can pick up whatever extras I need when we get to France."

* * *

They said their goodbyes at the airport. Then Alex and Julie boarded the smaller Dalton International jet that had flown Blake to San Antonio and the newly-weds crossed the tarmac to the larger, twin-engine Gulfstream V.

The captain met them at planeside and tendered his sincere best wishes. "Congratulations, Mrs. Dalton."

"I…uh… Thank you."

Blake stepped in to cover his wife's surprise at hearing herself addressed by her new title. "I understand you just got back from Tuscany, Joe. Sorry you had to make such a quick turnaround."

"Not a problem. Alex and Julie were at the controls for most of the flight back, so the crew is rested and ready to go. We'll top off our gas in New York and have you basking in the sun a mere seven hours after that."

Blake made the swift mental calculation. Three hours to New York. Seven hours to cross the Atlantic. Another hour or more to contact Madame LeBlanc and travel to the villa DI maintained in Provence. Eight hours' time difference.

He was used to transatlantic flights, but he suspected Grace would be dead by the time they arrived at their final destination. Just as well. She could use the next few days to rest and get used to the idea of marriage.

So could he, for that matter. He'd lined up all his arguments, pro and con, before he'd flown down to San Antonio. Then Grace had opened the door in those cut-offs and he'd damned near forgotten every one. Only now could he admit that the hunger she stirred had him twisted in as many knots as her refusal to trust him with the truth. Helluva foundation to build a marriage on, he conceded grimly as he put a hand to the small of her back to guide her up the stairs.

A Filipino steward in a white jacket met them at the hatch, his seamed face creased into a smile. "Welcome aboard, Mr. Blake. I sure wouldn't have bet we'd be flying both you and Mr. Alex on honeymoons in almost the same month."

"I wouldn't have bet on it, either, Eualdo. This is my wife, Grace."

He bowed over her hand with a dignity that matched his years. "It's an honor to meet you, Ms. Grace."

"Thank you."

"If you'll follow me, I'll show you to your seats."

Blake had spent so many in-flight hours aboard the Gulfstream he'd long since come to regard it more as a necessity than a luxury. Grace's gasp when she entered the cabin reminded him not everyone would view it that way.

The interior was normally configured with high-backed, lumbar-support seats and generous workstations in addition to the galley, head and sleeping quarters. For personal or pleasure trips like this, however, the workstations were moved together to form an elegant dining area and the seats repositioned into a comfortable sitting area.

"Good grief." She gazed wide-eyed at the gleaming teak paneling and dove-gray leather. "I hope Dalton International isn't paying for all this."

"You're married to DI's chief financial officer," Blake replied dryly. "You can trust me to maintain our personal expenses separate and distinct from corporate accounts."

She flushed a little, either at the reminder that they'd

just merged or at the unspoken reminder that she *wouldn't* trust him with other, more important matters.

The pink in her cheeks deepened when they passed the open door to the sleeping quarters. A quick glance inside showed the twin beds had been repositioned into a queen-size sleeper complete with down pillows, satiny sheets and a duvet with DI's logo embroidered in gold thread. Blake didn't have the least doubt that Julie and Alex had put those sheets to good use every moment they weren't in the cockpit.

Different couple, completely different circumstances. Blake and *his* bride wouldn't share that wide bed. The reality of the situation didn't block his thought of it, though. Swearing under his breath, Blake was hit with a sudden and all-too-vivid mental image of Grace stretched out with her arms raised languidly above her head, her breasts bare, her nipples turgid from his tongue and his teeth.

"I've got a bottle of Cristal on ice, Mr. Blake."

He blinked away the searing image and focused on Eualdo's weathered face.

"Shall I pour you and Ms. Grace a glass now or wait until after takeoff?"

A glance at his bride provided the answer. She had the slightly wild-eyed look of someone who was wondering just what kind of quicksand she'd stumbled into. She needed a drink or two to loosen her up. So did he. This looked to be a *long* flight.

It wound up lasting even longer than either Blake or the captain had anticipated. When they put down at a small commercial airstrip outside New York City to refuel, a thick, soupy fog rolled in off the Atlantic and delayed their departure for another two hours. The same front that produced the fog necessitated a more northerly route than originally planned.

By the time they gained enough altitude for Eualdo to serve dinner, Grace's shoulders were drooping. The steward's honey-crusted squab on a bed of wild rice and a bottle of perfectly chilled Riesling revived her enough for dessert. When darkness dropped like a stone outside the cabin windows, however, she dropped with it.

The first time her chin hit her chest, she jerked her head up and protested she was wide-awake. The second time, she gave up all attempt at pretense.

"I'm sorry." She dragged the back of her hand across her eyes. "I shouldn't have piled wine on top of champagne. I'm feeling the kick."

"Altitude probably has something to do with that."

Blake's calm reply gave no hint of his thoughts. He'd never seduced a tipsy female, but the idea was pretty damned tempting at the moment.

"It's been a long day. Why don't you go to bed?"

Her glance zinged to the rear of the cabin, shot back. "Aren't you tired?"

"Some." He put the last of his willpower into another smile. "But Eualdo's used to me working my way across the Atlantic."

"On your wedding night?"

He had no trouble interpreting the question behind the question. "He's been with Dalton International for more than a decade," he said calmly. "You don't need to worry about what he'll think. Or anyone else, for that matter."

Her glance dropped to her hands. She played with the band of diamonds, and he added getting the ring resized to his mental list of tasks to be accomplished when they returned to Oklahoma City.

"Go to bed, Grace."

Nodding, she unhooked her seat belt. Blake's hooded gaze followed her progress. When she disappeared inside the stateroom, he downed the dregs of his Riesling and reclined his seat back.

Well, Grace thought as she crawled between the sheets fifteen minutes later, she could imagine worse wedding nights. The social studies teacher in her had read enough ancient history to shudder at some of the barbaric marriage rites and rituals practiced in previous times.

In contrast, this night epitomized the ultimate in comfort and luxury. She was being whisked across an ocean in a private jet. She'd found every amenity she'd needed in the surprisingly spacious bathroom. The cotton sheets were so smooth and soft they felt like whipped cream against her skin. Two million stars winked outside the curved windows built into the bulwark. The only thing she needed to perfect the scene was a groom.

With a vengeance, all those play-wedding scenes she and her cousin had enacted as girls came back to haunt her. Hope's marriage had brought her nothing but heartache and fear. Grace's...

Oh, hell! Disgusted by her twinge of poor-me self-pity, she rolled over and thumped the pillow. She'd made her bed. She'd damned well lie in it.

Now if only she could stop with the nasty urge to march back into the main cabin and reopen negotiations. As Blake had so bluntly suggested, the sex was certainly doable. *More* than doable. The mere thought of his hard, muscled body stretched out beside her, his hands on her breasts, his mouth hot against hers, made the muscles low in Grace's belly tighten.

She clenched her legs, felt the swift pull between her thighs. Need, fierce and raw, curled through her. Her breath got shorter, faster.

This was stupid! Blake was sitting just a few yards away! Two steps to the stateroom door, one signal, silent or otherwise, and he'd join her.

Sex could be enough for now, she told herself savagely. She didn't need the shared laughter, the private smiles, the silly jokes married couples added to their storehouse of memories.

And it wasn't as though she'd arrived at this point unprepared. Teaching high school kids repeatedly reinforced basic truths, including the fact that each individual had to take responsibility for his or her protection during sex. Grace had seen too many bright, talented students' lives derailed by their biological urges. She wasn't into one-night stands and hadn't had a serious relationship in longer than she cared to admit, but she'd remained prepared, just in case.

So why not ease out of bed and take those two steps to the door? Why not give the signal? She and Blake were married, for God's sake!

She kicked off the sheet. Rolled onto a hip. Stopped. The problem was she *wanted* the shared smiles and silly jokes. *Needed* more than casual sex.

"Dammit!"

Disgusted, she flopped down and hammered the pillow again. She was a throwback. An anachronism. And thoroughly, completely frustrated.

She didn't remember drifting off, but the wine and champagne must indeed have gotten to her. She went completely out and woke to a knock on the stateroom door and blinding sunlight pouring through the window she'd forgotten to shade. She squinted owlishly at her watch, saw it was the middle of the night Texas time, and had to stifle a groan when another knock sounded.

"It's Eualdo, Ms. Grace. Mr. Blake said to let you know we're ninety minutes out."

"Okay, thanks."

"I'll serve breakfast in the main cabin when you're ready."

She emerged from the stateroom a short time later, showered and dressed in a pair of white crops and a gauzy, off-one-shoulder top in a flowery print. A chunky white bracelet added a touch of panache. She figured she would need that touch to get through her first morning-after meeting with her groom.

Blake unbuckled his seat belt and rose when she approached. Except for the discarded tie and open shirt collar, he didn't look like a man who'd sat up all night. Only when she got closer did she spot the gold bristles on his cheeks and chin.

"'Morning."

"Good morning," he answered with a smile. "Did you get any sleep?"

"I did." God! Could this be any more awkward? "How about you?"

"All I need is a shower and shave and I'll be good to go. Eualdo just brewed a fresh pot of coffee. I'll join you for breakfast as soon as I get out of the shower."

He started past her, then stopped. A rueful gleam lighting his eyes, he brushed a knuckle across her cheek.

"We'll figure this out, Grace. We just need to give it time."

* * *

Time, she repeated silently as the Gulfstream swooped low over a dazzling turquoise sea in preparation for landing. Despite her inner agitation, the sweeping view of the Mediterranean enchanted her.

So did the balmy tropical climate that greeted them. Grace had watched several movies and travel specials featuring the south of France. She'd also read a good number of books with the same setting, most recently a Dan Brown–type thriller that had the protagonists searching for a long-lost fragment of the Jesus's cross at the popes' sprawling palace in Avignon. None of the books or movies or travelogues prepared her for Provence's cloudless skies and brilliant sunshine, however. She held up a hand to block the rays as she deplaned, breathing in the briny tang of the sea that surrounded the Marseille airport.

A driver was waiting at the small aircraft terminal with a sporty red convertible. After he'd stashed their bags in the trunk, he made a polite inquiry in French. Blake responded with a smile and a nod.

"Oui."

"C'est bien. Bon voyage."

Grace glanced at him curiously as he slid behind the wheel. "You speak French?"

"Not according to Cecile."

Right. Cecile. The chef who owned the restaurant where Alex and Julie had hosted their rehearsal dinner. The gorgeous, long-legged chef who'd draped herself all over Blake. That display of Gallic exuberance hadn't bothered Grace at the time. Much. It did now. With some effort, she squashed the memory and settled into the convertible.

Blake got behind the wheel. He'd changed into khakis and a fresh shirt and hooked a pair of aviator sunglasses on his shirt pocket.

"Just out of curiosity," she commented as he slipped on the glasses, "where are we going?"

"Saint-Rémy-de-Provence. It's a small town about an hour north of here." A smile played at the corners of his mouth. "A nationwide transportation strike stranded Mother there during one of her antique-hunting trips about five years ago. She used the downtime to buy a crumbling villa and turn it into a vacation resort for top-performing DI employees and their families."

Grace had to grin. That sounded just like her employer. Correction, her mother-in-law. Delilah Dalton possessed more energy and drive than any six people her age.

"The place was occupied most recently by DI's top three welding teams and their families," he added casually. "But Madame LeBlanc indicated we'll have it to ourselves for the next two weeks."

Not so casually, Grace's heart thumped hard against her ribs. The combustible mix of lust and longing she'd had to battle last night had been bad enough. How the heck was she going to get through the next two weeks? Alone. With Blake. Under the hot Provencal sun and starry, starry nights.

Slowly she sank into her seat.

Six

A little over an hour later Blake turned off the auto-route onto a two-lane road shaded by towering syca-mores. Their branches met overhead to form a green tunnel that stretched for miles. The rocky pinnacles of the Alpilles thrust out of the earth to the left of the road. Sun-drenched vineyards and olive groves rolled out on the right, flashing through the sycamores' white, scaly trunks like a DVD run in fast-forward.

As delightful as the approach to Saint-Rémy was, the town itself enchanted Grace even more. Eighteenth-century mansions that Blake called *hôtels* lined the busy street encircling the town proper. Dolphins spouted in a fountain marking one quadrant of the circle, stone goddesses poured water from urns at another. In the pedestrians-only heart of the town, Grace caught glimpses of narrow lanes crammed with shops and open-air restaurants that invited patrons to sit and sip a cappuccino.

Blake noticed her craning her neck to peer down the intriguing alleyways. "We'll have lunch in town," he promised.

"I'd like that."

She studied her groom as he negotiated the busy street. He fit perfectly against this elegant eighteenth-century backdrop, Grace decided. The corporate executive had shed his suit and tie but not his sophistication. Sunlight glinted on the sleek watch banding his wrist and the light dusting of golden hair on his forearm. The aviator sunglasses and hand-tailored shirt left open at the neck to show the tanned column of his throat only added to the image.

"Madame LeBlanc will meet us at Hôtel des Elmes," he added as he skillfully wove through pedestrians, tourists and traffic.

She took a stab at a translation. "The Elms?"

"The Elms," he confirmed. "It used to be called the Hôtel Saint Jacques. Legend has it that the original owner claimed to have invented, or at least improved on, the scallop dish named in Saint James's honor."

Grace had to think for a moment. "Aha! Coquilles St. Jacques!"

"Right. You'll be pleased to know the current chef at the *hôtel* has followed in his predecessors' footsteps. Auguste's scallops au gratin will make you think you hear heavenly choirs."

The easy banter took them up to a pair of tall, wrought-iron gates left open in anticipation of their arrival. Once inside, Grace understood instantly the inspiration for the villa's new designation. Majestic elms that must have been planted more than a century ago formed a graceful arch above a crushed-stone drive. The curving drive wound through landscaped grounds dotted with statuary and vine-shaded arbors, then ended in a circle dominated by a twenty-foot fountain featuring bronze steeds spouting arcs of silvery water.

And looming beyond the fountain was a masterpiece in mellowed gray stone. The Hôtel des Elmes consisted of a three-story central wing, with two-story wings on each side. Wisteria vines softened its elaborate stone facade, drooping showy purple blossoms from wrought-iron trellises. Grace breathed in the purple blossoms' spicy vanilla scent as Blake braked to a stop.

The front door opened before he'd killed the engine. The woman who emerged fit Grace's mental image of the quintessential older French female—slender, charming, impossibly chic in silky black slacks and a cool linen blouse.

"Bienvenue à Saint-Rémy, Monsieur Blake."

"It's good to be back," he replied in English.

After the obligatory cheek kissing, he introduced Grace. She must have been getting used to being presented as his wife. She barely squirmed when Madame LeBlanc grasped both her hands and offered a profuse welcome.

"I am most happy to meet you." Madame's smile took a roguish tilt. "Delilah has long despaired of getting her so-handsome sons to the altar. One can only imagine how thrilled she must be that Alex and Blake have taken brides within a month of each other. *Quelle romantique!*"

"Yes, well…"

Blake's arm slid around Grace's waist. *"Trés romantique."*

His casual comment fed the fantasy of a honeymoon couple. Madame LeBlanc sighed her approval and handed him a set of tagged keys.

"As you instructed, the staff will not report until tomorrow, but Auguste has prepared several dishes should you wish them. They need only to be reheated. And the upstairs maid has made up the bed in the Green Suite and left for the rest of the day. You will not be disturbed."

"Merci."

If the villa's grounds and exquisite eighteenth-century exterior evoked visions of aristocrats in silks and powered wigs, the interior had obviously been retrofitted for twenty-first-century visitors. Grace spotted high-tech security cameras above the doors and an alarm panel just inside the entryway that looked as if it would take an MIT grad to program. The brass-accented elevator tucked discreetly behind a screen of potted palms was also a modern addition.

While Grace peeked around, Blake carried in their few bags and deposited them in the marbled foyer. "Would you like the ten-cent tour, or would you rather go upstairs and rest for a while first?"

"The tour, please! Unless…" Guilt tripped her. "I'm sorry. I zoned out on the plane, but you didn't. You're probably aching for bed."

Something shifted in his face. A mere ripple of skin across muscle and bone. Grace didn't have time to interpret the odd look before he masked it.

"I'm good." He made an exaggerated bow and swept an arm toward the central hall. "This way, madame."

Grace soon lost count of the downstairs rooms. There was the petite salon, the grand salon, the music room, the library, the card room, an exquisitely mirrored ballroom and several banquet and eating areas in addition to the kitchens and downstairs powder rooms. Each contained a mix of antiques and ultramodern conveniences cleverly integrated into an elegant yet inviting whole. Even the painted porcelain sinks in the powder rooms evoked an eighteenth-century feel, and the copper-and-spice-filled kitchen could accommodate cooks of all ages and eras.

The pool house with its marble columns and bougainvillea-draped pergola was a Greek fantasy come to life. The shimmering turquoise water in the pool made Grace itch to shed her clothes on the spot and dive in. But when they went back inside again and started for the stairs to the second floor, it was the painting of deep purple irises displayed in a lighted alcove that stopped her dead.

"Ooooh!" Grace was no art expert, but even she could recognize a Van Gogh when it smacked her between the eyes. "I have a poster of this same painting in my bedroom."

Blake paused behind her. "That's one of my mother's favorites, too. She donated the original to the Smithsonian's Museum of Modern Art but had this copy commissioned for the villa."

He was only an inch or two from her shoulder. So close she felt his breath wash warm and soft against her ear. The sensation zinged down her spine and stirred a reaction that almost made her miss Blake's next comment.

"This is one of the more than one hundred and fifty paintings Van Gogh painted during his year in Saint-Rémy. There's a walking tour that shows the various scenes he incorporated into his works. We can take it if you like."

"I would!"

The possibility of viewing sunflowers and olive groves through the eyes of one of the world's greatest artists tantalized Grace. Almost as much as the idea of viewing them with Blake.

Hard on that came the realization that she had no clue if her new husband was the least bit interested in impressionist art. Or what kind of music he preferred. Or how he spent his downtime when he wasn't doing his executive/corporate lawyer thing. She'd known him such a short time. And during those weeks he, his twin and his indomitable parent had focused exclusively on Molly and the hunt for the baby's mother.

Could be this enforced honeymoon wasn't such a bad idea after all. The main participants in every partnership, even a marriage of convenience, needed to establish a working relationship. Maybe Delilah had their best interests at heart when she'd arranged this getaway.

Maybe. It was hard to tell what really went on in the woman's Machiavellian mind. Withholding judgment, Grace accompanied Blake on a tour of the second story. He pointed out several fully contained guest suites, two additional salons, a reading room, even a video game room for the children of the Dalton employees and other guests who stayed at the *hôtel*. At the end of the hall, he opened a set of double doors fitted with gold-plated latches.

"This is the master suite." His mouth took a wry tilt. "Otherwise known as the Green Suite."

Grace could certainly see why! Awed, she let her gaze travel from floor-to-ceiling silk wall panels to elegantly looped drapes to the thick duvet and dozens of tasseled pillows mounded on the four-poster bed. They were all done in a shimmering, iridescent brocade that shaded from moss-green to dark jade depending on the angle of the light streaming through the French doors. The bed itself was inlaid mahogany chased with gold.

Lots of gold. So were the bombe chests and marble-topped tables scattered throughout the suite.

"Wow!" Mesmerized by the opulence, she spun in a slow circle. "This looks like Louis XV might have slept here."

"There's no record the king ever made it down," Blake returned with a grin, "but one of his mistresses reportedly entertained another of her lovers here on the sly."

Grace couldn't decide which hit with more of a wallop, that quick grin or the instant and totally erotic image his comment stirred. As vividly as any painting, she could picture a woman in white silk stockings, ribboned garters and an unlaced corset lolling against the four-poster's mounds of pillows. A bare-chested courtier with Blake Dalton's guinea-gold hair leaned over her. His blue eyes glinted with wicked promise as he slowly slid one of her garters from her thigh to her knee to her...

"...the adjoining suite."

Blinking, she zoomed out of the eighteenth century. "Sorry. I was, uh, thinking of powdered wigs and silk knee breeches. What did you say?"

"I said I'll be in the adjoining suite."

The last of the delicious image fizzled as Grace watched her husband open a connecting door. The bedroom beyond wasn't as large or as decadent as that of the Green Suite, but it did boast another four-poster and a marble fireplace big enough to roast an ox.

"It's almost noon Saint-Rémy time," Blake said after a quick glance at his watch. "If you're not too jet-lagged, we could reconvene in a half hour and walk into town for lunch."

"That works for me."

Calling herself an idiot for staring at the door long after it closed behind him, Grace extracted her toiletries from her tote bag and carried them into a bathroom fit for a queen. Or at least a royal mistress.

Maybe it was the glorious sun that sucked away her sense of awkwardness. Or the lazy, protracted lunch she and Blake shared at a dime-size table cornered next to a bubbling fountain. Or the two glasses of perfectly chilled rosé produced by a vineyard right outside Saint-Rémy.

Then again, it might have been Blake's obvious efforts to keep the conversation light and noncontroversial. He made no reference to the circumstances of their marriage or Grace's adamant refusal to betray her cousin's trust. As a consequence, she felt herself relaxing for the first time in longer than she could remember.

The still-raw ache of her cousin's death shifted to a corner of her heart. Jack Petrie, Oklahoma City, even Molly moved off center stage. Not completely, and certainly not for long. Yet these hours in the sun provided a hiatus from the worry she'd carted around for so many months. That was the only excuse she could come up with later for the stupidity that followed.

It happened during the walk back to their *hôtel*. Blake indulged her with a stroll through the town's pedestrian-only center, stopping repeatedly while she oooh'ed and aaaah'ed over shop windows displaying Provence's wares. One window was filled with colorful baskets containing every imaginable spice and herb. Another specialized in soaps and scented oils. *Hundreds* of soaps and oils. Delighted, Grace went inside and sniffed at products made from apple pear, lemon, peony, vanilla, honey almond and, of course, lavender. A dazzling display of stoppered vials offered bath oils and lotions in a rainbow of hues.

The clerk obviously knew her business. She sized up the diamonds circling Grace's finger in a single glance. With a knowing look, she produced a cut-crystal vial from a shelf behind the counter.

"Madame must try this. It is a special blend made only for our shop."

When she removed the stopper, an exquisitely delicate aroma drifted across the counter. Lavender and something else that Grace couldn't quite identify.

"The perfumers extract oil from the buds before they blossom. The fragrance is light, *oui?* So very light and yet, how do you say? So *sensuelle.*"

She waved the stopper in the air to release more of its bouquet. Grace leaned forward, breathing deeply. She knew then that whatever else happened in this marriage, she would always associate the scent of lavender with sunshine and brilliant skies and the smile crinkling the skin at the corners of Blake's eyes as he watched her sniffing the air.

He didn't remain an observer for long. Sensing a sale, the shopkeeper dipped the stopper again. "Here, *monsieur,* you must dab some on your wife's wrist. The oil takes on a richer tone when applied to the skin."

With a good-natured nod, Blake took the stopper in one hand and reached for Grace's wrist with the other. His hold was loose, easy. As light as it was, though, the touch sent a ripple of pleasure along her nerves. The ripple swelled to a tidal wave when he raised her arm to a mere inch or so from his nose.

"She's right," he murmured. The blue in his eyes deepened as he caught Grace's gaze. "The warmth of your skin deepens the scent."

Warmth? Ha! She'd passed mere warmth the moment his fingers circled her wrist. And if he kept looking at her like that, she suspected she would spontaneously combust in the next five seconds.

Thankfully, the shop clerk claimed his attention. The distraction proved only temporary, however. Eager for a sale, the woman urged another test.

"Dab a little dab behind your wife's ear, *monsieur*. It is of all places the most seductive."

Grace's internal alarm went off like a klaxon. Every scrap of common sense she possessed urged her to decline the second sample. The sun and the wine and this man's touch were bringing her too close to the melting point. So she was damned if she knew why she just stood there and let Blake brush aside her hair.

The crystal stopper was cool and damp against the skin just below her earlobe. An instant later, her husband's breath seared that same patch of skin. Their only physical contact point was the hand caging back her hair. If the shock that went though her was any indication, however, they might have been locked together at chest and hip and thigh. Thoroughly shaken, Grace took a step back.

The abrupt move brought Blake's head up with a snap. He didn't need to see the confusion on his wife's face to know he'd crossed the line.

The line he'd been stupid enough to draw! He was the one who'd assured her they would work things out. He'd spouted that inane drivel about giving their arrangement time.

To hell with waiting. He ached to drag Grace out of the shop, hustle her back to The Elms and strip her down to the warm, perfumed flesh that was sending his senses into dangerous overload.

"Monsieur?"

The shop clerk's voice cut through his red haze. Before Blake could bring the woman into focus, he had to exercise the iron will that allowed him to appear calm before judges and juries.

She finally appeared, smiling and eager. "Do you wish to purchase a vial for your so-lovely wife?"

God, yes!

At his nod, she whipped out a sales slip. "Do you stay here in Saint-Rémy?"

He knew his address would up the asking price by at least half but was beyond caring. "We're at Hôtel des Elmes."

Her glance sharpened. "Ahhh. I recognize you now. You came to Saint-Rémy last year, *oui?* With... Er..." She broke off, then recovered after an infinitesimal pause. "With your so very charming mother."

Riiiight. Blake seriously doubted his twin had timed a visit to the villa to coincide with one of their mother's protracted stays. Alex and Delilah were both obviously well-known in town, however, so he didn't bother to correct the clerk's misconception.

"We'll take a bottle of that scent."

Beaming, she rattled off the price for a three-ounce bottle. He was reaching for his money clip when Grace gave a strangled gasp.

"Did you say two hundred euros?"

"Oui, madame."

"Two *hundred* euros?"

"Oui."

"That's like..."

Blake paused in the act of peeling off several euro notes while she did the mental math.

"Good grief! That's almost three hundred dollars

U.S." Horrified, she closed her hand over his. "That's too much."

A pained look crossed the salesclerk's face. "You will not find a more distinctive or more delicate scent in all Provence. And..."

Her glance cut to Blake. When she turned back to Grace, a conspiratorial smile tilted her lips.

"If I may say so, madame, your husband does not purchase this fragrance for you. He is the one who will detect its essence on your skin. If it pleases him..."

Her shoulders lifted in that most Gallic of all gestures, and Grace could only watch helplessly as Blake dropped the euro notes on the counter.

Seven

Even with Grace's seductive scent delivering a broad-side every time Blake turned his head or leaned toward her, he didn't plan what happened when they returned to the villa. His conscience would always remain clear on that point. When he suggested a swim, his only intent was to continue the easy camaraderie established during lunch.

What he *hadn't* anticipated was the kick to his gut when Grace joined him poolside and slipped off her terry cloth cover-up. He'd already done a half dozen laps but wasn't the least winded until the sight of her slender, seductive curves sucked the air from his lungs.

"How's the water?"

Blake tried to untangle his tongue. Damned thing felt like it was wrapped in cotton wool. "Cool at first," he got out after an epic struggle. "Not so bad once you're in."

Oh, for God's sake! Her suit was a poppy-colored

one-piece that covered more than it revealed. Yet he was damned if he could stop his gaze from devouring the slopes of her breasts when she bent to deposit her towel on the lounger. That unexpected jolt was followed by another when she turned to dip a toe in the water and gave him an unimpeded view of the curve of her bottom cheeks.

"Yikes!" She jerked her foot back with a yelp and zinged him an indignant look. "You think this is *cool?* What's your definition of *cold?* Minus forty?"

He grinned and tread water as she dipped another cautious toe. Her face screwed into a grimace. She inched down a step, her shoulders hunched almost to her ears. Eased onto the next step. The water swirled around her calves, her thighs.

"Coward," he teased.

She took another tentative step, and his grin slipped. The water lapped the lower edge of her suit. The bright red material dampened at the apex of her thighs and provided a throat-closing outline of what lay beneath.

"Oh, hell."

He barely heard her mutter of self-disgust. Or felt the splash when she gathered her courage and flopped all the way in. She bobbed up a moment later, her hair a sleek waterfall of pale gold. Sparkling drops beaded her lashes. Laughter lit her eyes.

Something inside Blake shifted. He didn't see the woman who'd lied to him and his family by omission, or the conspirator who'd withheld crucial information about the mother of his child. There were no shadows haunting the eyes of this laughing, splashing water sprite. For the moment at least, no memories constrained her simple pleasure. It was a glimpse of the woman Grace must have been before she took on the burden of her cousin's secrets. An even more tantalizing hint of the woman who might reemerge if and when she shed that burden.

Without conscious thought, Blake realigned his priorities. Convincing his bride to trust him remained his primary goal. Getting her into bed ran a close second. But keeping that carefree laughter in her eyes was fast elbowing its way up close to the top of the list.

"All right," she gasped, dancing on her toes. "I'm in. When does it get to 'not so bad'?"

"Do a couple laps. You'll warm up quick enough."

She made a face but took his suggestion. He rolled into an easy breaststroke and kept pace with her. She had a smooth, clean stroke, he noted with approval, a nice kick. Two laps turned into three, then four. Or what would have been four.

She made the turn, pushed off the wall at an angle and submarined into him. They went under in a tangle of arms and legs. She came up sputtering. He came up with his bride plastered against his chest.

"Sorry!"

Blinking the water out of her eyes, she clung to him. They were at the deep end, in well over their heads. Literally, Blake thought, as her thighs scissored between his. Maybe figuratively.

Hell, there was no maybe about it. He wanted her with a raw need he didn't try to analyze. She must have seen it in his face, felt his muscles tighten under her slick, slippery hands. She looked up at him with a question in her eyes.

"According to our contract," he got out on a near rasp, "any and all physical contact must be by mutual consent. If you don't want this to go any further, you'd better say so now."

After a pause that just about ripped out Blake's guts, she clamped her lips shut and matched him look for look. With another growl, he claimed her mouth.

The kiss was swift and hot and hungry. If he'd interpreted her silence wrong, if she'd tried to push away, Blake would've released her. He was almost sure of that. She didn't, thank God, and he threw off every vestige of restraint.

They went under again, mouths and bodies fused. When they resurfaced, Blake kept her pinned, gave two swift kicks and took them to the wall. He flattened her against the tiles, using one hand to hold them both up while he attacked one strap of her suit with the other. The skin of her shoulder was soft and cool and slick. The mingled scents of lavender and chlorine acted like a spur, turning hunger into greed.

He switched hands, yanked down the other strap. She was as anxious now to shuck her bathing suit as he was to get her out of it. A wiggle, a shimmy, a kick, and it was gone. His followed two heartbeats later.

Her breast fit perfectly in his palm. The flesh was firm and smooth, the tip already stiff from the cold water. He rolled the nipple between his thumb and forefinger and damned near lost it when she arched her back to give him access to her other breast. He hiked her up a few inches, devouring her with teeth and tongue while he slicked his hand down her belly.

"Oh, God!"

Moaning, Grace threw her head back. She'd agreed to this. Had spent more than a few hours tossing around the idea of casual sex with this man. But this—this was nowhere near casual! Blake's mouth scorched her breasts, her shoulder, her throat. And her heart almost jumped out of her chest when he curved his fingers over her mound and parted her crease. She moaned again as he thrust into her and, to her utter mortification, exploded.

The orgasm ripped through her. She rode it blindly, mindlessly, until the spasms died and she flopped like a wet rag doll against his chest.

The thunder in her ears didn't subside. If anything, it grew louder. Only gradually did Grace realize that was Blake's heart tattooing against her ear. Gathering her shattered senses, she raised her head and curved her lips.

The skin at the corners of his blues eyes crinkled as he started to return her smile. Then she wrapped her legs around his hips and his expression froze. Slowly, sensually, she lifted her hips, positioning herself.

"Wait," he got out on a strangled grunt. "We need to take this inside."

"Why?"

"Protection. You need pro…" He broke off, hissing as she angled her hips. "Grace…"

He didn't say it, but she guessed he was thinking of Molly. She certainly was.

"It's okay," she said, breathless and urgent. "I'm covered."

He reacted to that bit of news with gratifying speed. Planting a foot against the tiles, he propelled them toward the shallow end. The sparkling water cascaded over his shoulders and chest as he took a wide stance and hefted her bottom with both palms.

A fresh wave of desire coiled deep in Grace's belly. Eager to give him some of the explosive pleasure he'd given her, she wrapped her legs around his waist. She didn't want slow. Didn't want gentle. When he thrust into her, she slapped her hips into his and clenched every muscle in her body.

He held out longer than she had. Much longer. Grace was close to losing control again when his fingers dug into her bottom cheeks. He went rigid and jammed her against him at an angle that put exquisite, unbearable pressure right where she wanted it the most. With a ragged groan, she arched into another shuddering, shattering climax. This time she took him with her.

Jet lag, a lack of sleep and the most intense sex he'd ever had combined to plow into Blake like an Abrams tank. He remembered helping Grace out of the water and savoring the view before she wrapped herself in one of the villa's blue-and-white-striped pool towels. He vaguely recalled diving back in to retrieve their bathing suits. He wasn't sure whether he'd suggested they stretch out in one of the loungers inside the vine-covered pergola, or she had. But the next time he opened his eyes, the sun had disappeared and hundreds of tiny white lights made a fairyland of the pool area.

He sat up, blinking, and scraped a hand across a sandpaper chin. The movement drew the attention of the woman on the lounger beside his.

"What time is it?" he asked, his voice still thick with sleep.

"I'm not sure. My internal clock is still set to Texas time." She glanced at the canopy of stars outside the pergola. "I'm guessing it's probably nine or nine-thirty."

Blake winced. Great! Absolutely great! Nothing demonstrated a man's virility like taking four or five hours to recharge after sex.

"Sorry I passed out on you."

"No problem." His obvious chagrin had a smile hovering at the corners of her mouth. "I napped, too."

Not for long, apparently. She'd used some of the time he was out cold to change into khaki shorts and a scoop-necked T-shirt. Her hair looked freshly washed, its shining length caught up in a plastic clip.

"Have you eaten?"

"I was waiting for you."

He was still in the swim trunks he'd brought up from the pool. They were dry now and rode low on his hips as he pushed off the lounger and reached out to help her up.

"Let's go raid the kitchen."

The hesitation before she took his hand was so brief he might have imagined it. He couldn't miss the constraint that kept her silent, though, once they'd settled in high-backed wrought-iron stools at the kitchen's monster, green-tiled island. As Madame LeBlanc had indicated, the chef had left a gourmand's dream of sumptuous choices in the fridge and on the counters. Grace opted for a bowl of cold, spicy gazpacho and a chunk of bread torn from one of the long, crusty baguettes poking out of a wire basket. Blake poured them both a glass of light, fruity chardonnay before heaping his plate with salad Niçoise and a man-size wedge of asparagus-and-goat-cheese quiche warmed in the microwave.

He forked down several bites of salad, savoring its red, ripe tomatoes and anchovies, eyeing Grace as she played with her bread, waiting for her to break the small silence. He had a good idea what was behind her sudden constraint. Morning-after nerves, or in this case, evening-after.

She validated his guess a few moments later. Drawing in a deep breath, she tackled the thorny subject head-on. "About what happened in the pool…"

He sensed what was coming and wasn't about to make it easy for her. "What about it?"

"I know we put the possibility of sex on the table when we negotiated this, uh, partnership."

"But?"

She looked down, crumbled her bread, met his gaze again. "But things just spun out of control. I'm as much to blame as you are," she added quickly. "Now that I've had time to think, though, it was too quick, Blake. Too fast."

"We'll take it slower next time."

The solemn promise almost won a smile.

"I *meant* it was too soon. I'm still trying to adjust to this whole marriage business."

"I know." Serious now, he laid down his fork. "But let's clarify one matter. Things didn't just spin out of control. I wanted you, Grace."

Color tinted her cheeks. "I'll concede that point, counselor. And it was obvious I wanted you."

"I understand this is an adjustment period for you, however. For both of us. We've a lot yet to learn about each other."

The deliberate reference to her hoard of secrets brought her chin up. "Exactly. Which is why we should avoid a repetition of what happened this afternoon until you're comfortable with who I am and vice versa."

What the hell would it take to get her to trust him? Irritation put a bite in Blake's voice. "So we just revert back to cool and polite? You think it'll be that easy?"

"No," she admitted, "but necessary if this arrange-ment of ours is going to work."

He swallowed the bitter aftertaste of anchovies and frustration. "All right. We'll take hot, wild sex off the agenda. For now."

* * *

Grace spent the second night of her honeymoon the same way she had her first, restless and conflicted and alone.

While moonlight streamed through windows left open to a soft night breeze, she punched the mounded pillow and replayed the scene in the kitchen. She'd been right to put the brakes on. The way she'd flamed in Blake's arms, lost every ounce of rational thought... She'd never gone so mindless with hunger before. Never craved a man's touch and the wild sensation of his hard, sculpted body crushing hers.

She'd had time to think while Blake dozed this afternoon, and the fact that she'd abandoned herself so completely had shaken her. Still shook her! She'd witnessed firsthand the misery her cousin endured, for God's sake. Had helped Anne run, hide, struggle painfully to regain her confidence and self-respect. Grace couldn't just throw off the brutal burden of those months and years. Nor could she dump it on Blake's broad, willing shoulders—much as she ached to.

No, she was right to pull back. Revert to cool and polite, to use his phrase. They both needed time to adjust to this awkward marriage before they took the next step. Whatever the heck that was.

It took a severe exercise of will, but she managed to block the mental image of Blake pinning her to the tiles and drop into sleep.

She remained firm in her resolve to back things up a step when she went down for breakfast the next morning.

The villa's staff had obviously reported for duty. The heavenly scent of fresh-baked bread wafted from the direction of the kitchen, and a maid in a pale blue uniform wielded a feather duster like a baton at the foot of the stairs. Her eyes lit with curiosity and a friendly welcome when she spotted Grace.

"*Bonjour,* Madame Dalton."

"*Bonjour.*"

That much Grace could manage. The quick spate that followed had her offering an apology.

"I'm sorry. I don't speak French."

"Ah, *excusez-moi.* I am Marie. The downstairs maid, yes? I am most happy to meet you."

"Thank you. It's nice to meet you, too."

She hesitated, not exactly embarrassed but not real eager to admit she didn't have a clue where her husband of two days might be. Luckily, Blake had primed the staff with the necessary information.

"Monsieur Dalton said to tell you that he takes coffee on the east terrace," Marie informed her cheerfully. "He waits for you to join him for breakfast."

"And the east terrace is…?"

"Just there, madame." She aimed the feather duster. "Through the petite salon."

"Thanks."

She crossed the salon's exquisitely thick carpet and made for a set of open French doors that gave onto a flagstone terrace enclosed by ivy-drenched stone walls. A white wrought-iron table held a silver coffee service and a basket of brioche. Blake held his Blackberry and was working the keyboard one-handed while he sipped from a gold-rimmed china cup with the other.

Grace stopped just inside the French doors to drag in several deep breaths. She needed them. The sight of her husband in the clear, shimmering light of a Provencal morning was something to behold. A stray sunbeam snuck through the elms shading the patio to gild his hair. His crisp blue shirt was open at the neck and rolled at the cuffs. He looked calm and collected and too gorgeous for words, dammit!

She sucked in another breath and stepped out onto the patio. "Good morning."

He set down both his coffee cup and the Blackberry and rose.

"Good morning." The greeting was as courteous and impersonal as his smile. "Did you sleep well?"

Right. Okay. This was how she wanted it. What she'd insisted on.

"Very well," she lied. "You?"

"As well as could be expected after yesterday afternoon."

When she flashed a warning look, he shed his polite mask and hooked a brow.

"I zoned out for a good four hours on that lounge chair," he reminded her. "As a consequence, I didn't need much sleep last night."

And if she bought that one, Blake thought sardonically, he had several more he could sell her.

He didn't have to sell them. The swift way she broke eye contact told him she suspected he was stretching the truth until it damned near screamed.

She had to know she'd kept him awake most of the night. She, and her absurd insistence they ignore the wildfire they'd sparked yesterday. As if they could. The heat of it still singed Blake's mind and burned in his gut.

In the small hours of the night he'd called himself every kind of an idiot for agreeing to this farcical facade. It made even less sense in the bright light of morning. They couldn't shove yesterday in a box, stick it on the closet shelf and pretend it never happened. Yet he *had* agreed, and now he was stuck with it.

It didn't improve his mood to discover she'd dabbed on some of the perfumed oil he'd bought her yesterday. The provocative scent tugged at his senses as he pulled out one of the heavy wrought-iron chairs for her.

"Why don't you pour yourself some coffee and I'll tell Auguste we're ready for... Ah, here he is."

At first glance few people would tag the individual who appeared in the open French doors as a graduate of Le Cordon Bleu and two-time winner of the *Coupe du Monde de la Patisserie*—the World Cup of pastry. He sported stooped shoulders, sparse gray hair and a hound-dog face with dewlaps that hung in mournful folds. If he'd cracked a smile anytime in the past two years, Blake sure hadn't seen it.

The great Auguste had been retired for a decade and, according to Delilah, going out of his gourd with boredom when she'd hunted him down. After subjecting the poor man to the full force of her personality, she'd convinced him to take over the kitchen of Hôtel des Elmes.

Blake had made his way to the kitchen earlier to say hello. He now introduced the chef to Grace. Auguste bowed over her hand and greeted her in tones of infinite sadness.

"I welcome you to Saint-Rémy."

Gulping, she threw Blake a what-in-the-world-did-I-do look? He stepped in smoothly.

"I've told Grace about your scallops au gratin, Auguste. Perhaps you'll prepare them for us one evening."

"But of course." He heaved a long-suffering sigh and turned his doleful gaze back to Grace. "Tonight, if you wish it, madame."

"That would be wonderful. Thank you."

"And now I shall prepare the eggs Benedict for you and *monsieur,* yes?"

"Er, yes. Please."

He bowed again and retreated, shoulders drooping. Grace followed his exit with awed eyes.

"Did someone close to him just die?" she whispered to Blake.

The question broke the ice that had crusted between them. Laughing, Blake went back to his own seat.

"Not that I know of. In fact, you're seeing him in one of his more cheerful moods."

"Riiight."

With a doubtful glance at the French doors, she spread her napkin across her lap. He waited until she'd filled a cup with rich, dark brew to offer the basket of fresh-baked brioche.

"We've got dinner taken care of," he said as she slathered on butter and thick strawberry jam. "What would you like to do until then?"

She sent him a quick look, saw he hadn't packed some hidden meaning into the suggestion, and relaxed into her first genuine smile of the morning.

"You mentioned a Van Gogh trail. I'd love to explore that, if you're up for it."

Resolutely, Blake suppressed the memory of his mother ruthlessly dragging Alex and him along every step of the route commemorating Saint-Rémy's most famous artist.

"I'm up for it."

<u>Eight</u>

Grace couldn't have asked for a more perfect day to explore. Sometime while they'd been over the Atlantic, August had rolled into September. The absolute best time to enjoy Provence's balmy breezes and dazzling sunshine, Blake assured her as the sporty red convertible crunched down the front drive. It was still warm enough for her to be glad she'd opted for linen slacks and a cap-sleeved black T-shirt with I ♥ Texas picked out in sparkly rhinestones. She'd caught her hair back in a similarly adorned ball cap to keep the ends from whipping her face.

Blake hadn't bothered with a hat, but his mirrored aviation sunglasses protected his eyes from the glare. With his blue shirt open at the neck and the cuffs rolled up on his forearms, he looked cool and comfortable and too damned sexy for his own or Grace's good.

"I wasn't sure how much you know about Vincent

van Gogh," he said with a sideways glance, "so I printed off a short bio while you were getting ready."

"Thanks." She gratefully accepted the folded page he pulled out of his shirt pocket. "I went to a traveling exhibit at the San Antonio Museum of Art that featured several of his sketches a few years ago. I don't know much about the man himself, though, except that he was Dutch and disturbed enough to cut off his left ear."

"He was certainly disturbed, but there's some dispute over whether he deliberately hacked off his ear or lost it in the scuffle when he went after his pal Gauguin with a straight razor."

While Blake navigated shaded streets toward the outskirts of Saint-Rémy, Grace absorbed the details in the life of the brilliant, tormented artist who killed himself at the age of thirty-seven.

"It says here Van Gogh only sold one painting during his lifetime and died thinking himself a failure. How sad."

"Very sad," Blake agreed.

"Especially since his self-portrait is listed here as one of the ten most expensive paintings ever sold," Grace read, her eyes widening. "It went for $71 million in 1998."

"Which would equate to about $90 million today, adjusted for inflation."

"Good grief!"

She couldn't imagine paying that kind of money for anything short of a supersonic jet transport. Then she remembered the painting of the irises at the villa, and Blake's casual comment that his mother had donated the original to the Smithsonian.

She'd known the Daltons operated in a rarified financial atmosphere, of course. She'd lived in Delilah's rambling Oklahoma City mansion for several months and assisted her with some of her pet charity projects. She'd also picked up bits and pieces about the various megadeals Alex and Blake had in the works at DI. And she'd certainly gotten a firsthand taste of the luxury she'd married into during the flight across the Atlantic and at the Hôtel des Elmes. But for some reason the idea of forking over eighty or ninety million for a painting made it all seem surreal.

Her glance dropped to the diamonds banding her finger. They were certainly real enough. A whole lot more real than the union they supposedly symbolized. Although yesterday, at the pool...

No! Better not go there! She'd just get all confused and conflicted again. Best just to enjoy the sun and the company of the intriguing man she'd married.

A flash of white diverted her attention to the right side of the road. Eyes popping, she stared at a massive arch and white marble tower spearing up toward the sky. "What are those?"

"They're called *Les Antiques*. They're the most visible remnants of the Roman town of Glanum that once occupied this site. The rest of the ruins are a little farther down the road. We'll save exploring them for another day."

He turned left instead of right and drove down a tree-shaded lane bordered on one side by a vacant field and on the other by tall cypresses and the twisted trunks of an olive grove. Beyond the grove the rocky spine of the Alpilles slashed across the horizon.

"Here we are."

"Here," Grace discovered, was the Saint-Paul de Mausole Asylum, which Van Gogh had voluntarily entered in May 1889. Behind its ivy-covered gray stone walls she glimpsed a church tower and a two- or three-story rectangular building.

"Saint-Paul's was originally an Augustine monastery," Blake explained as he maneuvered into a parking space next to two tour buses. "Built in the eleventh or twelfth century, I think. It was converted to an asylum in the 1800s and is still used as a psychiatric hospital. The hospital is off-limits, of course, but the church, the cloister and the rooms where Van Gogh lived and painted are open to the public."

A very interested public, it turned out. The tour buses had evidently just disgorged their passengers. Guides shepherded their charges through the gates and up to the ticket booth. After the chattering tourists clicked through the turnstile single file, Blake paid for two entries and picked up an informational brochure but caught Grace's elbow once they'd passed through the turnstile.

"Let them get a little way ahead. You'll want to experience some of the tranquility Van Gogh did when he was allowed outside to paint."

She had no problem dawdling. The path leading to the church and other buildings was long and shady and lined on both sides by glossy rhododendron and colorful flowers. Adding to her delight, plaques spaced along the walk highlighted a particular view and contrasted it with Van Gogh's interpretation of that same scene.

A depiction of one of his famous sunflower paintings was displayed above a row of almost identical bright yellow flowers nodding in the sun. A low point in the wall provided a sweeping view of silvery-leafed olive trees dominated by the razor-backed mountain peaks in the distance. Van Gogh's version of that scene was done with his signature intense colors and short, bold brushstrokes. Fascinated, Grace stood before the plaque and glanced repeatedly from the trees' gnarled, twisted trunks to the artist's interpretation.

"This is amazing!" she breathed. "It's like stepping into a painting and seeing everything that went into it through different eyes."

She lingered at that plaque for several moments before meandering down the shady path to the next. Blake followed, far more interested in her reaction to Van Gogh's masterpieces than the compositions themselves.

She was like one of the scenes the artist had painted, he mused. She'd come into his life shortly after Molly had, but he'd been so absorbed with the baby it had taken weeks for him to see her as something more than a quietly efficient nanny. The attraction had come slowly and built steadily, but the shock of learning that she'd deceived him—deceived them all—had altered the picture considerably. As had the annoying realization that he'd missed her as much as Molly had when she'd left Oklahoma City.

Yet every time he thought he had a handle on the woman, she added more layers, more bold brushstrokes to the composite. Her fierce loyalty to her cousin and refusal to betray Anne's trust irritated Blake to no end but he reluctantly, grudgingly respected her for it.

And Christ almighty! Yesterday's heat. That searing desire. He knew where his had sprung from. His hunger had been building since… Hell, he couldn't fix the exact point. He only knew that yesterday had stoked the need instead of satisfying it.

Now he'd found another layer to add to the mix—a woman in a black T-shirt and ball cap thoroughly enjoying the view of familiar images from a completely different perspective, just as Blake was viewing her. How many variations of her were there left to discover?

The question both intrigued and concerned him as he walked with her into the round-towered church that formed part of the original monastery. In keeping with the canons of poverty, chastity and obedience embraced by the Augustinian monks, the chapel was small and not overly ornate. The enclosed cloister beside it was also small, maybe thirty yards on each of its four sides. The cloister's outer walls were solid gray stone. Arched pillars framed the inner courtyard and formed a cool, shady colonnade. Sunlight angled through the intricately carved pillars to illuminate a stone sundial set amid a profusion of herbs and plants.

"Oooh," Grace murmured, her admiring gaze on the colonnade's intricately carved pillars. "I can almost see the monks walking two by two here, meditating or fingering their wooden rosaries. And Van Gogh aching to capture this juxtaposition of sunlight and shadow."

The artist couldn't have hurt any more than Blake did at the moment. The same intermingling of sun and shadow played across Grace's expressive face. The warm smile she tipped his way didn't help, either.

"I know you must have visited here several times during your stays in Saint-Rémy. Thanks for making another trek with me. I'm gaining a real appreciation for an artist I knew so little about before."

He masked his thoughts behind his customary calm. "You're welcome, but we're still at the beginning of the Van Gogh trail. You'll discover a good deal more about him as we go."

She made a sweeping gesture toward the far corner of the cloister. "Lead on, MacDuff."

They spent another half hour at Saint-Paul's. The windows in the two austere rooms where Van Gogh had lived and painted for more than a year gave narrow views of the gardens at the rear of the asylum and the rolling wheat fields beyond, both of which the artist had captured in numerous paintings. The garden's long rows of lavender had shed their purple blossoms, but the scent lingered in the air as Grace compared the scene with the plaques mounted along the garden's wall.

At the exit she lingered for a good five minutes in the spot reputedly depicted in *Starry Night,* arguably one of the artist's most celebrated canvases. The glowing golden balls flung across a dark cobalt sky utterly fascinated her and prompted Blake to purchase a framed print of the work at the gift shop. She started to protest that it was too expensive but bit back the words, knowing the stiff price wouldn't deter him any more than the price of the perfumed oil he'd purchased yesterday.

They stopped at the villa to drop off the purchase, then spent a leisurely two hours following the rest of the trail as it wound through the fields and narrow lanes Van Gogh painted when he was allowed to spend time away from the asylum. The trail ended in the center of town at the elegant eighteenth-century *hôtel* that had been converted to a museum and study center dedicated to the artist's life and unique style.

After another hour spent at the museum, Blake suggested lunch in town at a popular restaurant with more tables outside than in. Grace declared the location on one of Saint-Rémy's pedestrians-only streets perfect for people watching. Chin propped in both hands, she did just that while Blake scoped out the wine list. He went with a light, fruity local white and a melted ham-and-cheese sandwich, followed by a dessert of paper-thin crepes dribbling caramel sauce and powdered sugar. Grace opted for a crock of bouillabaisse brimming with carrots, peppers, tomatoes and celery in addition to five varieties of fresh fish, half-shelled oysters, shrimp and lobster. She passed on dessert after that feast, but couldn't resist sneaking a couple of bites of Blake's crepes.

They lingered at the restaurant, enjoying the wine and shade. Grace was sated and languid when they left, and distinctly sleepy-eyed when she settled into the sun-warmed leather of the convertible's passenger seat.

The crunch of tires on the villa's crushed-shell driveway woke her. She sat up, blinking, and laughed an apology.

"Sorry. I didn't mean to doze off on you."

"No problem." He braked to a halt just beyond the fountain of leaping, pawing horses. "At least you didn't go totally unconscious, like I did yesterday."

A hint of color rose in her cheeks. Blake sincerely hoped she was remembering the wild activity that had preceded yesterday's lengthy snooze. He certainly was. The color deepened when he asked with totally spurious nonchalance if she felt like a swim.

"I think I'll clean up a bit and see what's in the library. You go ahead if you want."

"I'll take a pass, too. I've got some emails I need to attend to."

"Okay. I'll, uh, see you later." She swung away, turned back. "Thanks again for sharing Van Gogh with me. I really enjoyed it."

"So did I."

This was what she'd wanted. What she'd insisted on. Grace muttered the mantra several times under her breath as she climbed the stairs to the second floor.

Tugging off her ball cap, she freed her wind-tangled hair and tried a futile finger comb. When she opened the door to the Green Suite, she took two steps inside and stopped dead.

"Omigosh!"

Starry Night held a place of honor above the marble fireplace, all but obscuring the faint outline of whatever painting had hung there before. The print's cool, dark colors seemed to add depth to the silk wall coverings. The swirling stars and crescent moon blazed luminescent trails across the night sky, while the slumbering village below created a sense of quiet and peace. The dark, irregular, almost brooding shape dominating the left side of the print might seem a little sinister to some, but to Grace it was one of the cypress trees Van Gogh had captured in so many of his other works.

She walked into the suite, took a few steps to the side and marveled at how the stars seemed to follow her movements. Then she just stood for long moments, drinking in the print's vibrant colors and thinking of the man who'd obviously instructed it be hung where she could enjoy it during her stay.

Okay, no sense denying the truth when it was there, right in front of her eyes. Blake Dalton was pretty much everything she'd ever dreamed of in a husband. Smart, considerate, fun to be with, too handsome for words. And soooooo good with his hands and mouth and that hard, honed body of his.

She could fall in love with him so easily. Already had, a little. All right, more than a little. She wouldn't let herself tumble all the way, though. Not with her cousin's memory hanging between them like a thin, dark curtain. As fragile as that curtain was, it formed an impenetrable barrier. Grace couldn't tell him the truth, and he couldn't trust her until she did.

Sighing, she turned away from the print and headed for the shower.

The curtain seemed even more impenetrable when she joined Blake for dinner that evening. As promised, Auguste had prepared his version of coquilles St. Jacques. It would be served, she'd been informed, in the small dining room. *Small* being a relative term, of course. Compared with the formal dining hall, which could seat thirty-six with elbow room to spare, this one was used for intimate dinners for ten or twelve. Silver candelabra anchored each end of the gleaming parquet-wood table. Between them sat a silver bowl containing a ginormous arrangement of white lilies and pink roses.

Blake had dressed for the occasion, Grace saw when she entered the room. She felt a funny pang when she recognized the suit he'd worn at their wedding. He'd opted for no tie and left his white shirt open at the neck, though. That quieted her sudden jitters and let her appreciate his casual elegance.

He in turn appeared to approve of the sapphire-colored jersey sundress that had thankfully emerged from her suitcase wrinkle-free. Its slightly gathered skirt fell from a strapless, elasticized bodice. Earrings and a necklace of bright, chunky beads picked up the dress's color and added touches of purple and green, as well.

"Nice dress," Blake commented. "You look good in that shade of blue."

Hell, she looked good in any dress, any shade. Even better out of one. Manfully, he redirected his thoughts from the soft elastic gathers and refused to contemplate on how one small tug could bring them down.

"Would you care for a drink before dinner?" He nodded to the silver ice bucket on its stand. "There's champagne chilling."

"Who can say no to champagne?"

The wine was bottled exclusively for The Elms by the small vintner just outside Epernay Delilah had stumbled across a few years ago. She got such a kick out of presenting her friends and acquaintances with a gift of the private label that her sons had given up trying to convince her not everyone appreciated their champagne ultra brut.

With that in mind, he filled two crystal flutes, angled them to let the bubbles fizz and handed one to Grace.

"What shall we drink to?"

"How about starry nights, as depicted so beautifully by the print you had hung in my bedroom? Thank you for that."

"You're welcome." He chinked his flute to hers. "Here's to many, many starry nights."

He savored the wine's sharp, clean purity but wasn't surprised when Grace wrinkled her nose and regarded her glass with something less than a connoisseur's eye.

"It's, uh…"

"Very dry?"

"Very something."

"They make it with absolutely no sugar," Blake explained, smiling. "It's the latest trend in champagne."

"If you say so."

"Try another sip. Mireille Guiliano highly recommends it in her book *French Women Don't Get Fat*," he tacked on as additional inducement.

"Well, in that case…" She tipped her flute. The nose scrunch came a moment later. "Guess it takes some getting used to."

"Like our marriage," he agreed solemnly, then smiled as he relieved her of the drink. "We're learning to be nothing if not flexible, right? So I had another bottle put on ice just in case."

He made a serious dent in the ultra brut over dinner. Grace limited herself to one glass of the semi-sec but didn't debate or hesitate to accept a second serving of Auguste's decadent scallops au gratin. The chef himself presided over the serving tray and forked three shell-shaped ramekins onto her plate. Blake derived almost as much pleasure from her low, reverent groans of delight as he did from the succulent morsels and sinfully rich sauce.

The awkward moment came after dessert and coffee. Blake could think of a number of ways to fill the rest of the evening. Unfortunately, he'd agreed to take wild, hot sex off the agenda. He had *not* agreed to table slow and sweet, but he gritted his teeth and decided to keep that as his ace in the hole.

"I think there are some playing cards in the library. Want to try your hand at gin rummy?"

"We could. Or..." Her eyes telegraphed a challenge. "We could check out the video room upstairs. I saw it had a Wii console. I'm pretty good at Ubongo, if I do say so myself."

"What's Ubongo?"

"Ahhhh." She crooked a finger, batted her lashes and laid on a heavy French accent. "*Come avec moi, monsieur,* and I will show you, yes?"

A month, even a week ago, Blake would never have imagined he'd spend the second night of his honeymoon frantically jabbing red buttons with his thumbs while jungle critters duked it out on a flat-screen TV and his bride snorted with derision at each miss...or that each snort would only make him want her more.

He fell asleep long after midnight still trying to decide how getting his butt kicked at Ubongo could put such a fierce lock on his heart. But he didn't realize just how fierce until the next afternoon.

Nine

When Grace came downstairs, Blake was pacing the sunny breakfast room with his phone to his ear. He speared a glance at her gauzy peasant skirt topped by a white lacy camisole, waggled his brows and gave a thumbs-up of approval.

She preened a little and returned the compliment. He'd gone casual this morning, too. Instead of his usual hand-tailored oxford shirt with the cuffs rolled up, he'd chosen a black, short-sleeved crew neck tucked into his tan slacks. The clingy fabric faithfully outlined the corded muscles of his shoulders and chest. Grace was enjoying the view when he finished one call and made a quick apology before taking the next.

"Sorry. We've just been notified of a possible nationwide transportation strike that could affect delivery from one of our subs here in France. I've got the plant manager on hold."

She flapped a hand. "Go ahead."

That discussion led to a third, this one a conference call with Alex and DI's VP for manufacturing. Although it was still the middle of the night back in the States, both men were evidently working the problem hard. Grace caught snatches of their discussion while she scarfed down another of Auguste's incredible breakfasts.

Blake apologized again when he finished the call. "Looks like I'll have to hang close to the villa this morning while we refine our contingency plan. Alex said to tell you he's sorry for butting into your honeymoon."

Her honeymoon, she noted. Not his.

"No problem," she replied, shrugging off the little sting. "I want to do some shopping. I'll walk into town this morning."

When she left the villa an hour later, she saw vehicles jammed into every available parking space along the tree-shaded road leading into the heart of town. They were her first clue something was happening. The bright red umbrellas and canvas-topped booths that now sprouted like mushrooms in every nook and cranny of the town provided the second.

Delighted, Grace discovered it was market day in Saint-Rémy. Busy sellers offered everything from books and antiques to fresh vegetables, strings of sausages and giant wheels of cheese. A good many of the stalls displayed the products in the dreamy colors of Provence—pale yellows and pinks and lavenders of the soaps, earthy reds and golds in the pottery and linens.

She wandered the crowded streets and lanes, sniffing the heady scents, eagerly accepting free samples when offered. She bought boxed soaps for friends back in San Antonio, a hand-sewn sundress and floppy-brimmed hat exploding with sunflowers for Molly, a small but exquisitely worked antique cameo brooch as a peace offering for Delilah.

She'd thanked the dealer and was turning away when a wooden case at the back of the umbrella-shaded stall caught her eye. It held what looked like antique man stuff—intricately worked silver shoe buckles, pearl stickpins, a gold-rimmed monocle with a black ribbon loop.

And one ring.

Compared with the other ornate pieces in the case, the ring was relatively plain. The only design on the wide yellow gold band was a fleur-de-lis set in onyx. At least, Grace assumed those glittering black stones were onyx. She learned her mistake when the dealer lifted the ring from the case to give her a closer look.

"Madame has a good eye," he commented. "This piece is very old and very rare. From the seventeenth century. Those are black sapphires in the center."

"I didn't know there *were* black sapphires."

"But yes! Hold the ring to the light. You will see the fineness of their cut."

She did as instructed and couldn't tell squat about the cut, but the stones threw back a black fire that made Grace gasp and gave the dealer the scent of a deal in the making. He added subtle pressure by dropping some of the ring's history.

"It is rumored to have once belonged to the Count of Provence. But the last of the count's descendants lost his head in the Revolution and the rabble sacked and burned his *hôtel,* so we have no written records of this ring. No—how do you call it? Certificate of authenticity. Only this rumor, you understand."

Grace didn't care. She'd walked out of Judge Honeywell's office wearing a band of diamonds. Blake's ring finger was still bare. She didn't need a certificate to rectify the situation. Those shimmering black sparks were authentic enough for her.

"How much is it?"

He named a figure that made her gulp until she realized it was a starting point for further negotiations. She countered. He shook his head and came back with another price. She sighed and put the ring back in the case. He plucked it out again.

"But look at these stones, madame. This workmanship."

"I don't know if it will fit my husband," she argued.

"It can always be resized."

He dropped his glance to the sparkling gems circling her finger. His expression said she could certainly afford to have it fitted, but he cut the price by another fifty euros. Grace did the conversion to dollars in her head, gulped again and tried to remember the exact balance in her much-depleted bank account.

She could cover it. Barely. Squaring her shoulders, she took the plunge. "Do you take Visa?"

The velvet bag containing the ring remained tucked in her purse when she returned to the villa. A local official had delivered documents couriered in from some government source, and Blake had invited her to join them for lunch. The woman was lively company and was delighted to learn Blake intended to show his bride Saint-Rémy's ancient Roman ruins. She also warned they must go that very afternoon, as the archeological site could be affected if the transportation unions went on strike the following day as they'd threatened.

Grace couldn't see the connection but didn't argue

when Blake said he was satisfied with his review of the contingency plans and was free to roam for a few hours. Before they left the villa, though, he made sure his mobile phone was fully charged, then tucked it close at hand in the breast pocket of his shirt.

The monuments she'd spotted through the trees yesterday were even more impressive up close and personal. Blake parked in a dusty, unpaved lot filled with cars and what turned out to be school buses. Grace had to smile at the noisy, exuberant teens piling out of the buses.

"I've taken my classes on a few field trips like this one," she commented. "It's always tough to judge how much of what they'll see actually sinks in."

Not much, Blake guessed. At least for the young, would-be studs in the crowd. As both he and his brother could verify, the attention of boys that age centered a whole lot more on girls in tight jeans than ancient ruins.

Boys of any age, actually. Grace wasn't in jeans, but she snagged more than one admiring look from the male students and their teachers as she and Blake joined the line straggling along the dirt path to *Les Antiques*.

The two monuments gleamed white in the afternoon sun. Blake couldn't remember which triumph the massive arch was supposed to commemorate—the conquest of Marseille, he thought—but he knew the perfectly preserved marble tower beside the arch had served as a mausoleum for a prominent Roman family. Luckily, descriptive plaques alongside each monument provided the details in both French and English.

Blake wasn't surprised that the teacher in Grace had to read every word, much as she had on the Van Gogh trail yesterday. Peering over the heads of the kids, she glanced from the plaque to the intricate pattern decorating the underside of the arch.

"This is interesting. Those flowers and vines repre-sent the fertility of 'the Roman Province,' aka *Provence*. I didn't know that's where the region's name came from."

Two of the teens obviously thought she'd addressed the comment to them. One turned and pulled an ear-bud from his ear. The other tucked what looked like a sketchbook under his arm and asked politely, *"Pardon, madame?"*

"The name, Provence." She gestured to the sign. "It's from the Latin."

"Ah, oui."

Blake hid a smile as the boys looked her over with the instinctive appreciation of the male of the species. They obviously liked what they saw. And who wouldn't? Her hair was a wind-tossed tangle of pale silk, and the skin displayed all too enticingly by the white lace camisole had been warmed to a golden tan by the hot Provencal sun. Not surprisingly, the boys lagged behind while the rest of their group posed and snapped pictures of each other under the watchful eyes of their teachers.

"You are from the U.S.?" the taller of the two asked.

"I am," she confirmed. "From Texas."

"Ahhh, Texas. Cowboys, yes? And cows with the horns like this."

When he extended his arms, Grace grinned and spread hers as far as they would go. "More like this."

"Oui?"

"Oui. And you? Where are you from?"

"Lyon, madame."

The shorter kid was as eager as his pal to show off his English. "We study the Romans," he informed Grace, his earbud dangling. "They were in Lyon, as in many other parts of Provence. You have seen the coliseum in Arles and the Pont du Gard?"

"Not yet."

"But you must!" The taller kid whipped his sketchbook from under his arm, flipped up the lid and riffled through the pages. "Here is the Pont du Gard."

Grace was impressed. So was Blake. He'd visited the famous aqueduct a number of times. The kid's drawings captured both the incredible engineering and soaring beauty of its three tiers of arches.

One of the teachers came over at that point to see what his students were up to. When he discovered Grace was a teacher, he joined the kids in describing the Roman sites she should be sure to visit while in the south of France. He also provided her a list of the architectural and historical items of interest he'd tasked his students to search out at *Les Antiques* and the adjoining town of Glanum.

"What a good idea," Grace exclaimed as she skimmed the Xeroxed four pages. "It's like a treasure hunt."

"The class searches in teams," the teacher explained. "You should join us. You will gain a far better appreciation of this site."

"I'd love to but..." She threw Blake a questioning glance. "Do we have time?"

"Sure."

"We can team up."

Blake gauged the boys' reaction to that with a single glance. "You and these fellows do the hunting," he said easily. "I'll follow along."

List in hand, she joined the search. Her unfeigned interest and ready smile made willing slaves of her two teammates. Preening like young gamecocks, they translated the background history of the first item on the list, and crowed with delight when they collectively spotted the chained captives at the base of the arch representing Rome's might.

Blake found a shady spot and rested his hips against a fallen marble block, watching as Grace and her team searched out two additional items on the arch and three on the tall, pillared tower of the mausoleum. He wondered if the boys had any idea that she let them do the discovering. Or that her seemingly innocent questions about the translations forced them to delve much deeper into the history of the site than they otherwise would have. Those two, at least, were going home experts on *Les Antiques*.

The hunt took them across the street and down another hundred yards to the entrance to Glanum. Unlike the arch and mausoleum, access to the town itself was controlled and active excavations were under way at several spots along its broad main street. Despite the roped-off areas, there was still plenty to explore. The students poked into the thermal furnaces that heated the baths, clambered over the uneven stones of a Hellenistic temple and followed the narrow, twisty track through the ravine at the far end of town to the spring that had convinced Gauls to settle this site long before the Romans arrived.

Grace was right there with her team, carefully picking her way down a flight of broken marble steps to the pool fed by the sacred spring. The fact that she could translate the Latin inscription dedicating the pool to Valetudo, the Roman goddess of health, scored her considerable brownie points with the kids. The delight they took in her company scored even more with Blake.

He could guess the kind of dreams those boys would

have tonight. He'd had the same kind at their age. Still had 'em, he admitted wryly, his gaze locked on his wife.

The hunt finished, Grace exchanged email addresses with her teammates and their teacher before walking back to the car with Blake.

"You were really good with those kids," he commented.

"Thanks. I enjoy interacting with teens. Most of them have such lively minds, although the mood swings and raging hormones can be a pain at times."

Their footsteps stirred the dust on the unpaved path. A car whizzed by on the road to the mountain village high up in the Alpilles. The scents of summer lingered on the still air. Blake grasped her elbow to guide her around a rough patch, then slid his hand down to take hers.

He saw her glance down at the fingers interlacing hers. A small line creased her forehead, but she didn't ease her hand away until they reached the convertible. Blake chalked the frown up to the unsettled nature of their marriage and started to open the passenger door for her. She planted her hip against the door, stopping him.

"I bought you something while I was in town this morning." She fished a small velvet bag out of her purse. "It's not much. But I saw it and thought of you and our time here in France and… Well, I just wanted you to have it."

When he untied the strings, a heavy gold ring rolled into his palm. The fleur-de-lis embedded in its center flashed a rainbow of sparks.

"The dealer said it's an antique. He thinks it once belonged to the Count of Provence, but there's no documentation to support that claim." She looked from the ring to him with a mix of uncertainty and shyness. "Do you like it?"

"Very much. Thank you."

The heartfelt thanks dissolved both the shyness and uncertainty. "You're welcome."

The inquiries Blake had run into her finances told him she must have maxed out her credit card to buy the ring, but he knew better than to ruin the moment by asking if she needed a quick infusion of funds. He showed his appreciation instead by tilting the design up to the light.

"The stones are brilliantly cut."

"That's what the dealer said."

"He said right. You rarely find sapphires with so many facets."

"How'd you guess they're sapphires?"

Grinning, he lowered the ring. "Mother has me take care of insurance appraisals and certificates of authenticity for all her jewelry. She's got more rare stones in her collection than the Smithsonian."

"I don't doubt it. Here," she said when he started to slide it on. "Let me."

She eased the ring onto his finger, then hesitated with the band just above the knuckle.

"With this ring…"

The soft words hit with a jolt, ricocheting around in Blake's chest as she worked the ring over his knuckle. It was a tight fit, but the gold band finally slid on.

"…I thee wed."

Grace finished in a whisper and folded her hand over his. Blake didn't respond. He couldn't. His throat was as tight as a drum.

"I can recall every minute in Judge Honeywell's office," she confessed on a shaky laugh. "I can hear the words, replay the entire scene in vivid Technicolor. Yet…"

She glanced around the dusty parking lot, brought her gaze back to his.

"This is the first time I feel as though it's all for real."

"It is real. More than I imagined it could be back there in the judge's office."

His hand tightened, crushing hers against the heavy gold band. She glanced down, startled, then met his gaze again.

"Let me take you home and show you just how real it's become for me."

Blake had no doubts. None at all. He made the short drive to the villa on a surge of adrenaline and desire so thick and heavy it clamped his fists on the steering wheel.

Uncertainty didn't hit until he followed Grace up the stairs and into the cool confines of the Green Suite. When she turned to face him, he half expected her to retreat again, insist they go back to cool and polite.

He'd never wanted a woman the way he wanted this one. Never loved one the way he did his bright, engaging, sun-kissed bride. The fierce acknowledgment rattled him almost as much as the hunger gnawing at his insides. He could slam on the brakes if he had to, though. It would damned near kill him, but he could do it. All she had to do was…

"Lock the door."

It took a second or two for his brain to process the soft command. Another couple for him to click the old-fashioned latch into place. When he turned back, she reached for the top button on her camisole.

His uncharacteristic doubts went up in a blaze of

heat. With a low growl, he brushed her hands aside. "I've been fantasizing about popping these buttons since you came downstairs this morning."

He forced himself to undo them slowly. He wanted the pleasure of baring the slopes of her breasts inch by tantalizing inch. But his greedy pleasure splintered into something close to pain when he peeled back the cottony fabric and revealed the half bra underneath. With a concentration that popped sweat on his brow, he slid the camisole off her shoulders.

Damn! He was as jerky and eager as any of the adolescents they'd encountered this afternoon. Grace was the steady one. She displayed no hint of embarrassment or shyness when the camisole slithered down her arms and dropped to the carpet.

She reached back and unhooked her bra. The movement was so essentially female, so erotic and arousing. Blake ached for the feel of her smooth, firm flesh against his. But when he dragged his shirt free of his slacks, she copied his earlier move and brushed his hands aside.

"My turn."

Just as he had, she took her time. Her palms edged under the shirt, flattened on his stomach, glided upward. Blake bent so she could get it off over his head. His breath razored in, then out when her hands slid south again. A smile played in her eyes when she found his belt buckle.

"I've been fantasizing about *this* since I came downstairs this morning."

"Okay, that's it!"

He had her in his arms in one swoop and marched to the bed.

Ten

The session in the swimming pool had sprung the beast in Blake. This time, he was damned if he would let it slip its leash. He kept every move slow and deliberate as he dragged the brocade coverlet back and stretched Grace out on the soft, satiny sheets.

He took his time removing the rest of her clothes, and his. As he joined her on the cool, satiny sheets, his eyes feasted on her lithe curves. Tan lines made a noticeable demarcation at her shoulders and upper thighs. The skin between was soft and pale and his to explore.

"Too bad Van Gogh isn't around to paint you." He stroked the creamy slopes and valleys. "You would have inspired him to even greater genius."

"I seriously doubt that."

"Well, you certainly inspire me. Like here…"

He brushed a kiss across her mouth.

"And here…"

His lips traced her cheeks and feathered her lids. "And here…"

Mounding her breast, he teased the nipple with his teeth and tongue until it puckered stiff and tight. Blake gave the other breast equal attention and got a hint of the anguish Van Gogh must have suffered over his masterpieces. He was feeling more than a little tormented himself as he explored the landscape of his wife's body.

She didn't lay passive during the investigation. She flung one arm above her head, brought it down again to plane her hand over his shoulder and down his back. Fingers eager, she kneaded his hip and butt.

Blake felt the muscles low in his belly jerk in response but refused to rush the pace. His palm slid over her rib cage, down her belly. Her stomach hollowed under his touch, and a knee came up as he threaded the dark gold hair of her mound. He slid one finger inside the hot, slick lips, then two, and pressed the tight bud between with his thumb.

Her breath was a fast, shallow rasp now. His was almost as harsh. And when she rolled and nudged him onto his back, it shot damned near off the chart.

She went up on an elbow and conducted her own exploration. Just as slowly. Just as thoroughly. His chin and throat got soft kisses, his shoulder a nuzzle and a teasing nip. She followed by lightly scraping a fingertip down his chest and through hair that arrowed toward his groin.

"Now here," she said with a wicked grin as her fingers closed around him, "we have a real masterpiece."

"You won't hear me argue with that," he returned, his grin matching hers.

She gave a huff of laughter and stroked him, gently at first, then with increasing pressure. The friction coiled him as tight as a centrifuge, but he was confident in his ability to extend this period of mutual discovery awhile longer yet. Right up until she bent down, took him in her mouth and shot his confidence all to hell and back.

His breath left on a hiss. Everything below his waist went on red alert. He managed to hang on for a few moments longer but knew his control was about to blow.

"Grace…"

The low warning brought her head up. Her lips were wet and glistening, her eyes cloudy with desire. When he would have reversed positions, she preempted him by hooking a leg over his thighs. She guided him into her, gasping when he thrust upward, and dropped forward to plant her hands on his chest. The skin over her cheeks was stretched tight. Her hair formed a tangled curtain. Blake had never seen anything more beautiful or seductive in his life.

"Forget Van Gogh," he said gruffly. "Not even he could do you justice."

He shoved his hands through her hair and brought her down for a kiss that was as fierce as it was possessive.

Grace came awake with a twitch. Something rasped like fine sandpaper against her temple. Blake's chin, she decided after a hazy moment. Unshaven and bristly. Deciding to ignore the movement, she burrowed her nose deeper into the warm crevice between his neck and shoulder.

"Grace?"

"Mmmm."

"You awake?"

"Nuh-uh."

"No?"

He shifted, and the chin made another scrape. Grace

raised her head and squinted at the dim shadows wreathing the room.

"Whatimeizzit?"

"Close to six, I think."

"Jeez!"

Her head dropped. Her cheek thumped his chest. She tried to drift back into sleep but laughter rumbled annoyingly under her ear.

"Not a morning person, I take it."

"Not a 6:00 a.m. person," she mumbled, sounding sulky even to herself.

"I'll keep that in mind for future reference."

It took a few moments for that to penetrate her sleepy fog. When it did, she pushed up on an elbow and shoved her hair out of her eyes. She wasn't awake enough to address the subject of the future head-on. Or maybe she just didn't have the nerve. Still a little grumpy, she went at it sideways.

"Are you? A morning person, I mean?"

"Pretty much." An apologetic smile creased his whiskery cheeks. "I've been awake for an hour or so."

She groaned and would have made a dive for the pillows, but he shifted again. She ended up lying on her side, facing him, with her head propped on a hand and her thoughts hijacked by a worry about morning breath. She ran a quick tongue over her teeth. They didn't feel too fuzzy. And her lips weren't caked with drool, thank God! She refused to think about her uncombed hair and unwashed face. Or how much she needed to pee.

Blake, of course, looked totally gorgeous in the dim light. A lazy smile lit his wide-awake blue eyes, and he was tantalizingly naked above the rumpled sheets. He even smelled good. Sort of musky and masculine and warm.

When she finished inspecting the little swirl of dark gold hair around his navel and brought her gaze back to his face, she saw his smile had taken on a different slant. Less lazy. More serious.

"I did some thinking while I was lying here waiting for you to rejoin the living."

She guessed from his expression what he'd been cogitating over but asked anyway. "About?"

"Us."

The arm propping her up suddenly felt shaky. Did he want to alter their still-evolving relationship? Renegotiate the contract? After last night, she was certainly open to different terms and conditions. Still, she had to work to keep her voice steady.

"And what did you conclude, counselor?"

"I want to make this work, Grace. You, me, our marriage."

"I thought we were making it work."

"Bad word choice. I meant make it real."

He reached over to tuck a tangled strand behind her ear. She held her breath until he'd positioned it to his satisfaction.

"I want to spend the rest of my life with you. You and Molly and the children we might have together."

Oh, God! Were they really having this discussion with her teeth unbrushed and her face crumpled into sleep lines? She couldn't fall on his chest again, lock her mouth on his and show him how much she wanted the exact same things.

"Hold on."

Surprise blanked his face at the terse order. A swift frown followed almost instantly as she threw off the sheet.

"I'll be right back."

She spent all of three minutes in the bathroom. When she emerged, he was sitting with his back against the padded silk headboard. The scowl remained, but the fact that she was still naked seemed to reassure him. That, and the joy she didn't try to disguise when she scrambled onto the bed and knelt facing him.

"Okay, I can respond properly now. Repeat what you said, word for word."

He hooked a brow and repeated obediently, "I want to spend the rest of my life with you."

"Me and…" she prompted.

"You and Molly and the children we might have together."

A giddy happiness gathered in her throat, but she had to make sure. "And you can live with the fact that I won't…can't tell you Anne's secrets?"

"I don't like it," he admitted honestly, "but I can live with it."

"Then I say we go for it. Molly, more babies, the whole deal."

The laughter came back, and with it a tenderness that made her heart hurt.

"Whew! You had me worried there for a moment."

"Yes, well, for future reference, you probably want to wait until I've brushed my teeth to spring something like that on me."

"I'll add that to the list," he said as she framed his face with both hands.

She reveled in the scrape of his whiskery cheeks, amazed and humbled at the prospect of sharing the months and years ahead with this smart, handsome, incredible man. Every tumultuous hope for their future filled her heart as she leaned in and sealed their new contract.

* * *

Given the rocky start to her marriage, Grace would never have believed her honeymoon would turn into the stuff that dreams are made of.

Last-minute negotiations averted the threatened strike, so no further business issues intruded and Grace had her husband's undivided attention. As she'd already discovered, he woke early and disgustingly energized. She wasn't exactly a sloth, but she did prefer to open her eyes to sunshine versus a dark, shadowy dawn. They compromised by making love late into the night, every night, and in the morning only after she'd come fully alert. Afternoons and early evenings were up for grabs.

They also spent long hours learning about the person they'd married. Grace already knew Blake liked to read but until now had only seen him buried behind *The Wall Street Journal* or *The New York Times* or the latest nonfiction bestseller. She raided the library on one of Provence's rare rainy afternoons and wooed him away from the real world by curling up with a copy of one of her all-time favorites. He didn't exactly go into raptures over *Jane Eyre* but agreed the heroine did develop some backbone toward the end of the story.

Grace returned the favor by digging into the bestseller he'd picked up at a store in town that stocked books in English as well as French. Although she had a good grasp of American history, she never expected to lose herself in a biography of James Garfield. But historian Candace Millard packed high drama and nail-biting suspense into her riveting *Destiny of the Republic: A Tale of Madness, Medicine and the Murder of a President.*

Aside from that one rainy afternoon, they spent most of the daylight hours outside in the pool or in town or exploring Provence. The Roman ruins of Glanum had fired Grace's interest in the area's other sights. The coliseum at Arles and arch of ramparts in Orange more than lived up to her expectations. The undisputed highlight of their journey into the far-distant past, however, was the gastronomical masterpiece of a picnic Auguste had prepared for their jaunt to the three-tiered Pont du Gard aqueduct. They consumed truffle-stuffed breast of capon and julienne carrots with baby pearl onions in great style on the pebbly banks of the river meandering under the ancient aqueduct.

They jumped more than a dozen centuries when they toured the popes' palace at Avignon. Constructed when a feud between Rome and the French King Philip IV resulted in two competing papacies, the palace was a sprawling city of stone battlements and turrets that dominated a rocky outcropping overlooking the Rhône. From there the natural next step was a visit to Châteauneuf du Pape, another palace erected by the wine-loving French popes to promote the area's viticulture. It was set on a hilltop surrounded by vineyards and olive groves and offered a private, prearranged tasting of rich red blends made from grenache, counoise, Syrah and muscadine grapes.

Each day brought a new experience. And each day Grace fell a little more in love with her husband. The nights only added to the intensity of her feelings. The unabashed romantic in her wanted to spin out indefinitely this time when she had Blake all to herself. Her more practical self kept interrupting that idyllic daydream with questions. Like where they would live. And whether she would transfer her teaching certificate from Texas to Oklahoma. And how Delilah would react to the altered relationship between her son and Grace.

Her two sides came into direct conflict the bright, sunny morning they drove to the open-air market in a small town some twenty miles away. L'Isle sur la Sorgue's market was much larger than Saint-Rémy's and jam-packed with tourists in addition to serious shoppers laying in the day's provisions, but the exuberant atmosphere and lovely old town bisected by the Sorgue River made browsing the colorful stalls a delight.

For a late breakfast they shared a cup of cappuccino and a waffle cone of succulent strawberries capped with real whipped cream. They followed that with samples of countless varieties of cheese and sausage and fresh-baked pastries. So many that when Blake suggested lunch at one of the little bistros lining the town's main street, Grace shook her head and held up the paper bag containing the wrapped leek-and-goat-cheese tarts they'd just purchased.

"One of these is enough for me. All I need is something to wash it down with."

He pointed her to the benches set amid the weeping willows gracing the riverbank. The trees' leafy ribbons trailed in the gently flowing water and threw a welcome blanket of shade over the grassy bank.

"Sit tight," Blake instructed. "We passed a fresh-fruit stand a few stalls back. They mix up smoothies like you wouldn't believe. Any flavor favorites?"

"I'm good for anything except kiwi. I can't stand the hairy little things."

"No kiwi in yours. Got it. One more item to add to our future reference list."

The list was getting longer, Grace thought with a smile as she sat on the grass and stretched out her legs. Other people were scattered along the bank. Mothers and fathers and grandparents lounged at ease, with each generation keeping a vigilant eye on the young-sters tempting fate at the river's edge. A little farther away one young couple had gone horizontal, so caught up in the throes of youthful passion that they appeared in imminent danger of locking nose rings. Their moves started slow but soon gathered enough steam to earn a gentle rebuke from two nuns walking by on the side-walk above and a not-so-gentle admonition from a father entertaining two lively daughters while his wife nursed a third. His words were low and in French, but Grace caught the drift. So did the lovers. Shrugging, they rolled onto their stomachs and confined their erotic exchange to whispers and Eskimo nose rubs.

Grace's glance drifted from them to the mother nurs-ing her child. As serene as a Madonna in a painting by a grand master, she held the baby in the crook of her elbow and gently eased the nipple between the gummy lips. She didn't bother with a drape or cover over her shoulder, but performed the most natural task in the world oblivious to passersby. Men quickly averted their eyes. Some women smiled, some looked as though they were recounting memories of performing this same act, and one or two showed an expression of envy.

The scene stirred a welter of emotions in Grace she'd thought long buried. She'd prayed during Anne's trou-bled marriage that her cousin wouldn't get pregnant and produce a child to tie her even more to Jack Petrie. So what did Anne do after escaping the nightmare of her marriage and slowly, agonizingly regaining her self-respect? She fell for a high-powered attorney, turned up pregnant, panicked and ran again. Only this time she didn't run far or fast enough to escape her fear. Anne landed in a hospital in San Diego, and her baby landed in Grace's arms.

Grace had done her damndest not to let Molly wrap her soft, chubby arms wrap around her heart. It had been a losing battle right from the start. Almost the first moment she held Anne's daughter in her arms, she'd started working a contingency plan in her mind. She would keep Molly under wraps while she let it leak to friends that she was pregnant. Once she was sure word had gotten back to Anne's sadistic husband, she would take a leave of absence from her job and play out a fake pregnancy somewhere where no one knew her. Then she'd raise Molly as her own.

Instead, her dying cousin had begged Grace to deliver the baby to her father. Grace had conceded. Reluctantly. She understood the rationale, accepted that the child belonged with her father. The weeks Grace had spent with the Daltons as Molly's temporary nanny had only reinforced that inescapable fact. But the bond between her and Molly had become a chain around her heart. She'd dreaded with every ounce of her soul breaking that chain and walking away from both the child and the dynamic, charismatic Daltons. Now the chain remained intact.

Drawing up her legs, Grace rested her chin on her knees. She still needed to put a contingency plan into operation. She couldn't take the chance that Anne's sadistic husband might discover Grace had married a man with a young baby. Petrie would check Blake out, discover he wasn't a widower, wonder how he'd acquired an infant daughter just about the same time Grace came into his life.

She would contact a few of her friends in San Antonio, she decided grimly. Imply she'd met someone late last year, maybe during the Christmas break, and had spent the spring semester and summer vacation adjusting to the unexpected result. Then Blake Dalton had swooped in and convinced her to marry him.

Those deliberately vague seeds would sprout and spread to other coworkers. Eventually some version of the story might reach Jack Petrie. It should be enough to throw him off Molly's scent. It had to be!

Lost in her contingency planning, she didn't hear Blake's return until he came up beside her.

"One strawberry-peach-mango combo for you. One blueberry-banana for me."

She moved the sack with the tarts to make room for him on the patch of grass. Legs folded, he sank down with a loose-limbed athletic grace and passed her a plastic cup heaped with whipped cream and a dark red cherry. They ate in companionable silence, enjoying the scene.

The Sorgue River flowed smooth and green just yards away. The young lovers were still stretched out nose-to-nose. The father was hunkered down at the river's bank within arm's reach of his two laughing, wading daughters. His wife held the baby against her shoulder now and was patting up a burp.

Grace let a spoonful of her smoothie slide down a throat that suddenly felt raw and tight. This baby looked nothing like Molly. Her eyes were nowhere near as bright a blue, and instead of Mol's golden curls, she had feathery, flyaway black hair her mother had obviously tried to tame with a jaunty pink bow. Yet when she waved tiny, dimpled fists and gummed a smile, Grace laughed and returned it.

Blake caught the sound and followed her line of sight. Hooking an elbow on his knee, he watched the baby's antics until she let loose with a burp that carried clearly across the grass. After another, quieter encore, her mother slid her down into nursing position.

When Grace gave a small sigh, Blake studied her profile. He wasn't surprised by what he saw there, or by the plea in her eyes when she turned to him.

"I've had an incredible time in Provence," she said slowly. "Every day, every night with you has been a fantasy come true."

She threw another look at the baby, and he read her thoughts.

"I miss Molly, too," he admitted with a wry grin. "Let's go home."

Eleven

His mind made up, Blake moved with characteristic speed and decisiveness. While he and Grace threaded through the crowded market to their car, he used his cell phone to run a quick check of flight schedules for Dalton International's air fleet. The corporate jet was on the wrong side of the Atlantic, so he booked first-class seats on a commercial nonstop flight to Dallas leaving late that afternoon. With the time differential and the short hop to Oklahoma, they would get home at almost the same hour they departed France.

That left Grace barely an hour to throw her things together and say goodbye to Auguste and the rest of the staff. Blake's farewells included exorbitant gratuities for each member of the staff and a promise to bring madame back for a longer stay very soon.

The rush of leaving and her eagerness to get back to Molly carried Grace halfway across the Atlantic. Having Blake beside her in the luxurious first-class cabin staved off fatigue during the remainder of the trip. His low-voiced, less than complimentary commentary on the action flick they watched together had her giggling helplessly and the other passengers craning to see what was on their screens.

Fatigue didn't factor in until after the plane change in Dallas. Fatigue, and a serious case of nerves about coming face-to-face with Blake's mother again. Delilah had let loose with both barrels at her last meeting with Grace. The note from her that Alex delivered in San Antonio had much the same tone. She hadn't been happy about the hurry-up wedding and warned that she'd have something to say about it when the newlyweds returned from France.

Grace couldn't imagine how the redoubtable Dalton matriarch would react to the altered relationship between her son and his bride. Delilah must have known Blake proposed for strictly utilitarian reasons. Mostly utilitarian, anyway. Would she believe his feelings could undergo a major shift in such a short time? Probably not. Grace could hardly believe it herself.

By the time they turned onto the sweeping drive that led to Delilah's Nichols Hills mansion, dread curled like witches' fingers in her stomach. Then the front door flew open and she saw at a glance she'd underestimated Delilah. The older woman took one look at them and gave a whoop that boomed like a cannon shot in the brisk September air.

"I knew it!" she announced gleefully as they mounted the front steps. "No one can resist the fatal combination of Provence and Auguste. Especially two people who were so danged hot for each other."

"Don't you ever get tired of being right?" Blake drawled as he bent to kiss her cheek.

"Never." Blue eyes only a shade lighter than her son's skewered Grace. "And that's something for you to remember, too, missy. Now get over here and so I can give my newest daughter-in-law a hug."

Enfolded in a bone-crunching embrace and a cloud of outrageously expensive perfume, Grace made the instant transition from employee and former nanny to member of the family. She was so grateful to this fierce and occasionally overbearing woman that she found herself battling tears.

"Thank you for trusting me with Molly and for…and for…everything."

"We should be thanking you." The hug got tighter, Delilah's voice gruffer. "You brought Molly to us in the first place."

Both women were sniffling when they separated. Embarrassed by her uncharacteristic descent into sentimentality, Delilah flapped a hand toward the stairs.

"I expect you want to see the baby. She's up in the nursery. I just heard her on the monitor, waking up from her nap."

The last time Grace had climbed this magnificent circular staircase was as an employee in Delilah's home. She couldn't quite get a grip on her feelings as she ascended them alongside Blake, anxious to embrace the baby now making come-get-me noises from the room on the left at the top of the stairs. Nerves played a major role. Excitement and eagerness bubbled in there, too. But mostly it was sheer incredulity that she now had the right to claim this man and this child as hers.

When they swept into the nursery Delilah had furnished so swiftly and so lavishly, Molly was standing up in the crib. Her downy blond hair formed a spiky halo and her blue eyes tracked their entrance with a touch of impatience, as if asking what took them so long.

Grace's heart melted into a puddle of mush at the sight of her. It disintegrated even more when Molly gave a gurgle of delight and raised her arms.

"Gace!"

Half laughing, half sobbing, Grace swept the baby out of the crib.

September rolled out and October came in with a nighttime temperature dip into the forties and fifties. As the weeks flew by, a nasty little corner of Grace's mind kept insisting this couldn't last. Sometime, somehow, she would pay for the joy she woke up with every morning. But her busy, busy days and nights spent in Blake's arms buried that niggling thought under an avalanche of others.

Their first order of business was finding a house. Rather than move Molly's nursery to Blake's bachelor pad during the hectic process of inspecting available properties, they accepted Delilah's invitation to occupy the guest wing of her mansion. So naturally both Molly and Delilah went with Grace to check out the possibilities when Blake got tied up at work. Julie, too, when she wasn't flying or distracted by the business of setting up the home she and Alex had recently moved into.

Grace worried at first that Delilah might try to push her toward something big and splashy, but her mother-in-law was motivated by only one goal. She wanted her granddaughter close enough to spoil at will. So she was thrilled when Grace settled on a recently renovated half-timbered home less than a mile from the Dalton mansion. The two-story house sat well back from the street on a one-acre lot shaded by tall pines. Grace had fallen in love with its oak floors and open, sunny kitchen at first sight, but balked at the five bedrooms until Blake convinced her they could convert one to an entertainment center and one to an exercise room unless and until they needed it for other purposes.

Once the house was theirs, Grace faced the daunting prospect of filling its empty rooms. She thought about tackling one room at a time, but Delilah graciously offered the services of her decorator to coordinate the overall scheme.

"Take her up on it," Julie urged during a weekend brunch at their mother-in-law's.

The two brides lolled on the sunlit terrace, keeping a lazy eye on Molly in her net playpen while their husbands checked football scores in the den. Delilah had taken her other guest to the library to show him some faded photographs she'd unearthed from her early days working the oil fields with her husband. Grace found it extremely interesting that Julie's irascible partner, Dusty Jones, had apparently become a regular visitor to the Nichols Hills mansion.

"The decorator is good," her new sister-in-law asserted. "Really good."

Grace could hardly disagree. She'd lived in these opulent surroundings for several months as Molly's nanny. The Lalique chandeliers and magnificent antiques suited Delilah's flair and flamboyance, but Grace had lived in constant dread of Molly spitting up all over one of the hand-woven Italian silk seat cushions.

"Trust me," Julie urged. "Victor will help you achieve just the look you want. He understood right away that I wanted to go clean and uncluttered in our place. I've agreed with almost everything he's suggested so far."

"Surprising everyone concerned," Grace drawled, "yourself included."

"True," the redhead agreed, laughing. "I do tend to formulate strong opinions about things...as Alex frequently points out."

Marriage agreed with her, Grace thought. She looked so relaxed and happy with her auburn hair spilling over her shoulders and her fingers playing with the gold pendant Alex had given her as an engagement gift. The figure depicted on the intricately carved disk was the Inca god who supposedly rose from Lake Titicaca in the time of darkness to create the sun, the moon and the stars. Julie, who'd spent several years ferrying cargo in and out of remote airstrips in South America, had told Grace the god's name but she could never remember it.

"Might as well bow to the inevitable and give Victor a call," Julie advised, stretching languidly. "If you don't, Delilah will just invite him for cocktails one evening and make the poor guy go over your house plans room by room while she pours martinis down his throat."

"Okay, okay. I'll call him."

The two women sat in companionable silence. They'd known each other for only a few months but had become friends in that short time. Marrying twins had solidified the bond. It had also given them unique perspectives into each other's lives.

Grace had worried that her being the one to provide indisputable proof that Blake was Molly's father might drive a wedge between the brothers. Or between her and Alex. Until those final DNA results had come back, the preponderance of evidence had pointed to Alex as the most likely father. He'd taken the baby into his heart and had rearranged his life around her. The home he and Julie had just moved into had been bought with Molly in mind.

Alex appeared to have adjusted to being the baby's uncle instead of her father. He was just as attentive, and every bit as loving. Still, Grace struggled with a twinge of guilt as his wife got up to retrieve the stuffed turtle Molly had chucked out of her playpen.

"Tell me the truth," she said quietly when Julie dropped into her chair again. "Did Alex resent me for keeping my cousin's secret?"

"He did, for maybe a day or two after Blake showed him the final DNA results. He's a big boy, though. He worked through his disappointment." Her eyes took on a wicked glint. "I might have helped the process by redirecting his thoughts whenever I thought they needed it."

"Yes, I bet you... Oops, that's Blake's phone. He said something about expecting a call from Singapore. This may be it."

She scooped up the device he'd left on the table and checked caller ID. The number was a local one.

"Guess it's not Singapore."

Evidently the caller decided his message was too urgent to go to voice mail. Grace had no sooner set the phone down than it buzzed again, this time with a flashing icon indicating a text message.

"I'd better take this in to him. Keep an eye on Molly for me."

"Will do."

Phone in hand, she followed the sound of football fans in midroar to the den. Hoping it was the Dallas Cowboys who'd precipitated that roar, Grace shifted the phone to her other hand.

She honestly didn't mean to hit the text icon. Or read

the brief message that came up. But a single glance at the screen stopped her dead in her tracks.

Have an update on Petrie. Call me.

Ice crawled along Grace's veins. The hubbub in the den faded. The papered walls of the hall seemed to close in on her. She couldn't move, could barely breathe as Jack Petrie's image shoved everything else out of her mind. Smooth and handsome at first. Then smooth and sneering, as he was the last time he'd allowed Grace to visit his home. *His* home. Not her cousin's. Not one they'd made together. The house was his, the car was his, every friggin' dollar in the bank was his, to be doled out to *his* wife penny by penny.

The ice splintered. An almost forgotten fury now speared through Grace. Caught in its vicious maw, she let an animal cry rip from her throat and hurled the phone at the wall.

The Dalton men came running almost before the pieces hit the floor. Alex erupted from the den first.

"What the...?"

"Grace!" Blake shoved past his brother. "Are you okay?"

She didn't answer. *Couldn't* answer. Fury still clawed at her throat.

"Has something happened to Molly?" He gripped her upper arms. "Alex! Go check on Julie and the baby!"

He could have saved his breath. His brother was already pounding down the hall.

"Talk to me, Grace." Blake's fingers bit into her flesh. "Tell me what's happened."

"You got a call. That's what happened."

"What?"

She wrenched out of his hold. With a scathing look, she directed his attention to the shattered phone. He frowned at the pieces in obvious confusion.

"It was a text message." She fought to choke out the words. "My thumb hit the icon by mistake. I didn't intend to read the message. Wasn't intended to read it, obviously."

"What are you talking about? What message? Who was it from?"

"I'm guessing your friend, the P.I. What's his name? Jerrold? James?"

His jaw went tight. "Jamison."

"Right," she said venomously. "Jamison. He wants you to call him. For an update on Petrie."

"Oh, hell."

The soft expletive said it all. Spinning, Grace stalked down the hall and almost bowled over the two who emerged from the library. Any other time she might have noted with interest that a good portion of Delilah's crimson lipstick had transferred from her mouth to Dusty Jones's. At the moment all she could do was snap a curt response when Delilah demanded to know what was going on.

"Ask your son."

She brushed past them, wishing to hell she'd pocketed the keys to the snazzy new Jaguar Blake had insisted on buying her. She needed to get out. Think through this shock. But the keys were on the dresser. Upstairs. In the guest suite. Grace hit the stairs, grinding her teeth in mingled fury and frustration.

By the time she reached the luxuriously appointed suite, she'd added a searing sense of betrayal to the mix. She snatched the keys off the dresser, digging the jagged edges into her palm, staring unseeing at other objects scattered across the polished mahogany.

"Going somewhere?"

She jerked her head up and locked angry eyes on her husband. "I'm thinking about it."

"Mind if I ask where?" he asked calmly.

Too calmly, damn him! She'd always admired his steady thinking and cool composure. Not now. Not with this hurt knifing into her.

"I believed you," she threw at him. "When you said you could live with my refusal to betray Anne's trust, I actually believed you!"

"I am living with it."

"Like hell!"

His eyes narrowed but he kept his movements steady and unhurried as he turned, shut the door and faced her again.

"When you wouldn't trust me with Anne's secrets…"

"I couldn't! Some of us," she added viciously, "hold to our promises."

"When you *couldn't* trust me with Anne's secrets," he amended, his mouth thinning a little, "I had Jamison keep digging. I know now her real name was Hope Templeton."

The telltale signs that he was holding on to his temper with an effort took some of the edge off Grace's own anger. The hurt remained.

"I only had one cousin. Her birth is a matter of record. I'm surprised it took your hotshot P.I. so long to discover her real name."

"I also know she got married at the age of seventeen."

"How did you…? I mean, we…"

"Altered the record? I won't bother to remind you that's a crime."

He was in full lawyer mode now. Legs spread, arms crossed. Relentlessly presenting the evidence. The two of them would have to have this out, Grace realized. Once, and hopefully for all.

Reining in the last of her temper, she sank onto the bed. "Go on."

"What my hotshot P.I. did not find was any record of divorce. I can only assume Anne was still married when she and I met. I can also assume the marriage wasn't a happy one."

"And how did you reach this brilliant deduction?"

He shrugged aside the sarcasm. "The fact that Anne had left him, obviously. And that she used an assumed name, presumably to prevent him from finding her."

Grace could add so much more to the list. Like Anne's aversion to public places for fear Petrie or one of his friends would spot her. Her bone-deep distrust of all men until this one. Her abrupt disappearance from Blake's life, even though she must have loved him.

"I had Jamison check out her husband," he said, breaking into the dark, sad memories. "According to Texas Highway Patrol records, Jack Petrie is a highly decorated officer with two citations for risking his life in the line of duty. One for dragging a man and his son out of a burning vehicle. Another for taking down a drug smuggler who shot a fellow officer during a routine traffic stop."

"You didn't contact him, did you?" Grace asked with her heart in her throat.

"No. Neither did Jamison. But he made discreet inquiries."

She breathed in, out. "And?"

"Jamison came away with the impression Petrie was a devoted husband who liked to show off his pretty young wife. Rumor has it he was devastated when she walked out on him."

Blake waited for her to deny the rumor. When she didn't, he got to the real issue. "That leaves Molly."

"She's your child, Blake!" The exclamation burst out, quick and passionate. "Not Petrie's!"

"I know that. Even without the DNA evidence, Jamison's sources confirmed Anne left her husband almost a year before she and I met. Still, they were married when she gave birth to Molly, and under the law…"

"To hell with the law! You've run the tests. If it ever came to a legal battle, you've got more than enough evidence to support your paternity."

She came off the bed, pleading now.

"But it doesn't need come to a battle. Anne's dead. Petrie has no idea she had a child. Just leave it that way."

"What are you so afraid of, Grace? What was Anne afraid of? Did Petrie hurt her? Use his fists on her?"

"I…"

"Tell me, for God's sake!"

She almost broke down then. She would have given her soul at that point to share the whole, degrading truth, but her promise hung like an anchor around her neck. All she would respond to was one specific question.

"It wasn't physical. Not that I know of, anyway. But mental cruelty can be just as vicious."

"All the more reason for me to protect Molly from this jerk."

He had the training, the extensive network of connections to enact all sorts of legal sanctions. She knew that. She also knew the mere fact he'd had an affair with Anne would drive Jack Petrie to a jealous rage. The man was a sadist. He'd strangled his wife with a warped kind

of love that others mistook for devotion. Anne was beyond his reach now, but her child wasn't. Or her lover.

"You've just proved my point," Grace countered
with a touch of desperation. "You think Anne's husband won't want vengeance? He'll try to milk you for
millions. Drag a paternity suit out in court for years.
Have you thought of that?"

"Of course," he snapped. "I'm not afraid of a fight,
legal or otherwise."

Okay. All right. She had to breathe deep. Slow down.
Remember she wasn't dealing with someone as unbalanced as Jack Petrie.

"Put your own feelings aside for a moment, Blake.
Think what a long, drawn-out court battle could do to
Molly. When she's older she'll be curious about her
mother. All she'd have to do is surf the Net. You can
imagine the headlines she'll stumble across. Billionaire's Love Child Center of Vicious Paternity Dispute.
Decorated Police Officer Calls Wife a Whore. Secretary Hooks Rich Boss with Sex And…"

"I've got the picture."

He got it, and he didn't like it. She didn't, either, but
they couldn't ignore it.

"Don't dig any further, Blake. Please! In a year, two
years, everyone outside our immediate circle will just
assume Molly's our child. Petrie won't have any reason
to question it."

He looked as if she'd punched him in the gut. Or
square in his sense of right and wrong. His eyes went
cold, his voice flat and hard.

"So you want to live a lie. Like your cousin."

For Molly's sake she gave the only answer she could.
"Yes."

Twelve

"She just can't bring herself to trust me."

Blake gripped his beer and ignored the buzz from the crowd gathered in the watering spot a few blocks from Dalton International's corporate headquarters. He and his brother had wrapped a bitch of a meeting with senior executives from Nippon Steel earlier that evening, then taken their Japanese visitors to dinner at one of Oklahoma City's finest steak houses. The Nippon execs had taken a limo back to their hotel, leaving Blake and Alex to lick their wounds over a beer and a bucket of peanuts before heading home to their respective spouses. Despite the round of tough negotiations, it was Blake's spouse who occupied his mind more than the Japanese.

"I accept that Grace promised to keep Anne's secrets," he said, stretching his long legs out beneath a tabletop littered with peanut shells. "I respect her for holding to that vow, but Christ! We've been married almost a month now and she still doesn't think I can handle this character Petrie."

Shrugging, Alex attempted to take the middle road on the subject he and his twin had already beaten into the ground a number of times. "Grace knows Petrie. We don't."

"We know enough! The bastard terrorized his wife and forced her into a shadow life. Now he's doing the same thing to *my* wife."

Frustration ate like acid at Blake's gut. It was doing a serious number on his pride, too. He yanked at the knot of his tie and popped the top button of his shirt before downing a slug of beer.

"Mother says Grace stays in the background at the charity functions she's involved her in and ducks whenever a photographer shows up. She does the same when we attend a concert or some black-tie affair. The woman is fixated on maintaining a low profile until our marriage is old news."

"So? You don't exactly chase after the spotlight yourself."

"Dammit, bro, you're not helping here."

"You wanted a sounding board, I'm doing my best board act." Peanut shells crunched as his twin leaned his elbows on the table. "I've told you what I really think."

"Yeah, I know. You think I should take a quick trip to San Antonio and confront this guy. Let him know who he'd be dealing with if he got any smart ideas."

"Correction. I think *we* should take a quick trip to San Antonio."

"It's my problem! I'll handle it."

"You're doing a helluva job with it so far."

Blake's lips drew back in a snarl. He managed to choke it off. Barely. Alex knew damned well he was spoiling for a fight. Obviously, his twin was prepared to step in and draw the punches.

"Well, at least you've got Jamison's sources keeping an eye on Petrie," Alex commented.

"I'm getting regular updates."

"Does Grace know?"

"She knows."

That had caused another rough scene. Grace argued that Petrie was a cop. Sooner or later he would pick up on a surveillance, become suspicious, track it to the source. Blake countered with the assertion that Jamison and his associate in San Antonio were pros. They wouldn't tip their hands. In either case, Blake flatly refused to turn a blind eye to a potential threat.

Grace had conceded that point. Reluctantly, but she'd conceded. Still, the fact they were living with this guy Petrie's shadow hanging over them locked Blake's jaw every time he thought about it. He'd promised his wife he wouldn't confront the man without talking it over with her first. That discussion was fast approaching. In the meantime, he and Grace each pretended they understood and accepted the other's viewpoint.

"I get that Grace saw firsthand the hell Petrie put her cousin through," Alex said, attacking the matter from another angle. "What I don't get is why she doesn't want to take him on. I didn't know Anne all that well, but I do know Grace. My sense is she's much stronger than her cousin was."

"Stronger, and a whole bunch more stubborn," Blake agreed with a grimace.

"She's also got us to do the muscle work. All of us. Mother and Julie want in on this. Dusty, too."

Momentarily diverted, Blake raised a brow. "Yeah,

what's with that? The old coot's at Mom's house just about every time I stop by there these days."

"They're consulting," Alex replied, deadpan. "As Julie's business partner and coowner of one of Dalton International's subsidiaries, Dusty prefers to talk shop with someone who worked the same oil patches he did."

"Oh, Lord! I'm not going to tell you the image that just jumped into my head. But…" Blake raised his beer. "Here's to 'em."

Grinning, the brothers clinked bottles. Alex signaled the waitress to bring two fresh ones before returning to the issue digging at them both.

"Back to Grace. She's got to know she can count on you, on all of us, to protect her from this asshole Petrie."

"She knows," Blake said grimly. "The problem is she thinks she's protecting us. Or Molly and me, anyway."

His brother winced. "That's got to stick in your craw."

"Like you wouldn't believe."

He didn't go into further detail. As a kid Alex had been the one to wade fist-first into battle. Blake had always had his brother's back, though, and Alex his. The fact that his wife didn't trust him to have hers rubbed him raw. Feeling the grate yet again, he circled his beer bottle on the littered table and sent a shower of peanut shells to the already carpeted floor.

"So how long are you going to play this by her rules?" Alex wanted to know.

Blake's head snapped up. The uncompromising answer came fast. "The rules change the moment I sense so much as a hint of a real threat."

Grace was perched on one of the kitchen counter stools when she heard the muted rumble of the garage door going up. She'd put Molly down for the night at seven-thirty and indulged in the sybaritic luxury of an hour-long soak in scented bath oil that evoked instant memories of Provence's hot sun and endless lavender fields. Barefoot and supremely comfortable in a well-washed, black-and-silver San Antonio Spurs jersey that came almost to her knees, she'd curled up with a biography of Van Gogh before deciding to treat herself to a bowl of double chocolate fudge ripple. After so many years of busy days in the classroom and nights grading papers, she loved having the time and the freedom to read whatever struck her fancy. She loved even more reading to Molly, which she'd started doing before they'd moved into the house Grace was having such fun furnishing.

All in all, her days were perfect. The nights came pretty darn close.

Grace had gotten past her anger over Blake directing his P.I. to dig into the past her cousin had tried so desperately to escape. She'd also recovered—mostly—from the stinging sense of betrayal that he'd done it after she'd begged him to let that past stay buried. She understood his rationale. She didn't agree with it, but she understood it.

Unfortunately, a difference of opinion on something so crucial couldn't help but affect their continually evolving relationship. The strain it had caused was like a small but irritating itch they'd mutually decided to ignore.

Despite the itch, they still took pleasure in discovering new facets to each other's personalities. The quirks, the unconscious gestures, the ingrained habits. What's more, they still shared the sheer joy of Molly.

And Grace's pulse still bumped whenever her husband walked into a room.

Like now. She swiveled the stool, cradling her bowl of double chocolate fudge ripple, and felt the flutter as Blake entered the kitchen through the utility room connected to the garage. He moved with the athletic ease she so admired and looked as classy as ever, although the open shirt collar and the tie dangling from his suit coat pocket added a definite touch of sex to the sophisticated image.

They hadn't reached the stage of casual, hello-honey-I'm-home kisses yet. Grace wasn't sure they ever would, although she knew darn well they couldn't sustain indefinitely the searing heat they'd ignited during their honeymoon. She felt it sizzle now, though, as he nudged her knees apart so he could stand between them and cupped her nape.

"Did you and Alex get your Japanese execs all wined and dined?"

"We did."

His palm was warm against her skin, his eyes a smoky blue as his head bent toward hers. Tipping her chin, Grace welcomed him home with a kiss that left her breathless and Blake demanding a second one just like the first. She gave both willingly, as greedy as he was, but had to jerk back when the fudge ripple threatened to slide into her lap.

Blake eyed the bowl's contents with interest. "That looks good."

"Sit down, I'll get you some."

"I'll just share yours."

"Hmmmm." Her brow furrowed in a mock scowl. "In the 'just for future reference' category, I don't usually share my ice cream. Or my fries."

"Noted. But you'll make an exception in this instance, right?"

Since he was still wedged between her thighs and didn't look as though he planned to move anytime soon, she yielded the point.

"Okay. Here you go."

He downed the heaping spoonful in one try, prompting a quick warning.

"Whoa! You'll get a brain freeze gobbling it down like that."

A slow, predatory smile curved his mouth. "No part of me is liable to freeze like this."

He moved closer, spreading her wider. The Spurs jersey rode up, and Grace felt him harden against her.

"I see what you mean," she got out on a gasp when he exerted an exquisite pressure at the juncture of her thighs. "No danger of frost down there."

Or anywhere else!

The pressure increased. The muscles low in her belly clenched. He splayed his hands on her hips to keep her anchored, and the wild, throbbing sensation built with each rhythmic move of his lower body against hers.

"Blake!" She tried to wiggle away but the counter dug into her back. "We'd better slow down. I can't... You've got me too..."

"Hold on."

Like she could? Especially when he spanned her waist and lifted her in a smooth, easy move from the stool to the counter. She didn't even realize she still held the now-melted ice cream until he took the bowl and let it clatter into the sink. Then the jersey came up and over her head. Her bikini briefs got peeled off. Her mouth was level with his now, her hips in line with his belt. She should have felt completely, nakedly exposed. All she experienced was the urgent need to get him naked, too.

"Your jacket... Shirt..."

He shed the top half of his clothing with minimum movement and maximum speed. The bottom half stayed intact as he buried a fist in her hair, and took her mouth with his.

There was something different in this kiss, in the maddening pressure he exerted against her. He was a little rougher, a little harder, yet somehow more deliberate. As though he could demonstrate some sort of mastery over her if he wanted to but chose to restrain himself. Or not. Grace didn't register more than that hazy impression before he replaced his lower body with his hand and drove everything resembling rational thought out of her head.

She came mere moments later in a burst of bright colors and pure sensation. The explosive climax arched her spine and brought her head back. She slapped her palms on the counter to support her taut, shuddering body, but her arms folded like overstretched elastic.

Blake scooped her off the counter before she went horizontal and carried her limp and still quivering with pleasure to the bedroom. When he shed the rest of his clothes and joined her in bed for the grand finale, he was so gentle and tender Grace completely forgot that odd moment in the kitchen.

It came back with a vengeance less than a week later.

Yielding to her mother-in-law's indomitable will, she strapped Molly into her car seat to drive her over to the Nichols Hills mansion for some grandmother-granddaughter time. Grace herself had been instructed to shop for a cocktail dress for the big-dollar fundraiser

Delilah insisted her sons and their wives attend the following evening.

"Which I really do *not* want to go to," she said via the rearview mirror to the infant happily banging a teething ring against the side window.

Her eyes on the baby, she had to jam on the brakes to avoid an SUV cruising past the end of the drive. The near miss rattled Grace and reminded her to keep her attention on the road. The brief visit with Delilah didn't exactly soothe her somewhat frayed nerves.

"You should get your nails done while you're out," her mother-in-law suggested after a prolonged exchange of Eskimo kisses with a joyously squealing Molly. "Your hair trimmed, too."

"I look that bad, huh?"

"You look gorgeous and you know it." She hitched the baby on her hip and skewered her daughter-in-law with one of her rapier stares. "Just not as glowing as you did when you got back from Provence. Don't tell me you and Blake have taken the sex down a notch already."

"I won't," Grace countered coolly.

"Don't get on your high horse with me, girl. If it's not sex, it has to be that business with Jamison. Look, I don't like to meddle in my sons' lives but…"

She paused and waited with a reluctant grin for Grace to finish snorting.

"Okay, okay. Meddling is my favorite occupation. But I thought you and Blake had come to an understanding on that matter."

"We have. More or less."

The older woman let Molly play with her sapphire-and-diamond wrist bangle and skinned Grace with another serrated look. "I'm only going to say this once. I'll never mention it again, I swear."

Grace believed that as much as she believed her former employer could keep her nose out of her sons' affairs. Once Delilah got the bit between her teeth, she kept it there.

"You did right standing by your promise to your cousin," she said, "but she's dead and you're married now. You need to decide where your loyalty lies."

Grace went rigid, her eyes flashing danger signals. They bounced off Delilah's thick hide.

"Go," she ordered brusquely. "Shop, have your nails done, and for God's sake think about what I just said."

Grace fumed all the way to the exclusive boutique she and Julie had discovered some months ago. She pulled into a parking slot two doors down and killed the Jag's engine, then sat with her fists gripping the leather-wrapped steering wheel.

She didn't need Delilah to lecture her about loyalty, dammit! She'd spent what felt like half her life and every penny of her income shielding Anne from her sadistic husband. If she closed her eyes, she could still see her cousin fighting desperately for her last breaths. Hear her rasping plea for Grace to take Molly to her father and please, *please* don't let Jack know about her.

Her knuckles whitened on the wheel. She stared at the shop window in front of the Jag. The window was bare except for a For Lease sign, but Grace barely noticed the empty expanse of glass and darkened interior.

Maybe…

Maybe the habit of protecting her cousin had become too ingrained. Maybe she'd been following instincts tainted by Anne's bone-deep fear when she should be trusting Blake's. He was calm and cool in a crisis. And more intelligent than any six people she knew. He could also wield resources every bit as if not more powerful than Jack Petrie's. Most important, he was Molly's father. He'd strangle anyone who tried to harm her with his bare hands.

Groaning, Grace dropped her forehead to the wheel. Heart and soul, she ached to hold to the promise she made her cousin. She couldn't. Not any longer. Delilah was right. She had to let go of Anne's past. Her future revolved around Molly and Blake. With a silent plea to her cousin to understand, she raised her head and fumbled in her purse for her cell phone.

She pressed one speed-dial key. Her husband's superefficient executive assistant answered before the second ring.

"Blake Dalton's office."

"Hi, Patrice, it's Grace. Is Blake free?"

"Hi, Grace. Sorry, but he's in the middle of a conference call with the Association of Corporate Counsel's executive committee. They want him to chair the next symposium, you know."

"Yes, I do."

"Shall I pass him a note to let him know you're on the line?"

"No, just tell him… Tell him I was thinking about my cousin and…"

Hell! She couldn't put what she wanted to say on a yellow call slip.

"Just tell him I called."

"I will."

"Thanks."

She tapped End, feeling much like Julius Caesar must have when he brought his legionnaires across the Rubicon. She couldn't go back now. She didn't *want* to go back. She'd charge full steam ahead with Blake and Molly and a life without the specter of Jack Petrie hanging over it.

She was still riding the relief of that decision when she emerged from Helen Jasper's boutique some time later. As usual, the shop owner's eye had proved as unerring as her taste. She'd purchased the entire line of a young Oklahoma designer she was sure would make a splash in the fashion world. Grace ended up buying not only a tea-length cocktail dress in dreamy shades of green, but two beaded tops and a pair of slinky palazzo pants with accessories to match. She'd also had Helen bundle up the outfit she'd worn into the store and now felt very autumnal in heavyweight linen slacks in cinnamon-brown, a matching tank top and a pumpkin-colored silk overblouse left unbuttoned to show off a faux lizardskin belt as wide, if not as clanky, as Delilah's.

Smiling at the thought of Blake's reaction to the backless and darned near frontless cocktail dress, she bunched her shopping bags in one hand and fumbled in her purse for the car keys. She popped the door locks, dropped her purse on the front seat and was about to add the shopping bags when a black SUV wheeled into the slot next to hers. The idiot driver cut into the space so sharply she had to quickly yank on the open door to avoid having it dinged.

Mentally giving him the bird, she bent to retrieve the tissue-stuffed bags her quick move had sent tumbling to the floor mat. When she straightened, she caught a glimpse of the other driver from the corner of one eye. He'd exited his vehicle but hadn't moved away from it.

A prickly sense of unease raced along her spine. He

was standing close to her Jag. Too close. A half dozen tips from the various self-defense articles she'd read crowded into her mind. She went with the only one she could.

Jamming her car keys between her fingers, she closed her fist to form a spiked gauntlet and started to turn. She didn't get even halfway around before something hard rammed against her shoulder blade and her world turned red.

Thirteen

"She doesn't answer her phone."

Blake paced his brother's office on the twentieth floor of Dalton International's headquarters. Wall-to-wall windows offered a different perspective of downtown Oklahoma City than that in his own office at the opposite end of the long corridor bisecting the CEO's suites. But Blake had no interest in the sweeping panorama of the round-domed capitol building in the distance or the colorful barges meandering along the river in the foreground. He took another few paces, his fists jammed in the pocket of his slacks.

"I've left three voice mails. The first was around ten-thirty, the last one a half hour ago."

Although it was now just a little past two, Alex understood his brother's concern. He'd spent several tense hours himself when Julie took off in search of a missing Dusty Jones, her cell phone died and Alex didn't know where the hell she'd disappeared to. When he reminded Blake of that knuckle-cracking episode, his brother shook his head.

"I thought of that, but her phone was sitting in the charger next to mine when I left the house this morning. It's fully juiced."

"And Mother didn't know where Grace was heading?"

"Not specifically. Just that she was going shopping and maybe to get her hair or nails done."

"That sure narrows it down," Alex said drily as he reached for the phone on the broad plane of his desk. "I'll call Julie. I remember her mentioning some boutique or other that she and Grace really like."

Luckily, he caught his wife on the ground between crop-dusting runs. Julie had come to a reluctant decision to quit flying agro-air, worried that its high concentration of chemicals could affect the baby she and Alex had decided to try for. She was in the process of training a replacement now—and acclimating the poor guy to the challenges and dubious joys of working with Dusty.

Blake tried to suppress his nagging worry while his brother explained the situation to his wife and scribbled a couple of numbers on a notepad before promising to call back once they'd located Grace.

"She said to try a boutique owned by a woman named Helen Jasper." Alex punched in the first number. "Also a nail salon on… Hello? Ms. Jasper? This is Alex Dalton."

He listened a moment and smiled.

"Yes, I am. Very lucky. So is my brother. That's why I'm calling, actually. We need to get in touch with Grace, but her cell phone's not working. She was going shopping, and Julie said to try your place." His glance cut to Blake. "She did? All right, thanks."

Some of the tension riding Blake's shoulders left when Alex reported his wife had spent several hours and what sounded like a big chunk of change in the boutique.

"She left a little before noon. Maybe she stopped somewhere for a leisurely lunch."

"Maybe." The tension ratcheted up again. "But I can't see her lingering over a long lunch without calling to check on Molly."

"Let's try this nail place. She could have…"

Alex broke off, frowning when the door to his office opened. His executive assistant sent him an apologetic look as Delilah swept in pushing Molly's stroller, unannounced as usual. The matriarch of the Dalton clan—and nominal president of DI's board of directors—saw no reason why she had to wait for an underling to grant her access to either of her sons.

She halted the stroller in front of Blake. "Your assistant said you were here with Alex."

He barely had time to absorb her knee-high boots, black leggings and rust-colored tunic cinched with a monster leather belt decorated with an assortment of dangling, clinking zoo animals in silver and gold before Molly gave a joyous screech.

"Da-da!"

His heart turning over, Blake responded to his daughter's outstretched arms by unclipping the stroller's safety belt and gathering her in his. She brought with her that ever-fascinating, always changing combination of baby smells. Today it was powder and strained peaches and a faint, yeasty scent he couldn't identify.

"Have you heard from Grace?" Delilah demanded while Molly planted wet kisses on his cheek.

"No, but we know she left her favorite boutique a couple of hours ago."

"I was just saying she may be treating herself to a late lunch," Alex put in.

"She wouldn't do that," Delilah asserted flatly. "Not without giving me a call first to check on Molly."

The skin at the back of Blake's neck stretched taut. His mother had just confirmed his own thoughts.

"Patrice said Grace left a message for you earlier," she continued. "She didn't communicate her plans for the rest of the day?"

"Just that she wanted me to call her."

"That's it?"

"No." Blake's jaw tightened. "After she didn't reply to my second voice message, I grilled Patrice. She said Grace mentioned wanting to talk about her cousin, then changed her mind and just asked Patrice to tell me she called."

"Her cousin?"

Despite the distraction of Molly's palm slapping his cheek, he didn't miss the sudden flicker of guilt in his mother's eyes.

"What do you know that I don't?"

"Well…"

With a sudden premonition of disaster, Blake passed Molly across the desk to her uncle and locked on his mother. "Tell me what you did."

"I didn't *do* anything," she huffed. "I merely suggested to my daughter-in-law that she might want to think about whether she owes her loyalty to her dead cousin or her very much alive family."

"Dammit! I told you not to interfere in this."

"You're raising a daughter," she fired back. "You

should know by now that being a parent gives you the inalienable right to interfere when necessary."

Too furious to counter that broadside, Blake strode to the windows. He knew damned well that Grace *did* think about where her loyalty lay. Continuously. The matter twisted her in as many knots as it did him.

Had she gotten fed up with the pressure he and now Delilah had put on her? Was that why she hadn't responded to his return calls? Had she decided she needed some downtime, away from the Daltons, mother and son?

Christ! Would she just disappear? Walk out of his life as Anne had?

The thought put a hard, fast kink in his gut. Just as fast, Blake unkinked it. There was no way Grace would do that to him. She had too much integrity, too strong a sense of fair play. They'd argued over this whole mess, sure, but she knew he loved her too much to let her just disappear from his life.

Didn't she?

Brought up short, he tried to remember if he'd articulated the actual words. Maybe not, but he'd sure as hell showed her how he felt. The fact that he couldn't keep his hands off her spoke louder than words. As if it were an implied-in-fact contract, the attorney in him asserted, she could certainly infer his feelings from his actions.

Right, the less legalistic side of his mind sneered. Just as he could now infer why she hadn't returned his calls.

Well, there was one possible reason he could address right now. Cell phone in hand, he brought up the address book and hit Jamison's number.

"It's Blake Dalton," he said tersely. "I need an update on Petrie."

"Got a report a half hour ago," the P.I. informed him. "I was just going to email it to you."

"Give me the gist."

"Hang on, let me pull it up. Okay, here it is. Electronic surveillance of Petrie's residence showed him returning there yesterday afternoon at fourteen-thirty hours. My associate checked with his source in his highway patrol unit. Petrie and his partner testified in court in the morning. Reportedly, he felt queasy afterward, said he was coming down with something. He took the rest of the day off and called in for sick leave again this morning, saying he had a doctor's appointment. Surveillance showed him leaving his residence in civilian clothes at oh-six-fifteen."

Blake's eyes narrowed. "Pretty early for a doctor's appointment."

"That's what I thought, too. I've got my guy digging deeper."

"Call me as soon as... Wait. Back up a minute. You said Petrie testified in court yesterday morning?"

"Right. On a drug-stop case that crossed state lines and involved the feds. I've got the specifics here if you..."

"I don't need the specifics. Just tell me which court."

"Bexar County, 73rd Judicial District," Jamison reported after a moment. "Judge Honeywell presiding."

It might not mean anything. Honeywell heard dozens of cases every week. But the possibility, however remote, that Petrie might have picked up something about Grace from the judge or his assistant put the crimp back in Blake's gut.

"Call your associate in San Antonio. Tell him to put everything he's got on this. I want him to know Petrie's exact whereabouts, like fast."

"Will do."

He palmed the phone and was just turning to update the others when Alex's intercom buzzed. Shifting Molly to his right arm, his twin reached for the phone. Blake felt a surge of hope that Patrice had forwarded a call from Grace to his brother's office. That hope sank like a stone when Alex flashed him a quick frown.

"Yes, I'll take the call." He jiggled Molly, waited a moment and identified himself. "This is Alex Dalton."

Blake cut across the office. He pressed against the front edge of Alex's desk as the groove between his twin's brows dug deeper.

"Right. Thanks for calling."

"What?" Blake demanded before Alex had dropped the instrument back on the hook.

"That was Helen Jasper, the woman who owns the boutique where Grace shopped this morning. She just went out for a late lunch break and spotted Grace's car parked a couple doors down from her shop."

His voice was as grim as his face.

"She looked in the Jag's window. Said she could see the bags from her store spilling off the front passenger seat. Grace's purse is on the floor with them."

Delilah took Molly back to her house while her sons set out across town. Alex navigated, and Blake drove with a fierce concentration that was only minimally directed at the road. He tried to tell himself there were a number of reasons Grace might have left the Jag parked outside the boutique for so long. But none of reasons he dredged up explained her leaving her purse inside, in full view of anyone tempted to smash a window and empty it of wallet and credit cards.

"There's the boutique," Alex said when Blake pulled into the parking lot of an upscale strip mall. "And there's Grace's Jag."

Blake screeched into a slot beside the midnight-blue sedan and jammed his own vehicle into Park. He carried a spare key to the Jag on his key ring and was aiming it to beep the locks when Alex put out a restraining hand.

"There could be fingerprints or fibers or other evidence."

Like blood. He didn't say it. He didn't have to.

"Sure you want to contaminate the scene?"

"I've driven this car dozens of times. My prints, clothing fibers and DNA are all over it, but I'll be careful."

As it turned out, the doors weren't locked. Blake used the underside of the handle to open one. The baby seat sat empty in the back with some of Molly's toys scattered beside it. The front passenger seat held a jumble of shopping bags. Additional bags had obviously tumbled off the seat onto the floor. Grace's purse lay half-buried amid the silver tissue paper and pale blue bags. Her cell phone was clearly visible in the purse's side pocket.

Jaw clenched, Blake moved to the rear of the vehicle and used the key to pop the trunk. His breath escaped in a hiss of sheer relief when he found it empty. Alex gave him a silent, sympathetic thump on the shoulder. Blake knew he'd imagined the worst, too, although the empty trunk provided only temporary respite from those grim scenarios.

"I'll call Harkins," Alex said curtly.

Phil Harkins was a friend as well as a supremely competent chief of police. Alex had his phone out when Blake yanked on his arm.

"Wait!"

He ducked under the raised trunk lid and came back up with a half-folded sheet of paper he'd missed on the first, anxious sweep. The message inside was scrawled in bold black ink.

You took my wife. I took yours. If you want to see the bitch alive again, you'd better keep this between you and me. A rich prick like you shouldn't have much trouble finding us. We'll be waiting for you.

Blake swore savagely and passed the note to Alex. His brother was still reading it when Blake's cell phone pinged. He checked caller ID, saw it was Jamison and cut right to the chase.

"What have you got?"

"Petrie flew out of San Antonio on a oh-seven-ten flight direct to Oklahoma City. He landed at eight-twenty, picked up one checked bag and rented a black Chevy Traverse from Hertz, Oklahoma tag six-three-two-delta-hotel-eight."

"Does the rental have a vehicle-tracking device?" Blake bit out.

"It does, but Hertz wouldn't give me access to their system."

"I'll take care of that."

He skimmed his contacts and pulled up Phil Harkins's number. The DA was in his office, thank God.

"Hey, pardner," he said with the affable geniality he showed to everyone except the worst of the bottom feeders his office prosecuted. "How's it hanging?"

"I need a favor, Phil. Fast, with no questions asked."

"Shoot."

* * *

Ten nerve-twisting minutes later, Harkins delivered.

"Hertz just transmitted the GPS tracking data. Your boy departed the airport, drove to your neighborhood and cruised your street. Didn't stop, but made a sharp U-turn at nine-fifty-four and drove to Nichols Hills."

Hell! He'd been following Grace. Blake was sure of it.

"He idled a block from your mother's place for eighteen minutes," Harkins recited, "then drove to your present location, where he sat for almost two hours."

Watching Helen Jasper's boutique. Waiting for Grace.

"Do your people have a lock on him now?" Blake asked, his insides ice-cold.

"Roger. He's heading south on I-35, three miles from the Texas border." Harkins hesitated. "I don't know what you have going on here, but I can ask the Texas Highway Patrol to make a stop."

Blake couldn't chance it. Petrie was a Texas state trooper. He could have his radio with him and be listening in on their net.

"No, don't alert the troopers. Just keep tracking him and let me know if he deviates from I-35." He shot his brother a fast look. "I'll be in the air."

Alex was punching the speed call number for his chief of air operations before Blake disconnected.

"What have we got ready to go?" He listened then issued a terse instruction. "Top off the fuel tank on the Skylane. We'll be there in fifteen minutes."

Blake didn't question the choice of a single-engine turboprop over one of Dalton International's bigger, faster corporate jets. Alex could put the Skylane down in a cow pasture if he had to.

* * *

They were in the air less than a half hour later. Alex laid on max airspeed and made a swift calculation.

"We should catch them between Austin and San Antonio...if that's where the bastard's headed."

Blake nodded, his eyes shielded by the sunglasses he'd put on to protect them from the unfiltered sunlight. He kept his narrowed, intent gaze trained on the wide ribbon of concrete cutting across the rolling hills and checkered fields below.

Petrie was down there, a thousand feet below and almost two hours ahead, driving a black Chevy Traverse. Blake could only pray he'd stuck to his end of the deal and had Grace sitting alive and unhurt beside him.

Fourteen

Grace shifted in the bucket seat, biting down hard on her lip when the SUV jounced over a rut. With her arms cuffed behind her, the ache between her shoulder blades had magnified to sheer torture in the interminable hour since she'd regained consciousness.

She turned her face to the window to hide a wince and searched for a landmark, any kind of a landmark. All she could see was a dense forest of stunted live oaks poking above an impenetrable wall of scrub. Refusing to give in to the desperation squeezing her chest like a vise, she faced front again and forced herself to speak coolly.

"Where are we going?"

Buzz-cut, tanned and clean-shaven, the outwardly all-American guy in the driver's seat wrenched his gaze from the single-lane dirt road ahead and shot her a look of smiling malevolence.

"I told you. You'll know when we get there. Now unless you want to talk to me about that rich bastard who screwed my wife…"

Grace set her jaw.

"That's okay, cuz. You'll be squealing soon enough. Now shut the hell up. I don't want to miss the turn."

This was how it had gone since Grace had come to, dizzy and nauseous and aching all over. Petrie had refused to tell her how he'd found her. Refused to do more than smile with amused contempt when Grace warned he wouldn't get away with snatching her off the street.

She knew without being told that kidnapping wasn't all he intended. He was a cop. He wouldn't leave a live victim to bring him down. She also knew he intended to use her as bait to get to Blake.

She'd been so careful! How had he made the connection between Blake and Anne? No, not Anne! Hope! She had to think of her cousin as Hope again, use that name when referring to her, or she'd feed into the rage smoldering behind Petrie's careful facade.

Ten minutes later Grace caught a glimpse of blue water through the screen of trees. Five minutes more, and Petrie slowed to a near crawl, then turned onto an overgrown dirt track. Grace had no idea how he spotted the track. There was no mailbox, no scrap of cloth tied to a bush, nothing but two sunken ruts cutting through the heavy underbrush.

Thorny vines and ranches scraped the SUV's sides. He was doing one helluva number on the paint job, she thought with vicious satisfaction, then gritted her teeth as the SUV bounced over the ruts and white-hot needles stabbed into her aching shoulders. She wanted to sob with relief when the brush finally thinned and the dirt track gave onto a clearing that sloped down to a good-size lake.

A cedar-shingled cabin sat at the top of the slope, well above the waterline. Cinder blocks supported a screened-in porch. Additional cinder blocks formed columns to hold up the roof that shaded the porch. Grace whipped her gaze from the cabin to tree-studded opposite shore and spotted two or three similar structures. Most looked as if they were boarded up. None was within screaming distance.

Petrie pulled well off the track, killed the engine and got out. Leaving his door open, he extracted something from the floor behind his seat. A rifle case, Grace saw. Hand-tooled leather. Padded handle. Housing for the high-powered hunting rifle she'd seen him clean at his kitchen table more than once.

The case terrified her. Not for herself. For Blake. He would come after her. Find her somehow. Walk right into Petrie's gun sight.

The terror spiked again when Petric got out and propped the rifle against the fender before extracting a soft-sided pistol case from his door's side bin. The case was half-zipped, providing easy access to the blue steel semiautomatic he slid out. It wasn't his service weapon. Grace had seen his state-issued black leather holster and Sig Sauer often enough to recognize the difference. This had to be a throwaway, one of those weapons reportedly confiscated during traffic stops that somehow never made it into evidence logs. Untraceable to the man who now coolly ejected the magazine and checked to verify a round was chambered before snapping the magazine back in place and thumbing the safety lock.

Just as coolly, he settled the pistol in the waistband of his jeans and picked up the rifle case. Grace's heart was racing when he rounded the hood, yanked open the passenger door and popped her seat belt.

"Let's go."

He hooked a hand around her upper arm and dragged her out, firing the pain in her shoulders to white-hot agony. It took every ounce of will she had not to moan as he hauled her up to the cabin. The screen door screeched when Petrie pulled it open, then groped above the main door for the key he obviously knew was there.

When he shoved Grace inside, the stink of old, dank blankets and used fishing tackle hit like a slap to the face. Grimacing, she inspected the dim interior. Bunk beds lined one wall. A rough-plank picnic table, a worn sofa with mismatched cushions and a lumpy armchair took up most of the remaining floorspace. The kitchen consisted of a counter with a sink, hot plate and half-size fridge. An unpainted door hung on its hinges at the far end of the room and gave a glimpse into a cubby-hole of a bathroom.

"Nice place you got here," Grace commented with a credible sneer.

"Belongs to a friend of mine. He's invited me up here a couple times to fish and drink. I know it offends your delicate sensibilities, but it'll do fine for what I have in mind, cuz."

"Stop calling me that, you dog turd. You and I are in no way related, thank God."

"You always were the feisty one."

She didn't like the slow, up-and-down look he gave her.

"I might just have to train you to heel, like I did Hope."

"You want to bet that's gonna happen?"

The face her cousin had once rhapsodized about being so strong and stamped with character now radiated nothing but amused contempt.

"We'll see how full of piss and vinegar you are when I'm done with you."

Dragging her across the room, he spun her so she was nose to nose with the rolled-up mattress on one of the top bunks. She felt him working the cuffs on her left wrist, felt it spring free and the screaming agony when her arm dropped to her side. She knew she had only three or four seconds to whirl and claw and fight for her freedom, but before she could do more than curl her numbed fingers Petrie had spun her around again. In a quick move he snapped the free end of the cuff to the metal pole supporting the upper bunk. Steel rattled against steel as the cuff shimmied down the pole.

"Make yourself comfortable, cuz. I figure we've got some time before the fun starts."

With unhurried calm, he placed the tooled leather case on the table, unzipped it and began to assemble his hunting rifle.

Grace watched him, her arms dangling uselessly at her sides. They felt as though they'd parted company with her aching shoulders. When the blood finally pulsed back into them, she angled around as far as the cuff would allow and yanked at the rolled-up mattress on the lower bunk.

"All right, Jack," she said after she sank onto the dank ticking. "You may as well tell me. I know you're itching to rub my face in it."

"How I found you, you mean? Or how I found out about my whore of a wife and the rich dick you married?"

"Both."

"Took some doing," he admitted as he snapped the rifle's bolt into place. "I've been searching ever since Hope walked out on me. Checking state and county court records, making calls to various police departments, screening NamUS—the National Missing Persons Data System," he clarified gratuitously.

Grace knew damned well what NamUS was. The data system was open to anyone with a computer. She'd screened it regularly herself for updates on her cousin.

"It wasn't until your marriage license popped in the Texas Vital Statistics database that I finally got a solid lead, though. I saw Judge Honeywell had married you and talked up his assistant. She gushed about what a handsome couple you'd made, how the judge and the Daltons went way back. I went right home from the courthouse and got on the computer."

He lifted his gaze, gave her a mocking smile.

"Found plenty of coverage about the Daltons of Oklahoma City but didn't see much mention of you. Made me think you were keeping a low profile for a reason, so I dug deeper and found a petition filed with the Oklahoma County clerk's office to establish paternity of the infant referred to as Margaret 'Molly' Dalton."

The smile took a hard twist.

"So I made some calls, cuz, and discovered a woman matching your description showed up at Dalton's mama's place almost the same day as the infant. I knew the kid wasn't yours. I'd been watching you too close. So there could only be one reason why you'd take a leave of absence from your job to work as a nanny."

The mask slipped, releasing the fury behind it.

"The brat is Hope's, isn't it? My whore of a wife had a kid by this guy Dalton, and noble, do-gooding Cousin Grace rushed to the rescue just like she always did."

"Jack…"

"Shut up! Don't even try to lie your way out of this. The kid's birth certificate was included in the paternity petition. Didn't take a genius to link her birth to the death certificate filed in the same California courthouse."

He shoved away from the table, the hate now a living thing. Grace tried not to flinch as he stalked across the room.

"She died out there," he raged. "Hope died, and you didn't even let me bury my wife."

"Jack, please. She…"

"Shut up!"

The backhand exploded against her cheek and slammed her head against the metal pole. Tasting blood, Grace fought to blink away the black spots blurring her vision.

"You're going to pay for what you did, bitch. You and Dalton."

With that implacable promise, Petrie went back to the table and picked up the rifle. Grace was still swallowing hot, coppery blood when the door banged shut and the screen door screeched behind him.

Her head swam. The whole side of her face hurt. She slumped against the metal post until she gritted her teeth and forced herself to think through the pain.

The cabin sat on a high slope that gave a commanding view of the only road in. Anyone approaching by boat would be similarly exposed. Grace couldn't wait for Petrie to pick Blake off. She wouldn't!

Breathing through her nose, she twisted to look up at the bunk above her. Its mattress was rolled up, too, revealing a crosshatch of springs hooked through the rectangular metal frame bolted to support poles.

No, wait! She blinked again, praying her still spinning head wasn't registering a blurred image. The frame wasn't bolted. With the first thrill of hope she'd felt since she'd regained consciousness, Grace saw the frame fit into Y-shaped supports.

If she could lift the frame out of the supports…

Slide the cuff up and off the pole…

She stretched out on the dank mattress and listened for any sound indicating Petrie's return, but all she could hear was the thunder of her own heart. Keeping a wary eye on the door, she rolled up on her hips and planted her feet against a corner of the frame above her.

It didn't budge. Jaw clenched, she pushed again. There was a squeak of rusted metal, an infinitesimal shift. Grunting with effort, Grace applied more leverage and got the frame half out of the support. The cry of the screen door made her drop it and her legs instantly.

"Had to set up a few electronic trip wires," Petrie informed her when he entered. With brutal nonchalance as he dropped some kind of a battery-operated device on the table. "We don't want your husband to burst in on us unannounced, do we? Now all we have to do is wait."

Neither Grace nor Petrie had any way of knowing his electronic sensors would work against, not for, him.

She lay in stark terror for what felt like hours, alternately praying the black box wouldn't beep and praying it would signal the arrival of an entire SWAT team. When the box finally gave two loud, distinctive pings, her heart stopped dead in her chest.

Then everything seemed to happen in fast-forward. She didn't have time to think, barely had time to choke back a sob before Petrie grabbed the rifle and charged for the door. He left it open, giving her a partial view of his body shielded by one of the concrete block columns and the rifle nested snug against his shoulder. Frantic, she rolled onto her hips and jabbed her feet at the upper bunk's metal frame.

"That you, Dalton?"

The answer came just as Grace got the corner of the frame off the supports.

"It's me. I'm coming in."

The frame dropped at a sharp angle, its rusted edges almost slicing into her face. She rolled out from under them just in time and somehow managed to keep the handcuffs from making more than a brief rattle. Petrie didn't hear it, thank God. His focus and his aim were both on the figure climbing the slope.

"Walk slow," he bellowed, "and keep your hands in the air."

Panting with fear and desperation, Grace eased off the bunk and then slid the cuff up, off the metal pole. The steel bracelet dangled from her other wrist as she searched frantically for a weapon, any kind of a weapon. The only thing within reach that wasn't nailed down were the fishing rods. If nothing else, she could slash and whip one of them. She scooped one up and was frantically trying to disengage it from the others when Petrie bellowed a warning.

"You can stop there."

Grace could see Blake now, unarmed, more than close enough for a high-powered hunting rifle to drill a hole through his heart.

"I got a score to settle with you, Dalton. I'm going to do it slow, though. I think maybe I'll put the first bullet in your kneecap."

"You can put a bullet wherever the hell you want, Petrie. Just let my wife go first."

"I don't think so, pal. She's got as much to answer for as…"

Two loud pings stopped him cold. Instinctively, he tilted his head an inch or two toward the intrusion detection device still sitting on the table. Grace knew that was all the break she'd get. She lunged through the open door, arm raised, fist wrapped around the rubber handle of the fishing pole, and lashed into Petrie's face with everything she had.

"Sunuvabitch!"

He flung out an arm, caught her broadside and sent her crashing. She slammed into the hard ground and caught only a brief glimpse of Blake hurtling past her in a flying tackle. She was rolling onto a hip, dazed and shaken, when a second figure burst out of the brush on the opposite side of the clearing and raced for the cabin.

Alex pounded past her onto the porch. Blake didn't need his brother's help, Grace saw as she staggered to her feet. He had Petrie on his back, straddling his hips while he smashed a fist into his face with lethal precision.

A dazed corner of her mind wondered how a corporate attorney could take down a trained cop. Then she remembered the tales Delilah had recounted about her sons' rough-and-tumble childhood in Oklahoma's oil fields and saw firsthand the rage her husband put into every blow.

Finally, Alex had to intervene. "That's enough. Jesus, you'll kill him."

He caught his brother's arm and hauled him off a now almost unrecognizable Petrie.

"He's… He's got another gun." Still winded from her fall, Grace steadied herself with a hand on the cinder blocks and gasped for breath. "In his waistband, at his back."

Blake rolled the man over and took possession of

the pistol. Thumbing the safety with practiced ease, he passed it to his brother.

"If the bastard tries to get up, blow his head off."

Then he was beside her, his blue eyes savage when he took in the bruise she knew had flowered after Petrie's backhanded blow.

"I'm okay," she said before he could spin around and add to the punishment he'd already inflicted. "Just winded...and scared."

"Me, too," he admitted hoarsely, cupping her unbruised cheek with a bloody palm. "God, I was terrified we wouldn't get here in time."

She didn't ask how he'd found her. The details didn't matter now. All she needed, all she wanted at that moment was to lean into his hard, welcoming body.

He held her off and looked down at her with grim intent. "I never told you I love you. That ripped at me the whole time we tracked you."

She managed a shaky smile. "Well, now that you're here..."

"I love you, Grace. I'm sorry it took almost losing you to make me realize how much. Maybe someday you'll forgive me for that."

"I will. I do. And you have to forgive me for almost letting my promise to Anne blind me to the promise I made you."

"I will. I do."

She went up on tiptoe and brushed her mouth over his—very carefully.

"I love you, too." She put her whole heart into the simple words. "So much I can't remember what it was like to *not* love you. Now take me home so we can clean our scrapes and bruises and start our marriage over."

Epilogue

Delilah insisted on celebrating her granddaughter's first birthday with her usual flamboyance and flair. As one of the Oklahoma City Zoo's most generous benefactors, she chose that as the venue for the momentous event and marshaled her entire staff to prepare for it.

Her social secretary drew up the guest list, which included fifty of Delilah's closest friends—all potential donors for a new exotic bird aviary—as well as every child enrolled in the Oklahoma City Special Olympics.

Louis, her majestic butler, came up with the design for the colorful invitations. They featured a talking parrot who squawked out the delights in store.

Her chef baked the six-layer jungle-themed main cake himself but graciously allowed a caterer to handle the rest of the menu items.

Naturally, Delilah also marshaled her daughters-in-law for party duty. She brushed aside the fact that Julie had turned over crop-dusting operations to her partners and the two additional pilots they'd brought on board. Julie's current responsibilities as director of flight operations for Dalton International kept her twice as busy, but Delilah blithely announced she could take the necessary time off to help with this once-in-a-lifetime event, as could Blake and Alex. Grace, who had delayed going back to teaching for a year or two, was totally immersed in the early preparations and event itself.

When the big day arrived, Delilah assigned her daughters-in-law the job of welcoming invitees and handing out goody bags crammed with beak-billed ball caps, macaw whistles, parrot sunglasses and canary-shaped marshmallow bars. Alex she put to work matching golf carts with drivers for kids who had difficulty walking. Blake had been tasked to assist a Special Olympics coordinator organize games suitable for children with varying disabilities. Bow-legged Dusty Jones and various volunteers from DI manned the lemonade, popcorn and cotton-candy stands set up throughout the zoo.

Even Molly participated. Spouting gibberish only she could understand, she played pat-a-cake with anyone who would reciprocate and toddled on wobbly legs after brightly colored beach balls in the infants' roller-derby. She also locked her arms around several other kids and refused to let go.

"She's at the hugging and kissing stage," Grace explained apologetically as she disentangled her daughter from a red-faced three year old. "C'mon, Mol-i-gans, it's time to blow out your candle and cut the cake."

Molly came into her arms with a smile so joyous that Grace's chest squeezed. She could see more of her cousin in the baby now. Not the frightened, cowed woman Hope had become, but the happy, laughing girl Grace had skated and played hop scotch and made mud pies with. Tears stung as she stood for a moment amid the bird calls and colorful chaos, nuzzling the squirming infant.

Oh, Hope! She's so bright and beautiful. Just like you.

Then she spotted her husband weaving his way through the crowd. A grinning boy in leg braces rode on his shoulders, waving energetically with one hand while he kept a death grip on Blake's hair with the other. When they reached his mother, Blake dipped so she could lift her son down and stopped to exchange a few words with her.

Grace's chest went tight again. Could her life be any fuller? Could her heart? This kind, thoughtful, incredibly sexy man filled every nook and cranny of her being. He and Molly and the child just beginning to take shape in her belly. She'd never dreamed she could feel such all-consuming happiness—and such a sharp stab of panic as when Molly gave a joyous cry and all but launched herself from her arms.

"Dada!"

Experience had taught Grace to keep a secure lock on the chubby little legs, thank goodness. Laughing in delight at her neat trick, Molly hung upside down until Blake righted her.

"Think you're pretty smart, don't you?"

"Smart," she echoed from the nest of his arms, adding to her growing vocabulary of one-syllable words. "Molly smart."

"Yes, you are. Very smart."

He angled her against his chest and slipped his free arm around Grace's waist. "Mother texted me with orders to convene for the cake cutting."

"Me, too. Guess we'd better comply."

They met Alex and Julie where the paths to the aviary converged.

"Un-ca!"

Molly reached out imperious arms and was duly passed to her uncle. While he and Blake led the way to the tables groaning with cake and other goodies, Julie fell into step with Grace.

"When are you going to tell Delilah you're pregnant?"

"We were thinking after the party might be a good time. She'll be too pooped to rush over to our house and start redecorating the nursery."

"Ha! Don't bet on it." The auburn-haired pilot hesitated for a moment, a rueful smile in her unusual eyes. "Listen, sweetie, I don't want to steal your thunder, but… Well…"

"Julie!" Grace swung around. "You, too?"

"Me, too, unless the stick I peed on this morning is defective."

"Omigod! This is wonderful! Delilah will have to divide her energy between the two of us!"

Julie burst out laughing. "I thought that advantage might occur to you. It certainly did to me."

They waited to spring the news on their mother-in-law until after the last of the guests had left. The family sat amid the party debris to catch their breath before pitching in to help the clean-up crews. Molly was sound asleep in the stroller parked between Grace and Blake. Alex sprawled long-limbed and loose at a picnic table with Julie beside him. Delilah drooped in a folding chair, sighing in ecstasy when Dusty pushed his battered straw Stetson back on his head and began to knead her shoulders. Weariness etched lines in her face but she essayed a smile as she surveyed the deflating balloons and animal-shaped confetti littering the scene.

"The party went well, don't you think?"

"I'd say so," Blake agreed lazily. "How much in pledges did you strong-arm out of your friends?"

His mother's smile turned smug. "Just over a hundred thousand. They could hardly balk when I promised my sons would match them dollar for dollar."

Neither son so much as blinked at this blithe reach into their pockets.

"Half goes to Special Olympics," Delilah continued, wincing a bit as Dusty's gnarled fingers found a knot. "The other half should cover the new exotic bird aviary. The Zoo Director was thrilled at the news."

Grace and Julie exchanged glances, then both women telegraphed unspoken signals to their husbands. Blake took the cue first.

"Grace and I have some exciting news, too."

Delilah shot upright and skewered Grace with keen blue eyes. "I knew it! You're pregnant!" Chortling, she twisted to give Dusty a triumphant grin. "Didn't I tell you that wasn't the flu that had her tossing up her breakfast last week?"

"Yep, you did."

The matriarch faced front again and trained her laser eyes on Julie. "What about you? I figure there was a reason you quit working with chemicals six months ago. You and Alex trying for a baby?"

"Not trying," Julie admitted. "Having."

"Whooeee!"

Dusty's gleeful shout made Molly jerk in her stroller. Startled, she puckered her lips and blinked once or twice, then settled back into sleep while the crop duster danced a quick jig.

"I'm gonna be a three-time grandpa. Not honorary, either," he added when he spun to a stop. Under his bushy white brows, his glance turned to Delilah. "Guess this would be a good time we tell 'em our news, Del."

"Guess so."

The sapphire bangle she always wore winked on her wrist as she reached for the thorny palm he held out to her. She didn't have to go into detail, though. Both sons and daughters-in-law were already on their feet.

"About time you made an honest man out of him," Alex said with a wide grin as he pulled her out of her chair and wrapped her in a fierce hug. He yielded his place to Blake, who echoed his brother's sentiments.

"We've been wondering when you two were going to come out of the closet. Literally."

To the amazement of all present, Delilah blushed a rosy red. Dusty merely beamed while Julie enveloped his bride-to-be in another hug.

"I'm so happy for you." Her laughing glance went to her former partner. "And if anyone can keep you out of the casinos, you old reprobate, it's Delilah."

Grace waited her turn, her heart so full it was almost a physical ache. She'd promised during Hope's last, anguished hours to deliver Molly to her father and make sure she was loved.

She is, Hope. So very loved.

So was Grace. She felt its embrace when she walked

into Delilah's arms and met her husband's eyes over his mother's shoulder.

Whatever happened, whatever came in the years ahead, this was one promise she and Blake would always keep.

* * * * *

STOLEN KISS
FROM A PRINCE

TERESA CARPENTER

Teresa Carpenter believes in the power of unconditional love, and that there's no better place to find it than between the pages of a romance novel. Reading is a passion for Teresa – a passion that led to a calling. She began writing more than twenty years ago, and marks the sale of her first book as one of her happiest memories. Teresa gives back to her craft by volunteering her time to Romance Writers of America on a local and national level.

CHAPTER ONE

PRINCE DONAL'S PLANE GOES DOWN IN WORST STORM OF THE CENTURY

Today the world prays as superstorm Allie rages, hindering search and rescue attempts from reaching the plane carrying Donal and Helene Ettenburl, Prince and Princess of Kardana. The royal couple left the principality of Pasadonia traveling with other dignitaries for a weekend of skiing in the French Alps. There was no indication when the plane left Pasadonia that the two cold fronts pouring rain and snow over most of Europe would collide into an ice storm. The death toll is in the hundreds and continues to grow as utility outages leave hundreds of thousands without power. A distress call came from the royal flight late Saturday morning and there has been no contact since. French officials have elite search and rescue teams ready to go as soon as weather conditions allow. Prince Julian Ettenburl met with the French officials and rescue teams en route to Pasadonia to be with his nephew, the royal couple's thirty-two-month-old son, Samson Alexander Ettenburl, who remained behind, a guest of the Pasadonia royal nursery. On the plane with Donal and Helene Ettenburl were…

JULIAN FLIPPED THE news screen off with a sharp flick of his thumb and dropped his phone in his pants pocket. He knew his purpose for being in Pasadonia. Knew the plans for rescue included not only France's best cold weather rescue crews, but Kardana's as well. He'd provided the best vehicles, the best equipment, the best people available to find his brother and the future king of Kardana.

The news of the crash nearly killed his father, already frail from a mild stroke a year ago. Julian needed to gather his family and return home as soon as possible. And that included his brother, lost on the side of a mountain. For now he'd settle for his young nephew.

The train trip, the only mode of transportation capable of managing any distance in the storm, had been interminable but had allowed him to make the arrangements for the searchers. Though Prince Jean Claude had invited Julian to wait out the storm in the comfort of the palace, Julian preferred to begin the return trip. He hoped the nursery staff had Samson ready to go.

He arrived at the nursery and was greeted with subdued courtesy by the Matron, a pleasant woman, her plump figure and serene smile giving her a motherly appearance.

"Your Highness. May I express my wish that your brother and all those on his plane will be found soon, safe and sound?"

"Thank you. May I see my nephew?"

"Of course. But Master Samson is sleeping." Matron advised him. "I hate to disturb him as he's been restless and distressed missing his parents. You may see him, but I recommend letting him sleep."

"Thank you, Matron." Julian inclined his head in acknowledgment of her comments. Fading sunlight flooded the large room through the many windows. Colorful rugs covered the gold marble floor, while masterpieces of fanciful art graced the walls. White furnishings added a crisp cleanliness to the room. He spotted three attendants besides the matron. He had no doubt Samson had received the best of care in these rooms.

"It is my desire to return to Kardana as soon as possible. Please have the Prince's things packed and ready to go. And have his nursemaid report to me." He was surprised not to spy Tessa, Samson's nursemaid, somewhere nearby.

She always seemed to be hovering about, eyeing him. With the encouragement of his sister-in-law. Tessa was a dear friend of Helene's, and always struck Julian as more of a companion than a child care specialist. He made it a point to avoid them both.

Now he hoped for Helene's safety.

"It's best he return home," he advised the woman before him.

Matron nodded. "It is good he will have people around him he knows. However, he is quite exhausted and likely to be very fussy if you wake him now. Might you wait for a bit?" Her gaze cut to something behind him and back again as she made her plea. "Perhaps after you have dined?"

"Unfortunately, time is an indulgence I cannot allow. Please take me to my nephew," he demanded, denying her request for a delay.

"Of course." With a sigh, she gestured toward a door behind him that led to another room.

In here the drapes were closed and the lights turned low. Samson slept in a low race-car-shaped bed in the west corner. An older child occupied a canopied daybed nearby. As Julian stood over him, Samson jerked in his sleep and his tiny brow pinched as if stress followed him into slumber.

So young.

So innocent.

So important.

Looking down on him, Julian felt totally inadequate to care for him. The thought that he might be responsible for raising this child to be King outright terrified him. He was a bachelor by choice. He liked his tranquil life behind the scenes. Being Minister of the Treasury suited him, the numbers, the strategy, the quiet.

One more reason to pray for his brother's safe return.

"Julian, *ami*." Princess Bernadette, a regal blonde, swept into the room. She flowed forward and embraced him in warm arms, kissing the air over both cheeks. "I am so sorry. Tell me you have good news of Donal and Helene?" He shook his head, his gaze going to the thin woman with short platinum blond hair, who followed the Princess into the room. Tessa. Good.

"There is nothing new to report. The weather prevents a full-scale search. America sent a SEAL team to help. They are leading a small group of extreme weather experts on an extraction expedition, but it is slow going and communication is spotty."

"At least it is something." She squeezed his hands. "Please know we pray for their safe return."

He nodded an acknowledgment. "You can un-

derstand I am anxious to return to France to oversee the rescue operations."

"Indeed." She looked down on Samson. "Poor
baby knows something is wrong. He has been
fussy. He will be happy to see you. He needs the
familiar and to be with family."

Right. Julian couldn't remember the last time
he'd held the child.

"Thank you for your care of Samson. It has
been a relief during these trying hours to know
he is in good hands. Now, however, we have a
train to catch." He nodded to the bed. "Tessa."

With a flick of pale blue eyes, the nanny
stepped up to the crib and reached for the toddler. Samson jerked awake. Blinked at Tessa then
Julian and let out a scream.

A shrill scream woke Katrina Vicente. She
sprang up in the small bed, her fuzzy mind immediately going to Sammy. The toddler wasn't
dealing well with his parents' disappearance. He
totally rejected his nanny. The dolt, and Katrina
didn't use the word lightly, had told the boy his
parents weren't coming back. Of course he went
into hysterics.

Tessa quickly realized her mistake and had
tried to correct herself by telling him his parents
were lost and everyone was looking for them,
but the not-yet three-year-old didn't comprehend

the nuances of the situation. All he knew was he wanted his mama and papa, and they weren't here.

From that point on he wanted nothing to do with Tessa. She was familiar but not his mother, and he was smart enough to know when he saw her it meant his mother wasn't back yet.

Hearing his screams she pushed to her feet, ready to take on the dark-haired man who'd dared to wake her charge.

"*Mon Dieu*." She rushed forward. "You best have a good reason for waking this child. Or I'll have your head." She sent a chastising glare toward the Matron, hovering behind the man's broad figure.

"K'tina." Sammy twisted toward her voice and held out his arms.

She reached for him, the pitiful wail wringing her heart.

"Who are you?" The man stepped back, turning so Sammy was beyond her grasp. He stared down his aristocratic nose at her. The deep timbre of his voice easily cut through Sammy's renewed screams even as the boy thrashed wildly in his arms. "Samson, be still, child."

"I am the one who got him to sleep." She'd worked so hard to get him settled. In total despair, he hadn't been sleeping or eating. The poor baby was completely out of sorts.

He'd been in the middle of a screaming fit when Katrina came on duty early the day before. As nursemaid to the children of Prince Jean Claude and Princess Bernadette, she had become well adept at soothing such scenes. She'd wrapped him in her arms and sang softly to him. He shrieked and thrashed, but she'd held him securely, rocking and singing as he cried. Finally he'd slept for a couple of hours. Bringing much-needed peace to the nursery.

From then on he'd latched onto Katrina and she'd gladly stayed to care for him. She managed to calm him some, got him to eat a little through the day, but he rarely slept more than a few minutes at a time before he woke screaming. Nightmares, Dr. Lambert diagnosed.

And now this man had awoken him from his first decent rest.

"He's going home," the man stated.

"Give him to me." Undeterred by the man's imposing stance, she invaded his space to reach the boy. Focused on the child's cries, she tried to take Sammy, but quickly learned she was no match for the man's strength.

"It's okay, baby." She stroked Sammy's light blond hair seeking to reassure him. "It's okay. Katrina is here."

"Mama!" Sammy cried out at the same time he threw himself backward in the man's arms.

Unprepared for the sudden movement, Katrina was unable to elude him, and his hard head conked into hers. Pain exploded across her temple and black dots grew into bigger dots until darkness threatened to overcome her. She swayed and felt a hard band circle her waist. Slowly the dimness receded, and she found Sammy was in her arms and she was in the stranger's. Her legs felt weak yet she had no fear of falling. In the background voices buzzed.

"Katrina!"

"My goodness."

"Call the doctor."

Sammy clung to her, his small head resting on her chest, his wails growing into full-fledged screams. Disoriented, she blinked up into rich amber eyes.

"I have you." Warm breath tickled her neck. He led her to the daybed she'd been sleeping in until a few minutes ago. "Sit. We must check out your head."

"Sammy first," she insisted, grateful to be off her feet. Though curiously disappointed to lose the security of his arms. The bump on the head obviously distorted her thinking.

Dr. Lambert arrived within minutes. Light bounced off his bald head, and bushy white eyebrows topped expressive eyes. He smiled kindly and spoke in English, the official language of

Kardana. "How is our little man tonight? I hear he actually got some sleep before trying to knock you out with his head. I'll want to look at you, too."

"I am okay, but Sammy has a sizable knot on the back of his head." She sent Prince Julian a chastising glare. Oh yeah, she'd finally recognized the gorgeous, dark-haired man. "But, *oui*, he slept for a couple of hours before he was disturbed."

"Well, let us see what the damage is."

The doctor had been by to see Sammy every day, so he didn't try to move the toddler from her lap. Instead he talked gently to the boy, telling him what he was doing and why. He felt the child's head, looked into his eyes and listened to his heart. And when he was done with the boy, he did the same with Katrina. Again without disrupting Sammy.

"Did you lose consciousness?" He shone a light in her left eye.

"No." Katrina carefully kept her attention on the doctor and not the tall, brooding man standing arms crossed over a broad chest on the periphery of her vision.

"She came close," a deep voice put in.

The reminder brought to mind the feel of his strong arms cradling her. She'd been pressed against his hard body, the warmth of his masculine heat reviving in her moment of weakness. The memory sent blood pounding through her veins, adding to the throb in her head.

She didn't care for the thought of spending the night in the medical wing, so hopefully the doctor wouldn't attribute her racing heart to the bump on the head.

No, that came from the brilliant action of telling the Prince of Kardana she'd have his head for waking his nephew.

Not that she hadn't meant the reprimand at the time. Sammy needed the rest. But he also needed family. Ever since Tessa disclosed his parents were missing, Katrina had taken to following the doctor's example of talking to Sammy, explaining what had happened and what was being done to find his parents. It seemed to calm him.

He may have a limited vocabulary, but he understood a lot more than he said.

The one thing she'd promised him, again and again, was his family would come for him and then things would be better. He'd be with people who loved him, who would care for him, who would do everything they could to bring his parents back to him.

Unfortunately Julian Ettenburl didn't quite fit that picture. *Warm and loving* were not words she'd use to describe him. *Cold and stoic* fit him better. And impatient. Though that was more a feeling than anything he did.

His utter stillness revealed nothing of what he felt, nor did his fine-hewed features or his intelligent hazel eyes under straight brown eyebrows. His brother was touted as the handsome one, being blond and eye-catching. A soldier in the royal corps, he was seen as a man of action, a man in control. The world viewed him as a true Prince Charming.

Julian was darker, his features more defined, his demeanor more brooding, a testament to his preference to shun the limelight. Having seen them both, Katrina found the younger brother more attractive if infinitely less charming. She ducked her head, not that she had any interest in him, or in any man.

She had little doubt the dark prince would wield his considerable power and influence to find his brother. Sammy, however, might get lost in the shuffle as his uncle concentrated on the bigger goal.

"A bit of a concussion for both of you." The doctor sat back and regarded her and Sammy. "And you're both exhausted. I recommend twenty-four hours rest at the minimum."

"Can he travel, Doctor?" Julian asked, squaring his shoulders into an even-sharper line. "He can rest on the train."

Katrina tensed at the suggestion. Sammy stirred against her, and she patted him softly, adjusting so she covered his ear with one hand while lightly running her fingers through his hair with the other. Surely the man didn't intend taking Sammy tonight?

"Your Highness, I understand your urgency to return to France and the search for your brother, but the boy is traumatized. He was told his parents weren't coming back."

At this news amber eyes met hers, his disapproval drilling deep into her. No question who he blamed. She swallowed hard but refused to look away.

The doctor went on. "Sammy is in distress. The staff has done their best, especially Katrina, but he's slept and eaten little since news of the crash reached us. With the addition of this head injury, I highly doubt he'll get the proper rest he needs on the train."

"Julian—" Bernadette moved to the prince's side "—we have rooms ready for you. Why not stay the night and see how Sammy is in the morning? The early train is at eight, not too big a delay."

No mention was made that if the inclement weather continued, travel might be impeded. There was no need. It didn't take a genius to figure the odds, and it was well-known that Julian

Ettenburl was off-the-charts smart. Yet after only a few minutes in his presence Katrina saw he wasn't a people person.

Why ever had he been the one to come for Sammy?

She supposed it spoke well of him. But not if he insisted on making the child travel before he was ready. A glance from the Princess had Katrina biting back her opinion.

He showed some sense when he nodded at Bernadette. "We shall stay the night. Though I would like Samson with me."

"Of course." Bernadette readily agreed as she sent Katrina a hopeful glance. "Your suite has two rooms. I'll have a crib set up in the second bedroom."

"Thank you. You are most gracious."

"I do hope you'll join us for dinner. Jean Claude has been closely monitoring the rescue operations. I know he would welcome a chance to speak with you."

"As I would him." The Prince sighed, showing the first sign of weariness. "Actually, I find I'm quite famished."

"Then we shall dine." She hooked her arm through his and drew him toward the door. "Our chef will be pleased with the opportunity to impress you. Unless you'd prefer to freshen up first?"

"No, that is fine." He paused to nod at Tessa. "Please see Samson settled into my rooms." His critical gaze slid over Katrina. "I prefer you resume his care."

"Of course, Your Highness." Tessa bowed her head in acquiescence.

Heat flooded Katrina's cheeks at his obvious censure. Arrogant beast. She was happy to see the back of him as Princess Bernadette led Prince Julian from the room.

Tears stung the back of her eyes. Exhaustion, she knew. She didn't usually let attitude get to her. She lived in a world of royalty, worked in the palace, where arrogance and entitlement were practically job requirements. She'd learned long ago not to let it bother her.

Tonight, as she fought to keep her eyes open, it hurt.

Dr. Lambert righted her when she listed to the side. "My dear, you need to find your bed."

"*Oui.*" Oh how she craved her own bed. But first she'd see to Sammy, despite his uncle's wishes. She wouldn't let his poor behavior dictate hers.

"Good, you're going to be sensible. Just as well you live here in the palace. With the concussion, you'll need someone to check on you periodically through the night."

She'd like nothing more than to follow the doctor's orders and head to her room, but in the past few days Sammy had stolen a part of her heart. He'd brought her back to life. She couldn't rest until she knew he was settled for the night.

"What about Sammy?" Tessa asked. "Should I wake him during the night?"

"Yes. Wake him and check his pupils. If you notice any oddities or if he starts vomiting, call for me."

Tessa nodded and reached for the sleeping Sammy. He awoke with a jerk and shrank away from his nanny with a weak cry.

Katrina stood, cradling him to her chest. He subsided against her, closing his eyes. "I will carry Sammy to the Prince's rooms and see him settled."

Tessa blocked her way. The nanny looked down her nose at Katrina. "I'll take him."

She eyed the taller, thinner woman. It hadn't skipped Katrina's notice the other woman had kept her silence when the Prince focused his blame on Katrina for Tessa's lapse of judgment in telling Sammy of his parents' disappearance. In Katrina's opinion, the woman was showing no better sense now than she had before.

"I do not think so." She moved to walk around the woman.

Again Tessa stepped into her path. "His Highness made it clear he wishes me to resume my duties. He will expect me to deliver Sammy to his rooms."

Sighing Katrina shifted Sammy in her arms, his deadweight beginning to weigh on her. "Look, I am too tired to deal with a crying fit because you want to impress the Prince. He is not even in his rooms. Let me put Sammy down. We all know he is more likely to go back to sleep if I do it."

"Sammy is my responsibility." Tessa continued to protest.

"And in a minute I am going to give him to you and go to bed." In no mood to argue, Katrina pushed past the woman. Sometimes exhaustion had its advantages. "Think about it. Would you prefer Prince Julian come back to a sleeping child or one awake and wailing in misery?"

Tessa had no response for Katrina's challenge because they both knew she spoke the truth. Which didn't mean Tessa accepted it graciously. As they fell into step behind the porter showing them to Prince Julian's rooms, every click of her heels shouted her dissent.

Let her sulk. It was Sammy Katrina cared about. Her head throbbed and her arms began to burn, but one look down at his innocent, tearstained face gave her the strength to continue on. In the end they arrived at the suite before the crib did, and she gratefully sank into a blue silk tufted chair.

The room, a lavish display of antique elegance in blue and gold, reminded Katrina of what she loved about the palace. Tradition and longevity were built right into the brick and mortar of the royal home. She remembered coming here with her father as a child and thinking the palace was the most beautiful place on earth. She'd had so much fun with the other kids in the nursery she'd told papa she wanted to come back and live here someday.

Three years ago, she moved in. She never dreamed it would be under such agonizing circumstances.

But she worked hard, and last year earned a position in the nursery. She loved working with the children. Especially the royal twins, Devin and Marco. Because of her black belt in karate she was often assigned to them. The three-year-old boys were full of mischief and mayhem, yet were so smart and loving they were impossible to resist.

Katrina jolted from a light doze to find Tessa standing over her. She blinked and saw through the open bedroom door off to the right that the crib had been set up.

Good. The last thing she needed was another encounter with the headstrong Prince.

CHAPTER TWO

JULIAN ABSENTLY SHREDDED a piece of bread, unable to focus on the fine meal provided by the palace's talented chef.

He kept reliving the moment when his nephew shrank away from him with a cry of distress. It tore at his heart both as the child's probable guardian and as a man. He and his father were the child's closest relatives. Samson should be reaching for him not seeking comfort in the arms of a stranger.

Even if those arms were soft and scented of apple blossoms. Or if the stranger protected him fiercely with flashing violet eyes and a fiery mane of bouncing curls. The woman barely reached Julian's shoulder, and she'd been ready to personally take his head for disturbing Samson's sleep.

Probably a guilty conscience.

Fury fried already-frayed nerves at the thought of the meddlesome chit causing Samson undue trauma by telling him his parents wouldn't be returning. Even if it proved true, that should have been his job and handled once the boy was back among family. And after Julian had a chance to discuss the matter with a professional so he knew the best way to approach the issue without doing the kind of damage Samson was currently experiencing.

"My friend, you should eat," Jean Claude, Prince of Pasadonia, urged him. "The next few days will be trying. You will need to be at full strength."

"The meal is delicious." Julian speared a succulent shrimp from the savory dish. "I apologize for my lack of appetite." He usually valued a gourmet meal, but preoccupation prevented him from fully enjoying the multicourse fare. Nonetheless he appreciated the royal couple's efforts. Plus they'd provided a safe haven for Samson during the travesty of the past two days.

Physically anyway. They obviously needed better trained nursemaids.

A soft touch settled over his fingers, and he looked into Bernadette's sympathetic gaze. "I know you have much on your mind. I cannot imagine how you are holding together."

"It is difficult," he agreed, wondering if he should pull his hand away from hers or just leave it until she retreated. He respected the offer of solace, but her touch made him uncomfortable.

These awkward moments were why he preferred to avoid social situations.

"I hope you know we support you whatever the outcome of the search." Jean Claude spoke bluntly. "Of course we hope the rescue will be successful, Donal and Helene are in our prayers, but I know you are already preparing for the worst. If there is anything I can do to help, you have only to ask."

"You know me too well, my friend."

He'd met the older man when he was fourteen and Julian's family visited Pasadonia to witness the crowning of the new ruler, Prince Jean Claude Antoine Carrere. He'd been kind to an awkward kid on an occasion when he could be forgiven for being overwhelmed by his own agenda. Their relationship had grown through the years, and Julian looked on Jean Claude as one of his closest friends and advisors. The fact he was a well-respected world leader only added to the value of his offer.

"My mind boggles at all that must be done. But in truth I cannot focus on anything beyond finding Donal."

"Understandable." Jean Claude nodded. "I have my experts watching the weather and will provide you with any updates as soon as I receive them."

"I appreciate it." Julian chafed again at the

delay keeping him from returning to France. "I'm anxious to get back to the rescue operations."

"Yes. It is unfortunate that Sammy's condition has delayed you. It is admirable of you to put his needs first. He has had a difficult time missing his parents."

Julian clenched his jaw in irritation. "It was upsetting to learn he'd been told of the crash."

"It was not intentional," Bernadette rushed to assure him. "Tessa—"

"Excuse me, Your Highness." Jean Claude's assistant appeared at his side and handed him a folder. "The current weather report. And the call you were waiting for is holding."

"I shall be right there." The Prince glanced at the report and then handed it to Julian. "Not much change. I have to take this call. We will talk before you leave in the morning. Bernadette."

The Princess gracefully stood and rounded the table. She stopped and kissed Julian's cheek. "Stay. Finish your meal. A porter will show you to your room."

He cleared his throat. "Don't worry about me."

She sighed. "But I do. Good night, *mon ami*. If you wish to get some air, use the courtyard. The press are everywhere."

The Prince and Princess left the room hand in hand, an obvious unit set to deal with whatever business awaited them.

For a moment Julian envied his friend. Usually an insular man, it might be nice to have someone to talk to right now. Due to his father's frail health, Julian couldn't burden him with his worries, and it would be inappropriate to discuss family affairs with outsiders.

No longer hungry, he followed the porter to his room. When the elevator opened on his floor, Samson's cries pinpointed Julian's destination.

He rushed forward then waited impatiently for the porter to open the door. Inside he found Tessa walking Samson, both were in tears. Julian briskly made his way toward the two only to come to a dead stop next to them. What to do?

"What's the problem?" he demanded.

"The doctor advised me to wake him and check his pupils. Only he wouldn't go back to sleep. He started crying, and nothing I've done has helped."

"K-k'tina." Samson's breath hitched on the wail, but his message was clear.

"He keeps asking for her," Tessa revealed, the plea in her eyes as heart wrenching as Samson's tears.

Julian set his back teeth. The woman had caused this problem; it went against everything in him to reach out to her for help.

Feeling helpless, watching both woman and child struggle, he racked his mind for something to do to right the situation. But for all his considerable knowledge and his massive IQ, he lacked experience dealing with women and children, let alone both in a state of distress.

Considering distraction to be an option, he tried to take the boy.

"No!" Samson screamed and hit out at him. "K'tina!"

Bloody hell, he rebelled against drawing that woman back into his nephew's life. She was the reason he suffered so. But this wasn't just a tantrum; this was a miserable child seeking solace from the one person he'd connected with during this crisis. How did Julian deny him?

Simple, he didn't.

He called for a porter seeking information about Katrina and found that she had rooms at the palace. Lucky for him or he'd be out scouring the streets of Pasadonia. He soon stood outside Katrina's room. He wished for a more formal form of address, but in all the confusion they hadn't been properly introduced.

A maid answered his knock. She bowed. "Your Highness."

"I need to see Katrina." He stepped past the maid into the room.

"She's sleeping," the young woman said softly. "I've followed the doctor's orders. I woke her just half an hour ago and she was fine."

"I'm not here about her injury."

Through the open door of the bedroom he saw the redhead. Light from the lounge fell across the bed and the lovely woman within it. Long lashes dusted creamy pale cheeks. Dark bruises under her eyes were a violation against the porcelain perfection of her features. Whatever she'd done, he couldn't deny she'd pushed herself beyond the expected to help Samson.

Suddenly it seemed wrong to ask more of her. But for Samson he must.

"I'm sorry to disturb her, but I need Katrina to come with me. My nephew needs her help."

"Oh." The woman looked uncertain and then nodded. "I will wake her." She slipped inside the room and closed the door.

He paced the small lounge, wishing he were anywhere but here.

People called him cold. And maybe he was. If preferring order and calm were attributes of being cold. He needed both to do the work he did. Overseeing his country's treasury, including both finances and security, required a clear head and a focus of purpose.

He could work under pressure but he rarely had to. He had the ability to see the big picture, to track patterns and trends. So he prepared and diversified and created contingency plans. Which allowed him to move before the market did.

Some said it was magic or worse called him

psychic. Bah. It was just the way his mind worked. He enjoyed learning things, and his brain absorbed knowledge like a sponge. He surprised himself with the facts he knew sometimes.

People, on the other hand, were a mystery to him. As was their penchant for displaying high emotions.

A bachelor at thirty, he'd been content in his role as the spare heir. Though his father occasionally addressed his desire for Julian to find a suitable woman and start a family, the pressure had lessened after Donal wed Helene and Samson was born.

Still, Julian was a man like any other, with the same needs. His position, however, called for discretion. He managed that by having a number of lady friends he escorted to the many functions his title forced him to attend. By spreading his attention around, no one—women or press—built up undue expectations.

He supposed his reputation for being cold kept him from being dubbed a playboy.

The woman, Katrina, threatened his hard-won detachment. His attraction to her stunning beauty just made him angrier over the whole situation. As did the intelligence he'd spied in her violet eyes. She struck him as being too smart to make the blunder she had. So what had she been thinking?

Shock, he imagined. But it was no excuse, not in her position.

He may not be able to do anything to help his brother, but he could make sure Samson was cared for. And if that meant disturbing the injured woman's sleep, he'd do it without remorse. She deserved no more rest than the child she'd traumatized.

The door opened and Katrina walked barefoot into the lounge. She wore a lush white bathrobe that brushed her bare pink-tipped toes. Under it was a white garment trimmed in lace cut nearly as low as the V of the robe.

His gaze jerked to hers from the soft swell of her breasts visible in that V. She was so pale there was very little difference between her skin and the white of her nightclothes. Except for the shadows he'd noted earlier.

"Is Sammy okay?" she asked in a voice husky from sleep, her brow furrowed in concern. "Have you called the doctor?"

"His injury is not the problem," he assured her, his brusqueness more for his benefit than hers. "Tessa woke him as instructed, but he will not go back to sleep."

She gave a resigned nod, the action making her head appear too heavy for her slender neck. There'd been no sign of softness or frailness when she attacked him in the nursery. Just fierce protection of Samson.

Now he saw how tiny she was, clearly no more than five-four at the most. At six-two he towered over her. The oversize robe didn't help. Nor did her fiery mane of hair, which she'd tamed into a braid that hung halfway down her back. But without makeup, her skin appeared starkly white against the vibrant color of her hair.

"Shall we go?" She moved forward, swaying slightly.

He ground his teeth, half tempted to send her back to bed. More than tempted to join her there. He dismissed the inappropriate thought, disgusted with his libido for rising up when his full attention should be on his brother's family.

Samson's needs came first.

"Where are your shoes?" he demanded, focusing on the practical.

She stopped and frowned, as if it took an effort to think. He was reminded she, too, had taken a knock to the head.

"I'll fetch them." The maid disappeared into the bedroom and returned a moment later with a pair of fuzzy slippers. Katrina slipped them on; her pink-tipped toes peeked through the end.

She rubbed her forehead. "Would you prefer I take the time to dress?"

Yes. There was something entirely too intimate about her in nightgown and robe.

"No." Again he thought of Samson, saw tear trails on pale cheeks. "Let's go."

He followed her from the room and was surprised when the maid also stepped into the hall.

"It is all right, Anna." Katrina bid the maid. "Thanks for watching over me. You can go now."

"Oh, but I have doctor's orders," the young woman protested.

Annoyed by the delay, Julian bit back his impatience to address the woman. "What are your instructions? I'll see she's cared for the rest of the night."

Clearly upset with the change in circumstances but unable to countermand his authority, Anna outlined the doctor's instructions. "You must wake her every few hours and ask her questions to make sure she is coherent. If she's not, or you notice anything strange about her pupils, or she gets sick, you need to call the doctor immediately."

As she spoke, he automatically looked into Katrina's eyes to check her pupils and found himself lost in the solemn depths. Blinking, he turned to the maid, acknowledged her instructions and sent her on her way. While he took care of that, Katrina started ahead of him.

Her actions caused him to scowl. Protocol demanded she follow him. Sighing, he decided to cut her some slack; she had a concussion after all. However, it didn't escape his notice she appeared to know the way.

Though it may only mean she'd asked after where Samson would be, Julian believed it was more than that. She'd probably been the one to put him to bed. He wasn't okay with that. He'd charged Tessa with taking the boy to his rooms, made it clear he'd wanted her to resume care of the boy.

Already his authority was being undermined.

Something he would not tolerate.

"Mademoiselle—" Damn. What was her name? He quickly closed the distance between them. "I wish to make myself clear. Your assistance with Samson is appreciated. That does not mean I will abide interference with my decisions regarding his care."

"Of course," she responded as she pressed the button to call the elevator.

"Are you mocking me?" he challenged, crowding her.

She blinked those big violet eyes at him as she shrank back, making him feel as if he'd chastised an innocent.

"No," she said, and entered the elevator. She moved into the corner, her toes curling into her slippers. She pulled the edges of her robe together and tightened the sash. "I know you want what is best for him." A wan smile lifted the corner of her mouth. "Otherwise I would not be here right now."

He searched her features for any hint of guile but saw only the ashen evidence of her exhaustion. She looked so fragile he thought of sending her back to her bed. Only the thought of Samson's suffering kept him resolute.

"Excellent." The elevator doors opened and he waved her forward. "As long as you understand."

They traveled the remainder of the distance in silence. Which made the sound of Samson's cries all the more grating as they approached the door to Julian's rooms.

Inside the suite, tears stained the cheeks of both Tessa and Samson. The nanny had been walking the boy, trying to soothe him, but upon his and Katrina's arrival, she began sobbing.

"I can't take anymore." She thrust Samson into Katrina's arms and fled.

Katrina didn't hesitate. She wrapped Samson close and started talking to him. "Hey, baby, it is fine. I am here. Does your head hurt?" She kissed his light curls. "Mine, too."

Though he continued to cry, there was no denying Samson preferred the redhead to the blonde. Instead of fighting the embrace by curling up and putting his arms and legs between his body and Tessa's, he clung to Katrina's lusher figure.

Finding the scene painful to watch, knowing this might just be the beginning of Samson's trials, Julian moved to the fireplace to start a fire. This was going to be a long night.

Katrina continued to coo to Sammy until his sobs lessened and eventually he sat up in her arms. She used the collar of the fluffy robe to wipe his pale cheeks. Poor baby, he had such a hard road ahead of him. Ever the optimist, even she had to acknowledge the chances of his parents surviving both the crash and the icy weather were long odds.

Still, she prayed and she hoped. Miracles happened every day.

"Mama? Papa?" Samson asked around a shaky breath.

Biting the inside of her lip, she shook her head. "We do not know yet."

Tears leaked from his eyes. "I want Mama."

"I know, baby. She wants to be with you, too. And look…" She walked to the fireplace where Prince Julian stood. "Uncle Julian has come to get you." She met brooding brown eyes. His discontent with her conversation showed in the stiff set of his shoulders. He'd soon learn Sammy did better with information than platitudes. "He is going to take you to where they are looking for Mama and Papa, and then he will take you home."

"Unca Julie." Boy studied man for a minute then surprised her by holding out his arms indicating he wanted to go to his uncle.

Julian's eyes went wide when she plunked the toddler in his arms.

"Uh, hum." He cleared his throat, clearly at a loss what to do with the boy.

"It is a good thing." She mouthed the words, not wanting to disturb the moment. Though she stayed close enough to be enveloped in the dual scents of manly musk and baby shampoo.

This was the first time Sammy had voluntarily gone from her to someone else. It showed a level of trust that boded well for the future.

"Mama? Papa?" He put the question to his uncle.

Julian paled. She understood his pain. It broke her heart every time she had to tell Sammy his parents weren't coming home yet.

Julian's gaze shot to her.

She shrugged and crossed her arms over her chest. "Talk to him. He is a sharp biscuit. He does not talk much, but he understands more than you might think."

Skepticism flashed over his aristocratic features before he turned his attention to Sammy.

He hoisted the child up in his arms so they were eye to eye.

"Samson," he began, and for a moment she worried he'd lecture the young Prince on duty and decorum. But Sammy's intent attention must have swayed him. "The best searchers in the world are looking for them." And then he added. "I want to see them, too."

More tears leaked down Sammy's cheeks. He reached out, grabbed Julian's ears and leaned his forehead against his uncle's. The two shared a moment of loss and hope.

The poignant picture had Katrina swiping at her own cheeks.

Emotion must have gotten to Julian, because he squeezed too hard causing Sammy to squirm. He turned and held his arms out to her.

She looked to Julian, hating to end the closeness between the two, but he seemed happy to hand Sammy off to her. Hoping the exchange was enough to allow the boy to settle into sleep, she carried him into the room where the crib had been set up.

He frantically shook his head and began to cry. "No. No tired."

Rather than force it she backed up. Right into a hard male body.

"Oh!" She swung around even as his hands went to her waist, and suddenly she found herself in the Prince's arms. She looked up, and up, past his stubborn chin to eyes of molten gold. Oh yeah, definitely the better-looking brother. And way too close.

"Sorry." She winced internally at the squeak in her voice as she stepped back. Or tried to. His fingers tightened on her waist, holding her still as his hot gaze strolled from the gapping neckline of the robe to the racing pulse in her neck, to the bite she had on her lip, to her eyes. She played it cool even as a shiver traced down her spine and her pulse raced.

Wrong time.

Wrong place.

Wrong man.

Wrong woman.

He obviously agreed, because his hands dropped and he stepped aside.

Breathing a sigh of relief she moved past him to pace the room. Julian moved to the fireplace to stoke the fire. Way wrong man. She'd spent enough time in the palace from childhood on to know the demands placed on royalty. And the price was too high. If she ever worked out her trust issues, she wanted a kind man and a simple life.

Two strikes against Prince Julian.

Okay, that wasn't totally fair. These weren't

the best circumstances. Obviously he was under a lot of pressure.

Her arms were beginning to burn from fatigue so she took a seat on the antique sofa and tucked Sammy comfortably against her. He denied it, but he was tired. Part of his objection was probably to the crib. He hated to be called a baby. But what he really craved was human contact.

Calling to mind one of his favorite stories, she began a tale about a train named Thomas while slowly running her fingers through his baby-fine blond hair. After all he'd been through, she hoped it wouldn't be long before he fell asleep.

Thanks to Julian. He might be brusque and rude, but she gave him points for putting Sammy's needs before his own. She knew he would have preferred to leave Pasadonia without ever seeing her again. Or more on point, without Sammy seeing her. Yet he'd come for her rather than let Sammy cry himself into exhausted slumber.

She smothered a yawn, forced her eyes open and skipped ahead in the story.

So maybe there was a little kindness buried somewhere inside the cold Prince.

CHAPTER THREE

JULIAN TAPPED HIS lip as he contemplated the two asleep on the sofa. Snuggled up in Katrina's arms, Samson appeared more at peace than Julian had seen him since arriving at the palace.

Thank God. He'd taken about all of the boy's distress that he could handle.

Blast Tessa for deserting them. He was counting on her to help him with the boy on the trip home. She'd best have herself pulled together by morning. If he needed proof he was ill prepared to handle his nephew, he received it tonight. Samson couldn't get away from him fast enough.

Julian wanted to strangle Katrina when she started talking about Donal and Helene to the boy. Yet when faced with a direct question from Samson, Julian couldn't lie. Giving the child false hope served no purpose beyond delayed pain. Best he prepare for the worst and be surprised by a miracle.

Which didn't change the fact he'd be better off if left in the dark about the crash in the first place.

Julian switched his gaze to the woman responsible for some of Samson's suffering. Her lap provided a comfortable resting place for the child, but Katrina sat in the middle slumped to the right with her head listing at an angle sure to cause a crick by morning.

Dare he risk moving them? For certain they'd be more comfortable in a bed. But as he considered the logistics, he doubted the success of getting them both to the desired destination still asleep, an imperative in his mind.

He admired the Victorian design of the sofa they occupied, but nobody could argue the merits of its long-term comfort. The bench had cushioning, but the tufted back curved higher on one end than the other. Her position in the middle offered her little support on either side.

He supposed he had the answer to his earlier observation. If he were the cold bastard everyone thought him, he'd simply leave the woman and child to their own devices. When she became uncomfortable enough, she'd wake and move to the bed taking Samson with her or putting him in his crib. Problem solved.

But Julian wasn't that cold. With a sigh he rose and approached the sofa. Settling into the corner he turned toward the sleeping pair and pulled woman and child into his arms.

"Hmm." She surprised him by opening drowsy

violet eyes and staring up at him. "I am going to go to bed," she assured him in a sleep husky voice.

He waited, but instead of moving away, she snuggled into him with a contented mew, shifting her hold on Samson to keep him secure.

"You smell good," she murmured.

Him? She was the one who smelled good enough to eat, making him wish he'd eaten more of his meal. Maybe then he'd be less tempted by her.

He closed his eyes and tried to pretend he was at home in bed. He pulled to mind a problem he'd been wrestling with before the fateful plane went down and changed his life. Neither solution worked. The subtle, sweet scent of apple blossoms and the soft feel of womanly curves cuddled in his arms brought his body to life.

He ignored the inappropriate reaction.

She was exhausted and injured, and he'd accepted the responsibility of her care. That was the extent of their connection.

"You're so warm."

He shook his head, a half smile lifting the corner of his mouth. "Go to sleep already," he said running his hand over the silk of her hair.

And closing his eyes, he followed his own advice.

Deep in the night, something disturbed Katrina. She stirred slightly and then purred softly. It had been a long time since she woke up in Rodrigo's arms. How she'd missed this connection, the feel of hard arms holding her close, the warmth of a man's nearness, the sensual tickle of his breath on her cheek.

She opened her eyes to find the room dark except for the dying embers in the fireplace. Sighing, she snuggled in, hugging him as she drifted toward sleep.

He smelled so good, of musk and man. Her brow furrowed as her foggy mind niggled at a sense of wrongness, but it hurt to think. He shifted beneath her and the thought fled. She realized his movement was what woke her.

Yes. The only thing better than sleeping in his arms was being awake and in his arms. A pain in her head followed the thought. Thankfully it didn't linger and she dismissed it. Better to focus on the man. Without opening her eyes she angled her head and kissed him.

He went completely still, his sleep-relaxed body going tense. Usually he took it from there. Not tonight.

Tease. She smiled and, opening her mouth, she touched her tongue to his lips, seeking more. His lips parted and she tasted him. She knew immediately this wasn't Rodrigo.

And while her mind struggled with why that was a good thing, the man gave in to her invitation, sinking into the embrace with an aggressive dance of tongues.

No, this was not Rodrigo. Everything about him felt right. Heat flooded her and she gave in to his demand, sighing in surrender as she wrapped her arms around him and sank into a depth of passion she'd never known before. Wanting more, she pulled him closer.

He slanted his head taking the kiss deeper, the fever higher. He threaded fingers through her hair, holding her still for him while his thumb feathered softly over her temple in a soothing caress.

She nipped at his lower lip with her teeth. She wanted that hand, his hands, lower, tracing her curves, igniting a true fire between them. She pressed closer trying to show him, and a squeak sounded between them.

"Oh my goodness." In an instant everything came flooding back.

The crash.

The toddler.

The man.

No, no, no. She'd let a man touch her. Almost as bad, she'd been smooching with the Prince!

"*Mon Dieu*, I am sorry." She pushed back and checked on Sammy, who'd been crushed between the two of them.

A scowl drew his tiny eyebrows together and

his mouth twitched a couple of times, but he didn't waken. Somewhere during the night, he'd switched his weight to Julian. Without looking at the Prince, she lifted Sammy carefully and carried him into his crib. Before leaving the room she switched on the light and checked his pupils, sighed in relief when she found them even and reactive.

Unable to delay further, she returned to the sitting room, where Julian stood by the mantel stoking the fire back to life.

"Your Highness," she began.

"Stop." He put down the poker and turned to face her, keeping his hands clasped behind him. "You have already apologized. Now it is my turn."

"No, please." How mortifying. "I kissed you. It is my fault. I woke up in your arms—which it was very sweet of you to let Sammy sleep." His dark brows lowered so she rushed on. "I thought you were my old boyfriend. Oh God. You smelled wrong, but you felt good—"

"You are babbling, *mademoiselle*—" His sigh reeked of exasperation. "What is your full name?"

"Katrina Lynn Carrere Vicente." She cringed as soon as the words left her mouth.

"Carrere?" Of course the name caught his attention. "You're a relative of Jean Claude?" His tone turned grim. "Please tell me you are not related to the Prince."

"Distantly," she confessed, "through my mother." She didn't mention her father was a close personal friend. No need to make matters worse than they were.

His head dropped forward causing thick strands of hair to fall over his wide brow. He muttered what sounded like, "It just keeps getting better and better."

Her sentiments exactly.

But the show of emotion lasted only a moment. He quickly drew himself up and straightened his shoulders.

"Mademoiselle Vicente you have my deepest apologies. I should never have touched you."

"Your Highness."

He shook his head. "I'll express my regrets to the Prince in the morning."

"No." Her eyes went wide in shock. She felt sick to her stomach. The last thing she wanted was for the royal family to know she'd forced herself on a guest. She couldn't handle another disgrace. She stepped forward in entreaty. "Promise me you will not."

"I must." His posture was rigid. "I have offended a member of his family."

"No offense. None." She assured him. "You were the perfect gentleman."

His eyes narrowed in censure. "I had my tongue down your throat. Hardly the actions of a gentleman."

"But you kept your hands above my waist. I wanted them on me—" She broke off as his eyes darkened and narrowed even more. What was she saying? So not the place to go.

"I promise I am not offended. It has been a tough couple of days for everyone, and we found a moment of comfort in each other. That is all that happened."

"Is that how you see it?" His shoulders relaxed slightly.

It was all she would allow herself to believe.

"Yes. You held Sammy and I while we slept, something we both needed desperately. Something I believe you needed, too. The kiss came from the comfort of that gesture. You are leaving in the morning. Can we not forget it ever happened?"

He studied her in silence so long her nerves grew rattled. Finally he beckoned. "Come here."

Leery, she forced apprehension aside to approach him slowly, until she had to tip her head back to look up at him. He stared down into her eyes, his gaze penetrating. Again he rattled her with his intensity. Would he agree to put her indiscretion aside?

"Yes?" she prodded.

"Just checking your pupils," he stated. "How do you feel? Any nausea?"

The question confused her until she remembered her concussion.

"No," she assured him. Did he think her injury affected her thinking? No, only her actions. It was the only excuse she could come up with for her uncharacteristic advances. "I am fine."

"So it would appear." He nodded formally. "Tessa is next door. You may use the bed in Samson's room."

"Thank you." At the mention of bed, fatigue washed over her. "I checked on Sammy when I put him down. He was doing fine."

"Good. That's good." He turned back to the fire, clearly dismissing her.

But she couldn't leave without knowing if he meant to speak to the Prince in the morning. The loss of her career was the least of her worries. She respected and honored the people in this household and wished no harm or embarrassment on them. Not again.

She couldn't bear her father hearing of this. The disgrace might well jeopardize his friendship with the Prince.

"Please, Your Highness." She dared to disturb him. "I must know if you plan to reveal my indiscretion to the Prince."

He stiffened but did not turn. "It shall be as

you requested. We simply shared a moment of comfort."

"Thank you." She backed away, eager to put this encounter behind her. There was much more to Prince Julian than his reputation gave him credit for. Tonight she could only be thankful for his mercy.

Sleep eluded Julian. He worried about Donal, his father, Samson, while thoughts of duty warred with his natural inclination to stay in the background. Every instinct he possessed rebelled against losing his brother.

At five in the morning, he gave up all pretense of trying to sleep and rang for coffee, a hot breakfast and an array of items for Samson and the nanny. In anticipation of an early departure he also asked for Tessa to be roused so she could pack and get Samson ready for travel. Next he called and advised his security detail of his plans.

One of the advantages of being in the palace was not having security underfoot every moment.

He'd dressed and packed his own bag when the knock came at the door. He glanced at the closed door of the temporary nursery as he crossed the room. There'd been no movement from that quarter, a hopeful sign Samson was getting the rest he needed.

Another knock sounded as he reached the door.

He opened it to find his meal and the lady of the palace awaiting him.

"Bernadette." He bent over her hand. "You look fresh and lovely, considering the early hour. To what do I owe this honor?"

She moved gracefully into the room. "I have something to discuss with you. I am hoping I might share a cup of coffee with you while you eat."

"Of course." He waved her toward the elegant cart the steward had situated near the window and pulled the desk chair around for her use. The steward produced another chair and Julian joined her.

"Thank you, Pierre." Bernadette smiled a dismissal.

"What do you wish to discuss?" Julian picked up his napkin.

"*Non, mon ami*, you must eat first," she insisted. "You barely touched dinner last night."

"I had a lot on my mind."

"As you will until Donal is returned to us. First rule of being a ruler—take care of yourself." She lifted a dome, revealing a hot plate of steaming eggs. "Take a few minutes and enjoy a peaceful meal. Then we shall talk."

Lifting the coffeepot he poured two cups and placed one in front of her. "What you have to discuss must be really bad." He tapped his cup against hers. "I believe it's best if I eat first." He dug into his vegetable omelet.

"Wise choice." She sipped, closing her eyes and taking a deep breath of the freshly brewed beverage. She flashed him a sheepish smile. "Jean Claude prefers tea. I like both so I usually defer to him. But I do enjoy a good cup of coffee."

"There's nothing better to jump-start the day," he agreed.

She chatted while he ate, managing to avoid any sensitive topic in the process. The weather, politics and his family were never mentioned. He admired her talent at putting him at ease, allowing him a few minutes peace while he enjoyed his meal.

When he finally set down his fork, she topped off their coffee and got to the point.

"I am afraid I have some upsetting news. Tessa came to see me last night and asked me to let you know she cannot return with you to Kardana."

"What?" He carefully set his cup in its saucer. This couldn't be happening. "That is unacceptable."

"I know the timing is bad." She placed her hand over his. "However, she is very distraught. You know Helene is a close friend."

"Samson needs her."

"Unfortunately she feels too overwhelmed to

resume his care. She was in tears as she requested an escort to take her home to England."

"She's left the palace?" Shock blocked all thought.

"Yes." Bernadette confirmed, and with a gentle squeeze she released him. "I hope you will not blame Tessa too much. The last couple of days have been very emotional. Sammy rejected her after she told him of the crash. She tried to help but—"

"Wait." Julian cut her off. "Are you saying Tessa told Samson his parents were not coming back? I thought Mademoiselle Vicente made the mistake of telling him."

"Oh no." Bernadette shook her head, visibly surprised by his assumption. "We were at our wit's end with Samson when Katrina came on duty. He was inconsolable for hours. She took one look at him, gathered him in her arms and began rocking him. And she talked to him."

"About Donal and Helene." Yes, he'd seen a sample of her frankness with the child last night. "He responded to what she told him."

"He did." Her admiration for Katrina came through in her earnestness. "He stopped crying to listen to her. And he finally slept for a short time. She did not leave his side until you arrived."

Her revelation stunned him, sent his mind reeling. Something he experienced rarely. It was unlike him to make assumptions. Then again, the circumstances of the past few days were far from the norm.

The tragedy of the crash had his emotions rising to the surface, yet he was helpless to do anything. Anger at Katrina for the distress she'd caused Samson had given him something to focus on and do something about.

Erroneously, as it turned out.

Not only was his indictment and coldness misplaced, they were an affront to Katrina and the royal house that opened its arms to a hysterical child suddenly thrust upon them. He'd personally witnessed Katrina's dedication yet discounted it in favor of his preconceived notions.

He cringed inside when he realized he owed her yet another apology.

"…I truly believe it is the best solution," Bernadette said. Her expression was expectant and Julian realized she'd carried on with the conversation while he'd been examining his conscience.

"I apologize, Bernadette, my mind wandered for a moment. Do you mind repeating your solution? I am most anxious to hear your suggestion. I cannot leave Samson here, but I am far from a nursemaid. Frankly, the thought of changing a nappy is terrifying."

"Quite a vivid picture." Her melodic laughter

lightened the mood. "But I think you are safe. Sammy is potty trained."

Finally, something in his favor.

"Plus, no apology is necessary."

How he wished that were true.

"As I mentioned before, Samson has become attached to Katrina. My suggestion is she accompany you back to Kardana and stay until Tessa is ready to resume her duties or you find a replacement."

"Oh no." Horrified at the idea, he summoned a polite smile. "I could not steal off with a member of the royal family. Katrina told me of her mother's relationship to the Prince."

"Really?" Bernadette's fine brown eyebrows lifted in astonishment. "How interesting. Katrina rarely reveals her connection to Jean Claude." She tapped a finger on the table as she eyed him thoughtfully. "You must have asked her."

"I did. Why does she keep it to herself? Is it a secret?"

"Heavens no." Diamonds flashed as the Princess waved a careless hand. "Jean Claude is very fond of his goddaughter. Katrina, dear child, does not care to take advantage of the relationship."

"Goddaughter." Just shoot him and put him out of his misery. Katrina conveniently left that little tidbit out when she garnered his promise to forget his slip in protocol last night.

"Yes. Jean Claude went to school with Dom Vicente. They are the best of friends. Katrina has been tripping around the palace since she was tiny."

"Vicente." Of course he recognized the name. He should have caught it last night, but the royal name distracted him. "We've met several times. I'm surprised I haven't heard of the relationship."

"That is at Katrina's request." Concern darkened her features. "She prefers not to draw the attention of the press."

A confession trembled on the tip of his tongue. Only the fact he'd given his word kept him from disclosing his actions.

Well, that and the fact the moment seemed too intimate to share. The few hours holding her were the only solid sleep he'd had in two days. Waking to her mouth on his, her taste and scent surrounding him, drew him into the passionate interlude. Yet her reference to comfort resonated with him.

He'd agreed to forget the incident because she'd been correct. Comfort had led to the embrace. He wouldn't regret the rest, so how could he condemn them for the kisses?

"She is wonderful with the children," Bernadette continued. "We would have been happy to have her without a degree in child development, but she insisted on meeting all the qualifications and more. We often have her assigned to the twins. Of course it does not hurt that she is family and has a black belt in karate."

The more she extolled Katrina's virtues, the more the muscles tightened across Julian's shoulders.

"You have made my case, dear Lady. I cannot take away such an important member of your household."

"Julian—" her eyes shadowed with sadness "—we insist. We want to help. This is one small thing we can do. How is your father?"

He released a deep sigh. Giving his father news of the crash might be the hardest thing Julian had ever done. It was a well-kept secret the King had suffered a stroke a year ago. Mild as the stroke was, it had been a slow road to recovery, with both Donal and Julian taking on more and more of the royal duties as their father tired easily.

His father shrank before his eyes when he learned Donal and Helene were missing and presumed dead. His first thought had been of Samson. He had urged Julian to journey immediately to Pasadonia and return his heir to Kardana.

"I will not lie." Though he must be ever cognizant of keeping up appearances, "It was a blow. As you can imagine, he is anxious to see Samson."

"Yes, of course. How is Samson? I have not

heard of any complications from his bump on the head."

He imagined not much happened in the palace she didn't know about.

"Both he and Mademoiselle Vicente were fine when I checked on them around three. Grumpy but fine."

Another tinkle of laughter sounded. "For certain it is no fun to be awoken in the middle of the night. Poor Julian. You have had it tough these last few days. What news do you have from France?"

"I'm told the storm is beginning to abate, but less so at the altitude of the projected crash site. The elite team should reach the area soon. They're hoping to have more to report later this morning."

"Knowing you wished to leave early, I checked, and the train will be delayed an hour or two while they clear a couple of sections of track. I also checked the travel advisory and many roads and passes are still closed, so the train is still your best choice."

"That's disappointing." The delay chafed at raw nerves.

"Jean Claude ordered our private train car be made ready for the trip. You will be more comfortable. Plus, it will save you from having to deal with the press on the trip. I know it is not what you wanted to hear, but at least the delays will give Katrina time to pack."

"Pack?" a sleepy voice asked. Julian turned toward the sound to spy Katrina coming toward them. His body stirred at the sight of her mussed red hair and sleep-tousled beauty. "Where am I going?"

"Do you really think this is a good idea?" Katrina nervously twisted the ring on her right hand as she questioned her Princess's sanity. They were in the bedroom of her suite. Katrina sat on her bed, fighting for composure as she marshaled arguments against Bernadette's calm insistence. "The press is all over this story. It is the perfect time for someone to come forward and cause irreparable damage, not only to the house of Carrere but to the Kardanians, as well."

"It is the perfect opportunity for you to learn you have nothing to fear. We worry about you, Katrina. You cannot hide in the palace forever, my dear." Bernadette folded a lemon-yellow sweater and placed it in the open suitcase. "Young Samson needs your help. It is obvious he has bonded with you. Of course we remain hopeful, but it is likely the poor child will need a strong advocate in the following days."

"It is not worth the risk. His family—"

"His family needs you." Bernadette came to

the bed and took Katrina's hands in her own. "King Lowell is rumored to be in ill health and the queen mother is in her eighties. If Prince Donal has perished in the crash, Julian will be engulfed with running the country. I fear they may lose sight of Sammy in their grief."

"The staff—" Katrina quickly changed the words at the disappointment in Bernadette's eyes "—are no substitute for family."

"No. And it may fall to you to remind them all of that. Though losing a child, a grandchild is terrible, they still have Sammy, and he is reason to persevere. Dear, I know your concern is not just for yourself."

"I would never do anything to hurt Jean Claude." Katrina rushed to assure her friend and mentor, the slip of the night before haunting her.

"I know." Bernadette squeezed her fingers. "He knows. We believe in you. It is time for you to believe in yourself. Now—" Bernadette rose and went back to the wardrobe "—let us finish packing. Julian is not a patient man."

No, patience did not describe the visiting Prince. Which only made the challenge ahead of Katrina harder. But she dared not argue further. Even she recognized there was a limit to testing a royal's goodwill.

Even her? Especially her!

She'd never been good at decorum. She'd had

too much freedom running wild about the palace as a child. Jean Claude adored his goddaughter, so she was given undo leeway. She learned her lesson three years ago when the misuse of that freedom and a lack of good judgment resulted in hurting those she loved most.

Licking her wounds, she'd retreated to the place she felt safest in the world. The palace. More specifically the palace nursery, where she tried to be a good example of decorum to the next generation.

Her stomach twisted at the possibility of bringing shame to her home once again. No matter what Bernadette said, Katrina knew she'd been a disappointment to Jean Claude, worse to her own father. She stiffened her spine. *Not this time,* she promised them in her heart. She would go with Prince Julian to help Sammy, and she'd mind her manners, follow protocol and be a model of perfect decorum.

If she stuck to the background, there was no reason anyone should notice her.

CHAPTER FOUR

KATRINA GLARED AT the broad shoulders of Prince Julian as she hitched Sammy to a more comfortable position on her hip. The man hadn't spoken two words to her since bidding the Prince and Princess farewell. Julian seemed happy enough to accept the offer of Katrina's services yet disinclined to look her in the eyes.

To the side and behind the royal party strode armed security officers of both Kardana and Pasadonia. She silently and obediently followed the directions given to her as they boarded the royal train car provided by Jean Claude. Inside, an officer stood guard over them while the rest of the Kardanian security force did a quick scan of the whole car.

She stood quietly, but Julian was obviously antsy.

"Down," Sammy demanded and wiggled in a bid to get his way.

"Not yet." She tightened her arms around him,

but he was strong and she nearly lost her grip on him.

"I'll take him." Julian cautiously lifted the boy into his arms. He met her gaze briefly. "Thank you for your patience and cooperation with the security. I know it can be trying."

"I am used to it." She shrugged. "I sometimes travel around town with the twins." Over the past year she'd ventured out twice.

"It is a pain," he declared, his opinion punctuated by the tense line of his shoulders.

"A necessary evil for your safety. For Sammy's safety," she calmly pointed out. Her closeness to the royal couple and their twins made her happy for the protection that kept them safe. "And because I am with you, for mine."

"Samson," he corrected her. "Unfortunately many people do not grasp that notion. Ha." He gave a harsh laugh, a rueful shake of his head. "This is a change. Usually it is I explaining the need for caution."

She eyed him, reluctant to be sympathetic when she was annoyed with him for ignoring her. But he had taken Sammy, who still chattered and wiggled in a bid for freedom. And generally she wasn't one to hold a grudge.

"I suppose that can be trying, as well."

"I'll tell you, it can be a real damper on a date." Long-felt aggravation rang through the words.

Her turn to laugh. "Poor baby."

He froze and looked down his nose at her. "You are impertinent, *mademoiselle*."

She flushed and looked away. "I am sorry."

"Your Highness," Neil, Julian's head of security, turned to them, "the space is secure."

"Thank you." The lift of a dark eyebrow let her know she'd been saved by the announcement. "What is your security plan?"

"A man at both entrances." The trim, dark-haired man responded. "St. James will be in the computer room, and I'll be roving. The trip to Lyon is expected to take four hours."

Julian nodded. "And the weather?"

"There's been no change. Reports indicate the storm is lessening, but the airport at Lyon is still closed."

"Keep me apprised if anything changes."

"Very good, sir." Neil bowed briefly and moved down the corridor.

Julian turned back to Katrina. "*Mademoiselle,* would you care to give us a tour?"

"My pleasure," she lied. Just a tiny fib actually. What she'd really like to take Sammy into one of the guest rooms and sleep. Instead she followed in Neil's wake down the narrow corridor running along the left side of the train from the back where they boarded.

"The car has three guest rooms." She opened

the first door on the right and showed him a small room with a double bed, the decor a sparse elegance equal to a high-end hotel. The second door revealed a room much like the first, in reverse order with twin beds.

"These two rooms share a bath with a full shower. With your permission, I'll sleep with Sammy in here." He nodded. Good. She had the nursery monitor with her, but she preferred to stay close to the child. Unfortunately, it also put her closer to Julian. *Not a problem,* she vowed. It wasn't as if there was the least likelihood he'd make a move on her.

His appalled reaction to her kiss this morning proved she was safe from him.

"The master suite is the next door down. You have a private attached bath. The entire train car is bulletproof, including all the windows, plus the master bedroom acts as a panic room should the car be breached. I am sure Neil will go over all the specifics with you."

She waved him ahead, and he stepped into an elegant oasis decorated in cream, tan and bronze. This room included a small seating area and a bar with a mini refrigerator. Next came the lounge with plenty of comfortable seating in dark leather followed by a half bath and the crew's quarters.

Upstairs, she showed him the domed observation lounge with big-screen TV, the formal dining room, kitchen, tiny computer room and crew's lounge. As with the guest rooms and lounge below, the furnishings here were tasteful and soothing. Plush silver-gray carpet cushioned every step, soft hunter green velvet covered the couch and chairs, while dark woods, fine crystal and a stunning black marble table added to the richness of the rooms.

"Quite the setup." Julian let Sammy down in the observation lounge and settled into an armchair. "Much more comfortable than the deluxe sleeper car I traveled in to Pasadonia."

"Indeed," Katrina agreed. "Princess Bernadette especially prefers traveling by train when they have the twins with them. There are gates attached to the top and bottom of the staircases."

Sammy ran to the large curved sofa fitted into the rear point of the train. He clamored up, plopped right in the middle and gave them a wide grin.

She caught her breath and exchanged a hopeful glance with Julian. The smile was the first she'd seen Sammy give.

"You like it, too, little one." Responding to his joy, she sat next to him, lightly threaded her fingers through his hair. "Or is it the freedom you like? You have been very good today."

The train began to move, slowly pulling away from the palace yard. At the motion Sammy's eyes grew large, and he looked up at Katrina for reassurance.

"It is okay." She smiled. "This is a train. It is like a house on wheels. We are moving—turn around and you can see."

The boy climbed to his knees then stood and looked out the back. She lifted up a hand to protect him from a fall. He pointed at the palace staff seeing the train off. Several waved. Sammy waved back. "Bye-bye."

"That is correct...we are going bye-bye. We have started our journey." She thought of adding their final destination of home, but didn't want to remind him of his parents when he was in such a good mood.

Suddenly Julian settled onto the green velvet on the other side of Sammy and turned to face her. After he had ignored her for most of the morning, his scrutiny unnerved her. Protocol prevented her from questioning him. Instead she kept her focus on Sammy, playing point and name until the boy got bored of the game and slid off the couch to run around the open space of the lounge.

"I understand I owe you another apology," Julian stated gruffly.

"Oh?" Katrina wondered for what.

Several items sprang to mind, rudeness certainly, and rushing her—he'd given her a whole hour to pack and say her goodbyes. This, after Princess Bernadette practically forced him to take Katrina with him. That had been an awkward scene. She had been no happier about the idea than he was, but Bernadette wouldn't be dissuaded and Katrina felt obligated to support her Princess.

"Yes. Bernadette explained it was Tessa who told Sam—" He stopped and eyed Sammy before continuing. "That Tessa was responsible for Samson's distress. I blamed you when I shouldn't have. You have my apology."

Her brows popped into her bangs before she quickly got her disbelief under control. "Um, well. She was in a state of distress herself," Katrina explained. "I believe she and Helene were—are friends."

"There is no excuse for her behavior." There was no give in his response. "She is the nanny of a royal Prince. His welfare needs to come before any other consideration."

"I agree. The child's needs should always come first. Sammy, stop. Stay in this end of the room." She scooted to the edge of the couch, ready to hop up if Sammy went any farther. "But shock can make us do stupid stuff."

He surprised her by sweeping a thumb over her cheek. "Very generous of you, considering you have taken the brunt of her thoughtlessness."

His touch threw her more than his stare. Obviously he meant to denote the shadows under her eyes. She'd be mortified if she could think beyond the sensation of his caress. She blinked up at him, striving to recall the topic of conversation. Oh yes, his apology.

"Sammy is the one who has suffered. Though we do not truly know how much he understands. He is not yet three. He probably does not fully comprehend what *missing* means."

"He's a bright boy. I've never heard reports of him acting up in this manner." Julian turned his attention to Sammy, who was climbing into a club chair and pounding on the table. "He knows something is wrong."

"Yes," Katrina agreed, relieved and yet curiously disappointed to lose Julian's regard. "I think he is reacting to the tension in those around him. He has been different since you arrived. This is the first time he has played, the first time he has smiled. You are familiar, someone from home. He feels more secure."

"He knew Tessa."

"She was fairly new as his nanny, was she not?" At least that's what Katrina had heard.

He nodded, his features etched in grim lines. "She assumed the role a couple of months ago. A farce if you ask me. The woman has no child care training."

"But he is a Prince!" she blurted, shocked by the revelation. Tessa might be Helene's friend, but Sammy was the son of a royal. He had many things to learn beyond the average child. More important, he must be protected at all costs. True, he had his own security detail, but beyond being proficient in protocol and decorum, his nanny should be able to defend him.

Yet even as she protested, she was not genuinely surprised. The other woman always struck Katrina as a tad uppity, as if handling potty duty was beneath her. But she tried not to judge. There were times when she wasn't too happy about doing potty duty, either.

"I am glad you understand," Julian stated. "I was wrong to blame you without knowing all the facts. That…is not like me."

"You have much to occupy you." With the apology, she found she could be gracious.

"Again you show your generous nature." He looked like he'd like to say more, but decided against it. His words turned quite formal as he continued. "I do not deserve your goodwill, but I will accept it. Along with my apology, please know you have my gratitude. Samson is lucky you were there to help him."

"It has been my honor." This time she spoke the truth. She would assist any child in distress, and these circumstances went beyond the norm.

In the midst of crisis she was happy to do her part. Plus Samson was special. He was a Royal Prince, a future leader of the world. Her actions reflected on her country and her Prince. It made her proud to have Prince Julian acknowledge she did well.

Suddenly lights started to flash through the room in a strobelike effect. Katrina jumped to her feet and looked out the window. The train had reached the Pasadonia Station. Unfortunately, the press had arrived before them.

Sammy came running and buried his face against her knees.

"Paparazzi," Julian snarled. "Vultures, all of them. Take Samson below."

She had already grabbed Sammy up and headed for the stairs. Neil met her at the top. "It is just the press," she told him. "I am taking him to the twin guest room. Can you make sure the blinds have been pulled down?"

"No." Julian spoke over her shoulder. "Use the master suite for him."

Confused, she looked up at him. "But—"

"He is the future of Kardana," he stated simply. "He requires the extra security the room provides."

Neil nodded an acknowledgment of the command and led the way below. He went ahead of Katrina into the master suite and made sure the window shades had been secured. While Neil collected Sammy's and her luggage, she took the toddler to the bathroom. Back in the main room Neil had returned. Julian had joined him.

The two men managed to shrink the room considerably with their sheer size. Their sheer presence. Yet they were nothing alike—one was a trained killer, the other a world leader. One lived life in the shadows, the other the limelight. Both were used to giving orders, but only one wielded power with the mere lift of an eyebrow.

And no one would confuse who was who.

Certainly not Katrina, who found it difficult to take her eyes off Julian. He stood, arms crossed over his chest, just inside the door. His amber gaze ran over her before he switched his attention to his head of security.

Feeling his gaze like a touch, she shivered. Luckily he'd turned before she gave herself away. She blamed the kiss. No matter how she tried, she couldn't forget the feel of his mouth on hers.

Did his lingering gaze mean he was remembering, too?

Putting the thought aside, she set Sammy down in the middle of the bed and moved forward to join the men.

Neil quickly took her and Julian through the changing of the master suite into a panic room. She carefully kept her distance during the process. She really needed to get her inappropriate attraction under control. When the lesson ended, the train was beginning to pull from the station leaving the paparazzi behind.

"Report," Neil ordered, obviously speaking to someone on the other end of his headset. "Beale, handle it," he directed, and then advised Julian, "A couple of men on the back stoop of the train, my lord. Most likely press. St. James reports no other suspicious activity. Please stay here while I assist Beale then make a sweep of the car just to be sure we have no other surprises."

Julian acknowledged his acceptance with a slight incline of his head. With a bow Neil exited the room.

"Relax, Miss Vicente. Knowing the mechanics of activating the panic room is just a precaution. We must be ever vigilant."

That was a relief. But the train picked up speed, drawing a question from Katrina. "How do you suppose Beale will handle it?"

Julian shrugged. "I expect he'll ask the unwelcome guests to disembark."

"But these trains get up to a speed of two hundred kilometers an hour." Her heart raced at the notion of debarking at such a speed.

"Occupational hazard. Something they should have considered before attempting to catch a ride."

"Your Highness!" At her shocked exclamation he gave her a tight smile.

"Do you imagine Beale throwing them from the train? No. If they refuse to leave while it is still safe, they will be restrained on the stoop and suffer a long, cold ride to the next station, where they will be charged for trespassing. We are not the monsters they are, Katrina."

"Of course not." She flushed because she had envisioned the exact scenario he outlined. To hide her reaction she strode over to the seating area and tried for a bit of grace as she sat.

Being around the palace since childhood, she well knew the press was anything but harmless. Rodrigo certainly proved just how far a paparazzo would go.

There was big profit in getting that money shot, a million euros or more, depending on how much skin or how scandalous the photo. That was the very reason she limited her assignments outside the palace. She more than most knew just how far a paparazzo would go for that money shot.

And this was not just any story. A missing Prince, an orphaned heir to the throne, these were stories of a lifetime.

Her nails dug grooves into the soft leather of her chair. Oh God, she should never have left the palace.

"Make no mistake." Julian warned her. "I have

no pity for the paparazzi. They are a relentless plague on society. Those men seek to prey on Samson's vulnerability, his moment of tragedy. I will protect him at all costs."

"I can see that." He'd already demonstrated the truth of his claim by putting Sammy's comfort and safety before his own on more than one occasion. Quite heroic of him actually.

Right. Her admiration for him was so not helping in her effort to fight her surprising attraction for the man.

"A single picture of Samson during this trip would set a photographer up for life. I will not allow him to be used in such a manner. Do not disappoint me in this matter, Katrina."

She glanced at Sammy, who'd fallen asleep on the big bed. So innocent, so dependent, so important. "You can trust him with me."

"I do." For a moment his brown gaze softened. "Or you would not be here. Goddaughter of Jean Claude or not." He gestured toward the bed. "Rest while you can."

Julian returned to the domed lounge, chose a large club chair. He leaned back and discovered the chair reclined. *Thank you, Jean Claude.* After a while Julian dozed but came awake when the train slowed. Neil appeared to advise him they were pulling into their first stop and they would be delayed while their car was transferred to a different line.

"St. James is posted outside Master Samson's room. I'll be escorting the trespassers inside, turning them over to the proper authorities." With Samson tucked safely away and their equipment confiscated, the men would be led through the car and delivered into the care of the French Transport Police.

Julian nodded his agreement. Once alone, he tried to make a few calls but was hindered by the limited mobile service. The third time his call was dropped he gave up and switched to text. He let his father know they were en route and gave his assistant instructions on several issues, including making arrangements for Katrina to have a room near Samson and the nursery. Once that was done, he used a digital remote to put a rugby game on. Unfortunately a bad glare on the screen sent him hunting up the control for the blinds.

"My lord." A middle-aged porter appeared. "May I be of assistance?"

Julian indicated the glare on the television. "I wish to close some of the blinds. Where are the controls?"

"They are here, sir." He opened a hidden panel on the half wall between the lounge and dining room. "Or you may use the controls on the remote." The porter approached and bowed slightly. "If I may, sir?"

He proceeded to show Julian what the digital remote controlled, which was everything from the telly and blinds, to the climate and fireplace. He could even activate the gate at the top of the stairs and summon staff, all without leaving his seat.

"Would you care for something to eat?" the porter asked.

"Not at this time." Julian thanked and dismissed the man.

With the shades at half-mast, the light in the room dimmed considerably, and before long Julian dozed again. Worry for his brother, for the kingdom, for Samson kept Julian from slipping into a full sleep. He prayed with all his heart for his brother's safe return.

To contemplate what must be done if the Prince and Princess perished felt like a betrayal of hope. But it must be done. Julian needed to be ready to make decisions and act as soon as his brother was found, dead or alive. Because the possibility existed that Donal would be found alive but grievously injured.

Plans whirled through Julian's head as he tried to anticipate every contingency. So much to think about, but as he slipped closer to sleep, his control over his mind slipped and thoughts of Ms. Vicente took over.

The look on her face when he intimated Beale would toss the pesky men of the press from the train had been priceless. How could she spend every day at the palace and remain so delightfully unaffected? In the middle of this hell he found her patience and generosity of spirit calming.

He had no business thinking about her, yet he never lost track of where she was.

Holding her in his arms last night had been a mistake. And not because she was a dear friend and royal Prince's goddaughter. No, it was because the feel of her had been burned into his memory. Her soft curves aligned perfectly with the hard contours of his body.

And the taste of her, all sweetness and honey, had seduced the sense right out of his head as he sank into the embrace. Who would have predicted she'd wake up and kiss him?

Though he was half-asleep, a frown formed as he remembered she'd thought him someone else. A former boyfriend.

Anger roused him as he awoke with one word roaring through his head. *Mine.*

CHAPTER FIVE

GIGGLES FLOATED DOWN the stairs. Katrina smiled at the sound. Sammy so deserved a break from the depression that had swallowed him these past few days.

She slipped through the gate, relatched it and followed the joyful noise to the domed lounge, where she found Sammy and his dignified Uncle Julian playing ball. Realizing the two hadn't heard her approach, she paused to watch.

Man and child sat on the floor, their legs spread wide, rolling a ball between them. Make that two balls. As she watched, Julian bent to the side and snagged a ball that had gotten away from him.

"'ou missed." Sammy laughed.

"Because you cheated," Julian informed him.

He'd discarded his jacket, rolled up the sleeves of his shirt and ditched his shoes. At first glance he looked as relaxed and carefree as the giggling boy. Only a closer examination revealed the worry and fatigue weighing on him.

He held up the ball. "Let's try this again. This

is your ball." He rolled it down to the boy. "And this is mine." He picked one up from between his long, silk-clad thighs. "You send yours to me while I send mine to you. You don't send them at the same time."

"More balls." Sammy hopped up and ran to the couch. He pulled out a drawer and found a ball twice the size of the baseball-sized balls they were currently using. He pushed the drawer nearly closed and plopped down in front of Julian.

Ball in hand, Sammy reared back as if preparing to throw the ball. She tensed, ready to intervene, but Julian pointed a finger at Sammy.

"What happens if you throw that ball?"

Sammy deflated a bit. "No play."

"That's right." Sammy subsided, and Julian didn't dwell on the near infraction. "You think you can beat me with three balls but I'm pretty fast. Prepare to lose."

"Go!" Sammy sent both balls rolling toward his uncle while Julian sent one his way. The balls went back and forth to the sound of Sammy's chatter until Julian pretended to fumble the two shot his way and they jumped the barricade of his long legs.

"I win!" Sammy shook his fists in the air.

Katrina grinned, enjoying the interaction. Then she bit her bottom lip, wondering if she should leave them to their play. When Sammy woke up forty-five minutes ago, he'd promptly made sure she was awake, too. After freshening them both up, she'd wandered out to the lounge, where she found Julian working on his computer. Not wanting to disturb the Prince, she turned Sammy around and headed for the stairs.

Julian had stopped her and offered to take the boy for a while to give her a break. She'd told him about the storage drawers full of toys and gratefully escaped. She used the time to do something totally for herself. She dug out a book, curled up in a chair and read for thirty minutes.

It looked like Sammy had enjoyed his time, too. To the extent that she really hesitated to interrupt his time with his uncle.

"Care to join us, Ms. Vicente?"

Julian's question ended her dilemma. She moved into the lounge, closing the toy drawer as she took a seat. "It is good to see you two getting along."

"Yes, it surprises me, as well." He sent her an arch glance.

Sammy popped to his feet and ran to her. He jabbered excitedly about his uncle and playing ball. She understood every two words or so. "What a good lad you are. I brought you some juice." She tucked him in the crook of the couch and handed him a drink pouch.

"That is your influence, not mine," she advised

Julian. Heart racing, she dared to address an issue of great concern to her. "Forgive me, my lord. It is obvious you are not at ease with children, yet you have worked to put Sammy at ease. I just wonder if there is any affection or if it is merely duty."

Julian slowly climbed to his feet. "You overstep yourself, Ms. Vicente."

The ice in his gaze nearly deterred her. But for Sammy she must persevere.

"Perhaps, but we spoke of Sammy having special needs in his care because he is a Prince, and this is true. But I feel it is also important to point out he is a child like any other and in need of love and affection."

"And you doubt the Cold Prince's ability to provide for him."

Oh dear, she'd hit a nerve.

"I have observed in high-profile families that structure, discipline and decorum often take precedent over emotional support when it comes to educating the children." She checked on Sammy, who sipped his juice. "I would not want that for Sammy."

"Samson," he corrected. "I survived such a childhood, Ms. Vicente," the Prince stated with cool reserve, turning to stare out the window at the passing scenery. "I can assure you my lessons in decorum and protocol have served me well through my entire life."

"Of course. I do understand the importance of such lessons." Oh yeah, she'd offended him. But Sammy deserved to have someone fight for him. Her time with him might be short, but she'd do what she could while she was here. "I just believe hugs and laughter offer balance to all the demands of his station."

"With any luck he won't have to suffer my clumsy attempts at affection much longer." The stiffness in his posture belied the levity of his words.

Her heart sank as his meaning struck her. She talked as if Sammy's parents were already gone. Shame on her for the appalling lack of tact. She'd allowed her concern for the boy to get the better of her.

"I am the clumsy one." She approached him slowly. "I have become fond of Sammy and I worry for him. But my timing is not so good. Have you heard any news of your brother and sister-in-law?"

"Nothing." She imagined the emotionless word held a world of pain.

"Oh, Julian, I am sorry. I have not given up hope for your brother and Helene. Truly. This is a bit of a soapbox for me. How duty takes precedence over affection. It is just so sad when I know it does not have to be so." Flustered over her faux pas, she let her mouth run ahead of her head. Yet as soon as she stopped, everything she'd just said reran in her head. "Now I am babbling when you are sad. What a puppy-head I am. And to make it worse I just called you Julian. I—"

He held up a hand. "Stop apologizing. A loss of hope is understandable. The crash, the cold, the distance—everything works against them."

He ran a finger over one dark eyebrow, the weary gesture a minute glimpse into his worry and despair. In the reflection of the glass she saw the anguish he kept so ruthlessly hidden. "Do not equate lack of affection with lack of emotion. I pray for Donal's safety while I prepare to take his place. Every directive, every word is the worst kind of betrayal."

Yet he was not allowed to let anyone see. His admission broke her heart.

Katrina checked on Sammy, found him lying on the floor playing with a dump truck and a racer. Satisfied he was occupied, she did the unpardonable. She touched a royal Prince without his consent.

"We shall pray together."

Warm fingers slid around Julian's hand. Shocked by the touch, by the comfort, he tightened his hold until he heard a gasp. Still, she made no attempt to pull away. Instead she squeezed back, answering his silent cry of need.

His gaze went first to her reflection, but it was not enough. Driven by a compulsion deeper than his will, he looked into violet eyes drowned in tears. He quickly turned back to the unseen view, undone by her unstinting compassion. He swallowed past a constriction in his throat.

Protocol dictated he rebuff and reprimand her.

He could do neither. The connection soothed him as little else could. Suddenly he understood what drew Sammy to her, and nothing would do but he stand silent and hold her hand as the train raced toward the answers he sought.

The helplessness and lack of news frayed his nerves. Rather he knew. Then he could do as he'd been trained and put emotion aside while he acted in the best interest of his country. Katrina might not approve, but there were times when duty served one better than affection.

"K'tina, I hungry." Too soon, Sammy wiggled his way between them.

Julian immediately and reluctantly released her. He felt her continued compassion in the weight of her gaze and the softness of her touch on his arm before she knelt down to meet Sammy eye to eye.

"I am hungry, too." She tapped the little boy on the nose. "Shall we see what cook has for lunch?"

His eyes lit up at the question. "I wanna cheese sanwiss."

Listening to their byplay, Julian pushed the button for the porter. A growl of his stomach made him aware of his own hunger.

The porter appeared. "How may I serve, my lord?"

"We should like lunch please." Julian ordered. "Has the chef anything prepared?"

"Grilled cheese sandwiches," the man announced without a blink. "Or a nice salmon steak with rice and steamed vegetables with a tomato bisque as a starter."

"Lovely." Katrina stood and looked down at Sammy. "Would you like soup with your sandwich?"

Sammy considered this, his nose wrinkling up as he contemplated the major decision. Finally he nodded. "I 'ike tomato soup."

"We'll start with the soup." Julian directed the porter, who bowed and went to advise the chef.

Katrina towed Sammy off to clean up for the meal, leaving Julian alone to pull himself together. He watched her disappear out of sight.

But unfortunately she did not leave his mind.

Young, smart, beautiful and impossibly idealistic, she was a very dangerous woman with her weapons of comfort and compassion. How easily she slid beneath his guard. She made him act against his nature at a time when he needed to be strong, be resolute. Another moment and he'd have kissed her.

Again.

Inexcusable. Yesterday it had at least been an accident.

He closed his eyes as he remembered the news that followed the incredible, unfortunate embrace. Katrina was Jean Claude's goddaughter. Taking advantage of her would not only be a betrayal of a friend, the insult might incite an international incident. Neither he nor Kardana could afford such at this time.

There would be no more intimate moments with Ms. Vicente.

Sammy came clambering up the stairs. Julian helped to seat him while studiously avoiding the nanny's regard. It was the way it must be.

Katrina absently pushed the salmon around her plate. He'd been remarkably kind after her earlier blunder. She'd felt so close to him for those few minutes they spent holding on to each other.

But in the time it took her and Sammy to wash up, Julian had distanced himself again. It shouldn't, but his coolness hurt. She knew better, of course. Any closeness between them was entirely in her imagination. He was a Prince. She had a shameful secret.

End of story.

Though she owed him one, she wouldn't embarrass him with another apology. No. She'd learned her lesson. It was best if she kept her distance. Reaching for her napkin, she wiped Sammy's face. From this point forward, her undivided attention went to the boy.

Twenty minutes into the tense meal, Neil appeared at the table with a satellite phone. "My lord, it is the French President."

For the space of a second Julian's gaze met hers. Then, stoic as a blank wall, he took the phone and moved into the lounge area. "*Bonjour, Monsieur le Président.*"

Katrina bit her lip, her attention switched from Julian's tense shoulders to little Sammy innocently eating his sandwich. If the president was calling, he must have news of Prince Donal. Sadly, Julian's posture did not hint at good news.

Heart going out to her charge, she gently ran her fingers through his soft hair. He grinned up at her then dropped the last of his sandwich on his plate.

"I done."

"Good boy." She wiped his mouth and handed him his lidded cup. "Now finish your milk."

He shook his head, his blond hair wisping about his face.

So not the time to press the issue. She stood and helped him from his seat. With a last look at Julian's broad back, she carried Sammy down to his room.

Katrina paced the master suite while her small charge lay on the bed and watched a movie on DVD. His eyes were already blinking and she knew he'd be asleep soon. Since his uncle's arrival, he'd really settled down and behaved rather marvelously.

Unfortunately, that was likely to end soon, as it did not appear as if the news Julian received was very encouraging. She wrung her hands, distraught on behalf of both child and man. What a devastating loss this would be for both of them.

She twisted the ring on her finger, feeling helpless as she waited to hear the exact nature of the news Julian received from the president. Yet the very fact it was the president calling seemed significant. She'd longed to stay, to be there for Julian, but the return of his reserve made such a move impossible. So she'd given him his privacy.

Equally as important was not letting Sammy overhear anything he shouldn't. They'd all learned that lesson. Too bad she wasn't as good at handling her own lessons, like the slight problem of remaining impartial.

Her mother showed concern when Katrina first told her she wanted to be a nanny at the palace. Of course she'd only been eight years old. Still, she remembered her mother's words at the time.

"You have such a soft heart…I'm afraid you will get hurt. A nanny must care but not become attached. You, my dear one, care too much."

To this day that was her biggest problem. Sammy had already wormed his way into her heart and, by extension, his uncle. But her mother was right; it wasn't her place to become emotionally attached. If she hadn't exactly learned that particular lesson, she more than learned the one where she refused to allow herself to be used.

She nearly pulled the ring off, twisted it back into place. The problem with her and Julian was they kept forgetting she was the nanny. Her by getting too attached, and him because he saw her as Jean Claude's goddaughter. The reappearance of his stoic manner indicated he'd come to his senses. Now it was her turn.

A knock sounded on the door. She rushed forward to find Neil standing in the narrow corridor. She shook off a stab of disappointment.

"His Highness would like to speak with you in the lounge," he announced.

"Is it bad news?" she whispered, anxious to know what was happening.

"I don't discuss crown business." His bland expression didn't change, but the sadness in his eyes said what he would not.

"Of course." She acknowledged his discretion and took it as a reminder this was not her household. Harsh, but now was the time to get a grip and start separating herself emotionally from Sammy. And his uncle. "Will you sit with Sammy? He shouldn't be any trouble. I expect him to fall asleep soon."

Neil agreed and stepped inside. Katrina wiped her hands over her hips and headed for the lounge.

Julian stood, hands clasped behind him staring out the window. She experienced a moment of déjà vu and slowed as she remembered her new resolve to keep her emotions out of the job. She stared past him to the view, which consisted of a lot of snow and a smattering of trees. She doubted very much he saw any of it.

"Your Highness." She stopped a respectable distance behind him.

He tensed at the sound of her voice, making his posture even more rigid, if such a thing were even possible.

"Donal and Helene are dead."

At the stark announcement she closed her eyes, fighting the burn of tears. Though expected, it still hurt to hear the news. But she quickly persevered and focused on Julian. The words held a harsh quality, sounding as if he'd swallowed a handful of granite.

"My condolences," she whispered. And then, because that seemed so inadequate, she added, "What can I do to help?"

"We will be stopping to collect the bodies before traveling on to Kardana. There will be a delay while we wait for them to be delivered off the mountain. It could take a couple days. Jean Claude has approved the use of the train car for the full journey. You should prepare for an overnight stay perhaps more."

"Of course, my lord." So clipped, so unemotional. Her fingernails dug into her palms with the effort to stay uninvolved. "Will there be anything else?"

He turned then and her breath caught in the back of her throat. The clenched line of his jaw, the sheen of despair in his golden eyes told of his struggle for composure. Here was a man who had lost his brother.

"Yes." He stood straight and proud before her. "I realize it is highly inappropriate to ask." He fixated on a spot over her shoulder, as if unable to meet her gaze. "You are, of course, at liberty to refuse."

His uncharacteristic hesitancy tore at her heart, drew her forward. "What can I do?"

His eyes met hers, and his Adam's apple worked as he swallowed hard. "Would you hold my hand for a minute?"

CHAPTER SIX

"JUL—IAN." HER voice broke. Not hesitating, she went to him, wrapped both hands around his. He was cold, shaking. "I am so sorry."

"I didn't really believe it until now." His head bowed so his breath fanned over her cheek. "I knew the probability, but it wasn't real. My big brother is gone."

"He is in a better place," she offered, knowing it was too little, too mundane. She squeezed his hand, wished she could do more to ease his pain. No longer a Prince worried about duty, this was a man hurting for the loss of a dearly loved brother.

He shook his head less in denial than hopelessness. His forehead nearly touched hers, and she lifted a hand to his cheek and took the necessary half step to complete the connection, the comfort of skin to skin. A strangled noise came from his throat at the same time he clutched her to him.

"He's always been there for me. Such a bruiser, but he had the kindest heart. I don't want him to be gone."

"I know." She stroked his back; he shuddered under her palm. "You will always have him in your heart."

He didn't say anything more, just continued to hold her. She let him, holding him, too. So much stretched ahead of him. He'd been preparing for this—had felt guilty for doing so—but many would look to him now his brother was gone. Just as King Lowell had looked to his heir when he took sick last year. Those duties would now fall to Julian, as well. This time on the train might be his only opportunity to grieve in relative privacy.

Poor King Lowell. How awful to lose your son and heir. She could not imagine his sorrow, his grief. She'd seen him on the news yesterday talking of hope and staying strong while rescuers searched and the weather hampered efforts. Surely having Julian and Sammy home would bring him some measure of comfort.

Tears welled and overflowed, sliding down her cheek. She made no effort to stop them. Tightening her arms around Julian, she buried her face in his chest, allowing the fine silk of his shirt to absorb the wetness. In response, the arms that enfolded her were strong, and the cheek that rested against her temple held its own dampness.

"My father broke on the phone," he whispered.

"Just broke down and cried." She heard how his father's pain cut him deeply.

Okay, this was so not the way to achieve distance in their relationship. And she didn't care. His pain touched her. It would take a colder person than her to ignore his bid for comfort.

"It is okay for him to cry," she assured him in case the tears embarrassed him. "Even kings are allowed to mourn their sons."

"He would hate for anyone to know."

"His secret is safe with me." She backed up and gently cleaned his face with a tissue from her pocket. "Your secret is safe with me."

"How am I going to tell Sammy?" he demanded, voice raw.

"Wait," she suggested. "There is no need for him to know yet. Wait until he is home, surrounded by those he knows and loves in a familiar setting. I believe it would be less traumatic in those circumstances."

"Perhaps." He closed his eyes as if the weight of the decision took total concentration. "I am no good at these flash decisions. I like to gather my information, act from a position of knowledge."

"Making quick decisions is really no different. You just use the information you have. And then you gather more knowledge so you are better informed the next time you have to act."

"So wise." He kissed the back of her hand; the

heat of his breath tickling over her skin made her shiver, distracting her for a moment. The old-fashioned gesture was definitely not meant to be shared between employer and nanny. And then he turned her hand over and kissed the palm.

Her breath caught. Oh my.

He regained her attention when he framed her face in two large hands and lifted her gaze to his.

"Thank you." His thumbs feathered over her cheeks collecting the last of her tears. "You are a very giving woman."

"No one should be alone at such a time." She lifted her right hand and wrapped her fingers around one thick wrist, not knowing if she meant to hold him to her or pull him free.

"It's a dangerous trait." The thumb of the hand she held continued to caress her cheek, though he seemed almost unaware of the gesture.

"Why?" she breathed.

"Someone may take advantage of you."

A knot clenched her gut. Someone had. The harsh memory threatened to destroy the moment. She should step back, return to her duties. But she didn't. Because of the glint of vulnerability in his eyes.

Instead she bit her bottom lip and stayed put. For the first time she successfully stayed quiet. Perhaps because she needed this moment as much as he did.

"There is only you and me here." She blinked, noting the look in his eyes had changed. The pain lingered but awareness joined the grief. "Are you going to take advantage?"

"Yes." He lowered his head. "I am." And he pressed his mouth to hers. He ran his tongue along the seam of her lips then nipped her bottom lip. "You tempt me so when you torture this lip."

She opened her mouth to protest, but he took full advantage, sealing her mouth with his. Heat bloomed, senses taking over as sensation ignited passion. Large and warm, he dwarfed her, his strong body a shelter against the craziness of the past few days. He drew her closer, aligning her curves with his hard contours, taking the sensual escape to deeper levels.

For long moments she surrendered to his touch, to his heat, to his need. Lifting onto tiptoes, she looped her arms around his neck and got lost with him in a world without loss, without hurt, without protocol.

His thumb had found a new resting place, and her nipple peaked in response as a shot of raw craving ran through her. Too soon his hand shifted, moved down her side to the small of her back and lower. He cupped her derriere and lifted her off her feet. A trail of kisses led him to the curve of her neck. She arched into his hold.

Something vibrated against her thigh. A ring followed.

The real world beckoned.

Julian gently set her on her feet. But he stole a last kiss before he released her. He stepped back and pulled his phone from his pants pocket to check it.

She ran damp hands over her hips and took a step backward. She supposed it was something that he rejected the call.

She cleared her throat. "I should check on Sammy."

He nodded and crossed his hands behind his back in a formal pose. To remind himself of duty or to keep his hands to himself? "I suppose we're going to allocate this to comfort, as well."

"It would be best," she agreed, knowing as she did there'd be even less chance of forgetting these moments in his arms than their last embrace.

"Hardly logical." His eyebrows drew together.

"But for the best." She took another step back. "Do you not agree?"

He hesitated and then shook his head. "I'm not in a position to disagree."

What did that mean? Katrina stopped her retreat. Had the time in her arms meant more to him than a sensual escape?

But the moment was lost.

"You are right. It is best if we wait to tell Samson once we are home."

With that, he turned back to the window and lifted his phone.

The next two days were the worst of Julian's life. Waiting for his brother's body, and Helene's too, broke his patience. It took two days for them to be delivered off the mountain and be loaded into an attached cargo car.

His phone never stopped ringing. He accomplished much but recalled little of what he did. The weather improved enough that his assistant was able to fly down and join him, which helped tremendously.

Perhaps he should have flown Samson and Katrina on to Kardana, but he preferred to keep them with him. With his father's health issues, the raising of Samson fell to Julian now. It was right that the boy stay with him. That it kept Katrina close, too, was incidental. Or so he told himself.

That looking up and seeing her across the room calmed his frayed nerves had nothing to do with his decision. Nor did the memory of her kisses play any part in his decree. He'd be forever grateful for the comfort she gave him. He'd been hurting, and she got him past those horrible first moments.

To prevent Samson from being distressed, he'd

issued the order for no one to talk about his brother's passing. He kept all such discussions between him and his assistant for when they were working alone at the dining table upstairs in the dome.

"My lord—" the porter appeared next to the table "—you asked to be advised when we were within an hour of Kardana. We should reach the tunnel in an hour."

This would be the first time Julian had ridden a train through the twenty-three-mile rail and auto tunnel to the island of Kardana since the inaugural run.

"Thank you. Please advise Ms. Vicente."

"As you wish." He bowed and headed down the stairs.

Julian glanced at his assistant, Carl Brams, and met pale brown eyes through dark-rimmed glasses. Impeccable in a slate-gray suit, Carl didn't wait for instructions but reached for his mobile phone on the table.

"Security is already in place at the train station, but I'll alert them to our imminent arrival and ask them to advise his majesty. I'll also confirm the conveyance arrangements for transfer of the Prince and Princess."

"Remind them that Samson doesn't know. My father will want to see him. I do not want any slipups. This is too important."

As his assistant walked into the lounge area

to make his calls, Julian leaned back in his high-backed chair, away from the latest changes proposed for the initiative adding a police agency to Europol, the joint European law enforcement agency, which was currently investigative only. The vote would precede the International Peace Symposium in just under a month.

For the past few days his total focus revolved around collecting his family and returning home. But with that goal on the brink of reality, he realized how much he'd miss these days of quiet isolation.

Yes, he'd been connected to the world, and he'd stepped out to thank the French president for his assistance and expressed his gratitude to all those involved in the search and recovery operations. But for the most part this time on the train had given him an opportunity to mourn in private. More so than if he'd been at home.

A large part of that was due to the gentle solace of Samson's nanny. He purposely used the reminder of her position to aid in his constant battle to seek her out. Her quiet beauty and giving nature drew him like a bee to an apple blossom. Another time he may explore the potential of their heated embraces, but the chaos of his life made that a luxury he could ill afford.

Once they reached the palace, he expected to see little of her, something he both looked forward to and dreaded. Less temptation, but he'd miss their chats.

And the curve of her breasts in her prim, button-up shirts.

Plus the sweet sway of her derriere as she tended to Samson.

Heaven knew the taste of her already haunted him, and his arms felt empty without her in them. How could that be after such a short acquaintance? He could only hope the reverse would hold true, too, and out of sight would firmly put her out of his mind.

The plan held some flaws, as Julian intended to foster the growing relationship between him and Samson. The boy would need the extra care and attention after he learned of his parents' passing. To that end, Julian reluctantly made a note to address a replacement nanny for Samson as a top priority.

Carl returned to the table and time moved quickly from that point forward. Soon Julian exited the luxury train car and escorted Samson and his nanny through a storm of flashing lights and the thunder of hollered questions. The press swarmed the security barricades, aggressive in their demand for answers.

As prearranged, Julian paused to address the hungry mob of press. He stepped up to the microphone provided for the impromptu conference.

At his direction Carl continued onto the waiting limousine with Samson and Katrina. They'd managed to keep the news from the boy, and this was not how Julian wanted him to learn the truth.

"Kardana suffers a great loss as I return today with the remains of Donal and Helene Ettenburl, Prince and Princess of Kardana. My brother traveled to Pasadonia to attend a forum on ending world hunger. After the forum he and Helene decided to join a ski party on a jaunt to the Southern Alps. The storm that took much of Europe by surprise threw the plane off course and ultimately into the side of a mountain. There were no survivors. Prince Samson Alexander was left in the safety and care of the Prince and Princess of Pasadonia and returns with me today. An announcement of the funeral arrangements will be made soon. The royal family thanks you for your condolences and asks that you respect our request for privacy as we mourn for my brother and sister-in-law."

His statement made, Julian stepped away from the microphone. A barrage of questions followed his exit, and he happily left them for the press secretary. Within minutes he was sliding into the backseat of the limousine next to Katrina. Samson had been strapped into a car seat across from them next to Carl.

The fresh scent of apple blossoms drifted to

him as Katrina shifted to provide him with more room. He reached out to wrap a hand around her fingers, intent on holding her in place. Instead he pulled back and clenched his hand into a fist at his side. He'd just had this internal conversation. He was home. He could no longer allow the softness of her comfort.

"Look, Unca Julie." Samson pointed to something out the window. "That's by my house. K'tina, I home. Mama and Papa at home."

Julian met Katrina's gaze. His dismay was echoed in her violet eyes. He gave a slight shake of his head.

"Mama and Papa are not home yet. But you shall see your *grandpère*."

"The queen mother, Giselle, is also in residence." Carl informed the car.

"GiGi?" Samson asked tearfully, successfully distracted by mention of his great-grandmother. "She bing me a present?"

"I am sure she did." Julian flicked a glance at Carl, who pulled out his phone and began to text. Helped along by Katrina, Samson chatted on about favorite toys.

Julian turned his gaze to the window. Thoughts of the upcoming visit with his father occupied his mind. He hoped Father had found some peace in the past few days. Julian couldn't stand the thought of seeing his proud father broken. He feared witnessing it might destroy his own fortitude.

Katrina stared at her hand on the black leather seat, at the darker hand next to it but not touching her. Julian confused her. He obviously found comfort in her touch. A fact she took satisfaction in. It felt good knowing she was helping someone through a difficult time.

Yet now he held back. Which made her question, had it been her touch that soothed him, or just the warmth of human-to-human connection? She wished she knew, but it didn't really matter. The forced intimacy of the train trip was over. Best if they both retreated to their separate corners.

The royal Kardana palace was a fairy-tale castle set right in the middle of the capital city. Surrounded by beautiful garden grounds and made of brown stone, the huge house had turret-topped towers on both ends of the front of the manor. Gables and spires abounded and a broad two-tiered stone staircase led to a spiked gate.

Katrina craned her neck to see everything as the car turned into the curved drive leading to the main entrance. "It is beautiful," she breathed.

"It's home," Julian answered. He leaned toward her and lowered his voice. "We will encounter many people on our way through the palace. People may be upset and not watch what they say. Please take care as we go."

"I will do my best," she promised, but now they were here and the logistics came into play, it seemed delaying telling Sammy might not have been the best course to take. When she quietly mentioned her worry to Julian, he gave a half shrug.

"Too late to change things now. Between the two of us, we'll make sure it's okay."

Hearing him pair them as a team warmed her. She held the feeling to her as she followed Julian through the beautiful royal residence. She was awestruck by the museum quality antiques and art. She longed for time to linger and admire, to explore.

Thinking of Sammy, she stayed close to Julian. The staff they passed, nodded respectfully and showered sympathetic looks on Sammy, but no one mentioned his parents or the accident.

"K'tina, down please." He wiggled to be put down.

"Not yet, sweetie. First we need to see *grand-père*."

"My lord—" a portly man in a formal black suit met them in the grand hall "—his majesty and the queen mother are in the formal parlor."

He bowed and led the way to a door off a long hallway. He announced, "His Highnesses, Prince Julian and Prince Samson. And nanny, Ms. Vicente."

Carl stopped at the door, which made Katrina hesitate, but Grimes, the butler, gave her an encouraging nod, so she followed Julian's broad back through the opulent room. A mix of stunning antiques and modern comfort, the cream and burgundy room was both elegant and welcoming.

Lowell Ettenburl, King of Kardana, sat in a cream and gold high-backed chair. An imposing man with a full head of thick gray hair, his grief showed in the slump of broad shoulders and shadowed brown eyes.

"Julian." A sheen grew in his eyes, and he stood to embrace his remaining son.

The two men clung to each other and Katrina heard a few mumbled words. Her throat tightened as tears threatened. Finding the sight too profound to watch, she looked away, to give them privacy and to gather her composure.

She met the sad blue eyes of a grand dame. Dressed in a suit a shade darker than her eyes, she sat in a companion chair to the King. Short and a little plump, only her regal demeanor and rigid posture kept her from being swallowed by the thronelike seat. White hair wound around her head in an elaborate yet refined bun. Her lined face was made up to perfection. But the best cosmetics in the world could not hide the bone-deep sorrow as she watched her son and grandson.

"GiGi!" Sammy exclaimed. This time she had no hope of containing him as he practically jumped from her arms. He ran the short distance to his great-grandmother, climbed into her lap and wrapped his tiny arms around her neck.

The starch went out of the woman as she melted with love. She hugged Sammy so tight he protested and squirmed free of the embrace. But he sat in her lap and chatted away.

Katrina felt awkward standing there amidst the family in such a private moment of grief. The feeling magnified when Julian and the King moved a few feet away and began a hushed conversation.

"I rided on a train with K'tina," Sammy informed his great-grandmother. "I played ball with Unca Julie." Then, with total indignation, "Mama and Papa wen bye-bye and not come back!"

And while the room wheeled from that, he smiled with simple guile. "GiGi bring me present?"

Giselle blinked back tears as she hugged the boy to her again. "*Ja*, I always have a present for *Meingeliebterjunge*. It is in my room." Her beloved boy wiggled away and hopped to the floor. He grabbed her wrinkled hand and tugged. The queen mother patted the seat beside her, groping for a dainty handkerchief.

"Sammy, let GiGi rest now." Katrina took a quick step forward.

Sammy stared up at his great-grandmother before turning big eyes to Katrina. "Why GiGi sad?"

"She has missed you," she explained, keeping it simple. "Would you like me to take him?" she asked quietly.

"*Nein*, he is fine. I am comforted having him near." The older woman waved to a cream sofa. "Miss Vicente, please have a seat. You must forgive me…I am distracted."

"I understand." Katrina settled on the edge of her seat.

"*Oma*, forgive me." Julian bent and kissed his grandmother's cheek and then turned to include the King. "The fault is mine. *Vater*, *Oma*, this is Katrina Vicente from Pasadonia. She has been a great help with Samson's care."

Katrina immediately popped to her feet and curtsied to the King.

"Miss Vicente." He patted her hand then gestured for her to resume her seat as he reclaimed his. "Welcome. We thank you for your efforts on Samson's behalf."

"I am pleased to be of assistance. He is a delightful child."

"I spoke with Bernadette yesterday." Giselle dabbed at a lingering tear. "She described a situation that was less than delightful."

"Yes, well, Sammy was upset." He was the last one she blamed for any of this.

"Quite a shame, the fuss Tessa made." Giselle crossed her hands in her lap and tilted her chin up. "Such a disappointment."

Katrina said nothing to that. It wasn't her place.

"It matters not. We are home now." Julian took a place at the mantel. "And there is much to do."

Sammy sat quietly as he'd been taught, his little head moving with the conversation. His solemn expression worried her. He was taking everything in, but how much did he comprehend?

"Your Majesties, you have my deepest condolences." She purposely used a word Sammy wouldn't understand. "Princess Bernadette has released me to help for as long as you need me."

"Our Pasadonian friends have been very gracious. As have you, my dear," King Lowell said. "We have difficult days ahead of us and as you appear to have a calming effect on young Samson, we would appreciate your assistance while he adjusts to the news and we find a replacement for Tessa."

"Of course," Katrina agreed.

"Tessa go bye-bye," Sammy piped in, his brow furrowed. "Mama and Papa go bye-bye."

A look passed between the three royals.

"Ms. Vicente—" Julian offered her a hand up "—we need to take care of some family business with Samson. Grimes will give you a tour of the nursery and show you to your room."

"I understand." Everything inside Katrina rebelled. They were going to tell Sammy about his parents. And she'd been dismissed. She'd hoped to have more time to prepare him, though how do you really prepare for such news?

At the least she would have liked to be here for him.

Wasn't this why she'd come? To help him through the trauma? But no matter how close she'd gotten to Sammy, to Julian, these past few days, she wasn't family. Placing one foot in front of the other, she forced herself across the room.

"I wanna go with K'tina." It was a plaintive call.

She longed to answer the plea, to wrap him in her arms and buffer him from the coming confusion and pain.

The doors closed behind her.

CHAPTER SEVEN

FURY PROPELLED KATRINA through the palace halls.
The in-house physician had sedated Sammy.
Again. After being told the news his parents
wouldn't be coming back, ever, he went into a
screaming fit. The physician had been called and
the boy sedated. She hadn't liked it then, but had
understood to a small degree. Watching the boy's
distress was not easy, knowing he was hurting
saddened family and caregivers alike.

But there was no excuse, none, for continuing
to dope the child. Not for two days.

Grief needed to be dealt with. Smothering it
only delayed the process; it didn't relieve it. A
point she intended to make to Julian who, according to the doctor, had authorized the prescribed
regimen. She would already have voiced her opinion, but she hadn't seen him since the evening
meal the day they arrived. And there'd been no
opportunity for a private moment at that time.

She reached his office and addressed the pale,
dark-haired woman with dark-rimmed glasses

seated behind the desk. A nameplate listed her name as Marta. "I wish to see His Highness, Prince Julian."

"Nein." The woman didn't bother to look up from her computer. "His schedule is full."

Katrina gritted her teeth, knowing patience and courtesy would get her further than acrimony. "Carl—" The dark head shook again. "Then I wish to make an appointment with the Prince."

This earned her an exasperated examination ending in a scowl. *"Nein,"* Marta repeated dismissing her. "There is much demand on his time."

"I am here on a matter concerning Prince Samson," Katrina informed the woman as she gave her name. "It is of great importance."

Marta heaved a put-upon sigh. "Everything is of great importance," she muttered, and Katrina came to the conclusion this woman was used to working with Julian in his capacity as head of the treasury. A position, apparently, that required less decorum than Prince Regent. But she picked up the phone and called through to the inner sanctum.

After a brief exchange, she hung up and announced, "His Highness will come to the nursery to see you."

"When?"

Marta scowled. "When he can."

Katrina supposed that would have to do. She

thanked the woman and returned to the nursery. She paced as she watched over a very still Sammy. She'd already addressed her concern to the Queen Mother, but the older woman had faith in the elderly doctor. She made it clear she felt the sedation was easier on Sammy than the distress.

His listlessness scared Katrina.

"Sammy, time to wake up." She sat on the bed and gently ran her fingers through his hair. Hourly she tried to wake him. But he didn't stir. Hadn't stirred for the past three hours. She shook his shoulder and called his name louder. Nothing. Fear for him made her determined not to leave his side.

Just let the doctor try to give him another dose. The whole palace would hear her protests.

Her only hope was to persuade Julian of the danger of continuing to sedate the toddler.

An hour later she sat tapping her nails in the elegant nursery sitting room furnished in pale greens and yellows. No bright colors or playful pictures here. No toy boxes or riding horses. It was a beautiful room, but a sad nursery. With the door open onto the bedroom it allowed her to keep an eye on Sammy in supreme comfort.

Finally Julian strolled in followed by Neil. "Ms. Vicente, what is so urgent that it demands my presence?"

She surged to her feet. "Ju—Your Highness, thank you for coming. I am concerned for Sammy."

"Samson," he corrected as he moved deeper into the room. "We are in Kardana now. You must call him Samson."

She bit back a groan. Not exactly the sympathetic attitude she'd hoped for. "He is not yet three," she protested.

"He is a Prince." It was a bald statement of fact. One that did not invite argument.

If that's how he felt, he had the wrong girl for the job. All her frustration and fear exploded in a tirade. "He is a young boy who just lost his parents. He needs love and attention, understanding and patience, structure and routine."

Each word brought her one step closer to him until she invaded his space. She vaguely registered him signaling Neil, and the other man leaving the room. Mostly she focused on having her say.

"Now is not the time to lecture him on the burdens of the crown. Now is when he needs to be held and told he is loved."

"You called me here to tell Samson I love him?" His tone held the cutting edge of ice. "Do you have any idea what I'm dealing with right now? Funeral arrangements, press releases, the realignment of my duties, taking on the military, updating myself on world issues, the pending Europol vote. I'm a tad busy to be stopping by the nursery every five minutes to pamper a grieving child."

"So it is okay to drug him?" she tossed at him. "Just put him to sleep and your conscience is free for you to go about your duties?" Disappointed, she retreated a step. "After the time you spent together on the train, I expected better of you."

"Drugged?" He demanded. "What are you talking about?"

"I am talking about the doctor sedating Sammy. I am talking about the future king of Kardana being kept insensible to the point he cannot be awakened. Tell me, Prince Regent, how do you suppose the citizens of Kardana would react to such a picture?"

"You forget your place, Ms. Vicente." He walked past her to glance in at Sammy asleep in his bed. "You forget I saw the distress Samson went through before. Yes, I authorized the palace doctor to give him a mild sedative to ease him through the trauma. I was assured he would suffer no ill effects."

She crossed her arms over her chest, hugging herself as she paced over the floral antique carpet. Her ire calmed somewhat at his assurance. She had to remember she was speaking to a royal Prince.

"I am sorry, but see for yourself." She waved

him into the bedroom. "It is four in the afternoon and he's been asleep for hours. I could barely rouse him to eat lunch. He was lethargic and then he went right back to sleep. It is not healthy. Some sedatives are addictive. I am sure this is not something you want for Sammy, ah, Samson. The doctor—"

Julian's raised hand stopped her. The imperious gesture raised her hackles, but he was doing as she suggested and moving into the next room to check on his nephew. She bit her lip and followed.

"Hey, Samson." Julian sat on the bed and ran his hand over the boy's head. "Wake up."

As with her, there was no response. He tried repeatedly to awaken Sammy, but got little more than a drowsy protest. When Julian glanced at her, she saw real concern in his honey-brown eyes. "This is not good.

"Neil," he called as he lifted the child into his arms. The security officer appeared in the doorway. "Bring Dr. Vogel to me. And have Grimes bring me a change of clothes."

Neil bowed his head and disappeared. Katrina saw the elbow of another agent as he took over point on guarding Julian. She was surprised to see such close security inside the palace and wondered if there was something he was dealing with that he hadn't mentioned in his list of issues. But seeing him carry Sammy into the bathroom distracted her from the random thought.

"Here, hold him." Julian handed the limp child to her.

"What are you doing?" She cradled Sammy to her as Julian removed his jacket and went to work on the buttons of his white silk shirt.

"We need to wake him up." He reached into the shower and turned on the water before stripping off his shirt and tossing it over the sink. His wallet went on the counter. The muscles in his broad back and arms flexed as he kicked off his shoes and removed his socks. He might be a numbers man, but he definitely kept in shape.

Catching on to Julian's plan, Katrina began to disrobe Sammy. The pants and underwear came off with a tug, a sign he'd lost weight over the past few days. The shirt was a tougher matter as it needed to go over his head and his deadweight made it difficult to maneuver.

"I've set it at cool not cold. I don't want to freeze the lad. If that doesn't work, I'll adjust it." Julian finished setting the temperature and turned to help. He yanked the shirt off, and gathering Sammy into his arms, he stepped into the tub under the full blast of the water. He was soaked in seconds.

Sammy startled when the first rush of spray hit him. And still it took him a few minutes to come completely awake and begin to struggle in his uncle's arms. Katrina used the time to gather towels. Julian hadn't closed the curtain, so she dropped one on the floor to absorb the splashing. The remaining three she kept on hand for the bathers.

"Let him get mad," she advised Julian. "The adrenaline will help fight the effects of the sedative."

He nodded, indicating he'd heard, but kept his attention focused on containing the slippery child.

Enthralled, Katrina watched. And what a sight. Saturated with water the heavy weight of Julian's trousers drooped down his hips to reveal the top of black knit briefs. Rivulets of water rolled over broad shoulders and down muscles bunching and flexing in his bid to keep the flailing Sammy from hurting himself. Or Julian. The boy had already landed a couple of good hits.

She supposed she should leave. Julian had the situation well in hand. Literally. But she was helpless to drag herself away. A wet, half-naked Prince Julian tempted her beyond good sense.

Besides the tub was slick; he could slip. Best she remain to catch him if he slipped. The visual of getting her hands on all that slick skin made her mouth water. She swallowed hard and began an internal lecture on the impropriety of lusting after her host and employer. Add in the royal factor, and it broke so many rules she lost count.

"Get a grip," she muttered.

"I have him." Julian shot her a glance over his shoulder. "But I now have a healthy respect for the term *greased pig*. Chasing them is a favorite event at our Harvest Festival each May. Do you suppose it's been long enough?"

"Yes." She leaned in and got misted with spray as she turned off the water.

Then she enveloped Sammy in a big white towel and took him from Julian. The boy shivered in her arms. She rubbed briskly over his little body and turned for the bedroom. She spotted the other towels and picked up one to offer Julian, but when she looked back, he was unzipping his pants.

He lifted one dark eyebrow.

Heat flooded her cheeks. She dropped the towel back on the counter and made a quick escape.

In the bedroom, she tugged a new shirt and pants from the wardrobe and dressed the irate child.

"Unca Julie stupid." Sammy announced.

"Uncle Julian was helping you." She corrected the boy. Her hands shook with relief at seeing him alert and talking. "You were asleep and would not wake up. Uncle Julian took you into the shower so the water would revive you."

He considered that while she put his right shoe on. "What *revive* mean?"

"It means wake up." A deep voice answered from the bathroom door. Julian stood there attired in a towel tucked low on his hips. "How you doing, lad?"

Sammy eyed his uncle. "You waked me up in the shower."

"Yes."

"Why was I sleeping a lot?"

"The doctor gave you some medicine," Katrina explained when Julian seemed at a loss for an answer. "But Uncle Julian is not going to let him give you the medicine anymore."

"It was bad medicine?"

"No, but medicine is different for everyone because everyone is different. You are little and Uncle Julian and I are bigger, so we can take something that may not work as well for you."

"Cause I little?"

"Yes." Good enough for the child's explanation anyway.

"Is that my present from GiGi?" He scrambled to his knees on the bed and pointed. A large gift bag with a smiling puppy on the front sat on a table inside the door to the sitting room.

"Yes," Julian confirmed. "You can open it if you like."

The boy was across the room in a shot, pulling a good-sized dump truck from a cloud of tissue. "A tuck!" He dropped to the floor and began to play.

Tears stung the back of her eyes. Distracted by the rude awakening in the shower and now the gift from his great-grandmother he was happily occupied, but he'd soon remember the loss of his parents.

And she would be there for him, she vowed silently. As heart-wrenching as his pain was to witness, she preferred it to the unresponsiveness of overmedication.

"Hey." Warm fingers wrapped around her hand. "He's okay."

"Yes." Rather than gape at Julian's naked chest, she looked down to where his large hand engulfed her smaller one. She'd missed his touch. The heat coming off him warmed her, and she felt the shaking ease. "I am sorry for the things I said, but seeing him so listless scared me."

"You were right to call me." He dropped her hand to run his fingers through his damp hair. "I should never have let it get to this point."

"You cannot be everywhere doing everything." She remembered his secretary's muttered comment about everything being of the utmost importance. Obviously there was a high demand for his time. "I know you are busy." She dared a glance through her lashes. "Every time I see you, I am apologizing for something new."

He lifted her chin on a finger until he looked into her eyes. Lowering his head, he kissed her softly, sipping at her lips until she longed to throw her arms around his neck and demand more. Instead he lifted his head and ran a finger along her cheek.

"And I always seem to be kissing you. We should both refrain from these activities." His gaze rested on Sammy. "No apology is necessary. I thank you for calling my attention to his condition. It is telling that he hadn't opened his gift yet."

A knock sounded and the door from the hall opened admitting Neil and a heavyset, older gentleman with an arrogant expression.

She started at the men's entrance and stepped back, creating a discreet distance between her and the Prince. Hopefully they would not consider it a guilty motion.

As he had earlier, the doctor gave Katrina a dismissive glance. "My Lord, how may I be of service? *Ja*. I see the child is awake. You wish me to give him another dose to make him sleep." He tapped the old-fashioned black leather bag he carried.

"No," Julian bit out. "I want you to pack your things. You are dismissed from your position."

"Your Highness, I do not understand," Dr. Vogel blustered. "What have I done to deserve this?"

"You recommended sedating Samson without advising me of the dangerous side effects. Plus, I authorized an original sedation after we told him and he was in a state of distress. I did not know you were continuing to medicate him."

"I thought to save him upset." The doctor defended his actions.

"Grieving is a natural part of the healing process," Katrina said. The man just rubbed her wrong.

He turned on her, causing her to flinch. She had the feeling he'd like to strike her.

"Quiet, upstart," he snarled. "It is not your place to speak now." To Julian he said, "Sire, you must not listen to this foreigner. She is not a trained medical professional, yet she tried to interfere in my treatment of the boy. I have served your family well for many years."

"Count yourself lucky she contacted me. I have been displeased with my father's progress. With this incident I am assured I am making the right decision." In nothing more than a towel, Julian projected total confidence. "Have your resignation delivered to me by five this afternoon. At five oh one, you'll be handed termination papers."

The pompous man's cheeks reddened, his outrage and anger escalated to such a degree Katrina worried for *his* health.

At the door, the doctor delivered a parting shot. "Prince Donal would never have treated me with such disrespect."

"No." Julian didn't miss a beat. "If he'd seen his son an hour ago, Donal would have killed you."

With nothing more to say, the man disappeared. At a nod from Julian, one of the security officers peeled away to follow the doctor.

"My Lord, your clothes." Grimes filled the empty doorway.

Julian looked down at his naked pecs as if surprised to remember he lacked clothes. She wished she could forget. His near nudity distracted her terribly. Wicked fantasies kept playing with her mind. Even as Dr. Vogel bellyached, she'd half wished the loosely knotted towel would drop.

With a last appreciative glance, she gathered up Sammy and moved him to the sitting room to give Julian some privacy.

A few minutes later, impeccably dressed once again, he came through the lounge to say goodbye to Sammy. She received a nod. "Ms. Vicente, I'll see you at supper."

And then he was gone.

Sammy came to show off his new truck. She smiled her approval and made appropriate truck sounds. He grinned and drove off humming, "Zoom, zoom."

Katrina stared at the closed door. Julian's formality felt cold, wrong. Yet necessary. She believed her father and Princess Bernadette would approve her actions regarding Sammy's condition. Not so much the kiss that followed.

Julian was right; they needed to refrain from such activities.

"What is this I hear about you cavorting with the nursemaid from Pasadonia?" King Lowell demanded when Julian answered his father's summons the next morning.

Julian sat down across from his father in his personal sitting room before responding. He shouldn't be surprised. His father had informants all over the palace, not least of which was Grimes.

"*Cavorting* infers a bit of fun. I can assure you there was nothing pleasant about the experience." He explained the circumstances, ending with his dismissal of Dr. Vogel. No need to mention the kiss. That was between him and the entirely too touchable Ms. Vicente.

"Was it necessary to get rid of the doctor?"

Lowell plucked at his robe. He hadn't felt up to assuming his duties for the day. Julian worried about his pallor.

"I felt so, yes. I requested referrals from the Royal Kardanian Hospital and have three interviews set up for this afternoon. I've given the times to your assistant. I'd like you to sit in."

Lowell frowned but waved his hand in an accenting manner. "Back to the matter of this girl. Julian, you are usually an exemplary model of decorum. Now is not the time to become lax in your duties. The world has their eyes on us. How we act now will be how we are perceived in the future. There can be no rumors surrounding our house."

"I am aware of that." Julian really did not need the lecture. He was mindful of the inappropriateness of his intimacies with Katrina. He fought off resentment as he resolved again to keep their encounters professional. "There is nothing between me and the nursemaid."

He frowned. It felt wrong to dismiss her as a mere employee. "However, I would like to invite her to sit with the family during the funeral."

"I hardly find that appropriate," his father protested with a scowl. "It would only add credence to the speculation already brewing."

"I disagree. Grandmother set the precedent of treating Kat—Ms. Vicente as a guest by inviting her to join us for meals. This would merely be an extension of that. It promises to be a long, hard day. Samson will do better having her there."

"She is a nobody. She cannot sit with the royal family."

Julian hesitated, knowing Katrina disliked using her association with Prince Jean Claude. He also knew she would not put her comfort before Samson's.

"She is not quite—" not at all "—a nobody. It may help you to know Katrina Vicente is a relative of Prince Jean Claude Carrère, and his goddaughter."

Lowell's head cocked at that news. "Really?" he asked in a tone of great interest. "She told you this?"

"Reluctantly. It is not something she plays on. Princess Bernadette confirmed it in a separate conversation. Apparently Jean Claude is quite fond of her."

"Very well, then. She may sit with the family. But I expect total decorum from you."

"Yes, sir." Julian bowed as he prepared to take his leave. He was happy to see a little color in his father's cheeks.

"Send in my valet. I may as well get dressed if I am to attend those interviews."

"Of course." Unsure of what put the fire under his father, Julian made his departure. Whatever it was, he was pleased by the effects.

CHAPTER EIGHT

LITTLE HAPPENED TO test Katrina's new resolve over the next week. Well, if you didn't count re-occurring fantasies of Julian haunting her shower.

She threw all her energies into caring for Sammy. His mood fluctuated wildly from hour to hour, tearful and missing his parents one moment, to quiet and preoccupied the next, with a few incidents of happy and playful.

She rarely saw Julian. Yes, he made an effort to visit Sammy every day. But the visits were spontaneous and never lasted long. And, of course, he gave his attention to Sammy. Which pleased her. Truly. She had no business wishing for more.

Anticipation pulsed through her as she dropped her gym bag on the bench of the women's shower room. She'd loved having access to the palace gym during her stay, and truly looked forward to her daily workout while Sammy napped. The time worked out well. At midmorning she generally had the gym to herself, which gave her full use of the equipment and the mat.

Today she heard someone pounding away in the main room as she changed into her gym gear. From the sound of it they were putting themselves through a punishing routine.

A few minutes later she pushed open the door and stepped into the main gym to find Julian—correction His Highness Prince Julian—in shirtsleeves and business slacks bloodying his knuckles on the punching bag.

"Oh my God." She glanced around as she rushed to the shelves against the wall and grabbed some gauze and tape but there was no sign of Neil or any of the security officers. Obviously Prince Julian had slipped his leash. A sure sign he'd prefer to be alone. A sentiment she could respect, except he was hurting himself.

She meant to tape his knuckles and then leave him to fight his demons.

"Your Highness." She approached him from the front and slightly to the side so he could see her.

He didn't look up, gave no sign he'd heard her.

She stepped closer, spoke louder. He rounded on her and she threw up a block.

He blinked her into focus. And all that anger centered on her. "Go away."

"I will," she assured him, keeping her tone brisk, following the example he'd set since their arrival in Kardana. With the exception of that one kiss. She held up the tape. "After I bind those hands up."

He turned back to the bag, started punching again. "Just leave."

"Your hands already look like hamburger."

"That was not a request, Ms. Vicente." It was a harsh dismissal.

"Of course, Your Highness." She nodded and moved away. Halfway across the mat she stopped. He'd given her an order, but she couldn't—just couldn't—leave him like this, both bruised and hurting.

She knew the cathartic value of a hard work-out. She'd spent a lot of time in the gym when she lost her mother. At sixteen it was the only thing that kept her sane. But she managed to do it without damaging herself. Julian didn't realize what he was doing to himself. If he continued on, he might break a bone or two.

She swung around, planted her hands on her hips. "I cannot let you do this," she said hoping to get through his haze of fury. "Julian, please stop."

He didn't let up. "This has nothing to do with you. I told you to leave."

"You are angry. I understand. You have a perfect right to be upset."

He turned on her. "You don't understand squat!" His eyes were feral, his jaw clenched. "I didn't ask for any of this. I don't want to run the country."

"Okay."

"No, not okay." He raged. "I want my life back. The numbers. The quiet. The shadows."

"Yes." She well understood the appeal of the shadows. This was good. He was talking. Well, venting. Anger was a natural part of the grieving process. But he'd denied it until now. He'd been so controlled since he heard the news of Donal's death, so focused on doing his duty. The pressure had been building, a volcano ready to burst. No doubt his hands burned like lava.

"I don't know how to be a father." He paced away and back. "Sammy deserves better."

"There is no one better."

"Don't patronize me. My brother is dead."

"Feeling sorry for yourself will not bring him back."

Fury burned in his narrow-eyed glare. He dismissed her to return to the punching bag. "I told you to go."

"No." She saw he had no intention of stopping. She lifted her chin. "You want me to leave, make me."

He laughed, an ugly sound unlike anything she'd heard from him before. "Get out before you get hurt."

"I have a black belt in karate." She stepped

back, bowed, and then assumed a fighter's stance. Let him use his arms and legs for a while and give his knuckles a rest. "You will not hurt me."

His dark brows lowered. "I'm not going to fight you."

"Afraid a girl will put you on the mat? You should be." She challenged him with a palms-up wave. "Fight me."

He advanced on her. "I'll remove you myself."

He tried, but she blocked his every move, forcing him to fight her or back off. And he was too riled to back off. She suddenly found herself in full defense mode. He had skills, a mix of martial arts, and he was good. He made her work, but she was better.

She knew she could take him down. She just preferred he come to his senses rather than put him on his back. But she might have no choice. He kept coming. And he was strong. She'd lose her advantage if she let him tire her.

Time to go on the offense. Verbally and physically.

She put him on the defense, made him work. And when he was sweating, she talked to him, "It is not your fault. It is no one's fault."

"Sammy could have died. That would have been my fault."

Her heart broke at the pain in his voice. She should have known the medicating of Sammy would weigh on Julian, but he'd handled the incident so competently and Sammy was doing so well, she'd put it behind her. For Julian it had been one more thing already crowded onto his broad shoulders. No wonder the volcano finally blew.

Enough of this. She hooked his ankle with a quick kick and sent him sprawling on the mat. He caught her arm and took her with him. She landed on his solid chest.

"Ah, sorry." She tried to roll off him, but he held her in place. She stilled and looked down upon him. Anguish pinched his features, replacing the anger driving him.

"You saved him, Julian. Focus on that. Because I can promise you, it is not the last scary moment you will have. Children have a way of putting themselves in peril's way."

"*I* put him in peril."

Okay, this was just wrong. Julian had every right to his pain, even to his anger. Being beaten down by despair was another thing altogether. Bad for Julian. Worse for Kardana. Sympathy would only drag him further down the path of self-pity.

"*Oui.* You also put him in the shower. Get over it. The end result is what counts."

He rolled her off him. "Thanks for the sympathy."

"Sammy gets my sympathy." Thankful to be

free, she used the momentum to rotate onto her feet. "He has lost his parents."

"And I lost my brother." Julian climbed to his feet, turned his back to her. "I'll be glad when the funeral is over and we can get past this."

"Mourning Donal is not what bloodied your knuckles. Nothing so noble. This little tantrum is over the loss of your freedom. Your life has changed through no fault of your own, and you just want it to be done so you can get over it and move on." She flinched internally, being intentionally brusque didn't come easily to her. "What you do not realize is grief is not something you get over, it is something you get through."

Good gracious, next she'd be kicking defenseless little kittens. But sometimes you needed to be curt to be kind. She stomped to the door.

"You want to be alone, fine. Tape your own hands." She let the door swing closed behind her.

Just after three, Katrina strolled into the formal parlor holding Sammy's hand. In his other arm he clutched his new dump truck.

When the time came for her to leave Kardana—which may be sooner rather than later after the scene with Julian in the gym this morning—Katrina was adamant that she would leave Sammy with a firm foundation in his new family environment. She didn't know how it had been when his parents were there, but except for Julian's visits, Sammy had very little interaction with his immediate family.

Perhaps it was too painful for his grandfather and great-grandmother to see him in these first few days of mourning, and she respected that they were grieving. But Sammy needed them. And she honestly believed they needed Sammy.

Distraction and purpose were great alleviators of pain.

Under the circumstances, she decided to take Sammy to them. So she discreetly checked around and found out where the royal members of the household spent their time.

She learned King Lowell's regimen included a walk through the gardens most mornings, but today was not one of those times. But GiGi took tea in the formal parlor every day at three. So here they were.

"GiGi," Sammy cried out upon spying his great-grandmother. He ran forward, but stopped before he reached her and gave a very nice bow. "Thank you for my new truck."

"You are welcome, Samson." Giselle forced a smile, her deep pink lipstick stark against the pallor of her skin. She placed both hands in her lap; one held a lace-edged handkerchief. "What lovely manners you have today."

"We pracus," he advised her.

"Practiced." Katrina corrected. "He wanted to thank you for his gift. I hope you do not mind that we stopped by for a moment. Come along, Sammy."

"But I wanna biscuit," he protested, eyeing the goodies on the tea tray.

"We will request a snack when we get back to your rooms. We are disturbing *Oma*."

"Nonsense." The older woman waved her to a seat. "You will join me." She rang for an extra cup and some juice for Sammy before offering the boy a lemon biscuit. "Young man, let me see that truck."

He set the heavy toy in her lap.

"Oh my." She cringed slightly.

"Careful, Sammy," Katrina admonished him softly. "You have to be gentle with ladies."

"He's fine." Giselle ran a hand over his head. Color had come into her cheeks, and affection chased some of the sadness from her expression. "It is a fine truck."

"Look't this." Sammy demonstrated how the front scoop lifted toward the back. "And it's fast." He showed her that, too, while happily munching a biscuit.

A maid appeared with a second tea tray and the Queen Mother poured Katrina a cup of tea. Together they sipped while Sammy played.

"He appears to be doing well," Giselle observed after a few minutes. "I am happy for that."

"The distraction helps." Katrina settled her cup back in the saucer. "He is very fond of you."

"And the new truck." The wry comment was issued with a regal inclination of Giselle's gray head.

"Yes." Katrina laughed softly. "It is his favorite toy and has proved useful these past few days."

"I did not get it for him, you know. Someone else produced it."

"It does not matter. Regardless of who picked it out, it is your love that generated the gift. And he has taken great pleasure in it."

"It's kind of you to say so." She sent Katrina a sharp glance as she sipped from her fragile china cup. "I was concerned over the matter with Dr. Vogel. Quite distressed over his dismissal."

"I am sorry." Uh-oh. The visit was going so well, Katrina hated to see the benefit slide away because of her earlier actions. "Was he a friend?"

"Heavens no," Giselle denied with regal disdain. "The man is a bore. But he was familiar. And I believed he had our best interests in mind. But seeing Samson doing so well, I must wonder."

"The new pediatrician visited Sammy this morning. He seemed to like her. She saw no lingering effects from the sedation."

"Excellent. Please keep me advised."

"Of course." She set her cup on the table. "We should be going. I brought a book to read to Sammy in the garden. Thank you for allowing us to share your tea."

"You do not fool me, child." Giselle sent Katrina a shrewd glance as she gestured for the book. "I know when I am being manipulated. However, I recognize the good it does Samson. You may join me for tea tomorrow."

Katrina smiled and handed her the book.

Her walk through the gardens with the King proved equally as successful. When she happened across him, while pushing Sammy in his stroller, she saw grief weighed heavily on him, just as he leaned heavily on his cane. But seeing Sammy lifted his mood.

She asked if they might join him and before long she had him pushing the stroller and sharing memories of Donal and Julian playing knights and robbers about the lush grounds.

The stroller made him steadier on his feet, and they walked well past the time he usually allotted for his daily exercise. He told Sammy stories of his father while sharing some of the history of the palace. There was no mistaking the pride in his heritage.

Katrina finished the jaunt with promises Sammy would join him for his walk the next day.

* * *

Julian proved the hardest to pin down. Okay, she dragged her feet a little. But he did spend most of his time behind closed doors in his office. And he missed more meals than he made. Avoiding her? She finally resorted to joining him for breakfast at six so Sammy could start his day with his uncle.

She found him seated reading a newspaper on an east-facing terrace overlooking the expansive gardens. Dawn bloomed on the horizon and a chill lingered in the air.

A maid stood just inside the door. Katrina stopped. "Excuse me, Master Samson and I will be joining His Highness for breakfast."

"I will advise Grimes." She bobbed a curtsey.

Katrina smiled her thanks, swallowed hard and strolled out to the terrace. She saw the appeal of his chosen spot. It was a beautiful setting at a beautiful time. The deep navy of night gave way to a magenta edged with a rosy glow. Soon the sun would add a bright gold as the sky lightened. The garden reached clear to the terrace. Bougainvillea laced up the columns surrounding them, and newly bloomed rosebushes bordered the brick porch.

"Good morning." She greeted Julian with forced cheer. They had such a complex relationship. From moment to moment she never knew if he was going to kiss her or freeze her out. Today she just hoped for cordial.

He lowered one end of his paper and eyed her over the bend.

"Good morring, Unca Julie," Sammy echoed.

She ramped up her smile and childishly crossed her fingers as she ignored protocol to pull a chair out, seating first Sammy and then herself.

"Please, join me," he offered ruefully. But he did fold his newspaper and set it aside. "Good morning Samson. Ms. Vicente."

"My lord. I am being presumptuous, I know, and I did promise Bernadette I would be on my best behavior." She bit her lip a little over that confession. "But you are so busy and have made such a good effort to spend time with Sammy, I thought we should make some effort to come to you, too." She winced at the yellow bruising on his hands. "How are you?"

"Better than I have a right to be. The bandages came off yesterday. The doctor advises me I'm lucky I didn't break a few bones." He flexed his fingers. "That's because of you. I'm in your debt again."

"Not at all. We all need to vent occasionally." Not wanting to dwell on the incident in case he changed his mind, she changed the topic. "I see we have interrupted your reading."

"No. This—" he tapped the paper "—has become more habit than necessity these days. I now have advisors that present me with the news."

"You do not sound too pleased with the service."

"I like gathering my own information."

"Ah. And so you will." She glanced significantly at the paper. "Perhaps you will lose this need once you gain trust in your advisors. I imagine it will take time for everyone to work comfortably together."

"An excellent observation. You're very intuitive."

"No." A blush heated her cheeks under his focused attention. "Just a good listener."

"Yes," he mused. "I have noticed."

"What is giving you fits?" she asked, because obviously something was. "No need to give names or details. Generalities are sufficient."

He simply shook his head, his eyes never leaving her face. "You are a temptation, Ms. Vicente."

She bowed her head to avoid the intensity in his gaze. "I only mean to help."

"I can't deny I need help." Weariness flowed through his words. "Or someone to talk things through with. I wish my father were stronger."

"And perhaps he wishes he was needed more."

"Indeed?" His retort was sharp. "You know my father so well?"

"No, but we had a visit in the garden yesterday. I got the impression he sometimes feels useless."

"Quite the good listener," he observed. "That's ridiculous. He's the King."

"I know. But he is still human. And when we have been ill, we sometimes doubt our abilities. Once we let the reins slip away, it can be difficult to grasp them again."

"You're saying he wants to rule again but doesn't know how to regain his authority?" The notion clearly astounded him.

"Possibly. I hardly know for certain. I am just going on instinct. At the very least he might appreciate the distraction of a conversation."

"I hungry," Sammy announced.

"I am, too." Julian switched his gaze to the boy, and Katrina breathed again. "I'm having pancakes."

"Yeah. I wan' pancakes, too!" Sammy bounced in his seat. "K'tina wan pancakes?"

"Yes, pancakes and maybe some eggs and sausage."

"I wan' eggs and sausage," he demanded.

She laughed. "You want it all."

"I hungry." He nodded.

The maid appeared followed by a footman, both carrying trays they placed in the middle of the table. "May I make you a plate?"

"Thank you, Amy, we will serve ourselves," Julian responded.

"Allow me." Katrina began to lift lids and soon had full plates in front of everyone. Sammy glowed as he chomped on a pancake. He also had eggs and meat, along with some fresh berries. Julian had a much larger serving of the same. She stuck to eggs, sausage and a few berries.

Silence fell with the arrival of the food. Once a few bites were consumed, the quiet gave way to giggles as Julian teased Samson by trying to steal some of his berries. Katrina sat back and watched them have fun. Something she felt they both needed. These moments with his family really helped Sammy with his loss.

And from what he'd revealed, Julian would also benefit from a few minutes of levity. His phone rang, and she experienced a letdown, because truthfully, she enjoyed this time with the two of them. So much for applauding her own efforts.

But Julian surprised her by rejecting the call and responding with a text. For the next ten minutes he devoted himself to Sammy as they finished the meal. He talked to him like an equal, and Sammy responded well to him even when the topic turned serious.

"Samson, your Mama and Papa's funeral is tomorrow."

Sammy nodded solemnly. "K'tina told me. We are goin' say bye-bye to Mama and Papa."

"That's right." Julian wiped his hands and set the cloth napkin on the table. His gaze touched her before going back to the boy. "It will be a very long day. We want to say a proper good-bye, and the citizens of Kardana need to be able to say bye-bye, too."

"K'tina says lots of peoples loveded them." Sammy's bottom lip began to tremble. "But I loveded them most."

"Yes, we loved them best," Julian confirmed, reaching for the napkin he just discarded and wiping Sammy's cheeks. "You will have to be a big boy and sit still for a very long time."

"I be good," Sammy promised. "K'tina says I make Mama and Papa happy when I am good. She says they will smile at me from h'ven."

"She's right. Katrina is very smart." Julian threw her a thankful glance. "Come give me a hug."

Sammy hopped up and threw himself into his uncle's arm. He wrapped his little arms about Julian's neck and clung. Man and child comforting each other. She blinked back the sting of tears.

"Your Highness." A nursemaid named Inga stood at the end of the table. In her mid-twenties, the petite blonde showed sense and compassion the few times Katrina took Sammy to the nursery.

At her appearance, Julian kissed his nephew on the head and patted his back. "Sammy, Uncle Julian needs to talk to Katrina for a few minutes. Inga is here to take you back to your room, okay."

He looked ready to protest, but Inga stepped back and pointed to his tricycle. "I brought your bike, but you must be careful and stay close to me."

His eyes lit up. "Okay."

"Thank you, Inga." Julian nodded his dismissal.

Heart racing, Katrina watched Sammy ride away. What was this about? Was Inga her replacement? With the funeral tomorrow, was Julian thinking her services were no longer needed? She should be happy at the prospect of going home. Yet the thought made her stomach hurt.

"Katrina." Julian drew her attention away from the departing child.

"You are very good with him," she told him. "He still gets sad, but he is going to be fine."

"Yes. In large part due to you. *K'tina says,*" he mimicked. But he covered her hand with his. "I was surly earlier and I apologize. As you've guessed, I'm on edge. There are so many issues demanding my attention. I keep asking myself, what would Donal do? But the answer doesn't always feel right, and I end up arguing with myself."

"Julian, you must not do that to yourself." Unthinking, she turned her hand to thread her fingers with his. "Donal is gone. It is sad, but a fact nonetheless. Yes, he was well respected, but I urge you to follow your own way. You will not truly feel comfortable in the position until you do."

"You are probably right, but it is not as easily done as said. My advisors were his advisors, and they expect me to act as he would have. The Europol vote comes up soon and I'm being urged to approve the change as it has been presented. I agree with the primary purpose, but I have reservations about the execution of those changes."

"Then you must speak up," she urged him. "The advisors will adjust once you exert yourself. You are a highly intelligent man, a logical thinker. If you have reservations, others probably do, as well. And remember you have to live with your decision. If you do not speak up and the problems you foresee occur, how will you feel?"

He rubbed his eyebrow. "Not good."

"You wish to honor Donal, which is admirable, but how long will you act as his ambassador? Soon enough you will not know his opinion on issues and you will be forced to address the question or vote from your own perspective. You should just start now. Plus, who is to say Donal wouldn't have agreed with your position if you had discussed it with him? I believe the best way to impress your advisors is to be yourself."

"So wise. Am I supposed to tell them *K'tina says?*" he teased her.

She blushed. Blast her unruly tongue. But how did she hold back when he seemed so alone, so torn as he struggled to do right by his country and his brother. Since she'd already offered her unsolicited opinion, she added, "You are supposed to be true to yourself, to act on your own convictions. And talk to your father. You do not have to do this alone."

"Perhaps I'll do that. Thanks for the advice, but that is not why I asked to speak to you. The funeral is tomorrow. I want you to sit with the family."

Shock stole her voice, panic kicking her pulse into high gear. Never had she expected this possibility. Her palms grew clammy. To sit with the family would bring her to the attention of the press. Speculation would be rife and they wouldn't stop until they knew every detail of her life.

"No." She pushed her plate away. "It is a time for family. It would be inappropriate."

"I've already made the arrangements," he advised her as if she had no choice in the matter.

"Your father will not approve."

"I spoke with my father. He gave his approval."

"But no," she protested, "this is not right. I am not family."

"Katrina, it's okay. No need to get upset." He leaned in, cupped her hand in both of his.

Oh, she was in such trouble. His touch comforted and distressed her at the same time. She wasn't prepared for this moment. Had hoped never to have to tell him of her shame.

"I would rather not." She tried to dissuade him. "My presence will just provoke speculation when the focus should be on Donal and Helene. The whole country is mourning. They do not wish to see a stranger sitting with the royal family."

"It doesn't matter that you are not family. You are Jean Claude's goddaughter, a valued guest. People will understand. Sammy loves you. You, more than anyone, will be a comfort to him tomorrow."

Unfair. She'd do almost anything for the child, but appearing at the funeral with the young Prince would only bring more heartache down on the Ettenburl family, and they'd already suffered so much.

"It is best if I stay in the background," she insisted.

"He needs you." Julian was relentless in his persistence. He lifted her bowed head on one finger until she looked him in the eyes. "I need you."

"Oh Julian—" his image blurred as tears welled in her eyes "—I cannot."

'My dove, do not cry." His thumb swiped away an escaped tear. "Is this about the pictures?"

She froze, literarily went ice-cold. "You know?"

She couldn't look at him, couldn't think. How was it possible he knew about the pictures? Only a handful of people in the world knew. He was not one of them.

"Jean Claude told me before we left Pasadonia."

"Oh my God." She felt raw, exposed. Betrayed.

"He thought I should know of your concerns. It was an honorable move on his part."

"Honor?" She laughed harshly. The ugliness of the pictures flashed before her mind's eye. No wonder he felt free to kiss her. He thought she was easy.

"There is no honor in this matter. Everyone should have just let me stay home." She jumped to her feet. Home was exactly where she needed to go. "I am sorry you were made a part of my—" she swallowed hard "—unfortunate incident." She pushed her chair in, held tight to the finials. "I believe it is time for me to return to Pasadonia."

Pasadonia, but maybe not the palace. How could Jean Claude tell this man of her shame?

Had Bernadette known? Had her father? Her thumb went to her mother's ring, caressed the metal. She'd never felt so alone.

She stepped back, dipped into a curtsey. "By your leave, Your Highness." And then she fled. She didn't run, but moved with great purpose through the drawing room, down the halls, up the stairs to her room next to Sammy's suite. Happy to reach her refuge, she shoved the door closed.

And turned to find Julian looming large before her.

CHAPTER NINE

KATRINA BLINKED AT Julian. "How?"

"This is a sixteenth-century castle. There are many secret passageways throughout."

"So it is okay to invade my privacy?" She walked around him. "Please go away."

"No." He crowded her, forcing her farther into the room. "I'm sorry. I never meant to cause you pain."

"How could it not hurt?" She backed away from him, needing distance, needing to be alone to bind her wounds. "It was the most devastating time of my life. A stupid, shameful time."

"Katrina." He took a step forward. She took two back. He stopped, his expression anxious. "What happened?"

"You know." She wrapped her arms around herself to contain the pain, to hold back the tremors. Unable to look at him, she chose the ceiling instead. Such exquisite crown molding. "He told you. Just go. I am sorry for your loss, but I do not want you kissing me anymore. Despite what you think, I am not a loose woman. I will not be used in that way again."

"I don't think that." He sounded appalled. "How could I believe such a thing of you?" Now he sounded closer.

Damn him. He stood in front of her, too close, too solid, too concerned.

"You are the kindest, most giving woman I know. I think of you as smart, and intuitive, and gutsy. You're also sexy as hell, which is why I like kissing you." He cupped her cheek, rested his forehead on hers. "Jean Claude told me there was an incident in your past that resulted in some compromising photos being taken. He assured me all evidence of the documents has been purged, but you still fear they may reappear and cause an embarrassment. Now you tell me the rest."

"Is that not enough?" She tried to pull away, but he held her fast. With a sigh she gave up fighting. His heat, his strength were too much temptation. "It is best if I leave before the embarrassment can be visited on the House of Kardana."

"You're not going anywhere." His mouth moved across the skin of her cheek. At her ear, he whispered, "Tell me."

"I was young, stupid, naive. My junior year of university I met a man. He was so hot, so sophisticated. Totally out of my league. Yet he seemed to have eyes only for me. I should have known better, yet he flattered me, wooed me, fooled me. I thought I was in love, but he was a paparazzo intent on using me from the beginning."

"Bastard," he grated.

"Oh yeah. As soon as I started seeing him, he began hinting about visiting the palace. But I had a full load of courses, and maybe I sensed something was off deep down because I never took him. Thank goodness."

Julian drew her to the bed, sat beside her at the foot. "Where do the photos come in?"

She shook her head, and unthinkingly worked her mother's ring. "He drugged me—at a party— then took me back to my apartment, st-stripped me, and took some really ugly pictures. Some—" she drew in a steadying breath "—some of them included him doing things to me."

"Rape?" He choked out the question.

She closed her eyes, wished she could shut out the memories as easily. "The doctor said no."

He said nothing for several beats of her heart. She clenched her hands together in her lap waiting for his condemnation. He'd understand now why she should leave.

But he didn't push her away; he pulled her into his arms. "Tell me he is dead."

Bad, she was a bad, bad person, because his comment actually made her want to smile.

"When I woke up, the pictures were spread all around me. I was so sick, from the drugs, from the pictures. All I could think of was to call my dad. It was mortifying."

"And he advised Jean Claude."

"I begged him not to. But, of course, he had to. The Prince was very kind. I couldn't look him in the eye for months. But telling him was the smart thing to do. The extortionist didn't expect me to confess my shame so quickly, so they were able to capture him when he made his first demands."

"But he lives."

"Yes." She did smile this time. "In prison. For the rest of his life. Extorting a member of the royal family is considered treason in Pasadonia."

"Then he should be dead."

"So bloodthirsty," she chided him, burying her face against his neck, because deep down she felt vindicated by his reaction. "I admit at first I wanted him dead. He violated me. Not just my body, which was bad enough, but my life, my pride, my relationships, my future. He took it all from me."

"Not everything," Julian denied. "You fought back. You're a beautiful, courageous woman."

If only she believed him. "I am glad he lives. He destroyed my life. And I put him behind bars for the rest of his. My freedom for his—it is a fair trade."

"Katrina—" he lifted her face to stare into her eyes "—you don't need to fear him anymore. Jean Claude got rid of the pictures and all evidence of them. Do not give this psycho any more power over you. I want you with the royal family tomorrow."

"No." She shook her head, her shoulders, trying to get away from him. "This is the digital age. Nothing completely disappears anymore."

"Treason is a death sentence. If the man lives, he bargained the pictures for his life. You are safe from him. No one will ever see those photos."

"I am not worried about me." She stopped struggling to face him. "Do you not understand? I was the fool. I let that happen to me. If the pictures went public, I would be mortified. This is what I deserve. But it would not be me alone who suffers. The press would exploit my relationship with Jean Claude. Embarrassment to him, the Princess, my father, to you and your family is what I seek to avoid."

Oh lord, she hoped never to see such a look of defeat on her father's face ever again.

Julian kissed her.

He framed her face in his hands and took her mouth with his. His tongue breached the line of her lips and sank deep to tangle with hers. On a half sob she answered his demand, sinking into his arms. He felt and tasted familiar, safe.

But it was an illusion.

She pulled her mouth free. "Stop."

Safety was always an illusion.

"This is wrong." She struggled halfheartedly, but he rolled with her, pinning her back on the bed and pinioning both of her hands in one of his. His mouth went to the curve of her neck.

"What's wrong is your thinking." The breath from his words heated her skin. "You need a distraction to allow you to think clearly once again. You were a victim." He pulled the neckline of her yellow sweater back and licked her collarbone. "You deserve none of what happened to you."

"Julian, we cannot." She tried to reason with him when all she really wanted was for him to continue kissing her. "You have appointments."

"Today they wait for me."

She arched into his touch when his hand found the skin of her stomach and roamed up to cup a lace-covered breast. He meant to steal her thoughts and he succeeded. She couldn't think while his talented fingers worked her flesh. Could no longer remember why she wanted him to stop.

"Julian," she cried out.

"Shh, my dove." He levered up and over, releasing her in the process. He wiped tears from her face. "I would never hurt you." He kissed the corner of her right eye. "I'll stop if you truly want me to."

She looped her arms around his neck. "Do not stop! You make me forget when I am in your arms. You make me feel again."

"What of the boyfriend you thought me when you woke me with a kiss?"

She chewed her bottom lip, which earned her a soothing lick of his tongue. Had she once thought him cold?

"An aide to one of Jean Claude's ministers took an interest in me last year. He was attractive and nice. I thought I might...that enough time had passed. But I never made it past a few kisses."

He pulled back, watched her expression. "Tell me, Katrina, have I made you uncomfortable at any time?"

"No." Touched, she traced his jaw with her fingers. A little shy, she confessed, "There is no one but you when you hold me."

He liked that. "Then let us replace all the bad memories with good ones." His mouth settled on hers and his fingers went beneath the hem of her sweater to the button of her skirt.

"Wait." Her hands closed on his over the material. "Not everything. I—"

"Shh. No need to explain." He slowly worked at ridding her of her clothes, caressing and kissing her through the sensual striptease until she was down to her silky cream camisole. He made faster work of shedding his own clothes, and soon gathered her in his arms.

He made love to her with exquisite tenderness, worshipping her body from temple to toes. The softness of his touch teased, tormented, tantalized until she withered with want. She kissed his jaw, his neck, the ball of his shoulder, everywhere she could reach. She loved the feel of him, the taste of him, the freedom to come alive in his arms.

Sensation built with the brush of skin on skin, of muscles flexing, and hips rolling. Julian whispered his intentions and followed through like the true strategist he was. She thrilled to his every move, his exquisite care, his wicked demands.

"Julian," she cried out when he joined with her. And then rolled and put her on top, urging her to take her pleasure. She blinked, slowly grinned and wiggled to get her bearings.

"Have mercy," he groaned and cupped her bottom to help set her rhythm. And she reached new heights of sensation.

Taking him at his word, she moved, slowly, then faster, until sweat glistened on their skin and every breath was a gasp. "More," she demanded, biting his shoulder. "I want more."

"Then take more." Pulling her close he flipped them putting her under him. He reached new depths, drawing the passion tighter, the emotion higher. His kiss stole her breath, but she didn't care, only sensation mattered, only the race for ecstasy. And then he was there and taking her with him. She clung, body arched, and soared the exploding skies with him.

A short while later, when she'd almost caught her breath, Julian's cell phone rang in his pants pocket across the room.

Next to her he groaned.

She laughed and trailed her fingers down his truly magnificent back. "I thought I was hearing bells ring while we were making love." She lightly bit and then kissed his arm. "Turns out it was your phone. That is probably the tenth time it has rung."

"I'm going to burn the thing. Do me a favor and toss it in the fireplace."

"Right. And two seconds later your security detail would burst through the door. You know they are out there."

He lifted onto an elbow and met her eyes from mere inches away. "I know I don't want to leave you."

"I am fine." She kissed him softly. "Mission accomplished."

"Katrina —"

"Shh." She touched a finger to his lips. "I am fine."

"You'll sit with Sammy, with me, during the funeral?" he pressed.

"Yes. If you really wish me to. I will sit with you."

How could she abandon him, or Sammy, at such a vulnerable time? Much as she wanted to protect her secrets and keep her family from further embarrassment, she couldn't do it at the expense of an innocent child. But she would attend as Sammy's nursemaid. She must keep her association with the two totally professional. It was the only way to protect everyone she cared for.

The family met for breakfast the next morning. They ate in silence as the weight of the day loomed before them. Julian looked around the table.

His father wore a new suit, fitted to his leaner frame. He had a bit of color in his face from his walks the past few days. Julian worried about his stamina, but the proud jut of his chin boded well for his endurance. His Majesty the King of Kardana was a stubborn man of pride.

GiGi sat with a stiff posture and a pale complexion. Grief shadowed her eyes but was otherwise absent from her expression. She had experienced loss many times in her long life.

"Thank you, Ms. Vicente, for agreeing to sit

with Samson. It will be a long day for him." Lowell addressed Katrina.

"It is my honor, Your Majesty." She responded to the King, but her gaze met Julian's briefly before she went back to pushing eggs around her plate. "I am happy to help in any way I can."

"I also appreciate that you are joining us," GiGi added. "I hope I may call upon you if I need assistance."

"Of course." Katrina laid her hand over the older woman's. "Please let me know if you need anything."

Grimes came in then along with Julian's and his father's assistants, who began running through the day's schedule. The funeral procession would go from the palace to the cathedral two miles away where a full funeral mass would be performed for family and invited friends and dignitaries. The procession would then move on to the National Cemetery, and Prince Donal and Princess Helene would be laid to rest. Afterward, a grand reception would be hosted at the palace.

Julian watched Katrina while the day's obligations were outlined. He'd thought much on her revelations the day before. Truthfully, it preyed on his mind. She was so giving, so courageous, she deserved better than to live in fear of an eventuality that would never occur.

Since Donal's passing so much of what Julian

dealt with daily was reactive. He hadn't had a chance to get ahead of anything yet. And it chafed against his nature. She urged him to give it time. And so he would.

How he wished he'd met her at another time. Any other time.

The situation was just so difficult. He needed the comfort she offered, the gift of her passion, a gift beyond measure. Which tore him asunder, because being with her, no matter how brilliant it was, directly defied his father's decree to leave her alone.

He wasn't a rebel, never had been. But today he chose Katrina.

At the church, King Lowell escorted his mother to the front pew. Katrina followed behind, carrying Samson. Julian acted as pallbearer for Donal and then joined the family, sitting between GiGi and Samson.

A hint of apples reached him giving him a much-needed boost. Inhaling deeply he took great solace in having Katrina close by. He glanced over at her. She wore a severe sheath dress in unrelieved black. Her intent, he knew, was to downplay her appearance in the hopes of fading into the background. A corner of his mouth ticked up. Her pale skin and vibrant red hair made that impossible.

He checked on Sammy. He sat quietly with

Katrina's hand resting over his on his leg. The unity between them was a beautiful thing. Julian reached out and placed his hand over hers and Sammy's. Immediately the peace of that unity swelled to include him.

He gave the eulogy, a task more difficult than he'd anticipated. When he regained his seat, Sammy looked at him with solemn eyes and climbed into his arms to rest his head on Julian's shoulder. He welcomed the human contact. The boy had been remarkably well behaved. Julian credited Katrina's presence for that.

Even as he had the thought, she reached over and patted the boy on the back. Sammy sighed and closed his eyes. Julian expected he'd soon fall asleep. To show his thanks for her support he covered her hand with his, lacing their fingers.

She frowned and tried to pull free. He held firm as he turned his attention to the Minister of Defense, who was praising Donal's military career. Helene's father and a friend honored her memory with a few words. And then the service ended and it was time to move to the cemetery.

When he stood, Julian retained hold of Katrina's hand. She immediately shifted so her body hid the contact and discreetly, yet firmly, yanked her hand from his.

"Behave," she whispered.

He turned and passed a sleeping Sammy to her. "We have nothing to hide."

"Julian—I mean, Your Highness, please stop."

"My dove—" he ran his hand over Sammy's back, but he held her gaze captive "—if you call me Your Highness again, I will kiss you in front of everyone here. I don't do pretense well. Today is not the day for me to try."

"I prefer not to draw attention," she reminded him, insistent in her gentle way.

"Just so. I must attend my role as pallbearer." With a squeeze of her elbow he stepped out of the pew and took his place at the head of his brother's casket. *Soon, brother,* he thought, *you will be at rest. Be at peace. I will watch over Samson.*

"My dear Katrina." At the reception Princess Bernadette flowed up and kissed Katrina on the cheek. "You do us proud. And this little one, what a good boy you are." She caressed Sammy's cheek.

"Bernadette." Katrina relaxed for the first time in a very tense day. "I did not know you were coming."

"Of course we came. Donal and Helene were friends." She gracefully sank into a chair against the wall and Katrina took the seat next to her.

A waiter immediately appeared with a tray of wine. Bernadette took a glass but Katrina shook her head. Sammy squirmed around in her lap and rested his head on her chest. She looked down to see his eyes closing.

"But I thought Jean Claude was scheduled to visit Canada."

"For a presentation on health care," Bernadette confirmed. "He delayed the trip to attend the funeral, but he speaks tomorrow. We will have to leave soon. I have only a few minutes before he comes for me. Tell me how you are doing."

Terrible. I have fallen in love with my employer, a royal Prince and future world leader. Katrina longed to share her dilemma with her friend and mentor, but now was not the time. Plus Bernadette would encourage her to pursue her feelings when clearly Katrina could not risk the association.

"The Ettenburls have been very kind and welcoming."

"Julian has sung your praises to Jean Claude." Bernadette eyed Katrina over her wineglass. "He sounds quite smitten."

"Do not tease."

"I am not. Believe me, dear, it is not like Julian to enthuse over much."

Katrina's heart rejoiced at the other woman's words, but she remembered the need for decorum, which meant keeping her relationship with the

Prince strictly professional. "He is simply grateful for my help with Sammy."

Bernadette's alert green gaze swept over the room. "I'm glad we are not staying long. Tragedy is a great equalizer, but too many world leaders in one place is a dangerous temptation."

"Julian has great respect for Jean Claude. I know he will appreciate that you came."

"Hmm. Julian." The sparkling emerald gaze landed on her face. "You are not as indifferent as you would like me to believe."

Indifferent? No. In trouble, oh yeah. She was in way over her head. She couldn't breathe without thinking of the stolen moments in her bed yesterday. Sitting beside him in church and at the cemetery, smelling the yummy scent of man and soap, knowing he was hurting and being unable to touch him had been torture.

She eyed his broad-shouldered frame across the room. Expression somber, he nodded and talked, accepted condolences and moved from person to person, group to group. No one would guess how he hated this. How he yearned for it all to be over.

"You love him," Bernadette said softly.

Katrina cringed. "Am I so easy to read?"

"Yes." Bernadette leaned close. "It is part of your charm. I am so happy for you."

"Nothing can come of it." Katrina shook her head.

"He does not return your affections?"

"Yes." Flustered, she thought first of his passion, but he had not talked of his feelings. "No. I do not know. That is not the point."

"I would argue that is entirely the point. I know you, Katrina. This is about the pictures. You must put your fears aside. The pictures have been destroyed."

She bowed her head. "I know."

"But you do not believe. Do you think Jean Claude would lie to you about such a thing? That I would?"

"No." She lifted contrite eyes to her friend's face. "Of course not. But I fear there is no way of knowing for sure."

"There is faith. There is trusting in those who love you."

"It is for them I fear. I will not be responsible for bringing shame to my family again. I will most assuredly not add another royal family to the list of victims."

"You are not responsible. No one blames you. All your family wants is for you to be happy. You were always so fearless. Grab some of that old energy and go after what you want."

"Bernadette!" Katrina protested.

"You need a man you can trust, and he needs

some warmth in his life." Bernadette bumped
shoulders with Katrina. "It is the perfect match."

"I am here to help. Not for romance."

"My dear—" Bernadette ran her hand over the
sleeping boy's fine hair "—romance chooses its
own time."

Katrina smothered a yawn as she circled the buf-
fet table. Today started early and dragged minute by millisecond. Sammy, bless him, had been
a perfect angel. Of course he didn't understand
much of what went on, only that they were saying goodbye to his parents. Even at such a tender age, he knew his role as Prince demanded a
stoic public image.

She'd taken him to his room after saying goodbye to Bernadette and Jean Claude.

"Where is Sammy?" Julian appeared beside
her.

"There you are," she said. "I was looking for
you. Have you had anything to eat?"

He shook his head. "I haven't had two seconds
to myself. Samson?"

"I just came from putting him to bed. I will
not lie. I was tempted to escape to my room."
She didn't admit he was the reason she'd braved
the crowd. He looked great in his designer suit,
so regal. But he'd lost weight in the past week,
and she saw the fatigue he tried hard to disguise.

"No one would blame you." He curled a lock of her hair around his index finger. "I sent GiGi off to her rooms. Father insists on staying to the end. He's seated at the head of the room with Grimes stationed nearby. He'll advise me if my father begins to flag."

"It sounds like you have taken care of everyone but yourself." She handed him her plate and reached for a new one to fill up for her. And to put her out of his reach.

He'd become very touchy-feely today. His behavior threw her. She relished the intimacy at the same time she must reject it. Every touch, every nearness was noted. By the family, by visiting friends and dignitaries, by the staff. And worst of all, by the few members of the press admitted to the reception.

His attention seriously damaged her efforts to stay in the background.

"I'm not hungry." He belied his claim by eating a piece of ham. "I just want this day to be over."

"You gave a beautiful eulogy, *très* heartfelt."

"It was not difficult. My brother was a great man." He nodded at the British Prime Minister as he directed her with a hand in the small of her back to a table for two just outside the open terrace doors.

"Perhaps we should join another table," she suggested pointedly.

"No." He pulled out a chair for her.

"You are drawing undo attention to us."

"I wish for a few minutes' peace." She heard the weariness in his voice. "A few minutes when I do not have to make conversation, or accept condolences, or dodge ill-disguised political posturing. I can only get that with you. Is that so much to ask?"

Her lower lip suffered her indecision. This was not a good idea. But how could she deny him when she saw his need. When she longed to spend time with him, too.

"I suppose a few minutes could not hurt." She slipped onto the chair he held. "We are out of the way out here." Dusk loomed on the horizon washing the terrace in shadows. The scent of roses drifted on the cool spring air.

"Exactly so." His seat put him deep in a corner, somewhat obscuring his features.

She relaxed a little. "I will stay as long as you eat."

He sighed. "You drive a hard bargain." But he reached for his fork. The first two bites were to appease her, but then he really dug in.

With a small smile she picked up her fork. The quiet of the patio soothed her disquiet. Breakfast had been a long time ago, and she'd been too nervous to eat much. The food was delicious. The ham had a savory smokiness complimented by the fresh fruit and salad she tried, but it was the chocolate trifle that had her humming her approval.

"You must try this." She held out a bite, and he leaned forward to accept the decadent offering.

"Cook's trifle." He declared. "One of my favorites."

She pushed her plate into the middle of the table and they shared the remainder of the dessert.

"Thank you." He laid his hand over hers on the table. "I needed this."

Yes, he had. But a half hour of semi privacy merely teased. Seeing him relax only to tense whenever anyone came close to the terrace door or stepped out onto the terrace further along made her feel guilty for trying to deny him.

"You need more time." She flipped her hand under his. "After this is over, you should escape for a while. Just take off for the night."

"Lord, that's a great idea." His eyes lit up at the prospect of getting away. "I'll make the arrangements. Be ready at eight."

"Oh, but I—"

"You are brilliant." He lifted her hand to his mouth and kissed her palm. "I was wondering how I would make it through the end of the event, but knowing escape is near, I can handle anything."

"Julian." She pulled her hand away determined to disabuse him of his assumption. "I cannot—"

"Julian," a female voice interrupted.

Katrina looked up to find Tessa stepping up to their table. Katrina tucked her hands into her lap, but the lift of a dark eyebrow indicated Tessa had noticed her holding hands with the Prince. She received no other acknowledgment.

"Tessa." Julian politely rose to his feet to greet Samson's former nanny. "Thank you for coming to the services. Helene would be happy to know you were here."

"She was my friend. Of course I came." The woman tugged on the hem of her jacket, drawing attention to the way the designer suit flattered her slim curves. "I was hoping I might have a private moment with you."

Before he could refuse, Katrina stood. "I will check on your father."

"This will only take a moment," he objected.

"Take your time." She gathered their used plates and deposited them on a tray inside the door. A glance around revealed no one seemed to be showing any extra interest in her reappearance. Good. Hopefully that meant her *tête-à-tête* with Julian may have gone unnoticed.

Trying not to obsess about his conversation with Tessa, Katrina wove her way through the dwindling crowd to where Lowell sat at the head

of the room surrounded by well-wishers. She si-
dled up to Grimes.

"How is he doing?"

"He is tiring."

Weren't they all? And now she had to worry
over Julian's plan to escape. Yes, he needed the
break, but it was insane for her to go with him.

"Has he eaten?"

"He says he is not hungry."

"Hmm." Like father like son. "If you make him
up a plate, I will get it to him."

"I will see to it, *Fräulein*." He disappeared
without a sound, a neat trick on the marble floor-
ing. With his exit, she assumed his duty of keeping tabs on the King. The man was as stubborn
as his son.

Thoughts of Julian drew her gaze to the terrace door she just entered in time to watch Tessa
come storming inside. Oops, it appeared the conversation hadn't gone as she hoped. On her heels
came Julian. He headed toward the front of the
room, but was immediately surrounded and de-
tained. It would take him a while to make it to
his father's side.

"*Fräulein*." Grimes returned carrying a tray
of food and drink.

"Give me a minute and then bring the tray over.
Can you stand interference while he eats?"

"Child—" he gave a haughty nod "—I have done so for thirty years."

She realized the longtime steward must also be mourning. She gave his arm a small squeeze. "The family is lucky to have you."

Braving the crowd monopolizing the monarch, she loudly cleared her throat. "Excuse me, Your Highness," she said into the sudden silence. "May I have a word? It is regarding Master Samson."

"Of course." Lowell waved her forward. Happy with the success of her ploy, she moved to his side. She didn't expect him to make introductions. "It was very thoughtful of Jean Claude and Princess Bernadette to come to the services. It is a shame they could not stay long. But they are well represented by this young lady. Katrina Vicente is Jean Claude's goddaughter. She has been a treasure assisting with Samson, who understandably has had a difficult time adjusting."

She flushed as murmurs of approval echoed around her. She forced a conciliatory smile. "If you would give us a few minutes?"

To her relief, people melted back into the throng of visitors leaving her and the King alone.

King Lowell heaved a weary sigh. "My dear, what is this about Samson?"

"He is sleeping, lucky boy." She waved to Grimes. "He conked out after a bit of supper.

Speaking of food, I asked Grimes to get a plate for me. Do you mind if I eat while we talk?"

"Be at ease, my child." He gave his approval as the tray was set on a table between them. Grimes took up sentinel duty a few feet away.

"Oh my—" Katrina deliberately overplayed her part "—so much food, you will have to help me eat some of this."

King Lowell glanced from the food to Grimes's back. "I see. I have been set up. There is no issue regarding Samson."

"Not true." She held the plate up to tempt him. "He will be quite upset if you are too tired to walk in the garden with him tomorrow."

"Perhaps I will have a bite." He reached for a piece of roast beef. "We wouldn't want to disappoint the child."

"No," she agreed.

"You are a bit of a meddler, are you not *fräulein*?"

"I prefer to think of it as caring."

"I imagine you do. You can be quite subtle. But not tonight."

"You do not fool easily." She stole a berry from the plate. "And this is more entertaining. You looked like you could use a perking up."

"Hmm." He hummed his agreement. "It would appear you have us Kardanians wrapped around your finger."

"Hardly, Your Majesty." She gave a delicate snort. "You are a headstrong lot."

He laughed. "Just so. Ah, here comes Julian. I wonder if he has spoken with Tessa. When we spoke, she indicated she'd be interested in returning as Samson's nanny. I believe he would benefit from having someone familiar, don't you?"

CHAPTER TEN

"I ALWAYS THOUGHT of secret passages as being dark and creepy with dust and spiderwebs throughout." Katrina followed Julian's broad back through a narrow hallway. "This is well lit and tidy." She sniffed. "Are these walls cedar?"

"I have no idea. Donal and Helene used this passage to get to the nursery from their rooms. It's faster and more direct than taking the corridors. The servants also use them in matters of urgency."

"Convenient."

He glanced at her over his shoulder. "I recently had them clean the passages from my rooms to the nursery."

"Really?" Why had he felt the need to do so?

"*Ja*. After the episode with Dr. Vogel, I like to check on Sammy on my way to bed at night."

"Just Sammy?"

Julian stopped and turned to her. "Yes, my dove." He ran his thumb over the dent in her chin. "Yesterday was the first time I used the tunnel to access your room. I'm actually quite a decent chap."

"You—" she jabbed him in the chest "—are a blackguard of the highest order, sneaking me out of the palace."

"It was your idea." He kissed her briefly and resumed their trek through the inner labyrinth of the castle.

"I suggested you escape for the night. I was not proposing a lover's tryst."

"But this is so much better."

"You would think so, considering it is your idea. I really should have argued more. It was a tough day for Sammy." She fretted. "He may well have a restless night."

"We checked on him. He was out like a light." He led her down three flights of stairs and opened the door at the bottom. Fresh air wafted inside revealing the door opened to the outdoors.

This was her last chance to change her mind. To act with rationality and wisdom.

Her heart raced as he turned off the light and opened the door wider to look out. He grinned at her. And that's all it took. Stealing his excitement and joy was beyond her. She threw caution to the cool breeze streaming through the door.

Blood pumped wild and fast through her veins as adrenaline spiked. She hadn't felt this alive in years. She wanted this adventure. She wanted him. Craved time alone to explore the passion between them.

Bernadette had challenged Katrina to find her spine and go after what she wanted. She wasn't so selfish she'd risk a public relationship with him. But she could have tonight. A passionate gem to add to her memories before it was time to return home.

"The garage is just across the courtyard. My car is fueled and waiting. Neil knows we're going and has notified a guard at the gate that you are using my auto to drive an unwell guest home."

"You want me to drive?"

"Ja."

"Your car?" she clarified.

"Ja." His eyes narrowed in suspicion. "You can drive stick, yes?"

"Oui." She rubbed her hands together. "Let us go."

The moonlight showed the corner of his mouth notch up. "You do not wish to change your mind? Someone may see us and raise the alarm."

Her body was singing now. "Tease," she mocked him. "You would not let me change my mind."

"No," he agreed. His mouth claimed hers, searing her with a heated kiss. "Tonight you belong to me."

When he released her, she blinked up at him.

She licked her lips, tasting him, drew in a deep breath that filled her with his scent. And gave a wiggle to make sure the strength had returned to her legs.

"What are we waiting for?" she asked and ducked into the night.

Their escape went exactly as he outlined with no mishaps. The guard glanced at his slumped figure and waved them through the gates. The palace had been on high alert today with so many visitors, but most were gone and the security emphasis had been on vehicles arriving, not departing.

After a couple of blocks, Julian straightened in his seat. "You can pull over anytime and I'll drive."

"Oh no. I am having too much fun."

"Katrina."

She sent him a cheeky grin. But refused to pull over. Instead she followed the GPS to the edge of town where she rolled down the windows and punched the gas.

"Whee!" She laughed out loud as she took the expensive vehicle through a tight turn. "I love this auto."

Julian reached across and cupped the back of her head, threading his fingers in her hair. She thrilled to his touch; it was sensual and just a little primitive. Just like the wild ride through the hills. She reached the pinnacle and a view of the bay came into sight. Lights sparkled on the water of the bay, but behind it the North Sea was a vast void of blackness.

"My house is not far. It overlooks a secluded beach on the North Coast."

"We are going to your house?"

"That's the plan." He caressed her neck. "It feels good to be going home."

"I thought you lived at the palace."

"I have rooms there. It's convenient because of the many events I must participate in and when crown business runs long. But I prefer my own place."

"It looks like you will be spending a lot of time at the palace over the coming weeks."

"*Ja*. I will. I'll get used to it."

"Sammy really needs you," she felt compelled to say.

"I have not forgotten. Do not worry, my dove, I will take care of him. We are here." He pointed to a road to the left.

She drove down a long drive to a huge stone fence and an imposing gate. Julian leaned across her to press his thumb against the security pad. He smelled so good she gave in to impulse and took a nip of his jaw, which earned her a retaliatory kiss lethal enough to steal her breath.

"Just follow the lane up to the house," he whispered in her ear before settling back in his seat.

Her hands shook as she put the auto in gear and drove through the gates. After a couple of turns she came to a large two-story white and stone house that blended into the hillside and pulled to a stop in a stone portico. The door opened and a younger version of Grimes stepped out and opened her door.

"Welcome Fräulein Vicente."

"Allow me, Kristof." Julian came around the auto and took her hand. He helped her from the low-slung vehicle. "This is Kristof, my man of all things. He keeps my life in order."

"You give me too much credit, Your Highness."

He ushered her inside giving his manservant a raised brow look that made her think they shared a more informal relationship. "Kris, please bring us a tray of food and some wine. Then I wish not to be disturbed."

"Of course, my lord," Kris responded as he closed the door.

"Oh but—" Katrina dragged her feet. It seemed so rude to rush right off. Heat rose to her cheeks. Especially to the bedroom.

"Come, my dove." Julian drew her forward. "I will give you a tour. You can help me pick out Sammy's room."

"You plan to bring Sammy here?" With the lure

of a tour, she fell into step next to him through the white marble entry. She had assumed he'd leave Sammy in the palace nursery.

"I expect my schedule to be pretty full, but when I can get away, I'll want him with me. This is the living area." He waved her into a pillared room off the entry. A wall of windows brought the sea inside. She walked over to look out and admired the view of the bay. The furnishings were sleek and modern, light on white, esthetically beautiful but hardly child friendly. A fireplace gave the promise of warmth.

"I am happy to hear it. You will both benefit from the contact."

"Tessa asked for her position back," he told her.

A sense of dread welled up. Her stomach knotted as her fears resurfaced. Had he brought her here to tell her she was no longer needed as Sammy's nanny? To let her down easy?

"Your father mentioned she showed interest in returning. He seemed to think Sammy would do well with someone familiar."

"I agree, but it will not be Tessa." He continued the tour as they talked, showing her the dining room, an office, and the gourmet kitchen where Kristof prepared their meal before leading her up an open staircase.

His response had her emotions ricocheting

from one extreme to another in a matter of seconds. "Why not?"

"It was clear her interest was not in caring for Sammy." He gestured to a glass wall overlooking a pool. "The lower floor has a lanai. There's also a gym with a sauna, and Kristof's rooms are there along with additional servants' quarters when they are required."

She bit back a smile. "You mean your security detail."

She should have known he'd see through the other woman's shallow facade.

"They have been used for that purpose, *ja*." He showed her two bedrooms with en suite baths. Both rooms carried on the color scheme from downstairs and were starkly beautiful, but in her opinion the minimalism went too far. His suite was only slightly better in the fact it incorporated some color, gray and blue, and a few personal touches including a vivid painting of a storm at sea. The lavish bath with the large circular walk-in shower was the very definition of luxury.

It was good to be the Prince.

The view from his terrace took her breath away. The bay sparkled to the right, and in the far distance lightning flashed, highlighting clouds and sea as a storm rolled through. At the end of a long incline, waves crashed against a private beach.

"Lovely," she breathed. "You are closer to the coast than I realized."

Hard arms wrapped around her waist and drew her against his aroused body. "On a clear day you can see the British Isles from the roof deck. I'm on an inlet. Much smaller than the bay, but it protects me from the worst of the storms and has the benefit of the beach."

"You have a beautiful home." She leaned back, savoring his warmth. And the knowledge he wanted her.

"Hmm." He kissed her neck. "That sounds like there is a *but* attached."

"I just have a hard time seeing Sammy here. All the white, it is a little cold."

He stiffened and his arms dropped away. He moved to a table next to a two-person lounge and picked up a glass of wine from a tray of food-stuffs Kristof must have left while they were touring the house.

She hugged her arms to herself. What had she said to drive him away?

"Many people consider me to be cold." He sipped the wine, choosing to look at the view rather than her. "*Unemotional* is another word they use."

"Not me," she denied, walking toward him, stopping between him and the view. "You have never been unemotional with me."

"No," he agreed as he caressed her cheek. "You are a meddlesome creature. It is impossible to be unaffected by you."

She wrinkled her nose. "*Mon Dieu,* that does not sound like a compliment. Perhaps you are cold after all."

"You dare much. It is hard to believe you are cowed by a phantom photograph."

It was her turn to move away. "Sometimes our fears are irrational. It does not make them any less real." She stared out to sea, wished the past away. "I do not wish to discuss it."

"I dislike seeing you suffer needlessly. The type of photograph you described is worth a lot of money to the tabloids. If someone had them, they would already have sold them."

"Maybe they do not know who I am, or maybe they are waiting for me to gain in notoriety to drive the price up." Seeking to distract him, she turned and looped her arms around his neck. "We could play the maybe game all night. But I did not come here to talk."

Lifting onto her toes, she pressed her lips to his, tracing the line of his mouth with her tongue until he opened and all but consumed her with his immediate response. He tilted her head and deepened the kiss.

And all thoughts of phantom photos were lost under his sensual assault.

He swept her up, making her head spin, or was that just the intoxicating result of his touch. The Fates knew he drove all rational thought from her head. But tonight she didn't care. Tonight was all about giving in to passion, to the needs of her lover.

Lover.

Her mind stuttered over the word. Especially when she looked into the heated eyes of the Prince. Prince. Boy, when she deviated from the norm, she went totally off planet.

She'd denied herself for so long, unwilling to risk a closeness that would shatter the little confidence she'd reclaimed. But Julian's grief ignited her compassion, allowing him to breach the wall she'd built around her emotions and reach her vulnerable heart.

He set her on the lounge and joined her. Built for two, his bulk made it a tight fit, but she didn't mind. Her body took over, putting a brake on the rising panic. She didn't mind at all. The closer the better.

Yes, she shivered as he traced his hand over the curve of her hip. She'd worry about emotion tomorrow. Tonight was about sensation, about forgetting, about touching the stars.

"Are you cold?" He broke off the kiss to reach for a blanket, pulling it over the both of them.

"Not in the least," she assured him. But she

spied the tray of food behind him and on cue her stomach rumbled. "Goodness." She lifted one shoulder in a sheepish half shrug. "But I am hungry. I only picked at the food at the reception. Can we see what Kristof left for us?"

"But of course." He lifted the heavy tray with one hand and placed it on their laps. It contained roast beef, a choice of cheeses, soft bread cut into slices, some fruit and an assortment of biscuits.

"Oh my. This is a feast." She fed him a grape.

He chewed then selected a roll of thinly sliced roast beef, but after a few minutes she realized she was the only one attacking the tray of food.

"You are not eating."

"You made me eat at the reception. Plus, I am enjoying watching you." He ran the back of his finger along the line of her jaw. "There is only one thing I am hungry for."

Heat bloomed under the intensity of his gaze. His thoughtfulness in the face of his desire touched her. First he protected her from the cold and then he fed her, all while putting his passion on hold.

How could she have thought him cold or unfeeling?

Yes, there was a necessary reserve he kept between himself and the world, but a royal learned early in life that a certain level of distance was needed to retain any sense of self. Add Julian's natural inclination for order and control, his penchant for numbers and strategy, and his impatience with fools and incompetence, and it stood to reason he projected a cooler demeanor. It didn't make him cold.

His explosive passion taught her that.

More, the man cared, for his nephew, for his family, for his country. Perhaps too much. For all his cool reserve, he gave his full attention to whatever was before him. Nobody could fault him on his dedication.

And right now, all that lovely attention was focused on her.

She took the tray and leaned across him to set it on the table, then she stood and held out her hand. "Come. Let us feast."

Taking her hand, he surged to his feet and pulled her to him, claiming her mouth in a kiss that demonstrated just how hot-blooded he was. He took and she gave, her surrender becoming its own demand, for more, for hotter, for him.

A breeze blew a fine mist over the terrace. She gasped, the cold water a shock against her overheated skin.

"The storm is getting closer." She snuggled into Julian's warmth.

"Sometimes I like to sit out here and watch the storm roil across the sky. But not tonight." He solved the problem by sweeping her into his arms and stepping into the room. "Tonight I want to watch your face as the storm we create flashes through your eyes."

"Feast and storms," she teased, looping her arms around his shoulders. "Sounds like a soggy picnic."

He threw back his head and laughed. "So much for romance."

"I do not need romance." She stroked his jaw. "I prefer honesty."

"I, too, detest games."

"I know." She sighed as he set her on her feet beside the bed. "You are the most truthful and honorable man I know. Our time together is so limited." Her fingers went to the buckle of his belt. "Let us not waste time. Make love to me."

He caught her fingers, brought them to his mouth for a brief kiss. "You make me want to linger, to play. No time with you is wasted. I speak the truth when I say I want to watch you ignite in my arms."

He placed her fingers on the top button of his shirt then his went to work on hers. "I agree the time for talk is over, but I will not be rushed." He bent his head to nibble the exposed curve of her neck. "I intend to take my time."

So that was his plan. To take his time. He'd certainly been doing that. Giving her the tour, feeding her, all the while seducing her with soft touches and heated kisses. Slowly, surely, he'd gotten her all worked up. And now he wanted to put the brakes on again? No.

"Then we are at odds, lover." She grasped the edges of his shirt and pulled with all her strength. Buttons flew in every direction as the hard planes of his chest were revealed. "Hmm." She hummed her approval. "You take your time, but I am done waiting." And she dived in for a taste of all that yummy skin.

The muscles under her lips moved as he chuckled. "So contrary. You go at your pace and I'll go at mine." He lifted her head to press a kiss to her lips. "I am sure we will meet up in the middle."

She smiled and nipped his bottom lip. "Get naked. Now."

Surprisingly—considering his slower agenda—he complied. He shrugged out of his ruined shirt, stepped out of his pants and briefs. His socks flew over his shoulder and then she was finally in his bed. And while he slowly undressed her, she trailed her hands over every muscle and bulge, enjoying the feel of him, smooth in some places, hair roughened in others.

Every caress led to a need for more. Everything about him was vital, resilient, addicting. He was all male and he made her feel alive, feminine, empowered.

But with every slow, deliberate touch, she felt a

growing urgency. Even as she clung to him, time seemed so short. If this night was all they had, she couldn't waste a second.

She arched under the soft caress of his hands. With deliberate, unhurried determination he stripped her, carefully leaving her nearly sheer cotton camisole, and then proceeded to trace the curve of her body until he cupped her breasts under the soft fabric. With loving, torturous precision, his mouth tormented the tips through the cloth bringing her exquisite pleasure.

Okay, that slowed her down. Kind of hard to seduce him while she soared on sensation. Then again, maybe this was where they met up. He certainly had her attention. She dug her nails into his back and lifted into his touch, pushing her breast into his hand, wanting more, wanting it harder.

He didn't disappoint. But neither did he hurry.

"Beast," she taunted him. "Stop teasing me."

"Not teasing," he breathed against her ear. "Pleasing."

"Not fast enough."

"Why are you in such a hurry?" He slid his hand down her hip. "We have all the time in the world."

"But we do not," she corrected him. "Time is slipping away. We must hurry or we will lose this opportunity."

"Not a chance."

"But—"

"Shh, my dove. We have all night. And I won't be rushed."

How could he be so calm? "You could get called away at any minute."

"Is that what you're worried about? No need." He trailed his mouth along her collarbone. "No one will disturb me short of World War Three."

She pulled back, her eyes going wide. "*Mon dieu*, we have just jinxed the world."

He laughed, causing his body to rub against hers in interesting ways. "You are such a delight." A hard kiss destroyed her thought processes. "If this is the end of the world, then let us make it worthwhile."

"If this is the end of the world—" she rose up, and biting her lip, pulled her camisole up and off "—then I do not want anything between us."

His eyes glinted in approval, easing her anxiety. He rose up next to her, drawing her to him, offering her the shelter of his arms, replacing fear with wonder.

Sighing, she gave herself into his care.

His talented fingers sent her body arching again. His reverent touch making her feel cherished. And still he would not be rushed. Darn him. Her nerves sizzled. What he did to her defied rational thought. He went to her head like the finest champagne, making her tipsy on sensation.

Still a novice at lovemaking, she mimicked his every caress, doing unto him what he did to her, and soon she experienced the thrill of having him on the brink of losing control. He joined them with more urgency than care, and she loved how driven he was.

She wrapped him in her arms and rode the storm, feasting on his cry of fulfillment. And when the world exploded in a prolonged moment of bliss, World War Three could be raging outside and she wouldn't even know.

CHAPTER ELEVEN

DAWN JUST TOUCHED the horizon when Katrina strolled with Sammy onto the terrace for breakfast a week later. Disappointment bit deep when she saw the empty chair at the head of the table. No Julian.

She hoped he was only running late. This time alone with him—well, except for Sammy—had become a favorite time of day. Superseded only by the passionate nights when he managed to steal through the secret passage to light up her world.

The time was fast approaching for her to leave. Sammy had taken to Inga. And though he still ran to Katrina, the time would soon come when delaying her exit would be more detrimental than beneficial.

A maid arrived with a tray of food. She set it in the middle of the table, nodded and retreated.

Katrina had made two official appearances with Sammy, one with Giselle at a hospital luncheon and one with the royal family as King

Lowell accepted a Cross of Saint James awarded to Donal for his dedicated service to the Kardanian Armed Services. It was the highest honor a soldier could receive.

There hadn't been a dry eye at the ceremony, except for Sammy, who didn't understand. He'd been more upset by her tears than by the accolades heaped on his father. With the resilience of the very young, he was already moving on. Yes, he still missed his parents, but he was more concerned with what was in front of him than in those beyond his reach. It was both sad and encouraging.

And ultimately the best thing for Sammy.

She'd helped him through the transition, but soon she would become a part of what he needed to set aside in order to move forward.

But she wasn't ready to go.

She glanced at the terrace door, hoping to see Julian appear. This past week had been the happiest of her life. Not even having the press latch onto her connection to Jean Claude could dim the joy she took in Julian's arms. And the attention hadn't been that bad. The connection seemed to legitimize her presence at the funeral, and she was praised for her assistance during a difficult time.

Julian was quick to point out she'd worried over nothing.

She sighed. So far.

When everything was so good, she couldn't help worrying something would come along to spoil it.

"Where Unca Julie?" Sammy demanded. He did enjoy his mornings with his uncle.

"Uncle Julian is a busy man." She dished some hot cereal up for the boy and set it in front of him. "Hopefully he will be here soon."

Sammy nodded and dug into his food. Katrina waited for Julian for a few minutes but when he didn't appear, she made herself a plate of eggs and rashers and a bit of toast. After she caught herself glancing at the door for the third time, she reached for the paper set on the table in front of Julian's seat.

She flipped it open and froze. The paper shook until she dropped it onto her plate of half-eaten eggs. It wouldn't matter. She felt sick. She buried shaking hands in her lap as she reread the headline.

PRINCE JULIAN GRIEVES IN THE ARMS OF JEAN CLAUDE'S GOD-DAUGHTER. IS THERE A ROYAL WEDDING ON THE CARDS?

Under the caption was a picture of Katrina locked in Julian's arms. They were kissing, his hair was tousled and her clothes were in disarray. It was more than clear what they'd been doing and what they intended to do. They were on the balcony of Julian's home.

The blood drained from her face leaving her light-headed. She closed her eyes, unable to look at the picture of a special moment turned ugly. This was what she'd feared, becoming a public embarrassment.

It tore her up, knowing her father would see the image. And Jean Claude. And Bernadette. Worse, Julian and King Lowell had probably seen it. Was that why Julian wasn't at the table?

Of course it was. He was probably working on damage control right now.

No need to read the article.

Her stomach churned and spots formed before her eyes. Frightened because Sammy was there, and she was responsible for his care, she scooted back and put her head in her lap. Immediately the dots began to fade.

"K'tina okay?" Sammy climbed off his chair to pet her hair.

Great, a young child was comforting her. That really spoke to her state of mind.

Pulling herself together, she lifted her head and gave him a weak smile. "I am fine. Just a little tummy ache."

"You need medcin?" he asked, worry puckering his little forehead.

Damage control. That's what she needed, action to replace the helplessness that nearly incapacitated her from the moment she saw the newest life-destroying photo.

"No. Medicine will not help me." Her heart wrenched at his obvious concern. He was such a sweet boy, and the whole world now believed she'd used him to get to his uncle. The situation was intolerable. "Come on. Time to return to the nursery."

After dropping Sammy off with Inga, Katrina returned to her room and went straight to the secret passageway. This was the first time she'd used it without Julian, but she found the hidden lever and the door swung silently open.

A little nervous, she stepped inside. She remembered Julian pointing out his office when they were making their escape the night of the funeral. She hoped she could find her way.

The last thing she wanted to do was publicly approach his office. Not now the whole of Kardana knew they were lovers. The need for discretion became imperative as the forbidden embrace posted in full color flashed before her mind's eye.

Quickly making her way along the narrow corridor, she found the stairs and went down two flights then took the first passageway on the left.

She hadn't noticed the two times she was with Julian—the night of their escape and the memorable night he'd insisted on having her in his bed—just how many passages made up the inner workings of the castle. A person could seriously get lost in here.

Actually the prospect didn't overly worry her at the moment. In fact, disappearing held a certain appeal.

Except she wasn't that big a coward.

Keeping a low profile to prevent episodes such as this was one thing, leaving others to clean up her mess was another. She'd allowed her father and Jean Claude to call the shots three years ago because she'd been a traumatized innocent, but now she was an adult. She was responsible for her own actions.

She warned Julian this could happen, yet she'd let him seduce her into believing they were safe tucked away at his home. This just proved there was nowhere the press couldn't reach with their high-tech cameras.

At the third door down, she paused to listen. Nothing. Did that mean he wasn't in there, she had the wrong room or perhaps the rooms were soundproofed? Given the delicate nature and highly confidential conversations that took place in these offices, she suspected the third option.

Mon Dieu, that meant she'd have to open the

door to discover if Julian was inside. Crossing her fingers, she turned the knob and inched the door forward.

"Marriage?" Julian's voice.

She sighed, thank goodness. She pushed the door another inch and froze. From the small view of books and statuary she knew immediately she had the wrong room.

"Really, Father, when did you start believing the headlines?" The derision in Julian's tone stung. She more than anyone knew the headlines were a gross overstatement of the situation, still she had hoped for a little sympathy.

She backed up, intending to leave, but the sleeve of her sweater caught on the doorjamb. She tugged, but it held. Unfortunately, it was her right arm and she couldn't see where it caught.

The conversation in the room continued.

"I am not talking about the headlines. Though you should know the reaction of the people is quite favorable. They are pleased at the notion of a royal romance."

"Romance always catches the imagination of the people," Julian said dismissively. "It will pass as all gossip does."

Was it really that easy for him? Had he not considered her position at all? Katrina struggled with the captive threads. The sweater was already snagged beyond repair, but she dare not pull free and leave evidence of her presence behind.

"You deliberately misunderstand me. I am talking about a serious romance resulting in a real marriage creating a family for you and Samson."

"You're suggesting I get married to provide Sammy with a new mother?"

"My son, we have seen how fragile life can be. I am telling you it is your duty to marry and provide an heir."

"You have two...that's usually considered enough."

"Do not get flippant with me. This is important."

"This is too much." The movement of Julian's voice indicated he'd risen to pace. "I have all I can handle. I have neither the time nor the inclination to look for a wife."

Mon Dieu, that stung, too. For no good reason. She'd never presumed to think their relationship would go beyond this time and place.

Liar, her conscious scolded.

And, oh lord, it was true. She lost her heart to him when he asked her to hold his hand on the train. His vulnerability in that moment touched something deep within her. She'd been his ever since.

"You found the time to be with Katrina," King Lowell pointed out.

"You begrudge me a little distraction?" Frustration frayed Julian's control.

"Only when it comes at the expense of an international incident."

"Jean Claude is a friend. He knows I would never hurt Katrina."

Really? Katrina bit her lip. She wished she were so sure.

"Uh!" Her breath caught as she pricked her finger on the stubborn splinter holding her confined. Then suddenly the material gave and she was free. She checked to be sure no threads were left behind before fleeing to the safety of her rooms, tears staining her cheeks.

"Jean Claude is a friend. He knows I would never hurt Katrina," Julian claimed, making a mental note to return his friend's call as soon as he finished with his father. Which he prayed would be soon. This ridiculous conversation was a waste of his time. He would not be pressured by his father or anyone when it came to choosing a wife.

Hell, there were days since the crash when he felt like he had to schedule time to breathe.

The only peace he had these days were the scant hours he spent in Katrina's arms. In those precious minutes he felt no demand for his attention, no political pressure, no claim of duty, no need to be "on." She accepted him for himself and gave freely of herself.

He lacked any desire to hurt her. And even less to replace her.

When he saw the picture in the paper this morning, he knew it was bad. Knew Katrina would freak and his father would disapprove. The one thing he hadn't anticipated was a demand from the King to marry and provide a family for Sammy.

He should have. His father had been showing his fear of mortality lately. Muttering fatalistic comments and pulling back from his duties. Donal's passing only made it worse.

Julian refused to be the next victim.

"I would rather not test the theory of friend over family." Agitation lent a rosy hue to Lowell's pale features as he rejected Jean Claude's goodwill. Pulling rank agreed with him. He looked more robust than he had in months. "If you are not serious about the girl, send her home."

No!

The muscles in Julian's shoulders tightened. In full revolt he informed his father, "Out of respect for you as my father and my King, I have allowed you to dictate many things in my life. Who and when I marry is not going to be one of them."

"Julian, life is rarely fair. I know much is being asked of you, so I will drop it for now." Unperturbed by Julian's bid for independence, Lowell leaned back in his desk chair. "I have no doubt you will do your duty to the crown. The people and the press will serve as my heralds until you do."

"You forget, Father. I am a champion at ignoring the press." His reputation for being cold had been well earned in that regard. Finally it served a purpose. He observed his self-satisfied parent with narrowed eyes. "Since you are in fighting form this morning, you may take the meeting on educational reform. Speaking of duty, it's time you picked up some of the slack around here."

Leaving his father sputtering his outrage, Julian departed the King's office. He was late for breakfast with Katrina and Sammy. He reached the terrace to find their places cleared. Only his setting remained, sans the standard copy of the paper.

As he stood viewing the table, Grimes arrived with a folded copy of the paper on a tray.

"Sorry, my lord. Ms. Vicente quite destroyed the first copy."

Damn. He wanted to be with her when she saw the picture.

"Did she appear upset?" he demanded.

"Yes, she seemed quite distressed when she left here with Master Samson about twenty minutes ago."

"Thank you." Julian turned for the door.

"My lord," Grimes protested, "your breakfast."

He wasn't hungry. But he'd also learned long days required constant refueling. Julian swung back, grabbed a croissant, tore it in half and stuffed it with eggs and sausage. As he passed Grimes, he instructed, "You may clear the table."

On his way to the nursery he tagged Neil on his mobile phone. "Where is Katrina?"

"She's in the gym."

"Thanks." He adjusted his direction. Of course she went to the gym. She worked out daily. And the Lord knew he understood the need to pound out your troubles.

"My lord—" Neil caught Julian before he disconnected "—security picked her up in the passageway next to the King's office about ten minutes ago."

"Sh–" He bit off the profanity. "I'm going to the gym. See that we are not disturbed. Advise Carl my father will be taking the early meeting."

"The press secretary—"

"Everything waits."

"Yes, Your Highness."

Julian ended the call as he entered the gym and turned into the men's locker room. If he was going to go a few rounds with Katrina, he needed to be dressed for success.

* * *

Katrina landed a roundhouse kick in the center of the punching bag. It required little style but provided a satisfying impact. She followed up with a two-one punch. Yah, yah.

Pulling back, she swiped at her cheek with her arm.

Foolish girl. The gym was no place for tears.

She struck at the bag again. And again. Anger at her self-deception burned in her gut. Had she learned nothing from her past experience? Just because she had feelings for a man didn't mean he returned her regard. Obviously far from it.

At least Julian hadn't betrayed her. Small compensation as she dealt with the fact her feelings for the photographer were a mere pittance compared to what she felt for Julian. True love made a mockery of simple infatuation.

The incident in her past paled next to the heart-wrenching pain she currently fought to contain.

The disdain and frustration in Julian's voice as he dismissed any involvement between them echoed through her mind. He obviously didn't love her, yet she'd believed he held some affection for her.

Never had she felt so alone.

She abandoned the punching bag and sought to regain some sense of self by going through the discipline of her regular karate routine. She took a couple of deep breaths before beginning, flowing from one movement to another with rigid control, focusing mind and body on form and motion.

She'd need all her wits about her when the repercussions of the photo in today's paper began to rain down on her. If any pictures did remain from her past, now would be the time for someone to score big. Her name had been linked to two royal houses and she appeared to be the lover of a Prince. A compromising picture of her would be worth hundreds of thousands of dollars. If not more.

She should have stayed hidden in Pasadonia.

Halfway through the routine she became aware of Julian standing on the periphery of the mat. She ignored him in the hopes he'd go away.

He didn't. He let her get through the routine and then he stepped onto the mat.

"Nice moves," he said. "Excellent timing and balance."

She completed two more punches before replying. "I practice often." Without looking at him, she moved right into some quick kicks.

"You're upset."

She had no answer for the obvious.

She wondered at his conciliatory tone. Was he not upset?

"Katrina, I'm sorry you were alone this morning when you saw the paper."

"It does not matter." She gave him the truth. What difference would it make if he'd been there? None. The picture would be no less devastating with him by her side. And given what she'd heard she wondered how sincere his concern would have been?

He appeared in front of her, deftly catching the fist flying toward his face. "I need you to stop and talk to me."

In a flash, her pain turned to anger. He became her adversary. She retrieved her hand, reset her balance and attacked with a few round kicks that made him retreat. "I sent you sprawling to the athletic mat before, Your Highness. Perhaps you should leave."

"Katrina, we have much to speak of."

"Funny, I cannot think of a thing."

"I can be just as stubborn as you. I'm not leaving until we talk." He gracefully advanced on her. For the first time she noticed he wore gym clothes. He bowed formally and took up a basic karate stance. "I know you expect the photos from your past to make an appearance. That's not going to happen."

"So you have said. I can only pray you are right." She responded to his bow and immediately went on the offensive.

His defense and counterattack were perfect. She instantly recognized anger had affected his skills in their last bout and stepped up her game. She wouldn't make the same mistake. He had reach and strength on his side, but she had finesse and agility on hers.

Plus she was stronger than she looked. She made him sweat. Better, she made him breathless, which made it difficult for him to talk. She struck with an open palm, driving her point to the heart.

The next few minutes were spent in physical exertion as she fought to put him on his ass again.

It may be petty, but being dismissed as a distraction did that to her.

The longer they fought, the fiercer she became. Perspiration dewed her skin, stung her eyes, weakened her. Whereas the sweat caused his T-shirt to cling to taut muscles. The harder he fought, the better he looked. Bastard.

Grunts and yells filled the air along with the smack of skin on skin. Fury propelled her actions, but his reckless grin put her over the edge. She finally put him down, but he took her with him. She landed on his chest with a breath-stealing thud and a nasty sense of déjà vu.

Pushing against the granite planes of his chest, she fought to right herself. The hard circle of his arms kept her pinned in place.

"Let me up," she said, careful to keep all emotion from her voice.

"Not until you listen to me." He tightened his hold. "You expect the worst. But don't you understand? When the infamous photos don't appear, you'll finally be free."

"You sound awfully certain." She knew better. Her only chance at certainty was lack of exposure. And that option was now lost to her.

"It just makes sense," he said, his arrogance showing.

"None of this makes sense. Why would a paparazzo wait to sell a picture of us? The photograph in the paper was from the night of the funeral, more than a week ago. And your balcony overlooks the sea. The angle of that shot would have to come from the water." She dug her elbow into his sternum almost earning her freedom. "It is a near-impossible shot."

"Katrina." He rolled, putting her beneath him.

"No." She wedged her arms between them. She needed something, anything, to hold him at bay, to keep the pain contained. "You did this."

CHAPTER TWELVE

"THIS IS ALL your fault," she whispered. "Seducing me, making me feel safe, giving me hope."

She knew in her heart she was being unfair. That he meant to reassure her. Too late. Her confidence lay shattered at her feet. She pushed against his chest. "Let me up."

"Katrina, listen," he implored.

"No. Let me go." She attempted to roll him off her. His elegant hands framed her, holding her fast, preventing her from getting away. She went still. Wiggling would only embarrass them both.

"I can't stand for you to hide away from the world because of a past mistake," he explained, staring into her eyes, pleading for her to understand. "You're better than that."

"My life is none of your business." She looked away, unwilling to acknowledge his motives.

"It is as long as you are here in my palace."

"A problem easily solved." She pushed again, harder this time. "Let me up. I am going home."

He loomed large above her. "You aren't going

anywhere. You need to stop protecting yourself and live."

"Easy for you to say." She turned her head away. "My life is not a game. People I care about can be hurt." She couldn't think beyond the rage, the hurt, not with the heady scent and feel of him distracting her.

"If they truly care, they will be pleased to see you free of the weight hanging on you."

As if he truly cared. "They show their love by letting me make my own decisions."

"You mean they allow you to hide in the palace. Such a beautiful prison. I'm surprised you accept it. Surely it is too good for the severity of your crime."

"You do not know what you are talking about."

"I know you are a shining star but you hide in the background, afraid to draw attention to yourself lest you disturb the shallow life you've built around your fear."

Her chest tightened as the truth struck home. Her breath caught. She couldn't breathe but her mind reeled. She told herself her sacrifices were for her family, to prevent further pain or embarrassment coming to them, but in reality she'd just been punishing herself for failing them. What a disappointment she was.

"Katrina! Damn it, breathe." He lifted off her,

dragged her into a seated position. "I'm sorry. I didn't mean—"

"Stop. Do not pretend now." He may be right about her, but it changed nothing. She threw up an elbow to block him when he tried to draw her close again. "Do not pretend you care when I am nothing to you. Your time would be better spent looking for a wife."

He fell back on the mat beside her, nodded as if in confirmation. "You were in the passage near my father's office. You heard him instruct me to—"

"Look for a wife," she finished for him. She didn't question how he knew she'd been outside his father's office. At least part of the hidden passages must be under security surveillance. "Good luck with the search."

"I'm sorry if you were disturbed by what you heard. But you must know you have been a comfort to me. I was in no mood to discuss our relationship beyond that."

His reasonable explanation for what she'd heard did little to breach her anger and hurt. "I believe the word you used was *distraction*."

"Both are true." He propped up on an elbow, ran a finger down her cheek. She dodged away from his touch. "I told him, forget it, he didn't get to dictate who I married. I'm thirty-two years old.

I will not be told when and whom I shall marry as if I were a callow youth."

"How crass of him to think of Sammy at this time."

He narrowed brown eyes in ire. "Don't you start. With handling my responsibilities and Donal's, plus preparing for the Europol vote, I have no time to think between one meeting and the next. My visits with Sammy have to be scheduled into my day. And you are my hidden vice. I cannot take anything more being heaped on me."

Hidden vice.

She supposed that described their relationship exactly. And it did not have a good ring to it. Partly her fault, she knew. Her insistence on discretion certainly contributed to the hidden part. But acknowledging it didn't matter. She still felt used. Foolish. Shamed.

She'd let herself be seduced again.

Photographed again.

She couldn't take any more.

"Well, you will have one less vice to worry about. I am returning to Pasadonia."

"No." He pushed to his feet, pulled her up, too. He scrubbed his hands over his face, wiped the sweat on his pants. "I'm saying I couldn't think! While my father was talking I simply reacted, pushing back at him, denying all concept of courtship and marriage. Yet as soon as I left him and turned my thoughts to you, it all clicked into place."

"No." Stomach churning, she backed up.

"Ja." He pursued her hands reaching for her. She childishly put hers behind her back as she continued to retreat. He matched her step for step, catching her by the elbows when she tripped on the edge of the mat.

"Do not," she entreated.

"You are the answer, Katrina. You are gentle and caring, smart, funny and sexy. I can talk to you. Best of all Sammy already loves you."

Her heart broke a little with each word. It was all about the convenience, all for Sammy. "What about you?"

He cocked his head, his brows rising in question. "What about me?"

"Sammy loves me. How do you feel?"

His expression cleared. He hauled her close, kissed her temple, her mouth. "You know I care about you. Haven't I demonstrated how much each night in your bed?"

"You want me." She wormed her arms between them, seeking distance, needing the ability to think. "That is passion. It will fade."

"It hasn't," he stated with emphasis. "My need for you has only grown." A finger on her chin lifted her face to him. She stubbornly refused to look at him. "Katrina, will you marry me?"

Her gaze flew to his, and she saw amusement lurking in his amber eyes. Oh God. How sad was it that for a moment joy flared through her? Pretty pathetic, as proven by his humor at her expense.

Oh, she had no doubt he was serious. Lowell's point, after all, had been to provide Sammy with a mother figure. Who better than she? Hadn't she put her life on hold for the child? She loved the little guy, wanted the best for him. But this was one sacrifice beyond her.

"No." Pretending her heart wasn't breaking, she pulled away from Julian. "I am done being used by you."

"Harsh." He reached for her hand. She tucked it behind her. "You love Sammy. We're good together. We can make this work."

"We really cannot."

"Katrina. I want you for my wife."

"No, you want the comfort you find with me. Well, I am done being a diversion for you. You do not get to manipulate my life, turn around and insult me, and then expect me to fall all over myself when you propose. You think you know me and maybe you do, but you do not love me."

Sliding to the side, she gained her freedom, stepped away from him with hands fisted. "In a world where everything around you seems out of control you have found the one thing you can apply reason and strategy to solving. Well, my life is not a game and it is not the place for you to flex your leadership muscles."

Walking to the bench at the side of the room she grabbed up her towel. When she turned back, he stood in the middle of the mat, his features expressionless.

"Goodbye Julian."

Who did she think she was? Julian snarled to himself. He was a bloody Prince. Women didn't turn him down. Not now, not ever. His temper no cooler for a cold shower, he stepped out and grabbed a monogrammed towel.

She should be honored and thrilled by his proposal. Instead she acted as if he'd betrayed her.

Forgive him if he didn't see the tragedy in the photo making the papers. His father and Katrina were both overreacting.

Never a violent man, he'd experienced a rage unlike anything he'd ever known when she told him of how she'd been drugged and humiliated. He'd wanted to hurt someone. Do something. He'd been helpless to defend her.

So seeing her freed from her self-imposed isolation pleased him enormously.

Fury flared as he remembered the hurt and dejection on her face. With a sweep of his arm he cleared his bathroom counter. Bottles, soap, crystal dishes went flying across the room.

He left the disarray and marched to his closet, chose a new suit, a matching tie.

Damn her for treating his proposal as an insult.

So he hadn't been as smooth as he could have been. And maybe he should have chosen a better time. And place. She didn't have to attack his motives, his character. They were good together, both in bed and out. She loved Sammy. Was it so wrong to think they would make a happy family?

It all went to show he'd been impulsive in proposing. Far from the premeditation she accused him of, he'd reacted to her pain, allowing emotions to sway him, which was totally unlike him. When he looked at the circumstances logically, he reverted to the arguments he'd given his father.

He had a country to run. Marriage was a distraction he couldn't afford. The abrupt end to the love affair only proved a relationship was ill-advised at this time. He was too busy for a proper courtship, let alone marriage.

Besides, they just buried Donal and Helene. Bad enough Julian must fill his brother's boots on a political front. It was just wrong to insert Sammy into a new family unit as if his parents were interchangeable.

She wanted to go? Let her. He had more important things to do than chase after an ungrateful brat.

Julian shrugged into his jacket, straightened

his tie and left his suite. Katrina was right about one thing, it was time to put his considerable talents of reason and strategy to work on his country's problems.

Surprisingly, King Lowell seemed sad to see Katrina go. Good manners demanded she bid her host farewell. Giselle gave her a hug and wished her well, but the King showed her to the conversation area of his office and seated her in a Queen Anne Chesterfield armchair.

"I must thank you for all you've done for my family. You made a difficult time more bearable with your kindness and care."

"I hope you might let me visit with Sammy sometime," she asked humbly. "He has truly stolen my heart."

"Of course. Though, I do not think Sammy is the only one to steal his way into your affections. I have never seen my son so smitten." Lowell leaned back in his chair. "Today is the first time he has ever defied me outright." He smiled and shook a finger at her. "He disagrees with me plenty. But he is a strategist. He steps back, assesses. And always he comes with his arguments of logic and reason. Today he argued from a position of emotion."

Katrina fought to make sense of what the monarch said. Had he just confessed to matchmaking?

Was that his response to the picture in the paper? She supposed announcing a wedding was imminent would defuse the sordidness of the situation. Running would no doubt acerbate things, but it could not be helped.

"You play a dangerous game, Your Majesty."

"Julian has suffered much over the past month, and he has much yet to deal with in the months ahead. He would benefit greatly from having a strong woman by his side. One thing I have learned over my many years of ruling—there is a time for caution and a time to be bold, and you must be willing to live with the consequences of the choice you make."

King Lowell sighed, as if some of those many decisions carried some weight. "I wish Julian to be happy, so I felt the reward was worth the risk, but make no mistake there is a duty he must meet here. Sammy will be well cared for, but there is no replacement for a mother figure."

Katrina struggled against a rising confusion. The King's interference may have precipitated Julian's proposal, but the son's sins were all his own.

She knew the importance of a mother's presence in a child's life as she lost her mother at a vulnerable age. Even now she missed her. What she wouldn't give to talk to her mother for just a few minutes. She loved her father, but sometimes she wondered how different her decisions might have been if she'd had her mother longer.

"You are right. Sammy is lucky to have you and Giselle, but he deserves to have two loving parental figures."

For all Julian's faults, he had Sammy on his radar, and she had no doubts he would do right by his nephew. How like him to schedule Sammy into his day. His devotion could not be questioned, which meant he would eventually bow to duty and choose a wife.

She forced the thought of Julian with another woman out of her mind and rose to her feet. Time to go.

"I have taken up too much of your time. I just wanted to say goodbye and thank you for making me welcome."

"You are always welcome here. I fully expect to see you again soon. In the meantime I have ordered the royal jet be made ready and a helicopter is standing by to take you to the airport."

"But, Your Highness!" she protested in shock. "I cannot—"

He held up an imperious hand. "For your comfort, yes. But more for my son's peace of mind. He will not rest easy until he knows you are safely home."

Her last stop was the nursery. Sammy cried. "You go bye-bye like Mama."

"Shh, little man. Do not cry," she bade him. "I will still be your friend. I promise to come visit you." And she would. Soon. While Julian was away.

"No! Do not go," he implored, clinging to her, tears staining his cheeks. His distress wrenched at her already-broken heart.

"I love you, Sammy," she assured him. "You can always count on me. But the time has come for me to go home to my family."

"I don wan' you to go." He burrowed his head against her. Knowing there was no way to make him understand, she gave him a final hug and kiss and then handed him over to the waiting Inga.

"Take good care of him," she urged the other woman. Swallowing down tears, Katrina made her exit, glad to be going home.

The helicopter served as a white-knuckle distraction on the flight to the airport in Newcastle, England where the Royal House of Kardana kept their royal jet. Katrina barely noticed the well-appointed amenities surrounding her in the luxury jet. She sank into a soft cream leather armchair, pulled lush brocade drapes over her window and closed her eyes, shutting out the world.

If only her thoughts were so easy to shut down.

She kept seeing the cold descend on Julian's features as she threw his proposal back at him. She hadn't seen that expression on his face since he accused her of telling Sammy his parents were missing.

He'd been mistaken about her then, and he was mistaken now if he believed she'd be happy in an emotionless marriage.

Loving Sammy wasn't enough. Loving Julian wasn't enough. She deserved to be loved, too.

Longing for home, she prayed Jean Claude's claim was true and that the mortifying pictures taken of her three years ago were well and truly gone. Because more than anything, she wanted her life back.

"Ms. Vicente." A calm voice spoke next to her.

Katrina opened her eyes to see a lovely woman in her forties smiling at her.

"We're about to take off. Please buckle up." She went over a few safety issues, advised the length of the flight then asked if Katrina needed anything.

She shook her head. The only thing she needed was out of her reach.

"I'll check with you in flight," the woman offered and disappeared.

After buckling her seat belt, Katrina adjusted the crystal lamp next to her and reached for a magazine in the cherrywood console, determined to keep her mind occupied with something, anything besides Julian.

She failed, of course. And her spirits were low as she disembarked in Barcelona, the closest international airport to Pasadonia. She'd been informed another helicopter was waiting to take her on the final leg of her journey.

When she reached the bottom of the jet steps and looked up to see where she went next, she spotted the dignified man with dark red hair tinged with silver at the temples. He stood tall and broad, shoulders squared, hands clasped in front of him.

Emotions welled up, lodging in her throat. She flew across the tarmac into the waiting man's arms, felt them close protectively around her. And for that one moment in time everything was okay again.

"Daddy."

"Dear, you're going to have to call him sometime," Princess Bernadette advised Katrina a week later.

"Must I?" Katrina sighed, her gaze following the antics of Bernadette's twin boys as they pranced about the palace courtyard in the early-morning sun. Not even eight in the morning and Julian had called her twice. "He probably wants to know Sammy's favorite cereal. He will sort it out without me."

"Cereal?" Bernadette's stepdaughter, Amanda, joined them on the stone benches. A year and a half ago Jean Claude, and the whole country, had been surprised to learn he had a full-grown daughter. "I'm leaving if you're talking food." The American rubbed her baby bulge. "My doctor lectured me on my weight yesterday so my breakfast consisted of yogurt this morning."

"Pooh." Bernadette waved off the doctor's advice. "Those guidelines are based on an average woman's weight. You are so slim you need the extra calories for the good of the baby."

"You think so?" Amanda asked hopefully. "I don't want to do anything to hurt my baby."

"I agree with Bernadette." Katrina added her support. She'd avoided Amanda because of her notoriety, but Katrina had grown fond of her in the past week. "You are all baby. We can go for a walk after supper if it makes you feel better."

Amanda beamed. "It does. Thanks."

"Yes, well, sorry to disappoint, but there's no cereal. We're talking about the fact Katrina needs to call Julian. He's called her twice already this morning."

"Through his admin," Katrina clarified. "The man can't even be bothered to dial his own phone." That pretty much told her how he felt about her, which didn't amount to much. His real reason for calling was probably to gloat over the fact no pictures from her past had appeared to haunt her. Thank the good Lord.

Of course the press made a whole thing of her leaving Kardana, speculating on the relationship between her and Prince Julian and whether their affair was over or if she'd be returning soon. At the same time they exploited her connection to Jean Claude.

"That is a little punk—" Amanda wrinkled her nose "—even if he is a busy man."

"He would get more done if—"

He stopped fighting his own nature. Katrina barely kept from uttering the words. She bit her lip and shook her head at herself, angry because her first response to Amanda's comment was in defense of Julian.

"—if he delegated more," she finished lamely, which was also true. He might not deserve her loyalty, but she would not reveal private details she'd learned during intimate conversations.

She flushed a little under Amanda's direct regard. "You're not ready to talk to him yet," she declared. "I remember how I felt when I learned Xavier was only spending time with me because he was under orders to keep me close. I felt used and betrayed. I wanted nothing to do with him."

"Yes." Katrina shuddered with a sigh. For the

first time she felt someone understood what she was going through.

"Maman, Amanda," Devin called, "look at me." He did a somersault and landed on his back.

"Me too. Katrina, watch me." Marco outdid his brother by doing two flips.

Katrina and the others smiled and clapped. The boys grinned and frolicked some more.

"It was obvious the two of you were very much in love," Bernadette said. "Just as it is clear Katrina and Julian have something special between them." She squeezed Katrina's hand. "You so deserve to find happiness. Please talk to Julian."

"I will think about it." An easy promise to make as she thought of little else.

"I'm so happy to hear that," Bernadette said. "I feel responsible, you know, for insisting you go to Kardana."

"Do not." Katrina pleaded. "I am not sorry I went—"

"Your Highness." Bernadette's assistant approached. "If I might have a word?"

The Princess stepped away with the woman, viewed something on the tablet she carried. Bernadette's gaze lifted to meet Katrina's. Bringing the tablet with her she handed Katrina the digital device.

"This is why Julian is calling."

The screen was fixed on a tabloid site boasting a picture of Katrina and Jean Claude holding hands in the palace portico. The headline read:

KATRINA RETURNS TO PASADONIA.
IS SHE EXCHANGING ONE PRINCE
FOR ANOTHER?

CHAPTER THIRTEEN

KATRINA STARED AT the shocking headline. She had accompanied the twins as they saw their father off to a meeting, and Jean Claude had grabbed her hand and drawn her outside to ask how she was settling back into the palace.

"Katrina, I'm so sorry," Bernadette said. Behind her, Amanda ushered the boys inside with the help of the assistant.

"No." Katrina shook her head. "I am sorry. I brought this to your family."

"Don't you dare blame yourself for the shameful behavior of the paparazzi." Bernadette's temper flared. "You have suffered so much, but you can't give them power over you. Anyone who knows you will see it for the rubbish it is. For the rest, most people know these tabloids are more fiction than fact. Trying to fight them would only draw out the sensationalism."

"I know, but I hate that you and Jean Claude are drawn into my drama."

"Dear, if not you, it would be someone else.

Jean Claude is the trifecta for the paparazzi. He's a royal Prince, a world leader, a handsome celebrity. He will always be a prime target. As his goddaughter, that attention is extended to you."

Katrina knew Bernadette spoke the truth. Coming out of the shadows meant dealing with the press.

Her mobile phone beeped indicating a text message. Meeting Bernadette's gaze, Katrina reached for the phone. "Julian again."

The text read: ANSWER YOUR BLOODY MOBILE.

On cue the phone rang in her hand. This time she recognized Julian's number. Bernadette squeezed her shoulder and walked away, giving Katrina privacy. Sliding her finger across the screen, she tried for casual. "Hello."

"Katrina." Relief and ire both infused the word. "I saw the tabloid this morning. Are you okay?"

"Thank you for your concern. I am fine." And she would be.

"Bloody press can't leave us alone. Why didn't you take my call?" he demanded.

"You did not call." She took pride in the steadiness of her voice. "Marta did."

"You knew she called for me."

"I have found I am not inclined to wait for you." Oh, that felt good.

Silence sounded from the other end. "I do not care for this stubborn streak in you."

"Just because I refuse to be your puppet does not make me stubborn," Katrina protested.

"Woman, you are the embodiment of stubborn. And meddlesome, persistent, smart, giving, caring and sexy. I've missed you." A huskiness added weight to his statement.

Oh, she'd missed him, as well. So much. But she couldn't let the pain sway her. "How is Sammy?" she asked instead.

"Doing well. He likes Inga. He still asks after you. He wants to know if you're ready to come home."

She closed her eyes against the want. "I am home."

Julian threw down his phone and stood to pace. He was an intelligent man. So why did he still allow her to distract him? Why couldn't he concentrate?

A knock preceded his father's entrance into his office.

"Son—" Lowell took a seat in the more comfortable conversation area, forcing Julian to go to him "—I've heard of the tabloid article. How is Katrina doing?"

"How should I know?" Julian played it cool.

As he had done since she left, preferring to keep the fact he was slowly falling apart to himself.

"Because you phoned her up as soon as you saw it." Lowell rode the chair as if it were his throne. He nodded to Julian to sit. "I assume you spoke with her. Unless you lacked the intelligence to call her directly and had your secretary do it. In that case, she probably rejected your ass."

Julian ground his back teeth. He'd been in meetings, damn it. Which he would have happily have left to talk to her once she was on the line. He should be in a meeting now, but bollocks it all, he needed a few minutes.

He picked up the extension on the table in front of him and instructed Marta to push his day back thirty minutes. He hung up on her protest that his flight to the Peace Symposium left in two hours. Putting thoughts of the symposium and the Europol vote that preceded it aside, he sat back in his chair and drummed his fingers on the leather armrest.

"She said she was fine."

"Did she sound fine?"

Julian considered his father's question. How had she sounded? He had to think about it. He'd been too busy fighting the need to see her, to hold her, to analyze how she sounded. Now he did. A little shaky at first, but she'd grown in confidence.

"She did actually." Which drove him a little crazy. An unreasonable response. Why should he care if she missed him? "I told her Sammy wants her to come back," he revealed.

"Ah." His father nodded as if unsurprised, and then he lifted a bushy eyebrow. "You mean you want her to come back."

"Not at all," he denied. "We've been over this. My duty is to the country."

"Of course. It's for the best. What does she have to come back to?"

Julian rocked forward in his chair, buried his fingers in his hair. "I offered her a kingdom."

"Son—" the proximity of Lowell's voice indicated his father leaned forward to speak quietly to him "—to Katrina a kingdom is more a detriment than an inducement."

"Sammy," he said desperately.

"*Ja,* she loves the boy," his father agreed. "But Sammy wasn't enough to keep her here, and he won't be what brings her back."

"She loves me, too. I saw it in her eyes." Those incredible, violet eyes that revealed every emotion. He'd seen everything in the deep blue depths, from disapproval, to amusement, to anxiety, to passion, and yes love. Which left him with the question, "If she loves me, why did she leave?"

Lowell rose and patted him on the back. "Perhaps it's what she didn't see in *your* eyes."

* * *

"Katrina, you look lovely," Jean Claude said as he stepped into the lounge of their shared hotel suite. Looking smart and dignified in a tuxedo, he crossed the beige carpet of swirling leaves to kiss her cheek. "Thank you for agreeing to attend the gala with Bernadette and me."

"The Peace Benefit Gala is a worthy cause." She swirled the skirts of her lavender ball gown. "And who does not like a party?"

"You." He squeezed her hand, drawing her to the comfortable couch to sit with him. "In the past you have avoided social occasions, or stuck to the shadows. Tonight you've agreed to step into the limelight with us."

"Bernadette explained your press secretary felt a public appearance with the three of us would help discredit the image projected in the tabloids." She perched on the edge of the couch. If she sat back in this dress, she'd need a crane to get out. "I'm happy to help in any way I can. Especially as it is my—"

"Stop." He shook a finger at her. "It is nobody's fault. The paparazzi do not need a reason. If they have nothing to report or sensationalize, they will make it up. As you saw earlier this week. Now that you are a public figure, you will be targeted more often. You cannot fight them...you can only put out the image you want to project and hope the world sees the truth."

A public figure? Her? It seemed surreal, but she supposed the fact she received her own invitation to the Peace Benefit Gala confirmed her celebrity. The international event was well attended by the rich and famous, from actual royalty to Hollywood royalty. She pleated the tulle on her skirt. "What if the world does not see the truth?"

"Then that is their problem." His hand settled over her restless fingers. "You cannot let the press rule your life."

"I know." She lifted her gaze to meet his. "I have finally learned that lesson. It may just take a while to get used to it."

His gray eyes smiled. "We will help you as much as we can. Tonight all you have to do is smile and look like you're having a good time."

"I can handle smiling," she assured him. Looking happy might be harder to pull off. On the table her mobile phone vibrated. Probably Julian again. After talking to him two days ago, he'd persistently called, and she'd persistently refused to answer.

She required distance to get over him. Speaking with him only made it harder to get her emotions under control. Love for him squeezed her heart. If not for him she would never have had the confidence to step out with Jean Claude and

Bernadette tonight. Julian's faith and belief in her gave her the courage to believe in herself, to command her own power.

Tonight she was proud of herself. Despite her heartache, she must put Julian behind her and move forward.

Bernadette swept into the room in a figure-hugging designer gown in a deep ruby red.

"Darling—" Jean Claude rose gracefully and went to her "—you are stunning." He kissed her lightly on the lips. "I will be the envy of every man at the gala." He kissed his wife's hand and wrapped it around his elbow before extending his other hand out to Katrina. "Shall we go?"

Katrina gave her mobile one last glance, lifted her chin and joined Jean Claude and Bernadette on the pathway to her future.

Turned out looking happy came easily enough with Bernadette running an amusing commentary in Katrina's ear as they arrived in the limousine and began the press gauntlet known as the red carpet.

The television entertainment and media magazine professionals were all very positive and friendly, but it was still quite overwhelming. Katrina planted a smile on her face and stuck close to her friends.

Bernadette kept looking over her shoulder. At

first Katrina thought the other woman was just keeping tabs on her, but she finally realized she was watching for someone or something.

"Is everything okay?" she asked the Princess between interviews.

"Of course." Bernadette smiled brightly.

They were a quarter of the way down the red carpet, speaking with a British fashion personality about the designers of their gowns, when Katrina felt the heat of a masculine body slide in behind her and a man took possession of her hand. She knew instantly who it was. The way the fashion announcer lit up only confirmed her guess.

"And we are joined by Prince Julian of Kardana," the pretty blonde gushed. "How cheeky of you to sneak up on us. You look quite dapper this evening."

"Thank you. I'm happy to join my friends for such a worthy cause."

"Yes, it's brilliant to see so many lovely people here supporting peace."

The chitchat went on for a moment more and then Jean Claude led their party off the dais. As soon as they were clear, he offered Julian his hand. "My friend, it is good to see you."

After greeting the Prince and Princess, Julian lifted Katrina's hand to his mouth and kissed the back of her fingers. "I would choose to be no-where else this night."

"Is this part of the plan?" Katrina demanded, pulling her hand from Julian's. She stared daggers at Bernadette. "It would have been nice to have some warning."

"Julian called at the last moment and asked to join us. It seemed a nice touch to bolster the image we were going for. You would only have fretted if I told you."

Katrina was given no opportunity to respond as event personnel urged them along.

She should have expected something like this. Bernadette was happily married. She wanted everyone to have a loving family like she did. And for some reason she believed Katrina and Julian belonged together. Maybe it was that sense of responsibility she'd spoken of earlier for insisting Katrina accompany Sammy and Julian back to Kardana.

She felt surrounded by him. The reporters and cameras all but disappeared as she absorbed his heat, inhaled his scent, melted at his touch. She couldn't look at him, couldn't give him the satisfaction of knowing he got to her.

At the first opportunity she intended to take a firm hand and inform him he couldn't keep disrupting her life with his repeated calls and impromptu appearances. She'd finally conquered her fear; surely she possessed the strength to stand strong in putting their fling behind her.

Julian bent his head to whisper in her ear. "You may take me to task once we are inside."

She sent him an arch look over her shoulder that didn't quite connect with his eyes. "You can be certain I will."

So she smiled some more, talked endlessly about her gown, and carefully remained non-committal to any questions regarding her relationship with Prince Julian. A task made easy as he fielded all inquiries with a brash smile and misdirection.

Finally they reached the entrance and the receiving line. She greeted the dignitaries with somber courtesy and happily accepted a flute of champagne once she entered the ballroom. The bubbles tickled the back of her throat and sent a pleasant fizzle tingling through her.

Julian's hand at her waist constantly reminded her of his presence. A circumstance she needed to deal with immediately. She wasn't an actress. She had no hope of fooling the entire assembly of celebrities and world leaders into believing they were a couple.

"Time to chat." She grabbed his hand and drew him through the throng to French doors leading to a balcony lit by miniature lights threaded artfully amongst the crawling ivy.

He came willingly, practically pushing her out the door. She turned to him, but he was already yanking her into his arms. No time to protest before his mouth slammed down on hers. He ravished her with tender demand, taking the kiss deep. Equal parts possessive and obsessive, he pulled a response from her that had her arching onto her toes seeking to get closer to him.

Or maybe that was just her wanting more of him, reveling in his embrace, sinking into the feeling of safety, and home, and the rush of her blood through her veins as sensation built on sensation and she longed for more.

He nipped her bottom lip. The tiny sting of pain brought her back to her senses. And still it took a moment to gather the strength to push him away.

Finally she created an inch between them. That's all he'd allow, drat the man. And her breasts still brushed his chest with every inhalation as she fought to regulate her breathing, but the space existed, bringing with it the ability to think. Inch by inch she'd gain more.

Her sanity demanded it.

"Why are you here, Julian?" She met his gaze for the first time since his arrival. He looked happy, more at ease than she'd ever seen him. She gritted her teeth. How like a man.

"I'm here for the Peace Symposium. The Europol vote, remember."

"*Oui*. I meant why are your here at the gala? Balls are not your thing."

"You are here," he said simply. "We are on a date. I took your advice today."

"We are not on a date," she informed him emphatically. "What do you mean? We did not talk today."

"Only because you refused to answer my calls." He ran the backs of his fingers down her cheek. "You are so beautiful. A blind date, then. I'm courting you. I meant the advice you gave me about voting with my conscience on the Europol police initiative. I gave my argument and voted accordingly."

"You cannot court me. I rejected your proposal." The urge to hug him had her inching backward. "I am glad you decided to vote from the heart. It was the right thing to do. I can see the peace it has brought you."

"Any peace you see is because I'm with you. Do you realize we never officially dated?" He eliminated the ground she'd gained. "I must court you to change your mind. Turns out others agreed with me, and the initiative was recalled for further refinement."

"And you are celebrating by harassing me?" She took a full step back and came up against the bracket of his arms. Why did he have to make this so hard? Anguish leaked into her next plea. "You need to let me go."

"Never." She was in his arms again, being softly kissed.

What did he mean? Her heart swelled. With fear? With yearning? She couldn't tell the difference anymore.

"Do not play with me, Julian. Not about this. It is too important."

"Why would you think this?" He caught her chin on the edge of his hand, coaxing her into meeting his gaze. "Have I ever lied to you?"

She failed to recall a single instance.

A symphony added background music to their little drama as the dancing began inside. The lilting notes of Strauss's "The Blue Danube" started the event off with a waltz.

He held her close enough to mimic the dance, but neither of them moved as she scanned his face for a clue to his plan. She saw earnestness and sincerity, but dare she believe he cared?

"Come home," he demanded, all playfulness gone. "You belong in Kardana. With me. With Sammy."

"I love Sammy, but he cannot be why I return to Kardana." Bernadette was right, only Katrina could give her power away. She deserved to be wanted for herself, not for her child care capabilities.

"Then return for me," he directed her. "I know this thing with the press is my fault. I should never have brought you to their attention. I thought I was so smart, but I only hurt you. I'm sorry."

"Do not be. If I brought one thing home with me from Kardana, it is a realization that everyone has been right. I have been playing ostrich, hiding my head in the belief if I couldn't be seen, I couldn't be hurt."

"You're stronger than you think."

Wrong. But she refused to live in fear anymore. She was done living in a prison of her own making. Done hiding.

"You believed before I did." Taking back her power allowed her to see he'd been right. "I should have trusted Jean Claude, had more faith in myself." She did not care to be fodder for the press, but she no longer feared her violation would be splashed across the tabloids for all to see. "You have given me a peace of mind I would never have otherwise. For that I thank you."

"I'm glad. The lord knows there's no peace to be found without you. I need you, Katrina. I can't think clearly without you."

"That is only because you are unused to anyone challenging you," she advised him. "You will get over it."

"I don't believe I will," he muttered. "I need you to challenge me, to help me think. To give me the patience to deal with all the people."

"There is only one reason why I would return to Kardana."

"You have only to tell me," he commanded. "I will make it yours."

But he couldn't. There was no forcing love. It had to be freely given or it was not love at all.

"You want my help with Sammy," she reminded him.

"*Ja*. I do. But I was foolish to see that as a reason for marriage. Father put the idea in my head, and when I saw the picture of a future with you, it felt so right I bumbled my proposal by focusing on the wrong thing. And my pride was hurt when you rejected me."

He led her away from the door and the swell of music closer to the balustrade, where he bent down and kissed the curve of her neck. She shivered but refused to be distracted from his explanation.

"Go on," she whispered.

"I love you, Katrina. I may have a genius IQ, but emotions do not rely on intellect. I missed you like bloody hell. I couldn't concentrate. I couldn't sleep. I couldn't get you out of my head. Turns out you were the one helping me keep it all together. You stole my peace when you walked away."

"Julian."

"It took me a while to realize missing you had nothing to do with my pride and much to do with loving you." He brought her hand to his mouth, kissed her palm. The heat of his breath warmed her skin. The warmth reminded her of how caring he was with her and with Sammy, especially when he'd clearly been busy and grieving. And oh how patient and tender he'd been when they'd made love, how he cherished her when she bared herself to him.

"You truly love me?" Hope bubbled through her like the fine champagne she'd sipped earlier. Still, fear made her ask, "You are not just saying so to get me to marry you?"

He grinned at her, a beautiful smile full of affection. "I am saying it because I want you to marry me. But I can wait until I've courted you, until you believe me. I was so overwhelmed with running the kingdom I wasn't paying attention to what was happening with me. I fell in love, but I was afraid to admit my feelings because it was one more thing to deal with. And my brother had just died. The timing was wrong."

"What changed your mind?" Her heart raced as she began to believe.

"Seeing that picture in the tabloids, knowing it would hurt you. It killed me not being able to hold you, to help you through it. You said you were fine, but I knew you were being brave."

"I am fine," she corrected him. "I have decided fear of appearing in the tabloids or the press will no longer dictate how I live my life."

His brown eyes shimmered with tenderness. "I'm happy for you." He adored her with a kiss that went from gentle to heated in a flash. "You will need that attitude as my Princess."

Princess? Oh God. She was in serious trouble, because the notion only half terrified her. She shook her head.

"You are not going to stop pursuing me, are you?"

"No. Loving you, starting a life with you is the most important thing in my life."

"Then *oui*."

His expression turned half hopeful, half uncertain. "Yes, you will let me court you?"

Happiness was too big to be contained. She smiled and framed his face in her hands. "*Oui*, I will marry you."

He closed his eyes and laid his forehead on hers. His arms tightened to the point he squeezed the breath from her. She squeezed him back. It was impossible to be too close. And then he scooped her up and twirled her around, her skirts flying out behind her.

Suddenly he stopped, set her on her feet and

cupped her face. He wiped tears from her cheeks. "You're crying."

"Happy tears." She looped her arms around his neck. "They are happy tears."

* * * * *

THE MAID'S DAUGHTER

JANICE MAYNARD

USA TODAY bestselling author **Janice Maynard** knew she loved books and writing by the time she was eight years old. But it took multiple rejections and many years of trying before she sold her first three novels. After teaching kindergarten and second year for a number of years, Janice turned in her lesson plans and began writing full-time. Since then she has sold over thirty-five books and novellas. Janice lives in east Tennessee with her husband, Charles. They love hiking, traveling and spending time with family.

Hearing from readers is one of the best perks of the job!

You can connect with Janice at:
twitter.com/JaniceMaynard
www.facebook.com/janicemaynardreaderpage
www.wattpad.com/user/janicemaynard
and www.instagram.com/janicemaynard.

One

Wet yellow leaves clung to the rain-slick, winding road. Devlyn Wolff took the curves with confidence, his vintage Aston Martin hugging the pavement despite the windswept October day. Dusk had fallen. He switched on his headlights, drumming his fingers on the steering wheel in rhythm to the hard-rock oldie blasting from his Bose speakers.

No matter how fast he drove, he couldn't outrun his restlessness. He'd been on Wolff Mountain for a week, and already his father and his Uncle Vic were driving him batty. They had installed him as CEO of Wolff Enterprises two years ago, supposedly with their full trust at his back, but they loved playing Monday-morning quarterback.

It was easier when Devlyn was in Atlanta, ensconced in his fancy-ass office. Then the two Wolff patriarchs could only harass him via email and the phone. But giving up control of the company had been hard for them, and Devlyn did his best to make them feel connected, hence his frequent trips home.

His tires squealed as they spun slightly, seeking a connection with the rural highway. Devlyn knew these back roads intimately. He'd learned to drive here, had wrapped his first car around a tree not two miles up the road. For that reason alone, he eased off the gas.

At that instant, the glare of oncoming headlights blinded him as a car rounded the upcoming curve uncomfortably close to his lane. Devlyn tensed, gripping the wheel and wrestling his vehicle into submission. The other car wasn't so lucky.

Devlyn cursed as the little navy Honda spun past him, its white-faced driver momentarily visible, before the small sedan slid off the road and smashed into a telephone pole. Devlyn eased to a halt on the narrow shoulder and bounded out of the car, his heart punching in his chest as he dialed 911. By the time he hung up and reached the car, the driver was already opening her door. Air bags had deployed in the crumpled vehicle. The woman staggered to her feet, wiping ineffectually at a trickle of blood on her cheek. Even in the waning light of day, he could see a reddish mark on her cheekbone.

He grabbed for her as her knees gave out. "Steady," he said. The ground was the closest surface, unfortunately. She went down gracefully, like butter melting on a hot day. His arm was around her, but the gravel slope beneath their feet was uneven. It was all he could do to keep both of them from sliding down the embankment.

Crouching beside her, he pushed her hair from her face. "You okay?"

Her teeth were chattering. "You nearly killed me."

"Me?" His brows shot up in sync with his temper. "Lady, you crossed the center line."

Her chin lifted slightly. "I'm a very safe driver."

Glancing over his shoulder, he cursed. "Not from where I'm standing."

She shivered hard, and he realized with chagrin that this wasn't the place for such a conversation. "Your car is toast," he said. "The nearest ambulance service is forty-five minutes away at least. It will save time if we meet them in the next valley. I'll take you."

"So says the big bad wolf."

"Excuse me?"

She managed a smile, though her lips were blue. "Devlyn Wolff. What brings you here from Atlanta?"

"Do I know you?" He was acquainted with most of the people in this small section of the Blue Ridge Mountains, but occasionally someone new moved into the area. Then again, something about this woman was familiar.

"Not really," she said. Her nose wrinkled. "I'm getting wet."

He'd been so caught up in worrying about her that he hadn't noticed the rain. They were only half a mile from the driveway to Wolff Mountain, and thus his doctor cousin's clinic, but Jacob was out of town.

Grinding his teeth in frustration, Devlyn glanced at his watch. He had a late dinner meeting with a powerful, important investor in Charlottesville in less than two hours. But he couldn't possibly walk away from a woman who might be seriously injured. Wolff Mountain was isolated for a reason, but at times like this, the remoteness of his childhood home was a curse.

"Let me carry you to my car. You may be hurt more badly than you realize." Even as he said the words out loud, he winced inwardly. *Saint Devlyn to the rescue.* He wasn't a saint—far from it—but he had an unfortunate penchant for rescuing strays, be they animal or human. A tendency that had bitten him in the ass more than once.

She stood up, wavering only slightly. "That's very kind of you. But weren't you headed somewhere?"

Shrugging, he rose to his feet, as well. "I can reschedule."
And potentially lose twenty million dollars. He'd been coaxing
this particular venture capitalist into trusting him for almost
a year. So the moment was likely lost. But money was just
money, and he'd seen enough sports accidents in his college
days to realize that head injuries were not to be taken lightly.

If he could meet up with the paramedics quickly enough,
he might still be able to make his appointment. The woman
clearly knew who he was, so presumably she trusted him
not to be an ax murderer. He scooped her into his arms and
carried her toward his car. Her token protest was feeble. The
tremors that shook her slender body were undoubtedly a delayed reaction to the crash. She might have been killed.

His arms tightened around her, his breath hitching as
for a split second he imagined what could have happened.
Thank God she survived the impact. Her wet hair and clothing smelled of roses, an old-fashioned scent that suited her
somehow.

Once, he stumbled slightly, and her hand gripped a fist-
ful of his shirt, her fingernails digging into his skin. For a
second he flashed on an entirely inappropriate scenario that
involved him and her. Naked. In his bed.

He shook his head. Weird. Too weird.

He deposited her gently into the passenger seat and jogged
back to retrieve her purse. When he slid behind the wheel
and looked at her, she grimaced. "I'm not going to keel over,
I promise. The air bags did their job."

"Maybe so, but you look like hell."

Her jaw dropped. "Well, it just goes to show…"

"What do you mean?" He eased the car out onto the road.

"All the tabloids call you a billionaire playboy, but if that's
your slick line with women, they've got it all wrong."

"Very funny." He peered through the windshield and upped
the defroster. It was completely dark now. He turned off the

music, not sure if his tastes would soothe a woman who had been knocked around in an accident. The car was silent except for the swish of the wipers.

His passenger ignored him, her body nestled into the soft leather seat. Though she seemed relaxed, her arms were wrapped tightly around her waist.

A memory kept nagging at his brain. Something to do with this slight, mousy female. But try as he might, it wouldn't come into focus.

She sighed deeply. "I hate inconveniencing you. You could drop me at my mother's house."

"Is she home?"

"Not at the moment. But she'll be back in the morning. She drove down to Orlando to visit my Aunt Tina." She paused and winced when the car hit a bump. "I'm sure I'm fine."

"Don't be ridiculous. We Wolffs may have a reputation for being reclusive, but we're pretty tame when it comes down to it."

Her muttered retort was lost in the squeal of his brakes when he stopped short to avoid hitting a deer. The animal froze, peering at them through the windshield, before bounding into the woods.

Devlyn covered the remaining distance to the main highway and up over the small gap that led to a more populated area to the east, refusing to admit, even to himself, that he was rattled. "Not long now."

"I'm surprised you drive your own car. I thought the Wolff entourage relied on limos."

"I'm a control freak. I like taking the wheel."

Maybe he was imagining it, but he was picking up on some mixed vibes from his damsel in distress. Hostility, perhaps… as if she really did blame him for the accident. But even more than that, an odd intimacy, as if she knew more about him than he did about her. Devlyn was disconcerted. He was accustomed to women tucking their phone numbers into his pocket, not looking down their noses at him.

With one last call to 911, he flagged down the approaching ambulance and pulled off the road. He set the parking brake with a jerk. Before he could come around to offer assistance, his mystery lady was out of the car and heading toward the man and woman in uniform.

Damn her stubborn hide. He loped after her. If the professionals decided she needed to go to the hospital, Devlyn was off the hook.

In deference to the worsening weather, the responders left the gurney inside and had the woman stretched out by the time Devlyn approached. "Do you think it's serious?" he asked, speaking to the medic at the back of the vehicle.

She gave him that look reserved for clueless family members. "We'll know in a little bit."

The man inside bent over the patient, checking vitals. He began asking a string of questions. But one snagged Devlyn's attention right off. *Name?*

The mystery woman's eyes met Devlyn's across the space of several feet. She hesitated.

The question came a second time, more forcefully as the man frowned. *Name?*

Devlyn saw her inner struggle, and her capitulation. "Gillian Carlyle," she said clearly. Was that a glint of defiance Devlyn saw in her gaze?

Gillian Carlyle. Why did that sound so familiar? He didn't know this woman, did he?

While the medical exam continued, Devlyn analyzed the puzzle. Gillian's looks were unexceptional. Medium brown hair, darker brown eyes, pale skin, an angular figure. The cream angora sweater she wore along with a brown corduroy skirt and knee-length boots were not in any way provocative. She wasn't his type, not at all. So he knew they hadn't dated in some far-distant adolescent past. Yet for some reason, he was intrigued.

Finally, she was allowed to sit up. "Thank you," she said quietly. "I'm feeling much better now."

The ambulance driver began putting away all the equipment, addressing Devlyn over Gillian's head. "She told me you were the Good Samaritan who stopped to help her. Can you drive her home? She's gonna be okay. Lots of bumps and bruises, though. Make sure she's not alone tonight in case anything crops up that we missed. She should see her doctor for a follow-up visit tomorrow."

Devlyn groaned inwardly. Even if he dashed back up the mountain and took the chopper, he'd never make it now. "Sure," he said, with a smile that felt like a grimace. "I'd be glad to." In the boardroom, he had no trouble acting like a bastard. Not so much in real life.

He watched Gillian deal with the necessary evil of insurance info. Then he shepherded her back to the car, his arm around her narrow waist. Her bone structure was slender, though she was fairly tall. She fit against his shoulder as if she had been created for just that spot. In the flashing lights from the ambulance he could see that she was dangerously near the point of exhaustion.

How in God's name could he simply drop her off at a deserted house in her condition? "Is there anyone you can call to stay with you tonight? A friend? A neighbor?"

"No. But I'll be fine." She turned her head away from him.

He tucked her into the car and kicked the heat on full blast. If his big body was chilled, she must be freezing. Consigning his last hope of making the business meeting to hell, he sighed. "I'm taking you to Wolff Mountain. We have enough guest rooms for a small army. No one will bother you, but you'll have help close by if you need it. I'll call a tow truck in the morning and we'll see about your car."

She half turned to face him, her body visibly shaking. Moisture glittered in her eyes. "You don't even remember who I am, do you? Even after you heard me say my name. Take me home, Devlyn. I don't belong on your mountain."

And just like that, a memory clicked…

Devlyn recalled the day with painful clarity. It was the first anniversary of the terrible tragedy that had torn the Wolff family apart. On that particular sunny afternoon, Devlyn's father and uncle had insisted that their six combined children help scatter two urns of ashes over a newly planted rose garden on the side of the mountain.

For Devlyn, the process was gruesome and confusing. As soon as he was able, he fled to the secret cave that had become solace at his new home. A girl appeared from nowhere it seemed, staring at him with pity, pity he loathed.

"I'm sorry your mother died," she said. Her long, caramel-brown hair had been plaited into two identical braids that hung forward over her narrow shoulders.

Devlyn was embarrassed and humiliated. Boys didn't cry, especially not in front of girls. He ran a hand across his nose and was further mortified to see a smear of snot. "I hated her," he said abruptly. "I'm glad she's gone."

The girl's long-lashed eyes widened. "Don't be stupid," she said. "You can't hate your mother. She was beautiful. Like a princess. My mother lets me go into Mr. Wolff's bedroom sometimes when she's cleaning…if I'm really good. I love to look at Mrs. Wolff's picture on the wall." She held out her hand. "Here… I made you a card."

Devlyn's desperate anger swelled, determined to end this encounter. "You're not allowed," he shouted, knocking the small folded construction paper out of her hand. "Not anymore. This is my mountain, and you don't belong here. Go home."

Her face crumpled. He felt as if he had kicked one of the

new puppies that lived down at the stables. The silent misery on her delicate features only made him madder. "Go," *he screamed. "Go away."*

Devlyn felt anew the weight of guilt and remorse. For over two decades, he had carried the burden of knowing he had hurt a young girl with his hateful words. Now here she was. As if fate had given him a second chance.

He *could* pretend he didn't know her...could text a late arrival to his much-anticipated appointment and drop Gillian as quickly as possible. But his own cruelty stared him in the face. "Gillian," he said slowly. "Gillian Carlyle. It's been a long time."

Two

A quarter of a century had passed since Gillian had tried, in her own clumsy way, to extend sympathy to a hurting boy. But the passage of time had in no way dulled the memory of how she felt that day when the little rich kid kicked metaphorical sand in her face.

What made it worse was that she knew, even then, that he was right. Gillian's mother scrubbed toilets for a living. The Wolffs were richer than God. It was the first time Gillian had fully understood a difficult truth about the haves and the have-nots.

"It took you long enough," she said. The snarky retort was unfair, but she wasn't in a mood to be conciliatory. Though she no longer carried a chip on her shoulder, it had taken time and maturity to help her see that the Carlyles were every bit as happy as the wealthy Wolff clan in their fortress on the mountain. Maybe more so.

As a child, she had been tormented. She begged her mother

not to make Gillian go to work with her. But Doreen Carlyle had few options. Child care was not only expensive, but in a little wide-place-in-the-road like Burton, it was nonexistent.

Gillian was forced to see Devlyn occasionally, though each of them tried to ignore the other. Things were better when school started. Doreen put her young daughter on a bus before sunup for the long ride to the nearest consolidated school. And by the time Gillian returned home, her mother was finished with her shift at Wolff Castle, as the locals called it.

Gillian jerked herself out of the past, glad of the darkness that hid her turbulent emotions. She straightened in her seat. "It's really okay to take me to my mother's house. I promise I'll call someone if I start to feel worse."

It was the presence of a Wolff in the car, not her accident, that was responsible for the rapid pace of her heartbeat. Devlyn was a big man, broad through the shoulders and tall. The scent of his aftershave made her think of thick fir-tree forests and lumberjacks in flannel shirts, though the comparison was ludicrous.

Devlyn was an astute businessman, a shark in the turbulent world of financial greed. Despite the fact that her wits had been partially addled after the accident, she'd still been aware of his sartorial perfection, though he was perhaps a tad rumpled and sported a five-o'clock shadow.

He was the de facto ruler of the kingdom and, in that moment, Gillian hated him. When had he ever had to work for anything? When had he ever had to worry about money? Other than his mother's death years ago, admittedly a terrible loss, when had he ever known true hardship?

That wasn't fair perhaps. The Wolffs generously supported many worthy charities. Perhaps that chip on her shoulder still lingered as a splinter in her heart. And maybe she was manufacturing grievances in order to avoid admitting how much she was attracted to him.

Even as a teenager, on the few occasions she actually saw him, he had been breathtakingly handsome. Blunt, masculine features. Thick black hair with the sheen of a raven's wing. A white smile that flashed often. And a tough, honed body that exuded strength and confidence.

Little had changed except that now he was a man and not a boy. He had filled out, lost the slightly clumsy awkwardness of puberty. His gait was strong and sure, his movements sleek as the panthers that once roamed these hills.

He shot her a glance as he once again turned onto the road that led up to the entrance to Wolff Mountain. "I'm not arguing about this, Gillian. I'm sorry I didn't recognize you right off. But you have to admit that you've changed."

Did his gaze linger on her chest? Or was that her imagination? Surely not. She might be all tingly with perfectly natural feminine longing for a man who exuded an earthy sex appeal, but to think he had any interest in her was ridiculous.

Her instinct was to shoot back with a smart-ass comment about kidnapping, but she bit her tongue. Devlyn's mother and aunt had been snatched off a busy Charlottesville street, held for ransom and later killed. Kidnapping was not something to be joked about.

She shifted restlessly. Already her battered body bloomed with myriad aches and throbs. The paramedics had recommended an anti-inflammatory, but though she had some ibuprofen in her purse, she had nothing with which to wash them down. Suddenly, the idea of staying alone overnight held little appeal.

At the guardhouse Devlyn sketched a wave and waited for the huge mechanized metal gate to retract. Soon they were heading up the winding drive that served to isolate the Wolff clan from intruders.

She sighed deeply. "I'm not sure this is a good idea. I don't want to intrude on your family."

"They won't even know you're around…unless you want company."

"Why don't you have your own place here?"

He must have picked up on the faint, unintended criticism in her tone. "As you've already mentioned, I live in Atlanta," he said stiffly. "When I visit, I usually stay up in the big house with my dad and uncle." He paused. "If it would make you more comfortable, we can stay at Jacob's place. He and his wife won't care."

"He's the one married to the movie star, right? Ariel Dane?"

"Yep. She's a sweetheart."

Gillian's spirits plunged to a new low. The gorgeous, sexy Wolff men had their pick of models, heiresses and celebrities. It wasn't simply a matter of money. It was a lifestyle.

"I don't think it would be appropriate for the two of us to spend the night alone," she said, regretting the prim stuffiness in her words as soon as they left her mouth.

Devlyn snorted, and tried to pretend it was a cough. "I promise to be on my best behavior," he said, irony in every syllable. "But if it makes you feel more comfortable, we'll stay at the big house."

"Thank you."

By the time they pulled up in front of the massive structure that looked like Cinderella's castle on steroids, Gillian had trouble getting out of the car. Devlyn took her arms and gently pulled her to her feet. "Poor Gillian," he said.

The soft croon in his deep voice made her tremble. She was unable to protest when he scooped her up and carried her into the house. Striding through darkened hallways, he set a course for a back staircase that led to the second floor. Thankfully, they met no one on the way.

Devlyn paused before a half-open doorway. "This is my room. There's an adjoining suite with a door you can lock.

But if you need assistance during the night, you can text me or call me and I'll get you anything you need."

How about you, Devlyn Wolff? In the buff. Sliding on top of me and...

Her breath caught in her throat. She was suffering the effects of a long dry spell in the sex department. That's why she wanted to nibble his throat despite the fact that she felt as if she'd been run over by the proverbial truck. Proximity and deprivation. Simple explanations for the electric connection she felt to a man who was in no way an appropriate object of her fantasies.

Well, yes...for fantasy...in the abstract. But not at all healthy or practical to imagine him...and her...together... Oh, Lord. Her thighs clenched and her nipples tightened. She prayed he didn't notice.

His bed was neatly made. But a pair of jeans hung haphazardly over the back of an armchair, and a paperback crime novel lay upside down on the mahogany nightstand.

"I'm sure I'll be fine," she croaked.

Without acknowledging her comment, he took her, still in his arms, through the doorway into a room that was almost as large as his but was decorated in more feminine tones. Ever so gently, he set her on her feet. "Bathroom's through there. I'll see if I can round you up some clean clothes, and I'll call Jacob to see what medicine you can take."

Before she could catch her breath, he was gone.

She hobbled into the luxurious bathroom and stared in the mirror. If she'd had any illusions about her comparison to the female companionship usually enjoyed by Wolff men, they were shattered decisively by her reflection. Even on a good day, she didn't stand out in a crowd. Right now, she looked ghastly.

Stripping out of her rain-damp clothes, she adjusted the water and stepped into the shower. The hot pelting spray hurt in a good way, the steamy warmth penetrating her bones. Already, bruises were showing up on her too-pale skin. She'd taught a summer-school session instead of going to the beach with her girlfriends, and look where that had gotten her.

Knowing she didn't have the strength or the will to blow-dry her hair, and since she'd shampooed it the night before, she was careful to keep it from getting wet. As she stepped out of the shower and was drying off, a knock on the door startled her so much that she dropped her towel. "Don't come in," she cried, scrambling to cover her indecent bits.

A chuckle was her only answer. The door eased open a scant foot. One long-fingered, tanned hand reached in holding soft, clean clothes. The items landed on the counter with a muted plop, and the hand withdrew.

Gillian scurried forward and locked the knob with what sounded like a gunshot-loud click. She was pretty sure she heard Devlyn laugh again. The bounty he had provided included a set of lounging pj's…the kind you see in the Neiman Marcus catalog, the kind only rich women owned and wore.

The fabric was incredibly soft and warm, though not thick…some sort of cashmere blend. The cinnamon shade flattered her hair and added a snippet of color to her washed-out complexion.

She put on naughty silk panties that most likely belonged to Devlyn's sister, Annalise, then slipped into the top and pants. Devlyn hadn't added a bra. Gillian's own underwear tended toward cotton practicality. The new undies made her aware of the place between her thighs that throbbed as insistently as her injuries. And her breasts rubbed sensuously against the velvetlike fabric.

When she exited the bathroom, barefooted, she stopped short. Devlyn stood by the fireplace where a fire crackled with blissful heat. He had dragged a small table near the hearth, and it was set with an array of dishes. Her stomach growled audibly.

He held out a hand. "Come eat. And Jacob said you can double the usual dose of over-the-counter pain meds. If he were here, he could give you something stronger."

Shyness engulfed her. She had to force herself to approach him. "That will be fine. Don't worry about me."

He held out her chair, his arm brushing her shoulder as she sat down. "I can't seem to help it," he said wryly.

The carpet beneath her feet was soft as a cloud. She curled her toes into it and took a deep breath. "I know you didn't cause my accident," she said, looking up at him through downcast lashes. "I was just in a bad mood. I'm sorry."

He sat down as well, and poured each of them a cup of tea. The juxtaposition of his big, manly hands against the wafer-thin china teapot was incongruous and alarming. How could she keep him at arm's length if he didn't remain in the box she had labeled "spoiled rich philanderer."

She didn't want to like Devlyn Wolff. Not at all.

He took her lack of enthusiasm the wrong way. "It's herbal tea," he said. "No caffeine. But I can get you coffee if you'd rather have it."

Picking up the lovely ivory cup scattered with blue forget-me-nots, she shook her head. "I prefer the tea. Thank you."

He had fixed a tray of sandwiches as well—tiny, slightly ragged squares of white bread with the crusts removed. Peanut butter and honey.

Her whole body tensed. "Why did you make these?" she asked, her insides in a knot.

Devlyn shrugged, his expression moody. "As a penance, I guess. I remember watching you eat them in the kitchen when your mother was on her lunch break. I was jealous, you know. My mother never cooked anything."

Gillian didn't know what to say to that. No one *cooked* peanut butter. But she understood what he was telling her.

He waved a hand. "You need to eat something so the medicine won't upset your stomach."

Too late. The accident, this intimate tête-à-tête, Devlyn's unexpected domesticity...all of it had her in turmoil.

Mute and uncomfortable, she picked up a piece of sandwich, chewed and swallowed. The familiar tastes from her childhood opened a floodgate of memories. His hostility. Her feelings of inferiority. The emotions were as sharp and crisp as yesterday.

Yet he spoke of penance.

"You have nothing for which to apologize," she said slowly, eyeing him over the rim of her teacup. "You were hurting. We were both children." She didn't insult him by pretending not to understand what he was talking about. Their youthful confrontation in the cave all those years ago had clearly bothered him as well as her.

Devlyn wolfed down five mini-sandwiches to her two, and drained three cups of tea. For some reason, she was infinitely fascinated by the play of muscles in his throat as he swallowed. Everything about him was intensely virile, dangerously sexual.

When a woman became aroused by watching a man eat peanut butter and honey, she was in trouble. Big trouble.

He sat back in his chair and drummed his fingers on the arms. "I was hateful and cruel," he said quietly. His voice dropped an octave. "You were trying to express sympathy in the only way you knew how. I acted like a jerk."

She could almost see his frustration. "You were a kid. It was a long time ago. Forget about it."

"Have you?"

The sharp question caught her off guard. "I...uh...no," she muttered. "I never forgot."

After an awkward pause, he handed her some tablets. "These are nonprescription, but Jacob says they'll be the best thing for muscles aches. Take them now so you'll be comfortable in bed."

Their fingers brushed as the medicine changed hands. The word *bed* hovered in the air between them. She clenched her fist. "Thank you."

Without taking his eyes off hers, he covered her hand. "Now," he said hoarsely. "Don't wait. And quit being so damned polite."

She jerked away and swallowed the pills, almost choking because of the knowledge that he had touched her. It meant nothing… She was the one freaking out, not Devlyn. He was merely being a gentleman.

Avoiding his cobralike gaze, she scooped up a shortbread cookie. It melted on her tongue like ambrosia of the gods. "I'd forgotten how good these are," she moaned.

Devlyn reacted visibly to the involuntary sound she made. Feeling her cheeks heat in embarrassment, she bent her head and took another sip of tea. Was it just her, or was Devlyn reacting as strongly as she was to the odd sense of intimacy that shrouded the room in hushed layers?

Three

Devlyn couldn't remember the last time he'd spent this much time in a woman's bedroom without both of them getting naked. When Gillian made a surprisingly sexual response to cookies…goddamned sugar cookies, his sex hardened from zero to sixty in five seconds.

And she wasn't even pretty in the traditional sense.

He adjusted himself unobtrusively and ate another sandwich. Maybe if he kept his mouth full he could quit thinking about licking his way down that swanlike white-skinned neck. Good lord…

"So tell me, Gillian. What do you do for a living…when you're not smashing cars into trees?"

She stared at him with affront.

"Too soon?" He grinned at her, surprisingly entertained by the unexpected turn his evening had taken. The quick phone call to his investor had not been pleasant, but Devlyn was determined. The outlook might be grim, but he'd fought his way out of worse situations.

Gillian wiped her mouth daintily with a snowy cloth napkin, leaving a faint trace of pink color on the fabric. Seeing the stain from her lips, he imagined other oral scenarios. Perhaps because her lips were the only truly curvy thing about her. They belonged more to a porn star than to a quiet, wary-eyed, little mouse.

She curled her legs beneath her, drawing attention to slim thighs and a narrow waist. He wondered if he could span that waist with his two hands.

Gillian seemed blissfully oblivious to his baser instincts. "Do you joke about everything?" she asked, disapproval evident in her wide-set eyes.

He shrugged. "I'd rather laugh than cry."

And there it was again. That pesky, awful memory. *Hell.* He hadn't meant to bring it up again...or had he?

She cocked her head. "Why did I make you so angry that day?" she asked. "I've always wondered. Was it only because I saw you in tears?"

Any humor he'd tried to generate evaporated. He leaped to his feet and stoked the fire, throwing on another couple of logs for good measure. Leaning an arm on the mantel, he poked at the embers, wishing he didn't feel the same prodding at a place that would never heal.

"Sure," he said curtly. "That was it."

"You're lying."

He jerked around so quickly that he knocked over one of the andirons. Replacing it clumsily, he sat down hard in his chair, staring at her with bemused eyes. "I don't know what to make of you, Gillian Carlyle. So let's go back to my first question. What do you do for a living?"

"I'm a teacher. Third grade." Pride glowed on her face and in her voice until something stole it away, some weary acceptance of an unpalatable truth. "Or I was," she said, her tone subdued. "The county I worked for outside of Charlottesville cut forty positions last week. I was four years into a five-year tenure track."

"That sucks."

"Tell me about it."

Their eyes met, and they both burst into laughter. Devlyn realized in that instant that he had been wrong earlier. Gillian Carlyle wasn't plain. She was a beauty. But it was the hidden loveliness of the sea on a cloudy, windswept day. Only when the sun came out were the emeralds and sapphires and aquamarines revealed.

His brain whirred with sudden possibilities. "Is that why you're back home in Burton?"

"Partially. I begged my mother to move to Charlottesville with me when I got the job, but she never would. She loves the house where I grew up, and oddly enough, she loves Wolff Castle. She's very proud to be part of the staff here, and she doesn't want to leave."

"So why did you try to persuade her?"

"My dad was a carpenter. He died a few years ago when scaffolding at a worksite collapsed. Mama was distraught, and I wanted her where I could keep an eye on her. In case you hadn't noticed, there are no teaching jobs around here. Not many jobs of any kind for someone with my training."

"But she wouldn't move."

"No. And now she's glad she didn't. But that still leaves me in a tough spot, because I want to look after her, but I can't even take care of myself at the moment."

"Something will come up." He had an idea or two, but now was not the time. "Would you like another cookie?"

Her lips quirked. "I'm not stupid, Devlyn. I answered your questions. Don't you owe me the same courtesy?"

That amazing, adorably boyish smile flashed briefly. "I'm a stubborn SOB. Don't try to analyze me. What you see is what you get."

Her eyes widened as she caught the deliberately flirtatious innuendo. As he watched, her cheeks turned pink. And about the same time, a little frown line appeared between her brows. "I don't think you're a very nice man," she said slowly.

"Nice guys finish last. Don't you know?" He stood and messed with the fire again, irritated as hell that she put him on edge. She was a nobody. An unemployed elementary schoolteacher. A starchy, prissy, sexually repressed female.

Perhaps if he told himself often enough, he would believe it.

Gillian yawned suddenly, and he felt a lick of remorse. She'd been through a hell of a lot. It was long past time for her to be in bed. But not in his.

He stood up and held out his hand. "C'mon, little lady. You're drooping."

She stood and began stacking their dirty dishes.

"Leave them," he said, a hand on her arm. "The staff will get it in the morning."

Gillian froze, and immediately, he heard how his words must have sounded to her. Heat stained his throat. "I'm sorry," he said gruffly. "That was insensitive."

Gillian shrugged, causing the fabric of her top to mold to her bare, small, perfect breasts. He swallowed hard, caught unawares by a sudden driving urge to unbutton that top and look his fill.

She smiled wryly. "Don't be stupid. Your family provides a lot of great jobs for working-class people. That's not a bad thing."

But she didn't say it was good, either. He sensed her ambivalence and her fatigue. "Go to bed, Gillian. You're beat. We can talk in the morning, but if you need me during the night, don't play the martyr. I'm right next door."

Gillian tossed and turned for an hour, unable to sleep in a strange house. The medicine had taken the edge off her various pains, but her body still ached. At last, she climbed out of bed and went to the French doors, drawing the thick draperies aside and peering out into the dark.

A tiny crescent moon cast a dim light that filtered down like fairy dust among the trees that surrounded the house. When Wolff Castle was built, Devlyn's father and his uncle had been insistent that as little of the woods as possible be cut down. Consequently, the forest cloaked the enormous house like a security blanket, maintaining the privacy for which the Wolffs were famed.

The late-night scene was serene. Gillian's emotions were anything but. She felt trapped, claustrophobic. Even if she had the energy and the will to do so, she couldn't leave. Her car was crumpled at the bottom of the mountain.

Her mother's voice had been hard to read when Gillian called her to explain what had happened. Doreen Carlyle was well acquainted with all the members of the Wolff family, including Devlyn. And Devlyn's reputation with the opposite sex was no secret.

Women loved him. And he loved women. But never for more than a season, at best. Though he seemed like an open book, dark currents ran beneath his easy charm and his outrageous sex appeal.

Gillian curled her fist in a fold of cloth and shivered as her bare toes chilled on the flagstones that edged the doorway. Dare she go outside? Would anyone know?

Without another thought, she pulled her thick sweater over the fancy pajamas and shoved her feet into her boots. Even without a mirror, she knew she looked ludicrous. But she had to escape, had to prove to herself that she wasn't a prisoner. A small, spiral, wrought-iron staircase at the end of her balcony offered easy access to the level below.

The air was colder than she had anticipated. Rain had finally moved on, and indigo skies overhead were clear, allowing the temperature to plummet. Fall would soon give way to winter, especially at this elevation. She followed a pathway at random, not at all worried about being alone in the dark.

She was a country girl, born and raised in these mountains. Travelers came from across the globe to see the mystical and beautiful Blue Ridge, but for Gillian they were more like an old, comfortable friend.

As she meandered, she thought about the last time she had visited Wolff Mountain. She'd been a sophomore in high school, and in her economics class, they'd been doing projects about starting a business. Doreen Carlyle had asked Victor Wolff, Devlyn's uncle, if her daughter could interview him.

Gillian remembered how nervous she had been that day, but Victor Wolff, despite his gruff demeanor, had put her at ease. By the end of the conversation, they had been old buddies. He had a keen intellect and a knack for making money.

As she was leaving the house, preparing to negotiate the long, winding driveway in her fifteen-year-old Volkswagen Beetle, Gillian had come face-to-face with Devlyn Wolff. She remembered how her throat closed up, how hot color flooded her face. Neither of them spoke a word.

Devlyn seemed on the cusp of saying something urgent, but before he could tell her again that she didn't belong, she fled. And until tonight, that was the last time she had ever seen him in the flesh.

The press, however, was another story. Devlyn's exploits both in and out of the boardroom were legendary. He'd bought baseball teams, had at one time even dabbled with driving his own race car. The two Wolff patriarchs had put a quick stop to that, but even so, Devlyn deserved his reputation as a billionaire playboy…an out-of-date term, perhaps, but one that fit.

His wilder party days had tempered as he approached thirty, perhaps because he was being groomed to take over the reins of the family business.

Victor and Vincent Wolff started their families late in life, both of them at least fifteen years older than the beautiful wives they eventually lost.

Now, they were at a point where they wanted to enjoy retirement. So Devlyn was in control of everything. Nothing short of brilliant, he worked as hard as he partied.

Gillian was not immune to his appeal. But he was way out of her league. She preferred bookish, intellectual men, guys who were more like house-trained pets than wild, night-roaming creatures.

Devlyn was incredibly dangerous and yet so very attractive.

She hugged her arms around her body and decided she had had enough. Her limbs trembled with fatigue, and it was time for another dose of painkiller. Things always seemed so much worse at this hour…her bleak employment future, the lack of male companionship in her nunlike life…the hole in her emotions left by her father's passing.

Blinking back tears of self-pity that she refused to let fall, she turned and immediately tripped over a root, stumbling to her knees on the cold and muddy ground.

"What in the hell do you think you're doing?"

Devlyn's outraged voice startled her as much as the fall. In an instant, his hands were under her arms, lifting her effortlessly to her feet. Seeing the state she was in, he cursed beneath his breath and shrugged out of the thick, fleece-lined jacket he wore. He wrapped it around her and scooped her into his arms.

"You can't spend all your time carrying me around," she muttered. But it was a token protest at best. His warmth surrounded her even as his strength filled her with an odd contentment.

It was a false sense of security. She knew that. But for this one moment, this single, unlikely and unsettling reunion, she decided to pretend that she had a right to be here in Devlyn Wolff's embrace.

She had left the double, glass-paned doors to her room unlatched. After negotiating the narrow stairs, Devlyn deposited her on her feet long enough to remove her muddy boots and his shoes, before urging her inside, locking the doors and drawing the drapes.

Gillian had left a single lamp burning. The confusion in Devlyn's eyes mirrored her own. "I'm sorry I disturbed you," she said, the words stiff. "I couldn't sleep."

"Same here." Still he stared at her. "Sit down on the bed, Gillian."

He stepped past her, and moments later she heard water running in the bathroom. When he returned, he had a damp washcloth in his hands. "I said sit down."

She sat.

Why was she enabling his bossiness? She was a mature woman with a life that clicked along quite well. She didn't need a man to take care of her.

He took her fingers in his and gently wiped away the mud where she had landed, hands down. His touch was gentle but firm, removing the bits of leaves and grass that clung to her skin.

Next he removed his coat, the one he had wrapped around her. His eyes went to the muddy knees of her pajamas, and her stomach clenched. Surely he wouldn't—

"Lift your hips."

Like an automaton, she obeyed, watching the tableau unfold as he bared her legs and dragged the pants down to her ankles and away. "Get under the covers," he said.

Her face flaming with color, she obeyed, painfully conscious that he didn't even bother to avert his gaze. When she was covered from the waist down, she removed the sweater, managing to tangle her hair in the process. Devlyn disappeared into the bathroom a second time and came back holding a brush still wrapped in cellophane.

He sat down beside her, opening the package. "Turn away from me," he commanded.

She felt one hand settle on her shoulder. With the other, he dragged the brush through her hair. Her eyes closed and a whimper of delight escaped her lips. Her head lolled on her shoulders as the simple pleasure unfolded. Occasionally, as he encountered a knot, she felt his fingers sift through her straight, thick tresses.

Gooseflesh erupted all over her body, and her breasts grew heavy with arousal. Did he try this on all his women? God, the man was a genius. He never seemed to tire. The gentle pull of the bristles against her scalp went on and on. Sleepiness gradually replaced sexual excitement.

Dimly, she heard him speak soft words as he eased her onto her back. She felt hard, warm arms encircle her.

After that…nothing.

Four

Devlyn awoke abruptly, his internal alarm clock set for 6:00 a.m. For a moment, he was completely disoriented. And then everything came flooding back. Gillian Carlyle.

Though it was an anomaly to begin the day fully dressed in a woman's bed, the details were clear. He'd been driven by a combination of guilt and lust, determined to take care of the prickly woman who was a thorn in the side of his past.

He rubbed his gritty eyes, wishing he had the option of going back to sleep. But Wolff Enterprises expected him at the helm this morning, and he had already made one costly mistake because of this woman.

Gillian sighed in her sleep and nestled more closely into his embrace. He was on top of the comforter, hard and ready to take her. All she was wearing was a pajama top, and below the covers a next-to-nothing pair of panties. Unable to help himself, he slid a hand beneath the sheet and caressed her bottom.

Gillian sighed and turned to curl an arm around his neck.

Now her breasts were pressed snugly against his arm. He slid his fingers beneath the silk at her hip and felt her warm skin. His body throbbed with arousal. A few more inches and he would be touching her most intimate secrets.

Somewhere in the house he heard muffled laughter. The sound snatched him back to sanity. God in heaven. What was he doing? Had he learned nothing from the past?

He slid from the bed with all the care of a cat burglar hoping to elude detection. It took everything he had to turn his back on Gillian and return to his room. As he showered and dressed, he reminded himself of all the reasons he couldn't start something with his overnight visitor.

First and foremost was Gillian's clear discomfort about the fact that her mother worked for Devlyn's father. Devlyn could not care less, but even so, he acknowledged the difficulty of coaxing Gillian into his bed with little or no privacy for their fledgling relationship, especially when either or both of their parents might not approve.

Secondly, he owed Gillian more than a verbal apology for his shameful actions in the past. Acknowledging that he had been merely a boy when it happened was not enough. He was determined to clean the slate, and he knew just how to do it. He told himself that in this instance he was doing the right thing and not merely perpetuating his tendency to play hero to every woman who crossed his path needing help.

In college, he had supported his roommate's pregnant girlfriend, both emotionally and financially, when the father of her baby dumped her. That altruistic action on Devlyn's part had severed his relationship with a young man he had considered his best friend.

Not only that, the girl had latched on to the idea that lovers were interchangeable…and she set her sights on Devlyn. Only by graduating and moving hundreds of miles away had he been able to extract himself from the messy situation.

Unfortunately, it was a pattern that repeated itself in subsequent years. Every time he rushed in on his white horse to save the day, he got screwed. The secretary at work whose brother needed a job ended up hating Devlyn when he finally had to fire her worthless sibling.

Even worse was the fifty-something caterer who had accused Devlyn, over two decades her junior, of sexual harassment. He had offered to help her load her van after a staff Christmas party, and the woman had seen a chance to make a quick buck.

The Wolff lawyers settled out of court, costing the family an indecent amount of money. Now that Devlyn thought about it, it was a miracle that his dad and uncle had trusted him enough to make him CEO.

But despite his sometimes unfortunate judgment in dealing with the female sex, he was a whiz kid when it came to money matters. He'd earned his own first million, aside from the family business, by investments he'd made in his late teens.

The intensity and daily challenge of running the far-flung Wolff empire suited him perfectly. He was due back at his headquarters in Atlanta soon. Barely enough time to present his proposition to Gillian and ensure that he had finally made amends for the past.

So why was he obsessing over the image of long, slender legs and a sweetly curved bottom? The answer was simple. Logical or not, he wanted her, though she certainly deserved better than the flawed man he was.

Picking up his smartphone from the bureau, he took a deep breath and strode out into the hall. He had a dozen balls to juggle today, and he was already running behind. His personal life could wait.

Gillian rolled over and glanced at the clock, her muddled brain trying to understand why both hands pointed straight up toward the twelve. Then everything came rushing back. Her accident, the multiple disturbing and faintly erotic encounters with Devlyn Wolff. Her lack of a job.

Not the best memories with which to begin a day in which her body felt like an old woman's. She turned her head carefully, hoping to stave off the jackhammers that threatened to crush her skull. Though she was alone in the bed, the pillow beside her bore the unmistakable imprint of someone's head. When she tugged it closer for a sniff, the soft, expensive fabric emanated the unmistakable scent of Devlyn Wolff.

Holy cow. What had she done? Squeezing her eyes shut, she reached for images that hid in random corners of her brain. She remembered going outside. She even remembered Devlyn bringing her in and watching her take off her pants. At that point, things became hazy.

He had touched her hair…had lulled her to sleep. Then what? Surely the memory of his big, warm hand on her butt was a dream.

Stumbling into the bathroom, she splashed water on her face and noted in surprise the neatly folded pile of clean clothes that turned out to be a khaki skirt and a black scooped-neck T-shirt with a matching thin cardigan.

The clothes fit perfectly, which in itself was alarming. A man who could choose women's apparel with such an eye was a man with far too much experience in pleasing women.

Her boots were still muddy, perhaps beyond repair, but her stealthy benefactor had included a pair of black canvas espadrilles. The shoes were a little too large, but she stuffed tissues in the toes until she was certain they were snug enough to stay on her feet.

Feeling a bit too much like Little Orphan Annie, she finally opened the envelope that lay like a coiled serpent on the bedside table.

Please join me for lunch in the library at one. Devlyn.

The house was still and quiet, almost somnolent, as if everyone in the *Sleeping Beauty* castle snoozed for a thousand years. Thank God her mother was not scheduled to work today. Gillian's face would have given her away, her mother seeing at once that her daughter had fallen under the spell of a Wolff prince.

Gillian remembered the way to the library with ease. It was another place where Doreen Carlyle had kept her daughter entertained while she worked. Gillian had always been a compliant child, not one to make messes or break things. She had been more than content to curl up on the velvet-covered bench seat in the window alcove and read her favorite books for hours at a time.

In many ways, the Wolff Castle library had been her magic carpet, taking her to lands beyond the horizon, introducing her to characters whose lives were far more exotic than her own. The library had been her haven, her cozy nest. When she was there, she felt safe.

But nothing about today's visit inspired such warm, fuzzy feelings. When she opened the door, Devlyn was already in residence, his stance at the fireplace much like the night before in her bedroom. His lips curved in a welcoming smile, but his eyes were watchful.

"Good afternoon, Gillian. I hope you were finally able to get some sleep."

He was playing with her, trying to make her nervous. She knew beyond a shadow of a doubt that he had been the one to enter her room and drop off the clothes and the note.

"Yes," she said stiffly. "I did. I need to check on my car."

He shrugged. "Already taken care of…. The garage will drop it off at your mother's house by the end of the week."

She bit her bottom lip. "I'd like an estimate. So I can contact my insurance."

"Let me handle this. It's the least I can do. You know they'll jack up your rates if you submit it."

He had her there. And she couldn't afford the current payments, much less a rate hike. "I'll pay you back."

His brows narrowed in displeasure. "I said to forget it."

"You like ruling the world, don't you? Is there anyone who says no to you?"

Her sass seemed to amuse him. "Sit down, Gillian. Chef has prepared an autumn vegetable chowder that I'm told is to die for."

She joined him at the table, wondering what his family thought of his absence from the communal dining room. Of course, with Jacob out of town and the others perhaps tucked away in their own houses, maybe Victor and Vincent dined alone.

Devlyn picked up his spoon and dug in, polishing off his bowl of soup and three rolls before Gillian had barely started. It was hard to swallow anything past the constriction in her throat, even though Devlyn was correct about the delicious, hearty broth. Finally, the silence weighed too heavily for her to finish. She pushed back from the table and folded her hands in her lap.

The fire was warm—warm enough for her to discard her sweater. But she fancied she needed the extra layer of protection. "You left me a note," she said bluntly. "Why am I here?"

"I could have guessed you were a teacher, even if you hadn't told me."

The odd segue baffled her. "What does that mean?"

"You're uptight, bossy, no-nonsense…"

"And you've deduced all that in a mere twenty-four hours?"

"Less than that. I expect any moment to get my knuckles rapped with a ruler."

His air of masculine superiority set her teeth on edge. "That's an archaic reference."

"You don't know the tutors my father and uncle hired."

"Poor little rich boy." She regretted the words immediately. In many ways, the appellation was true…or at least had been in the past. Devlyn Wolff as a child and a teen had always seemed angry. And with good reason. He'd lost his mother violently. Been snatched away from the only home he had ever known and brought to this isolated mountain. Had not been allowed to attend school where he would have made friends. It was no wonder the six cousins were so close.

She didn't know how to characterize him now…that would require spending time together, a notion that alarmed and intrigued her at the same time. "We're getting off topic," she said, her voice firm…the one she used for recalcitrant boys on the playground. "What do you want to talk to me about?"

"I want to hire you."

Her hackles went up. "You apologized. I accepted. I don't need your charity simply because I'm unemployed."

"Before you ride that high horse off into the sunset, why don't you listen for a minute? I need to employ a teacher. It might as well be you."

Her stomach cramped. Did Devlyn have a child she hadn't heard about? "There are no schools anywhere near Wolff Mountain."

He grinned as if he had scored a hit. "My point exactly. Evidently you haven't heard, but the Wolffs are establishing a school in Burton."

"Thumbing your nose at the locals? No one around here can afford private tuition."

"Gillian, Gillian…" He shook his head. "I'm talking about a public school. And that's why I need you. It's a sticky proposition to make sure all of the accreditation requirements are fulfilled. And we've had a hell of a time convincing the administration that we'll stay out of the day-to-day running. But this is going to happen. The children of Burton have every right to attend school in their own community."

Gillian was stunned. What he said made perfect sense, but although the Wolffs were active in a number of charities, this project took benevolence to another whole level. "Whose idea was this?"

"It was a family decision. Too many of our staff worry that if one of their children gets sick, or falls on the playground, it would be a good forty-five minutes before they could get to the school. That's not acceptable. The economy is in the toilet. Money for new schools is scarce. We have the means to supply a need."

Gillian cocked her head, studying his face. He seemed genuinely excited and proud. "And you're spearheading the effort?"

"Mostly. Because I'm the one in charge. But all of us will step in at various points. Kieran's wife is a children's illustrator. She's planning to paint murals on all the walls. Jacob will design and outfit a small in-school clinic and hire a nurse. Gareth wants to build custom shelving for the library. I could go on..."

She held up a hand, feeling ashamed of her suspicions. On occasion, that chip on her shoulder about the rich gained weight again. "It's a lovely idea. I'm impressed. But I still don't see where I come in. It will be a long time until you're ready to hire teachers."

"I need a liaison...someone who will work side by side with me, but who knows how to communicate with state and local officials."

"But you work out of Atlanta."

"I'm here at least one weekend a month, sometimes two. Dad and Uncle Vic like to feel as if they are still part of the decision-making process. And I value their experience. But in regard to this school project, you'll be my point person. We'll work very closely together."

"I don't know what to say."

"Say you'll do it."

He named a salary that was over twice what she was making before the layoffs. Only a fool would turn down this opportunity, but then again, working with Devlyn Wolff would not be easy. He was charming and outrageously handsome and had a wicked sense of humor...all qualities that were destined to make a woman like Gillian fall into infatuation at the very least.

And she was pretty sure she wasn't imagining the sexual vibe between them. What was alarming was that if she succumbed, not only did she endanger yet another good job, but she risked getting her heart broken. "Who would you have hired if I hadn't come along?" It was hard to put her suspicions to rest.

"I hadn't gotten that far yet, but I called your principal this morning, and she speaks very highly of you...told me you were named 'Teacher of the Year' in your school last year. She's really upset about losing you."

"You investigated me?" The words ended on a screech of outrage.

"Your ID badge was sticking out of the side pocket of your purse. I'm a businessman. And despite your weird hang-ups, I'm not offering you this job because of something that happened when we were kids."

He could deny it all he wanted, but she was almost a hundred percent sure that Devlyn was the kind of man who needed to even the scales. This was his way of assuaging his guilt over the past.

Still, who was she to turn down a boon because of his

screwed-up motives? She needed a job. And this would be a good one.

"I'll do it," she said. "When do I start?"

Five

Devlyn high-fived his inner self, but managed to maintain a neutral expression. This was exactly the same feeling he got when he outwitted a difficult opponent in a business deal. He didn't probe too deeply at why it was so important to win over Gillian, but it was.

"You'll need to move in here," he said abruptly, thinking on his feet. The idea of having Gillian just down the hall made his pulse thud with anticipation.

She scowled, standing up and pacing with her arms wrapped around her waist. "That won't be necessary. The commute is not inconvenient."

"It's not your convenience we're talking about…it's mine. I'm a very busy man. When I can snatch a few minutes to discuss the school project, I'd like for you to be available."

Gillian's spine straightened and her chin lifted. "So in essence, you're hiring me to be at your beck and call."

He wanted to chuckle aloud. She was pissed. And it was

so much damned fun aggravating her. "Think of it more as a lawyer on retainer."

Her eyes shot daggers at him. Fuming, frustrated, she seemed about to burst with aggravation. "I'm not sure I trust you."

"You wound me." He put his hand over his heart. "What exactly do you think I have up my sleeve?"

"I don't know you well enough to tell."

"I'd like to get to know *you,* Gillian." He hadn't meant to say that. The words tumbled out uncensored, but they were true. Something about her seemed so real, so honest. In his experience, those were qualities rarely found in female companionship. Gillian knew as much or more about him, warts and all, than most people did. And he had an inexplicable urge to win her approval.

But the devil in him couldn't leave it alone. "I'll have a driver out front in fifteen minutes to take you to your mother's house so you can pack your things. I'd like you to be back on the mountain by five. I want to take you to see the property we've purchased…get your impressions."

She sat back down abruptly and started eating soup. "I'm not finished with my lunch. Better make it forty-five." She gave him a bland gaze that did little to disguise her intent. It was clear that she wouldn't be pushed around.

The businessman in him applauded her chutzpah. The hungry male took it as a challenge. This give-and-take was foreplay whether she realized it or not. The circumstances weren't ideal. He'd already made a list of "cons." But if Gillian felt the same sexual pull he did, he'd figure a way around the difficulties. He wasn't accustomed to denying himself when it came to women. Nothing permanent could come of this. He was not the pure, uncomplicated man Gillian needed for the long haul.

Devlyn Wolff, however, did *temporary* damned well. Gillian might try to hide her sexuality beneath generic clothing, but he could see the possibilities. And they excited him.

"Remember," he said, "You're agreeing to be here 24/7 anytime I'm in town. I want to get my money's worth."

Those big, beautiful eyes reflected shock and denial. "But you're not home all that often."

"At the moment, that's true. So we'll have to rely on emails and late night phone calls, won't we?"

"Late night?" Her voice squeaked.

"Some days that's the only time I can break free. Do you have a problem with that?"

She shredded a roll between her long, graceful fingers. "I don't suppose so. But I'm not sure what my mother will think about all of this."

"You've been on your own a long time, right?"

"Yes."

"Then what's the problem?"

She pursed her lips as if she had bitten into a sour spice. "You have quite a reputation in regard to the opposite sex."

"But ours is a business relationship. I'm sure your mother understands the difference."

"I guess…" Her hesitance aroused him as he imagined what it would take to coax her into his bed. In the past six months his schedule had been brutal. Workaholic was an understatement.

Life was too short not to play when the occasion presented itself. And Gillian Carlyle, as reserved and wary as she was, promised to be endlessly entertaining.

He glanced at his watch. "I'm afraid I can't drag this out any longer. I'm overdue for several phone calls. But I'll expect you back here at five…right?"

She nodded her head slowly. "I'll be here. You can count on it."

Devlyn forced himself to leave the room. If he pushed too

hard, she might decide to walk out, unemployed or not. And he couldn't have that.

He found his father, Vincent, and his Uncle Vic in Victor's study. Pipe smoke hung heavy in the air, and a chessboard sat between their armchairs, resting on a marble-topped table.

His father looked up when he entered. "Don't distract us. This is a hell of a game."

Devlyn took up residence on a sofa adjacent to the fireplace and pulled out his phone to begin working through emails. Soon he was immersed in the day-to-day operation of a global, multibillion dollar company. Some days it baffled him to realize the enormous enterprise he steered on behalf of the family. The responsibility was huge. But damned if he didn't love it.

Finally, the game wound to an end. Uncle Vic stood up and stretched. "I'm not too proud to say I need a nap. Didn't sleep worth crap last night. It's a sad day when a man can't drink coffee at midnight anymore."

Devlyn grinned. The two brothers were peas in a pod, always much alike in outlook, but bound together eternally by the horrific experiences of their young wives' deaths.

Neither had ever considered remarriage as far as Devlyn could tell. They had devoted themselves to rearing their combined six children far away from the limelight. It was a testament to their love and generosity that several of those children had returned to make Wolff Mountain their home.

Devlyn couldn't imagine staying here permanently, but at the moment, he was prepared to make some temporary changes. After his dad refilled his pipe and gave a few puffs that sent aromatic scent into the air, the old man perched on the other end of the divan.

His skin was leathery from years spent in the sun, but his dark eyes were as shrewd and sharp as ever. "What's on your mind, Devvie?"

The childish nickname didn't bother Devlyn. He knew his father respected him as an adult. He grinned. "What would you think if I set up a more permanent office here...for the next six months?"

His dad snorted. "You're up to something. I've seen that look a million times...starting with the first time you took off your diaper and smeared poo on the walls."

Devlyn winced. "For God's sakes, old man. Can we please not share that story? I'm almost thirty-one years old. It's embarrassing."

Vincent shrugged. "You'll always be my kid. Which is why I know you're plotting something. Details, boy. Give this old geezer a treat."

Devlyn's smile was wry. His father had the body of a much younger man. He ate an extremely healthy diet, despite the cigars. He was likely to live for another twenty years.

Devlyn grinned. "I just hired Gillian Carlyle to help us with the school project."

"The housekeeper's daughter?"

For some reason, the tops of Devlyn's ears got hot. "She's a fully certified teacher...comes highly recommended."

"Then why is she free right now?"

"Layoffs. Not her fault."

"Hmph."

"What?" He hadn't anticipated any guff about his decision.

"Are you thinking with your brain or your—"

"Hell, Dad." Devlyn cut him off quickly. "Give me some credit."

"I've seen the woman. She may be a tad more restrained in her clothing choices than your usual women, but there's a quiet beauty about her."

It was a little weird to hear his father say aloud what Devlyn had been thinking. "I'm hiring her for her expertise, not her suitability as a girlfriend."

"Then why move in here?"

Well, crap. The old man hasn't lost it.

"Okay," Devlyn admitted. "I don't hate the idea of getting to know her better. She's a quirky little thing. But we really do need her help. And we know she's not going to steal the silver or sell us out to the tabloids."

The Wolffs had endured their share of sensational gossip-rag stories. And outsiders were always an unknown quantity. Which made Gillian appealing in another way entirely. She was one of them in a sense.

His father stared a hole through him. "Who'll be minding the store in Atlanta?"

"A new kid. Well, new to management. I've been watching him. He's brilliant and driven. He lives for the job. I thought this would be a good opportunity to see what he can do."

"Okay, then. You have my blessing. And you know I'll enjoy having that ugly face of yours around." Vincent Wolff got to his feet. Devlyn rose out of respect and the two of them embraced briefly. It was awkward. Only in recent years had his dad been able to openly express paternal affection.

The past held too many ghosts, too many secrets. But Devlyn was all about the future.

Gillian was happy to find her mother home when she made the trip back down the mountain. The little one-level house where Gillian had grown up was as different from Wolff Castle as bologna from prime rib. But though genteelly shabby and quietly dated, it was home.

Doreen Carlyle embraced her daughter, smelling of Jergens lotion and fresh air. "Aunt Tina says hello. She wants you to go down for a visit while you have some flexibility."

"Welcome home." Gillian hovered as her mother put away three bags of groceries. For several years after Gillian's father died, Doreen had been a wraith, unable to imagine a world without her high-school sweetheart. But gradually she had returned to the world of the living, and Gillian would be forever grateful for her mother's resiliency.

Doreen hummed as she worked, a habit that used to annoy her daughter as a teenager, but now seemed like the most natural thing in the world. Gillian perched on a stool at the counter. "Have you heard anything about the Wolffs building a school here in Burton?"

Her mother paused momentarily, her back to Gillian, and then turned around, with a sheepish expression. "I heard about it for the first time last week, but I didn't want you to get your hopes up. It will be a long time until they are ready to start hiring teachers, honey."

"Devlyn Wolff offered me a job today."

Doreen sat down in a chair, a bag of sugar still clutched in her hands. "How in the world did that happen?"

"It's a long story. We ran into each other last night…I mentioned that I was out of work, and he offered me the job."

Doreen had a keen *mother* radar. "Gillian Elizabeth Carlyle. What have you done?"

"Nothing, Mama. I thought you'd be happy for me."

"Those Wolffs are my bread-and-butter, but I wasn't born yesterday. Devlyn Wolff is a rascal. And a skirt chaser."

"That's not fair. He can't help it if women pursue him because he's rich and gorgeous." Gillian found herself in the strange position of defending the man she had sworn to hold at arm's length.

"So you think he's gorgeous."

Gillian felt her cheeks flush. "I think everybody would agree on that."

"Hmm…" Her mother's assessing gaze appeared to see right through to Gillian's inherent ambivalence. It was thrilling to have a job. And Devlyn Wolff would be a fascinating boss. But the road ahead was booby-trapped with a thousand potential heartbreaks.

"There's one other thing…" She might as well get it over with.

"What?" Doreen's eyebrows rose, projecting alarm.

"He wants me to stay at the castle now and then…when he's there. So I'll be on hand when he has time to deal with the school project."

"Gillian, Gillian, Gillian." Doreen shook her head. "Do you remember that guy who gave you an engagement ring your sophomore year in college?"

"Yes, ma'am."

"I tried to warn you that he was using you."

"And I wouldn't listen." The boy had been far more interested in having Gillian cook for him and do his laundry than anything else. The engagement had lasted a mere four months.

"You're a grown woman now, entirely capable of making your own mistakes. But you're still my baby, and I still worry about you."

Doreen didn't mention the other debacle, and Gillian was grateful. In her first teaching job, the male principal had shown a marked interest in what Gillian thought was *mentoring* her. Unfortunately, the man had a reputation for inappropriate conduct with fresh-out-of-school young women. That situation had ended up with a sexual harassment lawsuit involving half a dozen new teachers.

Gillian had moved on to another school, but she had lost confidence in her ability to spot liars and con men. She didn't really think Devlyn Wolff fell into either category. But he was dangerous in an entirely different way. Devlyn's charm and knee-melting masculinity had the potential to make a female not care that he was leading her down the garden path.

A stint in Devlyn's bed, no matter how brief, might ruin

a woman for other men. That alone should be the cautionary tale to keep Gillian from doing something stupid.

She needed a job. Devlyn was prepared to pay her well for her expertise as an educator. Even if he flirted with her—and it seemed to be an inescapable facet of his personality—there was no way Gillian would allow herself to get sucked into believing that she was any more to him than a convenient warm body.

Surely she had learned her lesson. And Devlyn was an honorable man. He wouldn't pull anything sleazy...she knew that. The real danger was Gillian herself. All else aside, she had to remember that despite political correctness, princes didn't form lasting relationships with scullery maids, at least not in real life.

Gillian needed to meet a man who wanted what she wanted. Home, family, ordinary happiness. If she kept that in mind, all would be well.

Six

Devlyn found himself pacing the foyer at a quarter till five. What if she didn't come? He had rescheduled a late dinner with his investor from the night before, but in the meantime he had just enough of a window to take Gillian to see the land for the school.

The fact that he was anticipating her arrival with such emotion brought him up short. He knew himself fairly well, knew his tendencies to coddle women, to look after them. He'd been doing it with his sister, Annalise, since she was an infant in the cradle. Devlyn had been her protector, her white knight.

But he and his sibling had clashed during her late teenage years. Annalise was headstrong, and at that point in her life didn't take kindly to her brother interfering. Fortunately the two of them had mended fences a long time ago. His sister was one of his best friends.

With other women in his life—at least the ones he was attracted to—he'd never been able to maintain a platonic relationship. He was pretty sure he didn't want Gillian to be the first test case.

The front door opened abruptly, and Gillian burst through. Her expression was not exactly sweetness and light. *Grumpy* might be the word for it.

She set her overnight case on the floor. "Why am I here when you could have picked me up at my house and saved me a trip up the mountain?"

He grinned. "We're going to do an aerial reconnaissance first."

Her face went green. "Um, no. I don't do flying things."

"Come on, Gillian. It will be fun, I swear. And besides, you don't want me to dock your first paycheck already. You're on the clock…remember?"

"I think I may possibly hate you." Her glare might have intimidated another man. Devlyn took it as a challenge.

He laughed out loud, putting a hand beneath her elbow and escorting her out a side door and through the woods up to the helipad. "Climb in," he said cheerfully. Everyone was timid about being in a helicopter at first. But give her a few minutes airborne, seeing the verdant Virginia countryside from an eagle's eye view, and she'd be entranced.

Ten minutes into the flight Gillian had her head inside a barf bag. Losing her lunch…literally. The pitiful moan that reached Devlyn's ears made his stomach curl with guilt. How was he supposed to know she was serious? Did the woman never travel?

He stroked her hair tentatively, wincing every time she retched. "How about some water…that might help."

She shoved his hand away and threw up again.

Devlyn ripped off his headset and scuttled forward to crouch beside the pilot. "Land the damn chopper. Now."

The man looked at him incredulously. They were skimming over a thick forest. "It will be a few minutes."

"As quickly as you can." In the back of his mind lurked the knowledge that he was going to miss another shot at his investor. But circumstances were beyond his control.

Devlyn strapped himself back into his seat and rubbed Gillian's hair. He'd made some dumb-ass mistakes in his life, but this was near the top of his list. Was he destined to make Gillian Carlyle miserable?

After what seemed like hours, but must have been only five minutes or so, the helicopter floated to the ground, landing with a gentle thump in an overgrown field.

The chopper pilot gazed at Devlyn inquiringly. "You want me to wait until she feels better?"

Devlyn glanced at Gillian, who was huddled in her seat, eyes closed, face paper-white. "Not gonna happen. Head back to the castle. Tell them where we are. Send a car for us and a second driver to take both of them back."

While Devlyn helped Gillian out onto steady ground, the pilot gathered up a container of snacks and drinks, a thick canvas tarp lined on one side with reflective material and a another thinner, softer blanket. He stared at Devlyn in confusion. "We traveled as the crow flies, but it's going to be a half hour at least before someone drives here from the castle. Are you sure she'll be okay?"

Devlyn, his eyes on Gillian's wobbly stance, shrugged. "Don't have much choice. I'm not putting her back in that chopper. Hurry, man. As fast as you can."

After waiting for Devlyn and Gillian to move away to a safe distance, the pilot revved up the engine and lifted skyward. The wind wash from the rotors sent Gillian's hair flying in a halo around her head.

Silence fell, and Devlyn spread the tarp rapidly. "Sit down," he commanded. "You look like you're going faint."

"I need my purse," she said, her voice little more than a thread.

He stared down at the giant, black leather tote the pilot had left behind along with the few supplies. "What for?"

"Toothpaste." She swayed, going at least two shades whiter.

He grabbed her just as her knees gave out. "Easy. I've got you."

She curled into a fetal position, and he covered her with the thin fleece blanket. Her arm outstretched, she pointed. "I've got toothpaste in there."

With a sigh for her stubbornness, he rummaged in her things until he located a travel-size toothbrush and toothpaste. She also had hand wipes, baby lotion, tampons, two maps and an assortment of other odd *necessities*.

"Here," he said, holding out what she had asked for.

"Water bottle."

He watched, incredulous, as she scuttled to the edge of the tarp, opened the bottle and proceeded to brush her teeth, spitting into the grass. "I would have thought about kissing you anyway," he said, sitting back on his haunches until she finished.

That made her head whip up, her gaze wary as she wiped her mouth. "Don't be ridiculous. I could sue your family for sexual harassment and drag the Wolff reputation through the dirt." A raw throat made her voice husky.

"But you wouldn't. I know that and you know that. Come here, little schoolmarm. Let me hold you."

It was a testament to her misery that she didn't fight him. The sun was getting low, and the October day was cool and windy. They lay side by side on the tarp. Devlyn spooned her, tucking the blanket over and around them, his arm around her waist.

Gillian's fuzzy lavender sweater and gauzy print skirt in matching shades suited her. Her mostly straight hair tumbled across her face. He nuzzled her cheek with his. "I'm sorry," he said. "I'm going to listen to you from now on."

Her muffled laugh indicated disbelief. He drew her closer. "It's true. I shouldn't have bullied you."

"Why did you hire me?" she asked, the words almost inaudible. "The truth, please."

Where her bottom nestled against the cradle of his thighs, he was hard, aching. Every time he got close to her, his body went on high alert. It was disconcerting as hell. And inexplicable.

"I need an education professional to oversee details that are not my area of expertise."

"And you felt guilty because you were mean to me as a child and I was unemployed."

He stirred uneasily. "Okay…maybe. But that wasn't the primary reason."

"And you've been flirting with me. Explain that."

He concentrated on the pain from a rock that lay somewhere beneath his hip. "I like you," he said, unwilling or unable to expand upon that theme.

"Do you hit on every woman you meet?"

"Only the ones I want to take to bed."

She rolled onto her back without warning, shaded her eyes with one hand and stared at him. "Why me?"

"Why not?"

"That's not an answer."

"I don't have an answer," he growled, wondering why in the hell women had this insatiable need to pick everything apart. "Are you feeling any better?" Perhaps if he distracted her, she would change the subject.

"As long as you don't make me stand up anytime soon, I might live."

"There are lots of things we could do lying down."

"You are such a guy."

"Is that an actual complaint?" He touched her belly, just beneath the swell of her breasts. "I like you, Gillian Carlyle."

Her teeth mutilated her bottom lip. "No offense, but you're not really my type."

"And what is your type?" The scent of her shampoo was making him hungry. They were lying in the middle of some farmer's field, and all he could think about was lifting that fluffy, frilly skirt and taking her wildly.

"I want to get married."

Five simple words blunted his ardor.

"And I want to have children."

He removed his hand. "Is the biological clock that loud?"

She scooted to her side, leaned on an elbow and propped her head on her hand. Now they were facing each other. "It's a fairly normal goal for a woman my age. And you are clearly not a candidate for domestic bliss."

"What's wrong with a little recreational sex in the meantime?"

"You're like a hot fudge sundae," she said, a tiny frown creasing her brow. "They're a great treat on occasion, but if you're going to eat ice cream every day, vanilla is a much better choice. It's easy to get burned out on hot fudge."

"I'm sure such convoluted reasoning makes sense to you, but now all I can think about is licking chocolate sauce off your—"

She put a hand over his mouth. "Behave. You don't really want to do this."

"Oh, but I do." He licked her fingers, and her little *oh* of surprise hit him straight in the gut.

Instead of moving away, she stared at him. And he could swear that somewhere in those deep brown eyes lurked a snippet of interest.

She sighed. "Have you ever had a single serious relationship in your life?"

Perhaps she expected him to lie, but something about Gillian Carlyle made him want to be a better man. Starting with honesty. "No. Not really. And you?"

"A couple of false starts. But at least I believe in the concept."

"You're talking about love."

"Yes. And commitment."

"I'm not domesticated," he said. "I don't need dirty diapers and 3:00 a.m. feedings to be happy."

"But sex can make you happy?"

"I like to live in the moment. The future holds no guarantees. So, yes…on occasion, sex makes me happy."

He had her there. Saw it in her face. He reached out a hand and caressed her cheek.

"I've known you for years, Gillian. But I don't really *know* you. I'd like to change that."

"Why are you doing this?"

He'd never had a woman question his motives so deeply. "I'm not really sure. I've learned to rely on my instincts, though. They've served me well in business."

"And in your personal life?"

He shrugged. "I've made a misstep here and there. But don't we all when it comes to sex?"

"Not all of us take the smorgasbord approach. I've been with two men in my life, Devlyn. Can you even count yours with both hands and feet?"

"I don't sleep with men."

"Don't be a smart-ass. You know what I mean."

He should be angry. No other person of his acquaintance, male or female, would have the balls to cross-examine him about his sex life. But somehow he felt obligated to give Gillian the unvarnished truth. "It's complicated."

"I'm a smart woman."

Her steady gaze studied him and found him wanting. He rolled to his back and tucked his hands behind his head. The

October sky was so blue, it seemed unreal. At the far edge of the field a row of sugar maples flamed, red and orange, against an azure backdrop.

"You know that my father and my uncle didn't allow any of us to go to school."

"Yes."

"We were scarcely allowed off the property...and then only with bodyguards. For a horny teenage guy, it was hell. I dreamed about girls all the time."

"It must have been a strange sort of adolescence."

He laughed without amusement. "You could say that. The only way we were allowed to go away to college was if we used assumed names and swore never to tell a soul who we really were."

"I imagine that created a lot of difficult situations."

"Yeah. Ask Kieran sometime what it did to him. But anyway, I had decided that as soon as I got on campus I was going to screw the first girl who gave me a chance."

"And did you?"

His throat tight, he debated what he was about to say. No one knew this, not even his brother and sister. He couldn't look at Gillian, so he stared up at the sky.

Finally, he stumbled over the first few words. "The summer before I left home, my dad and Uncle Vic hired a husband/wife team to update the landscaping at the castle. The new employees were both in their early thirties, a young couple trying to run their own business and make a living. The woman was beautiful. And since she was working outside in the heat, she wore little shorts and halter tops..."

He swallowed, still able to see her even now. "I was obsessed with watching her. One day I was up in my bedroom with the window open. I heard the two of them arguing. And I saw him backhand her so hard she fell to her knees."

"Oh, Devlyn..."

"I flew down the stairs, ran outside, but he had disappeared. I really believe that if he had still been there I would have beaten him up. Hitting a woman... God, even I, green as I was, knew it was wrong."

"What did you do?"

"She was crying, almost hysterical. I tried to talk to her, but she was embarrassed. There was a big red mark on her cheek, and she didn't want anyone to see. I suggested taking a walk in the woods so she could calm down."

"And she agreed?"

"Yes. We were gone for a long time. I showed her the cave. I was so proud to be able to help her. I could tell that she was happy I was with her. We sat down near the entrance, you know, just cross-legged in the dirt. She told me that she was going to divorce him...that it wasn't the first time he had hit her. But she was worried about money. I don't know what made me do it, but I put my arm around her and told her that I would help her."

He felt Gillian's hand on his shoulder. "You don't have to tell me this," she whispered.

It was too late to stop now. Reliving it all made his stomach hurt. "I know I was naive, but I told her I had money of my own. In my room. That it wouldn't be a loan. She could have it, no questions asked."

"What did she say?"

"She started crying again. And then she kissed me."

Seven

Shock and distress left Gillian almost speechless. She was pretty sure she knew where this story was heading, and her heart bled for Devlyn.

He kept talking, almost as if he had forgotten she was beside him. "I didn't know what to do. It was weird and awkward and wonderful all at the same time. But she was married. And I knew that."

"She took advantage of you, Devlyn."

"Who's to say? I didn't waste much time weighing right and wrong. We undressed and then we…well, you know."

He fell silent. Gillian felt somehow as if the world had shifted on its axis. She didn't know Devlyn at all, not really. Except to understand that he had a streak of caring that ran soul deep when it came to women. He was a protector, a slightly tarnished, but decent knight.

"What happened afterward?"

"She stayed there while I ran back to the house and got the

money. I'd been doing odd jobs around the house for years, saving up to buy a car for college. My dad believed implicitly that young men should work for what they wanted."

"And it wasn't in the bank?"

"Our house was a fortress. I kept my earnings in a small wall safe in my bedroom."

"How much?" Gillian asked.

"I went back and handed her seven thousand dollars in cash."

"Please tell me she didn't take it."

His mouth was grim. "Oh, yes. She took it. And I never saw either her or her husband again."

"Do you think they deliberately set you up?"

"I don't know for sure. I've thought about it a million times over the years. I think it just happened. And with the money in hand, they took off. It's possible she even stayed with him."

A hint of nausea returned. Gillian knew without Devlyn saying the words that his first sexual experience had been tainted with guilt because of the woman's marital status. He had been seduced, plain and simple. Even if it truly was a spontaneous act on the woman's part, it was a terrible thing to do to a young boy.

"So what happened when you went off to college?"

A long silence ensued. Then Devlyn sighed. "Honest to God? I was scared. It occurred to me that I hadn't used a condom. So disease was a possibility. And there was even a chance that I had fathered a child. For months I lived in fear that she would show up on my doorstep."

Gillian scooted closer and wrapped an arm across his chest. "I'm so sorry. She took your innocence."

"Yeah, but what eighteen-year-old guy wants to be innocent?"

The words were flip, but she could hear the hurt that lingered, even now, more than a decade later. "But you found a girlfriend eventually?"

"Not a girlfriend. More like a series of one-night stands, mostly after keg parties." He covered her hand with his. "I was smart enough to use protection every time, but that was about the only bit of intelligence I exhibited. I lost count of how many girls I screwed the next two years."

Gillian didn't know what to say. He wasn't the only guy to sleep his way through college. But she sensed that the experience was a dark spot in his soul. Or he wouldn't be telling her in such detail. "You said two years...what happened after that?"

"I wised up...woke up one day in some dorm room I didn't recognize, and I realized that I'd had enough. Three months later, I met Tammi."

"Tammi?" He had said her name with affection.

"We met in an upper-level business class. I was doing advanced work. Tammi was a senior. The professor assigned a project and made us partners."

"And you fell in love with her."

Devlyn's chest rose and fell as he laughed. "Who's telling this story? You, or me? No, I didn't fall in love. But for the first time in my life, I had a female friend. It was novel, but nice. Tammi helped straighten out my head a little bit."

"Did you ever sleep with her?"

"Once, right before she graduated. But there were no fireworks. It was a bittersweet goodbye, nothing more than that. I hear from her now and again. She's a stay-at-home mom with three kids."

The little lick of jealousy Gillian experienced was unfounded, but real. And at that moment she realized the danger Devlyn represented. Already he had disarmed her with his painfully frank recitation. She wanted to hold him, to make up for the past.

But Devlyn Wolff was a grown man. And he didn't need Gillian's sympathy. What he wanted…apparently…was a convenient affair.

She got to her feet, wobbling only slightly. "Shouldn't the car be here by now?"

Devlyn stood as well, frowning. "That's all you're going to say? After I poured my heart out to you?"

She wrapped her arms around her waist, her stomach clenching with faint memories of her gastric distress. "You're trying to convince me that it would be fun to fool around while I'm working with you."

"Did I succeed?" That wicked, flashing grin was back.

"I'll consider it. You're a handsome man with a quirky sense of humor. And I'll be living in a town where the pool of eligible men is almost nonexistent. So maybe. But don't push. My mother works for your family. I'm not sure how I feel about that. Give me time to think about it."

"Fair enough." He smoothed her hair from her face, making her pulse stumble. "How about a kiss…just one…so we can test the waters."

"I'm not kissing you after I puked my guts out. That's not the kind of first impression a woman wants to make."

"Believe me. Guys aren't that picky. But in honor of your meticulous hygiene, how about I avoid your mouth?"

She took a step backward. "No." Devlyn Wolff touching her anywhere seemed like a really bad idea.

He circled her wrist with one big hand, his thumb on her pulse. "Relax, Gillian. I can't do anything to you out here in the open."

But that was a lie. He reeled her in, not stopping until her breasts were against his chest. She could either crane her neck to see his expression or rest her cheek on warm, starchy cotton that smelled like Devlyn. It was no choice at all.

Their heights were a good match. She fit nicely in his embrace. "Go ahead and do it," she said. "You're making me nervous."

He laughed. "Whatever the lady wants."

Nudging her head to one side, he nibbled his way from her ear to her shoulder. Gooseflesh erupted everywhere his teeth grazed her sensitive skin. When her knees began to tremble, her arms went around his neck for support.

Then it was no problem at all to return the naughty love bites Devlyn was inflicting. But when the tip of her tongue traced his throat at the opening of his shirt, he released her abruptly and staggered backward several steps.

He held out his hand. "I think we'll call that experiment a success." His cheeks were ruddy and his chest heaved.

In the distance a car horn tooted.

"Is that our ride?" Gillian turned, not sure if she was relieved or disappointed.

Two dark SUVs pulled up at the edge of the field. There was not much of a shoulder, so the vehicles were partway in the road.

Devlyn started grabbing up stuff. "C'mon. Let's not keep them waiting."

They tramped across the field rapidly, but Gillian held back when Devlyn chatted with the drivers. The sun was very low, casting lengthy shadows across the land. Would Devlyn still want to show her the property after dark? Surely not.

He turned and motioned. "I can send you back up the mountain with the guys, but if you feel like it, I'd like you to join me for dinner with an investor. I stood him up last night after you played pinball with that tree."

"I'll go back to the house." *And do what?* she wondered. Staying at the castle was really an awkward arrangement. Perhaps she could get her mom to come pick her up for the evening or ask one of Devlyn's drivers to take her directly to her mother's.

Devlyn frowned, evidently not hearing the answer he wanted. "Come with me," he cajoled. "He was really angry when I didn't show. You'll be proof that my Boy Scout good deed was the right thing to do. And besides…you're on the clock, remember?"

"That's not fair."

He grinned and opened the passenger door of the car he was preparing to drive, motioning for her to get in. "Dinner's on me."

She shook her head in mock disgust. "You must have been spoiled rotten as a kid."

His smile dimmed. "Let's just say that I like getting what I want."

She slid in beside him, conscious that her only hope of escape was driving away in the opposite direction. "And so do I. So one of us is doomed to disappointment."

Devlyn drove in silence, rethinking his strategy with Gillian. Perhaps having her at the castle wasn't the best idea. His family would be bound to notice if he started having sleepovers. And Gillian's mother was not likely to appreciate the son of her employer hanging around.

Life would be a lot easier if he could simply spirit Gillian away to his multimillion-dollar rooftop condo in Atlanta. But the job he had hired her to do was real. And needed to be done in and around Burton. Which meant that if Devlyn wanted to explore this surprising and compelling physical attraction, he was going to have to stay on the mountain much longer than he had originally intended.

He'd never had much respect for entrepreneurs who allowed pleasure to get in the way of business. But damned if Devlyn hadn't just entangled the two without the slightest bit of regret.

They pulled up in front of the restaurant in Charlottesville with five minutes to spare. Gillian fussed with her hair. "I'm not really dressed for a place like this."

"Don't worry," he said, handing his keys to the valet. "It's pretty dark inside."

"Very funny."

Horatio Clement was already seated. The man was a long-time family friend, at least a decade older than Victor and Vincent. He was a bachelor, had a stock portfolio that would make Bill Gates weep and was as tightfisted as Scrooge.

Devlyn's job was to cajole him into loosening the purse strings long enough to invest a healthy chunk of cash into Wolff Enterprises' latest expansion...a brand-new headquarters in Mexico City. With locations already on the West Coast and in London and Paris, the Wolffs owned a sizable chunk of real estate...high-tech offices that oversaw a multitude of interests from railroads to television stations to manufacturing.

Devlyn put his hand at Gillian's back, ushering her forward. "Hello, Horatio," he said. "I was hoping you wouldn't mind some feminine company this evening."

Horatio's bushy white eyebrows lifted. "Not your usual style, is she, Devvie boy?" He turned toward Gillian. "What's your name, girl?"

She shook his bony hand. "Gillian Carlyle. And you've hit the nail on the head, sir. I'm definitely not his type. But he's feeling guilty for running me off the road last night. That's why he missed your dinner appointment."

Devlyn ground his teeth. "I did *not* run you off the road. You were going way too fast."

Horatio snorted. "I've seen you drive, kid. I choose to believe this nice young woman."

Devlyn had no choice but to sit down and nurse his wounds. Before he could get the ball rolling, Gillian and Horatio were thick as thieves, the old man spinning one outrageous tale after the other, and Gillian egging him on with her contagious laughter.

It was going to be a long night.

Eight

Gillian hadn't expected to enjoy dinner, but Horatio was a darling. He had a snap in his eyes and a tart, wry humor that kept her on the verge of laughter as they dined on filet mignon, baby asparagus and giant, fluffy baked potatoes.

Devlyn spoke little, his expression hard to read. At one point, she stood and excused herself. "I know you gentlemen have business to discuss. I'm going to visit the ladies' room and then call and check on my mother."

When she returned five minutes later, Devlyn's face was a thundercloud, and Horatio had his arms crossed over his chest. The older of the two waved at Gillian. "I have some questions for you, young lady. Would you do business with him if you were me?"

Gillian hesitated. "I don't know all that much about finances…but I do know that Devlyn has a brilliant financial mind. Why else would his father and his uncle give him control of the company at his young age? My guess is that your investment will grow rapidly."

"Or it will disappear like smoke in the wind if this damned economy gets any worse."

"You can't take it with you, sir."

Devlyn froze. Had Gillian really said that?

For a split second nobody moved. Then Horatio threw back his head and roared with laughter. "This one's a pistol, Devvie. You'd better hang on to her."

Devlyn, accustomed to smooth-talking his way out of any situation, didn't know what to say.

Gillian stepped in like a seasoned negotiator. "With all that money you're going to make, I have a proposition for you."

Horatio eyed her sadly. "The doc says my ticker isn't strong enough to take those little blue pills. But I'm flattered, darlin'."

Gillian actually blushed. "Behave yourself. I'll bet you were a lot like Devlyn when you were his age. You loved the challenge of besting an opponent…the adrenaline rush. But that doesn't mean you have to walk away from the table. Say yes, Horatio. You know you want to."

The old man took a sip of his seventy-five-dollar bottle of wine. He stared at Devlyn. "I'll give you every cent I've got if I can have your little woman."

Devlyn scowled. "Not for sale, sir. And FYI, that request is politically incorrect."

"I'm eighty-six years old. I can say whatever the hell I want." But he patted Gillian's hand. "Sorry, sweetheart. No disrespect intended. You'll forgive an old man, won't you?"

She squeezed his gnarled fingers. "Of course. Now do you want to hear my proposition or not?"

His eyes twinkled. "Go for it."

"I don't know if you've heard, but the Wolff family is giving our little town of Burton an elementary school, K–8. We've never had one, and our children, even the youngest ones, have to ride the bus a long way every morning and afternoon. Why don't you donate several hundred thousand dollars toward the project, and we'll name the school after you."

She shot a worried look at Devlyn. "Can we do that?"

He sighed, fully aware that his business meeting had gotten entirely out of hand. "Sure. But he's supposed to be giving *me* money, not you."

Gillian waved a hand. "There's plenty to go around. Now be honest, Horatio. Wouldn't you like to leave behind a legacy that will benefit hundreds of children, maybe thousands in the long run? And you can be a consultant."

"Now wait a minute." Devlyn felt a noose tightening around his neck. It was happening again. He tried to help a woman in need, and suddenly his life was flying out of control. "I just hired *you*," he said, pointing at Gillian. "I can't afford another employee."

Horatio grinned, enjoying Devlyn's discomfiture. "I'll work for a dollar a day...and dinner once a week with Gillian. Alone."

"Five dollars a day, and no hanky-panky with my girlfriend."

Gillian's lips pursed. "I'm not your girlfriend. Office relationships seldom work out."

"We don't have an office...unless you want to go to Atlanta with me."

"Too far. I suppose I'll simply have to make do. Thank you, Mr. Clement. I think we have a deal. But you and Devlyn still have to agree on the Mexico thing."

Horatio shook his head. "It's a sad day when a grown man has to bring in a female to help shake down an old man. I'll be lucky to have enough left to pay for a nursing home."

Gillian's face fell. "I certainly don't expect you to jeopardize your own health and well-being, Horatio. I was presumptuous about the school. Close the deal with Devlyn. Don't worry about anything else."

Devlyn sighed. "He's kidding, Gillian. This *poor old man* could buy the state of Virginia if it was for sale. Don't waste time worrying about him."

Gillian glared. "Show some respect to your elders."

Horatio hopped into the conversation. "Yeah, Devlyn. Kiss my as—"

Gillian held up a hand. "Enough. Both of you are acting like children. Sign the darned papers and let's be done with this."

"We don't have any papers here," Devlyn said. "This is a gentleman's agreement, right, Horatio?"

Horatio stuck out his hand. "Let's get it over with, boy. Before she nags us to death. That's why women are no good in business."

Devlyn and Gillian groaned in unison.

Horatio managed to look innocent. "What did I say?"

Devlyn shook his adversary's hand and waved at the waiter for the check. "You're a scoundrel and a crook. But thank you, Horatio. You won't regret this."

Gillian learned a lot about Devlyn that evening. He could have conducted the same meeting at a boring office in thirty minutes. But instead, he'd taken the time to wine and dine a lonely octogenarian. And unless Gillian was mistaken, Devlyn enjoyed the mock battle as much as Horatio did.

In the car on the way back to the castle, a hushed silence reigned. Gillian didn't want to sleep under Devlyn Wolff's roof. And did he expect her to occupy the same suite as last night? The one with the connecting door to his room?

Perhaps agreeing to work with him had been a bad idea, but what choice did she have? It went against the grain to mooch off her hardworking mother, and any openings at area schools would likely only become available at the end of the year.

"How long have you known Horatio?" she asked, uneasy about Devlyn's mood. He was gregarious to a fault, so now that he was sober and quiet, she had to wonder what he was thinking.

He shot her a sideways glance, his gaze trained on the road ahead. "My earliest memory of Horatio comes from my fifth birthday party. He gave me a pony. Told me that a boy my age should learn how to ride a horse. I was petrified and determined not to show it. Horatio drove up the mountain once a week for six months until he was sure I could handle riding without getting hurt."

"He must love you very much."

"Yeah…beneath that crusty exterior, he's a teddy bear. But only in his personal life. He raised hell when he was still working."

"Did he ever have a family of his own?"

"He was married…when he was very young. My dad told me Horatio's wife died in childbirth. The two men had that in common, the loss of a spouse. I think that's why they became friends outside of the business setting. Horatio never found anyone else he could love like he loved his wife, so he's been on his own ever since."

"That seems so sad."

"He's not a hermit or a miser. He lives life. But he keeps her memory as a shrine."

"And your father…I know he and your uncle never remarried, but did they date at all…or have women friends?"

"If they did, I never knew it. They devoted themselves to my siblings, my cousins and me, to our safety, our education, our happiness. It wasn't always a smooth road. Dad and Uncle Vic suffered in the aftermath of the tragedy. In ways I was too young to understand. But they were determined that no harm would come to us."

"You were a lucky child."

"Indeed."

Despite the fact that he agreed with her, some intonation in his voice suggested bleak irony. She'd been around enough to witness his privileged lifestyle. And despite the constraints of being held a virtual captive on his mountain, it was still pretty great. The affairs of the Wolffs were generally known in Burton, but were there secrets to which she wasn't privy? "So what about you, Devlyn? Your cousins have started getting married. Will you be next?"

"Is that an offer?"

"Don't flatter yourself. You're way too bossy and stubborn."

"Pot. Kettle."

"I'll give you that one. We do share a few similar traits. But I have no desire to conquer the world one stock option at a time. I like what I do…being a teacher, I mean."

"Some people can't imagine shutting themselves up in a room for six or seven hours every day with twenty-five kids."

"I love them," she said simply. "And I love knowing that what I'm doing makes a real difference."

"And what about your personal life?"

"I already told you. I'll get married, I hope. I'd love to have a big family, maybe three or four kids. What about you? Tell me about your ideal woman."

"She's meek, brings me my slippers and agrees with everything I say."

Gillian laughed. "It's amazing you manage to get any female companionship at all. Of course the money and your looks account for some of it."

"I'm flattered."

"Don't be. Those are both negatives in my book."

"Says the woman who was unemployed just yesterday."

"Wow. You don't mind hitting below the belt."

"You're the one who said I'm not worth chasing."

"I said you weren't *husband* material. No woman wants a guy who's going to get hit on by all the PTA and soccer moms."

"Was there actually a compliment buried in there somewhere?"

They reached the bottom of the mountain and passed through the security gates. Gillian felt a squiggle of panic as they slid shut behind them. No way out…

"I'll be the first to admit that you're handsome and charming and probably the life of the party."

"But…?"

"I think I'm more suited to a nine-to-five banker with thinning hair."

He negotiated a hairpin curve with ease. "Should I feel threatened? Have you met this paragon of boredom?"

"Not yet. But I have a little time. You still haven't answered my question. When do *you* plan to marry and settle down?"

It was too dark now to see his expression. Tall trees flanked the road, blocking any ambient light.

"I don't. The business is my baby. My entire family trusts me to keep Wolff Enterprises profitable. It's an all-consuming job. I'd be a lousy husband and father."

His words were brusque, the tone flat. Something odd ran beneath the surface.

"Busy people get married all the time and raise families. Don't you want to carry on the Wolff name?"

"I have one brother and three cousins to do that. Drop it, Gillian."

She subsided into silence, disturbed by the notion that his vehement repudiation of marriage and fatherhood was something more than a bachelor's off-the-cuff aversion to commitment. But he'd made it clear that the topic wasn't open for discussion.

They pulled up beneath a stone portico and an employee took the vehicle away to be parked in one of the garages behind and below the main house. Gillian stood uncertainly, feeling a return of her earlier misgivings. She and Devlyn had not defined their working relationship. And for someone who planned her classroom activities to the minute, the lack of structure was extremely uncomfortable.

He shepherded her inside, leading her without words toward a part of the house she hadn't seen in years. "I want to show you something," he said. "Maybe it will help you understand why I want you to work with me on the school."

The room they entered was lined with file cabinets and a series of wall safes. Along another long expanse, a sophisticated computer setup blinked lazily. Devlyn went to one of the safes in the middle, punched in a code and opened the small metal door. Removing a box, he motioned for her to sit.

The room was not meant for relaxation. Her only option was one of two straight-backed office chairs. She perched there and stared at him. "What is it?"

His face impassive, he extracted a small item and handed it to her. Her stomach turned over. It was a child's clumsy attempt at a greeting card, at least a quarter of a century old. The edges of the paper were ragged with age.

She bit her lips, opening the missive carefully. As if it were yesterday, she remembered sitting at the kitchen table in her house, laboring over the complicated series of letters. "You kept this? But you were so angry."

He sat beside her. "After you left that day, I took it home. For some reason, I found comfort in it. I never showed it to anyone. I didn't want to be teased. You think I offered you a job because you needed one. And I did. It's serendipitous that someone with your skills and know-how is available to help us with the school. But most of all I wanted to say thank you."

"You don't owe me anything, Devlyn. My mother probably made me do that card for you."

"Doesn't matter. The point is that you reached out to me, and even though it's a bit overdue, I want you to know how much I appreciated it…still do, as a matter of fact."

He slid a hand beneath her hair, cupping her neck. "I know all the reasons we shouldn't get involved. You have weird hang-ups about your mother working here. I'm not a man who will give you babies and a minivan…and we face an appalling lack of privacy for what I have in mind. But fate has brought you back into my life, and I want you." He bent his head and found her lips in a warm, insistent, teasing kiss.

She tried to say his name, but he took her breath with his irresistible, coaxing mouth.

"Give me a chance, Gillian," he muttered. "Give *us* a chance."

Nine

Devlyn was pushing her. He knew it. And it wasn't his MO at all. He'd never had problems getting women. Much of the time, he had to shoo them away.

But Gillian did something to him. Perhaps it was because she had known him as a boy, had witnessed and understood most of the ins and outs of his life. The ups and downs. When he was with her he experienced a feeling of nostalgia, of peace.

When her lips moved beneath his, responding hesitantly, peace was the last thing on his mind. He groaned, deepening the kiss without conscious thought, plumbing the sweet depths of her mouth with his tongue, sinking his teeth into her bottom lip.

The position was awkward, both of them side by side in hard chairs. And the door was unlocked. All these realities flitted through his brain, even as his erection hardened painfully. "Come to my room," he muttered. "Please."

Gillian didn't say anything, perhaps because he wasn't allowing her to come up for air. Again and again he kissed her, his heart pounding and his head swimming. He was reaching the point of no return when Gillian put a hand on his chest.

"We have to stop, Devlyn. This isn't the place."

Even if the words were hoarse, they still had that schoolmarm tone that for some inexplicable reason turned him on. "That's why we're going to my room. Or hell, yours. I don't care." He cupped one breast in his fingers. Barely a handful. And yet the rush of tenderness that overwhelmed him only made him want her more.

She whimpered and pressed nearer, sending a rush of excitement like a tidal wave through his chest. Gillian wanted him. No doubt about it. But when he put his hand under her sweater, feeling the silk of bare skin, she shoved him away. "Enough."

It was sufficient to shock him back to his senses. The sound of voices in the hall made him curse. "I'm sorry. You make me crazy."

She cocked her head, straightening her hair with hands that trembled. "Why? I've seen pictures of the women you date… in society columns, in magazines, online. They're all tall and blonde and medically enhanced in the bosom."

"No one says bosom anymore."

"Answer me," she said.

It was the trace of hurt in her eyes that did him in. He rubbed his thumb over her bottom lip, its plump curve still damp from his kisses. "Aw, hell, Gillian. You've got something none of them have."

"What?" The vulnerability in her gaze belied the air of confidence that he usually saw in her.

He shrugged. "You belong here. You're part of Wolff Mountain. And that makes me feel…" He stumbled to a halt, not even sure what he was talking about.

At that moment, the door opened and Devlyn's father walked in. "I wondered where you were. How was the dinner? Did Horatio jerk you around?"

Devlyn rose, pulling Gillian to her feet as well, hoping he had his body under control. "He tried. Dad...this is Doreen Carlyle's daughter, Gillian. I'm sure you remember her. She used to spend time here when her mom was working."

Vincent Wolff was no fool. He stepped forward, hand outstretched. "Glad to see you, Gillian. I suppose you know that your mother is a valuable part of our staff."

"Thank you, sir. It's nice to see you again."

Vincent's gaze went from Gillian to his son and back again. Devlyn was pretty sure his father realized what he had interrupted, but he didn't do anything to embarrass Gillian.

"Did you need something, Dad?"

Vincent nodded. "I do. We need to talk about a labor issue I just got wind of in France. But it can wait."

Gillian slid past Devlyn toward the door. "You two go ahead. It's been a long day, and I think I'll go to my room. I assume it's the same one."

Devlyn tried to communicate his displeasure, but she was looking at his father. "Gillian, I'll bring you up-to-date on the school plan in the morning. Nine o'clock sharp."

She gave him a cool stare, one designed to put him in his place. "Yes, sir. I'll be there."

When the door closed, leaving Devlyn and his father alone, Vincent Wolff eyed his son with a gaze that revealed little of what he was thinking. Devlyn turned his back, feigning nonchalance, and scooped up the childish note as if it were nothing important. When he had returned it to the safe, he faced his father once again.

"What's the deal with Paris? I talked to the head of Human Resources last week and everything sounded fine."

"Forget about Paris. I want to know why that girl was here overnight."

Devlyn tensed, unused to being on the defensive with his father. As a rule, they got along really well. "She wrecked her car. Her mother was out of town. I thought she should stay until morning in case she had any residual effects."

"And how does that explain why I saw her suitcase a moment ago in one of our most beautiful guest suites, the one that happens to connect with yours?"

"I told you. I hired her. And I thought it would be more efficient to have her on-site since I'm juggling the Atlanta office, as well."

"You told me *you* were going to move in, not her. I've seen that look in your eyes," his father said quietly. "Gillian Carlyle is not one of your high-class, couture-clad socialites. She's a bright, levelheaded woman, but she's no match for you."

"You don't understand."

"So explain it to me."

"I like her."

"And?"

"And nothing."

"You're well beyond needing my approval of your bed partners, if you ever did. But I'm telling you right now. Don't mess with Gillian. All ethical considerations aside, your behavior could open us up to a lawsuit since her mother is on staff. It's too messy. Find someone else to entertain you while you're here."

"Nothing is going on."

"I saw your face when I opened the door. You want her. But you can't have her."

"That's between Gillian and me."

His father sat down in a chair, his face marked with fatigue. The sudden change in expression alarmed Devlyn. "You okay, Dad? Is it your heart?"

Vincent closed his eyes and inhaled, holding his breath for several seconds before releasing the air.

"It's not my heart. This chorus line of girlfriends you juggle is never going to change until you face the truth. We need to talk about your mother, Devvie."

Devlyn turned to stone, his heart still beating, but every muscle and sinew in his body rigid with emotional agony. "No, we don't. Not today. Not ever."

"I swear I didn't know, Devvie. Not until long after she was gone. I was working crazy hours, making money like a madman, and I missed what was happening under my nose. I'm so sorry, son."

Devlyn's lungs screamed for air. His legs barely supported him. Unwittingly, his father had resurrected Devlyn's own fears. Devlyn wasn't worthy of a relationship with a decent woman like Gillian. He was damaged goods. "It's in the past. Forget it." Wheeling around like a cornered animal, he bolted through the door.

Gillian unpacked her small suitcase and put her things in an antique bureau lined with delicate tissue scented with lilacs. The fragrance reminded her of the large bushes that bloomed alongside the castle driveway in spring.

After a phone call to her mother and another one to her closest teacher friend in Charlottesville, she found herself at loose ends. The flat-screen TV in the armoire held little interest, and the book she'd brought with her had hit a dull spot.

And then it came to her…she could revisit the library. Surely it would be empty at this time of night, and she remembered the way there, so she could hopefully go unnoticed.

She changed into soft, faded jeans and a long-sleeve cashmere blend sweater. Wearing thick, warm socks, she padded shoeless down the halls and through the corridors until she came to the room where she had spent so many happy times as a child.

The distinctive aroma of old books and pipe smoke drifted out as she hovered on the threshold. Smiling with delight, she slipped inside and quietly closed the door. With Devlyn, earlier, she'd been too on edge to enjoy her surroundings. Now she absorbed it all. Nothing had changed. With a little imagination, she could see herself at seven or eight, curled up in the window seat reading *Winnie-the-Pooh* or *The Secret Garden*.

She had been an excellent student, but shy and with few friends. Most of the kids in her grade lived in populated areas some distance from Burton. Gillian had always felt the sting of being different. As an only child, she didn't even have siblings for playmates.

Tiptoeing to avoid detection, she browsed the shelves. Someone had left a dim light burning, so there was just enough illumination to read titles. She stroked her hand over the leather spines. Victor and Vincent Wolff had amassed an incredible collection over the years. Art. Biography. Philosophy. History. A broad array of fiction. And of course, business. But it was the juvenile books that caught her eye. Several of them she vividly remembered reading...*The Velveteen Rabbit*. *Adventures of Huckleberry Finn*. *Little Women*.

On those times when Gillian had dug in her heels and refused to go to the castle after her encounter with Devlyn, Doreen had sometimes found a sitter, a neighbor, a friend. But she always brought home an armful of stories to be devoured and later returned.

Little Gillian adored books. Grown-up Gillian was equally enchanted. She found a worn copy of *Charlotte's Web* and took it with her to a burgundy, velvet-covered sofa flanking the empty fireplace. She would have preferred the cushioned window seat, but she wasn't willing to turn on anything brighter than the small lamp with the Tiffany shade that sat on a piecrust table at her elbow.

She loved the lamp. The mauves and greens and blues of the dragonflies almost seemed to glow. Settling into the cushions with a sigh of happiness, she began turning pages.

Devlyn wanted to run. He did, in fact, plunge into the forest and stumble as fast as his legs would take him down one of the many trails that crisscrossed the mountaintop. He thought about climbing in his car and driving fast as hell back to the anonymity of Atlanta where he was the boss and no one dared cross him. Where he could hide out in his sleek, impersonally decorated condo and forget about things he'd worked a lifetime not to remember.

But what would he do about Gillian? Send her down the mountain with no explanation? In the dark?

Damn it.

A rogue branch snagged his shoulder, ripping his shirt. The pain snapped him out of his downward spiral. He leaned against a huge tree, bent forward at the waist and bowed his head, hands on his knees, gasping for air.

All he could think about was seeing her...seeing Gillian. He gave himself a few minutes to regain his equilibrium, to put the monster back in the box. Nothing had happened. Nothing had changed. His dad might suspect, but no one knew for sure what demons lurked inside him. His defenses were intact. There was no reason for alarm. Slowly, he made his way back to the house.

Finding her room empty was a shock. The door to the hallway stood ajar a couple of inches. "Gillian?" He called her name several times, loud enough for her to hear if she was in the bathroom. But no answer. Where was she?

It took him thirty minutes to find her, his impatience increasing exponentially with every tick of the clock. He knew the huge, sprawling house from cellar to attic. His first guess was the warm, comfy kitchen…then the twenty-seat movie theater…finally the exercise room.

As he stood in the front foyer, grinding his teeth in frustration, suddenly it came to him. Little Gillian Carlyle spent many hours in one particular room. The library. He couldn't believe he hadn't thought of it before now.

When he got there, out of breath from his sudden sprint, the door was firmly shut. Was he wrong? Hoping not to startle her if she was inside, he gently turned the knob.

Shadows filled the room. The walls were lined with shelves that reached the ceiling. Many a time he had sailed one way and another on the moving staircase, despite remonstrations from his father. But less pleasant memories intruded.

This was also the room where he and his siblings and cousins had been given their lessons. Not allowed to attend regular schools because of the fear of kidnapping, all six children had been instructed in this room by a series of tutors…even in the summer. Victor and Vincent Wolff had high expectations for their offspring.

The worst times were the sunny, warm days. The pleasant library had become a prison. For a boy with energy to burn and an insatiable curiosity, having to finish lessons when the world outside beckoned had been little less than torture.

He shook off the memories and eyed his reason for coming. Gillian was asleep on the love seat, sitting up, her legs propped on a low coffee table. She had been reading. A book lay open in her hands, but her head had fallen to one side, her mouth curved in a faint smile.

Carefully, he sat down beside her and eased her into a reclining position, her head in his lap. She murmured something in her sleep, but didn't wake. A bruise on her cheekbone reminded him that she was surely still stiff and sore from the accident.

For a fleeting second he imagined what it would have been like had he found her dead in that car. The possibility chilled his blood. He would never have had a chance to apologize, but even worse than that, he could never have known the adult Gillian, with her prickly ways and her quiet charm.

Gently, he stroked her hair, fingers skimming now and again over the bruise. It troubled him, marring her creamy skin and reminding him that life was fleeting. God knew he and his family had learned that lesson the hard way. Because of the shared tragedy, over the years the Wolff clan had grown ever closer, a bulwark for each other against those who would seek to destroy them.

Gillian stirred and stretched. Then she froze when she realized where she was…and with whom. "Devlyn?"

"Never try to hide from a Wolff," he said, teasing her. "I'll always find you."

Ten

Gillian realized several things simultaneously. Devlyn's hand was under her sweater. She hadn't put on a bra when she'd changed clothes. And his fingers were tracing her ribs one at a time, higher and higher.

"I thought you were talking to your dad." The words came out on an embarrassing squeak.

His chest rose and fell on a sigh. "I was. We're done."

"He doesn't want me here, does he?"

"No. But not for the reasons you think."

Her stomach curled in embarrassment. "I'll go in the morning."

"No, you won't. We have work to do."

"The house belongs to your father and uncle. You're only visiting. It's not really your place to invite me to move in."

"It's my home, too. And besides, Dad's reservations would still exist even if you were staying at your mother's house."

"So he doesn't think I'm qualified to help with the new

school, is that it?" She'd suspected the job seemed too good to be true. And maybe it was. She didn't want to be beholden to the Wolffs. If her services weren't needed, she should go.

When she tried to sit up, Devlyn stopped her by the simple expedient of holding his large hand, fingers splayed, against her belly. "My dad trusts me to hire competent people."

"But?"

"He's worried that I'll seduce you and break your heart."

Vincent Wolff was astute. Even now, Gillian's emotions were dangerously involved. She looked into Devlyn's eyes and saw past the sophisticated man to the faint remnants of a vulnerable boy. Everything inside her strained toward him, ached to assuage his hurt and his guilt. Despite recognizing the risks, Gillian acknowledged in that one fraught moment that she wanted to become Devlyn's lover, for as long as it lasted.

Did that make her a bad person? Or even worse, hopelessly naive? "What did you tell him?"

"I said it was between us."

Devlyn had worn dress slacks to the meeting with Horatio. Unlike Gillian, he'd not taken the time to change. Beside her cheek, beneath the thin fabric, his sex was swollen, hard. If Gillian turned her head, her lips would be able to caress the length of him.

She had come to the moment of truth. A turning point that would require an odd combination of pragmatism and confidence. It was no decision at all. She took his hand and deliberately moved it upward to cover her breast. The connection of his palm to her sensitive flesh was electric. Devlyn groaned, his fingers tightening momentarily. Gillian experienced a rush of heat and desperate hunger that left her breathless.

Their eyes met. She reached up to touch his cheek. "It's okay," she said. "I know this is what it is. I want you anyway."

His expression was troubled, but his fingertips teased her

nipple as if they had a mind of their own. "I'll never lie to you, Gillian."

"I know." It wasn't him she worried about. He had been very clear about his motives, his plans for the future. Gillian would have to be the one to step back if she found herself in deep water. She wouldn't allow her heart to be broken. She was smarter than that.

"I love your skin," he muttered. "You're soft, so soft." Now both of his hands made mischief. She cried out when he pinched the tips of her aching breasts simultaneously and tugged. Fire shot from the point of contact to a place deep in her womb and below.

Her thighs clenched. "We need to move. To your bedroom." She was barely able to construct a coherent thought.

"Everyone's asleep. I'll lock the door." He slid from beneath her, and she felt his loss like a physical pain.

He was gone fleeting seconds. When he returned, she was standing up. She launched herself into his arms, delighting in the easy strength he displayed. She was neither tall nor short, but he pulled her to his chest and lifted her off her feet long enough to destroy her with a kiss that communicated yearning, masculine intent and heart-melting, disarming gentleness.

"Take off your shirt," she said. "I want to see you."

He chuckled at her urgency. "Bossy, bossy, bossy." But he obeyed, unbuttoning the top few buttons with maddening deliberation and then dragging the garment over his head and tossing it aside.

Her legs felt funny, like the time she had downed a glass of Long Island Iced Tea, not knowing what it was. But tonight she was stone-cold sober. And Devlyn Wolff was responsible for her sexual inebriation.

She put her hands on his wide shoulders, testing the resiliency of his skin, absorbing the warmth and power of muscle and sinew over bone. He stood rigid, his hands at his sides.

"You're so beautiful," she said, moving her hands across his broad chest. The light covering of hair made him look more primitive than the man she knew as a brilliant businessman. Half-naked, he exuded a force of will that thrilled even as it terrified.

She tasted one flat, copper-colored nipple. His whole body trembled. And still he didn't touch her. Her hands went to his belt. "May I?"

"Knock yourself out." It was a weak attempt at humor. The skin on his face stretched tightly over his cheekbones, his eyes squeezed shut as if he couldn't bear to watch her learning the planes of his body.

Clumsily, almost paralyzed by shyness, she unfastened his belt and drew it slowly through the belt loops. Her fingers settled on the tab of his zipper and stopped. His erection flexed against her touch, almost as if it were begging for her attention.

Devlyn grabbed her wrist. "No more. Not yet. I can't take it."

He went from passive to domineering so quickly, she was stunned. He grabbed handfuls of her sweater and dragged it over her head. Then he stopped, staring at her chest. "Sweet heaven. You're beautiful, Gillian. So damned beautiful."

He walked her backward until he could sit down, urging her forward to straddle his lap. She settled on top of him, leaned forward and put her hands on his shoulders. "Don't we have too many clothes on?"

"There you go again." He nuzzled his face in the valley between her breasts as if to reinforce the fact that he was teasing her. "Relax, honey. I'm in charge here."

She could have pressed the point. Sex was a two-way street. But in truth, she had no reason to doubt his ability to take over. When his mouth covered one aching nipple, brushing it repeatedly with his tongue and teeth, the rational part of her brain shut down. *Dear God.*

All that remained were the pleasure receptors. And they were in danger of overload. In her imagination, she had pictured Devlyn taking her hard and fast, demonstrating the same dominating force he wielded in the boardroom.

But she hadn't even been close. He treated her body as if it were a rare discovery, mapping it one sector at a time. Time was irrelevant. Devlyn feasted on her with the relish of a man coming off months of deprivation.

From her waist to her breasts, to the tender skin beneath and behind her ear, he kissed, he licked, he nipped, he stroked. Her breaths came in sharp pants, need building to the point of pain. "Please," she croaked. "I want more."

Unfastening the button at the top of her zipper, he slid both hands down inside her jeans beneath her panties and stroked her ass. "I think we're done with these," he said, his words guttural and harsh.

Pushing her to her feet, he dragged the denim down her legs, taking care to leave her lacy bikini in place. She wrapped her arms around her breasts, stricken by a return of shyness. She had been in relationships before. But never had she felt so exposed, so vulnerable.

Devlyn scooted to the edge of the sofa, cupping his hand over her mound. Slowly, making her want to scream in frustration, he began to finger her, sliding his thumb back and forth over the damp crotch of her underwear. She pressed her aching sex into his palm, begging wordlessly for release.

But he had a plan. One from which he would not stray. Curling his fist around the thin side of the bikini underpants, he stretched them so that he could drag the fabric back and forth across her most sensitive spot. The shock of it made heat pool in the place between her legs that ached so terribly. She writhed, moving closer. "Devlyn…"

Now he entered her with two fingers, not moving or thrusting. Merely letting her experience the mimicry of what was to come. She was wild with need, panting in her desperation. His thumb brushed the tiny nerve center that throbbed and burned, and she cried out, slammed by a climax that left her with no place to hide, no modesty, no maidenly dissimulation.

His arms were around her, supporting her as she rode out the last vestiges of pleasure. Limp and helpless, she barely had enough stamina to remain standing.

And then he started all over again.

Her panties disappeared in a flash. His arms encircled her hips, positioning his mouth at her center. "Again," he muttered. "I want you to come again."

Feeling him taste her so intimately was like nothing she had ever experienced. The rough pressure of his tongue, combined with the swollen remains of her last orgasm, brought her to the peak in record time. She tangled her hands in his hair, holding on as the insistent tide threatened to drag her under.

Shuddering and speechless, she clung to his shoulders. He stood and lifted her, stretching her out on the sofa. With jerky movements, he ripped off his pants and boxers and kicked them off with his shoes and socks. Foggy with the aftermath of what he had done to her, for her, she gazed up at him. He was primed and ready, his erection eager, bold.

"I want to touch you," she said.

He came down beside her, wedging his hips between her thighs. Leaning on one arm, he smiled. "I'm all yours."

She curled her fingers around his shaft, noting the way he winced as she did so. "Too hard?"

He grimaced. "Not hard enough." He nudged her legs apart even more, preparing to enter her, and then he cursed long and low.

"What? What's wrong?"

"No condom," he growled, his expression fierce.

She wanted him so desperately she couldn't think of anything but feeling him inside her. "It's the wrong time of the month. I should be fine," she pleaded, not prepared to wait another second.

"No," he said bluntly.

There was no question in her mind that he wanted her… badly. But as her head cleared, she realized that Devlyn was not prepared to take even the slightest chance of fathering a child.

It made sense. It was the responsible, moral thing to consider. But what sobered Gillian was that moments ago *she* was beyond coherent reasoning. Devlyn had been able to step back.

Which meant she was in more trouble than she realized.

Devlyn shuddered, waves of heat raking his body painfully. The lack of a condom had stopped him from making a terrible mistake. He didn't deserve Gillian's generosity, her sweet, seductive body. Not when he knew his terrible sentence, the inescapable truth of what his past had made him.

His shaft nestled against Gillian's moist folds. The head pulsed and throbbed, desperate to push inward toward bliss. He could almost feel the tight squeeze of her slick passage.

His brain told him to get up, but the rest of him said a big *hell no!* He was right where he wanted to be…or at least close. Beneath him Gillian was soft, so soft. His entire weight rested on her. He smelled the warm fragrance of her skin, the unmistakable nuance of arousal, his and hers.

The dimly lit room was still and silent but for the sound of his harsh breathing and the ticktock of the antique mantel clock. He felt its measured cadence in his chest. He couldn't look at her, didn't want to see her confusion, possibly her hurt.

If he had ever wanted a woman more, he couldn't remember. But then again, it was not his style to get so carried away that he reached this impossible impasse.

Gillian lay beneath him, mute...unmoving.

Exerting an almost superhuman amount of will, he forced himself up and away from her, every group of nerves and muscles screaming in protest. By the time he made it to his feet, he was sweating.

She watched him dress. Which did nothing at all for his erection, even though he had moved some distance away. He felt her gaze like a caress.

Though he half expected her to follow his lead, she still lay naked on the sensuous fabric of the sofa. She had flipped to her stomach, and the vision of her long, narrow back curving out into her smooth, rounded ass made him ache with lust.

Licking her lips, she whispered an innocent question. "Do you want me to come to your bedroom?"

He turned away from her, his head crammed with images from the past, his and hers. What right did he have to take her, knowing that the relationship would have more to do with expedience than permanence? Gillian represented all that was good and decent about women. He had deep scars, wounds that compromised his ability to love a woman, any woman. Would his selfishness bring her pain, despite her protestations to the contrary?

Clearing his throat, he walked to the nearest shelf, blindly removing a volume. "Get dressed. Please."

After a moment of what seemed like stunned silence, he heard the rustling that indicated her compliance.

Her voice startled him when she spoke. "What now? Look at me, Devlyn. What now?"

He faced her across a distance of several feet. Her hair was tumbled, her eyes shadowed with uncertainty and regret.

As he glanced down at the book in his hands, he felt an insane urge to laugh. The volume he had picked at random was Dostoyevsky's *The Idiot*. Was fate trying to tell him something? Sadly though, if he remembered his high-school lessons correctly, the hero in that story was a good but naive man unable to navigate a not-so-admirable world.

Devlyn was neither naive, nor particularly good. But for Gillian, he would try. He dropped the book on the desk. "I promised not to push you, and I broke that promise. Perhaps it would be wise to take a step backward. Our involvement could complicate things."

Even in the dim light he saw her pale. Her expression was hard to read. But the dark eyes that gazed at him so solemnly judged him and found him wanting. "I can make decisions for myself," she said. "I don't need you to protect me, Devlyn...not even from yourself."

Her dignity in the face of his unforgivable about-face shamed him. "It's not you," he said.

Fury shot from her eyes. "Oh, please. Surely you can do better than that? I understand that you don't want to take a chance without birth control. I get that. What I can't fathom is why you're shutting me out."

Even now he wanted her so badly he was close to begging. For forgiveness, for comfort, for sexual release. But he didn't deserve her. Not by a long shot. So how could he justify playing fast and loose with her emotional well-being?

His timing sucked. He should have realized from the beginning that he was headed down a dead-end road.

For one agonizing moment he had a vision of Gillian with a chubby, dark-eyed baby at her breast. The image pained him so deeply his eyes grew damp. Yearning constricted his chest. All he had to do was treat her decently, and she might fall in love with him. He could be the man to give her babies.

But even as the temptation faced him, he shoved it away. He couldn't give her children. He wouldn't. Of all the women he'd ever wanted, Gillian was the one he knew, beyond any doubt, who would love with a mother's pure heart, the one who would cherish her babies and stand by them as they grew.

One day soon a man would walk into her life, a man who could give her what she wanted...what she needed. That man was not Devlyn.

Moving with the painful limbs of an old man, he walked slowly past her to the door. "Good night."

She didn't answer. And she didn't follow.

And that was when he truly understood what he was giving up.

Eleven

Gillian cried herself to sleep, loathing the fact that Devlyn had reduced her to an emotional cliché. All night she slept in fits and starts, waking to find herself in a strange bed, and then reliving over and over the humiliating scene in the library.

He'd ruined it for her...that wonderful room. Never again would she be able to set foot inside it. Not without remembering the look on his face. Did he think she was trying to trap him somehow? Surely not. He had made his position very clear. Only a madwoman would believe she had the power to change him.

When the alarm went off just after dawn, she lay in bed, trying to find the courage to face the day. She didn't have the luxury of flouncing out of the house in a huff. The income from this job was not mad money, it was her livelihood...at least for now. If she was lucky, some teacher in the region would go on maternity leave at Christmas, and Gillian might get to finish out the year. And perhaps next fall things might be better.

None of that helped her now.

At eight on the nose, a polite maid brought coffee and scones along with juice and assorted jams. Gillian thanked her, uncomfortably aware that the young woman no doubt knew and worked with Doreen. It shouldn't matter, perhaps, but it did.

After devouring the lovely breakfast, Gillian dressed in a professional but understated outfit. A jacket and midcalf-length skirt, dark camel, with a silk blouse in a pumpkin-and-gold paisley print. Low-heeled, dressy boots in a neutral color finished what she now thought of as armor.

When she was ready, she sat at the lovely mirrored vanity and looked at herself objectively. The woman staring back at her was neatly turned out, but unexceptional. Brown hair, brown eyes, a small gap between her front teeth because her mom had not been able to afford braces.

Her mouth was perhaps her best feature, nicely shaped and usually smiling. The rest of her was ordinary. Like millions of other females in the world, she was not model material, but neither would her face scare children. And that was okay. She'd never yearned to be a beauty queen…except for once in seventh grade when she'd had a crush on a boy two years older than she was.

When she'd had the temerity to profess her undying devotion, he'd looked at her chest and told her that boys liked boobs.

The experience had been both heartbreaking and instructive. From then on out, she'd set her sights on more suitable romantic liaisons. Until now…

Running a brush through her hair, she made the mistake of thinking about Devlyn doing the same thing with a firm but gentle touch on the night of her accident. It would be easier if she didn't like him so well…if she could write him off as an insensitive jerk.

Glancing at her watch, she jumped up with a groan. The next few hours would require every bit of maturity and composure she possessed. She would *not* allow him to see how much last night's aborted encounter had upset her. He'd made his decision. As far as anyone was concerned, Gillian was working for the Wolff family, assisting them on a project. Nothing more.

As she stepped out into the hall, she hesitated. Devlyn had set a time for their meeting, but not dictated a place. Which forced her to search out the gentleman who oversaw *all* the staff and to inquire of him as to Devlyn's whereabouts.

The stuffy but efficient majordomo led her to the solarium, a lovely foliage-filled room with three glass walls that brought the brilliant sunshine and autumn panorama inside a warm and cozy enclosure.

Devlyn was there before her, a sheaf of architect's renderings spread out on a plain wooden table. Wearing dark slacks and a long-sleeve oxford cloth shirt with the sleeves rolled up, he looked casual, but professional. Gillian forced herself to walk toward him and perch a hip on one of the stools that flanked the work surface. "Is this the school?" *Stupid, Gillian. What else would he be showing you?*

He lifted his head, his eyes searching her face. "Good morning. How did you sleep?"

"Probably better than you." She winced inwardly. Drawing attention to their short-lived lovemaking wasn't productive…not at all.

His gaze was bland, as if he hadn't understood her sarcastic comment. But she could swear she saw his lips twitch with silent humor. "Take a look," he said. "See what you think."

She was forced to lean over the table, uneasily aware that he was far too close given the way things had ended the night before. She could smell his aftershave. The brush of his arm against hers made her shiver.

Marshaling all her concentration, she glanced down at the drawings of the new school. It was an impressive layout and far larger than she had expected. Though her brain didn't necessarily work in such a fashion, she tried to visualize what it would all look like when it was finished.

Devlyn tapped a corner of the paper with a pencil. "Well, what do you think?"

"It's beautiful, of course."

"But?"

"But what?"

He sighed. "I hired you to give us direction. You're a teacher. You've been in the trenches on a daily basis. Tell me what's missing...what needs to be changed."

Devlyn was right. Her expertise was what he had hired her to contribute. She nibbled her bottom lip. "Well..."

"Don't be bashful. I need the truth."

"In that case, I'd flip these two wings." She pointed to a section of the blueprints. "The low commodes are for the kindergartners, but you have them situated as the farthest grade from the lunchroom."

Devlyn nodded, his sharp gaze already assessing, dissecting. "What else?"

"If money is not an issue, it would be great to have a portico over the front entrance, so that on rainy days car riders could be loaded in the dry."

"What about the buses?"

"Generally they come to the opposite side of the school. But since you'll have at least five or six loading all at once, the best you can do is park them 'nose in' and make the overhang extend past the door of the bus."

She could almost see the wheels turning in his brain.

Devlyn erased a mark and jotted a note. "Next?"

"This is a sort of selfish request, but I don't see a teachers' lounge. Elementary faculty members seldom have time to use one, but it's nice to know it's there. You'd want enough room for several couches, a refrigerator, a microwave…and a couple of lunch tables."

"Would two tables be enough?"

"Yes. They'll be rotating in and out…and probably with only twenty-five or thirty minutes to eat. Less than that once they drop the kids off in the lunchroom."

Devlyn looked shocked. "Good lord. Are you telling me that public-school teachers don't get the traditional hour for lunch?"

Gillian laughed out loud. "What a lovely idea, but no. Who do you think would watch the classes?"

"I don't know." He shrugged. "Monitor people, maybe."

"If you can work that out, you'll have potential employees lining up in droves."

They studied the plans for another half hour, Devlyn firing insightful questions at her, and Gillian offering suggestions based on her experience. But suddenly, they both fell silent.

She moved unobtrusively to the right, trying to put space between them. Even in the midst of a business discussion, she was far too aware of him. But what he was thinking was a mystery.

He glanced at his watch. "I want to show you the property. But no helicopters this time," he said hastily.

"Good to know. Otherwise I would have been forced to resign on the spot."

"What do you do when you fly?"

He seemed genuinely curious. So she was stymied as to how to explain.

"I've never been in an airplane, Devlyn. So it hasn't been as issue."

"That's terrible," he said. "Can't your doctor give you something for the vertigo?"

"It's not a question of medication."

"Then what? Is it that you can't overcome the phobia?"

She looked down at the plans, anything to avoid his gaze. Embarrassment flushed her throat and heated her cheeks. "It's the money, Devlyn. My father was a carpenter. My mother is a housekeeper. I barely made it through school on scholarships and a variety of minimum-wage jobs. I've never had the opportunity to fly."

He was stunned. And as embarrassed as she was. Clearly, to a Wolff, it was difficult to imagine a life where remaining earthbound was the norm. "I apologize," he said stiffly. "I'm usually not so obtuse."

"I'm not offended. And truthfully, I'd love to travel someday. When I have the opportunity."

She could see him struggle. To be honest, she had wondered if the reason he was reluctant to follow through with a physical relationship was that he recognized the differences in their circumstances. Perhaps he imagined that she would expect expensive gifts...or even worse, thought that she would try to extract money from him somehow.

The incident when he was eighteen surely impacted his ability to trust. Especially when it came to women and his wealth. No matter how she and Devlyn tried to ignore it, there was a definite class difference. She was Cinderella to his Prince Charming. Though she wasn't the one employed by the Wolff family in a service capacity—her mother was—the stigma remained, at least in Gillian's mind.

Devlyn rolled up the plans and slid them into a large tube. "The architect is meeting us at the property in half an hour. I'll join you in the front foyer in ten minutes."

Gillian scrambled after him, but he had already disappeared, swallowed up by the enormous house. She darted to her bedroom, grabbed her purse and a notebook and spent her final two minutes trying to remember the most direct route to the castle's entrance.

It wasn't a castle, not really, but it definitely qualified as more than a mere house. Devlyn beat her to the rendezvous point, his gaze moody as he cooled his heels.

"Sorry," she said. "I'm ready."

Someone had brought the car around. She'd hoped to make the trip in one of the roomy SUVs, a vehicle with plenty of interior space. Instead, Devlyn had chosen to take the Aston Martin again. She slid into the low, comfy seat and tried to ignore the fact that his hard, masculine thigh was mere inches away from hers. He was a big man. But the car suited him somehow.

With a screech of gravel, they swung out of the drive and onto the long road that twisted and turned for a good two miles before reaching the highway below. The hands that gripped the steering wheel were tanned and lightly dusted with black hair. Remembering the image of those masculine fingers, dark against her fair skin, caused Gillian's breath to hitch. She shifted nervously, feeling the interior shrink even more.

Staring out the window, she searched for something to say. "May I ask you a personal question?"

He shot her a sideways glance. "I suppose."

"Was there a woman sometime in the past who tried to sue you for paternity?"

His jaw was rigid, the cords in his neck standing out. "No. What gave you that idea?"

Regretting her impulsive inquiry, she squirmed. His tone warned her to step carefully. "It's the baby thing. You're so adamant. It made me wonder."

The sunny morning had changed without warning, heavy cloud cover rolling in from the west. "I've never let any woman have the power to put me in that position. So it hasn't been an issue."

He wasn't going to give her anything more than that. The silence lengthened. It was almost a relief when heavy drops of rain began to pelt the windshield. The noisy deluge masked Gillian's discomfort. How could she ever understand Devlyn if he stonewalled her anytime a personal topic was broached? On the surface, he was an extrovert…charming, affable, a social animal.

But beneath the charismatic persona ran a vein of dark, turbulent emotion.

She told herself it didn't matter. Devlyn needed her skills as a professional educator. Everything else would have to be pushed aside if this arrangement was going to work. But she didn't know how to keep herself from falling for him.

The whole idea behind the new school was that it be built very close to the tiny community of Burton. Consequently, it didn't take long to reach the parcel of land the Wolffs had already acquired. A silver Porsche was parked on the side of the road when they arrived.

Devlyn reached across Gillian's lap and pulled a fold-up umbrella out of the glove box. "Here," he said. "Do you want a rain jacket? I think I have one in the trunk."

His face was so close to hers she could have leaned forward a few inches and kissed him. She licked her lips. "No. It's not really cold. I'll be fine."

The car windows had fogged up almost instantly when he cut the engine. Devlyn stared at her, his eyes stormy. The look in them was unmistakable. He wanted her. "Gillian…I…"

She put her hand over his mouth, surprised at her daring. "You don't owe me any explanations, Devlyn. And just so we're clear on this, I'm a big girl. I'm not looking for a husband this month…or even this year. So you're in no danger.

I've done enough thinking. When you want me, all you have to do is ask."

Sitting back in her seat, she glanced out the window. "He's waiting for us. The architect."

Devlyn cursed. "Let him wait."

Slowly, as if trying to draw out the pleasure, he slid a hand beneath her hair, cupping her neck and dragging her across the console. "My leaving last night had nothing to do with not wanting you." His lips were cool but firm. His mouth moved against hers as if he had never kissed a woman. The very innocence of the caress made her crazy.

"Forget last night," she muttered, trying to breathe. "All I care about is today." Tangling her fingers in his thick, soft hair, she kissed him back.

Twelve

It wasn't in Devlyn's nature to be indecisive. Second-guessing decisions—or hesitating in the heat of the moment—meant losing out in the business world. His utter confidence and knack for innovative leadership were the reasons his father and uncle had chosen him to pilot the enormous behemoth that was Wolff Enterprises.

If they could see the current state of his brain, they'd have him committed.

Beneath his hands, Gillian's skin and hair were soft. Her scent, light and floral, soothed him even as it aroused him. "I don't know what to do with you." He heard the raggedness in his voice, recognized his own utter confusion.

She pulled away, smoothing her hair. "We have someone waiting for us," she said, not meeting his eyes.

He sensed her vulnerability. Did she think he was playing some kind of sexual power game? She'd be shocked if she knew that he was as conflicted as she was.

"Fine. Let's go. But we're not done with this."

Before he could come around and help her, Gillian was out of the car with the umbrella over her head. The rain had eased to a gentle drizzle. She walked by his side as they approached the man who awaited them.

Sam Ely was tall, rangy and rich. Maybe not by Wolff standards, but still well-heeled enough to draw the attention of every available woman in Charlottesville. He'd started his own architectural firm at twenty-five and now ran a multimillion-dollar business.

Sam smiled at Gillian with a lazy grin. "Sam Ely." He stretched out his hand. "You must be our new *expert.*"

Devlyn watched, disquieted, as Gillian shook the architect's hand. "It's wonderful to meet you," she said. "Devlyn told me you're doing this project for half your normal fee. As a Burton native, I have to tell you how grateful I am."

Sam shrugged, a bashful *aw shucks* expression on his angular features. "I'm a sucker for little kids…what can I say? I'm honorary uncle to several of my fraternity brothers' kids…a dozen unofficial nieces and nephews already. And if my sweet grandma has her way, I won't be far behind in the procreation department."

Gillian laughed. "What does that mean?"

Sam took her elbow as they walked up a steep rise, leaving Devlyn to trail in their wake. "She's been setting me up with eligible women since the day I turned twenty-one. So far nothing has stuck, but any day now…"

"Is there someone special?"

He put an arm around her waist as she stumbled. "Take it easy. No…I'm still playing the field, but if I wait too long all the good ones will be taken."

The rain had stopped. Gillian lowered her umbrella and folded it up. "Somehow I doubt that will be a problem."

Devlyn snorted beneath his breath and wondered sourly if

Sam's slow Southern drawl was an affectation used to impress the ladies. Perhaps Devlyn should have thought twice about introducing Gillian at this stage in the game. He touched her shoulder, drawing her attention to the field ahead. "The stakes indicate the corners of the building. What do you think?"

The piece of property sat atop a small, flat-topped hill. Grading had not been a problem. The old farmer from whom they'd bought the land had plowed and planted this acreage for fifty years. There was plenty of room for the planned school, and even space for expansion one day, if needed.

Devlyn liked the idea that this verdant, grassy space would still be growing things...albeit children instead of corn and carrots. Gillian hadn't answered him. He turned and saw that her eyes were tear-filled.

"Thank you, Devlyn," she said, her words choked with emotion. "You're doing a very wonderful thing." She caught him completely off guard by hugging him tightly, her head tucked momentarily against his chest.

Over her shoulder his eyes met Sam's. The other man shrugged and smiled ruefully as if to say, *lucky guy*.

Devlyn allowed himself one quick squeeze and eased out of her grasp. He wasn't accustomed to indulging in personal moments during a business encounter. But then again, Gillian was teaching him new things about himself every day. The level of the regret he experienced in having to let her go was staggering.

Summoning his scattered brain cells, he motioned to the architect. "Let's walk room to room and I'll tell you how we want to tweak the design."

Gillian lingered behind the two men, turning in a circle to take in the view. Behind and above her, Wolff Castle sat somewhere atop its eagle perch, hidden from view by the forest that surrounded it. To the north, the Shenandoah Valley stretched for miles. Though the view today was shrouded in mist, she could visualize the panorama.

The school would be a showplace. She had seen the many windows in the drawings. Boys and girls of all ages would sneak peeks out of them in between assignments, dreaming of weekends and summers when they could run wild and free. This lush, remote, out-of-the-way spot was a great place to grow up.

Environmentally up-to-date, the school would generate much of its own electricity with solar panels and a wind turbine. Gillian had noticed a science lab in the plans, no doubt intended to be outfitted with sophisticated equipment. It warmed her heart to know that Burton's children, though from limited means, would have the opportunity and access to train for interesting careers.

The two men finished their circuit of the perimeter and returned to where she stood. Sam swept his arm in an arc. "I know it doesn't look like much yet, but I think you'll be impressed."

"I already am." Gillian glanced at Devlyn. "And I feel lucky to be part of such an exciting project."

Sam eyed Gillian. "How about I take you to lunch and I'll go over the blueprints with you…show you all the things I'm hoping to incorporate into the plans as we fine-tune them. You're welcome, too, Devlyn…of course."

Devlyn's handsome face darkened. "Not necessary. Gillian and I went over everything this morning."

Gillian wasn't stupid. Devlyn was staking a claim. Which made no sense at all, since he apparently didn't want to pursue a relationship with her. His arrogance was patronizing and ir-ritating. She gave Sam a big smile. "I'd still love to hear your ideas in more detail," she said. She shot Devlyn a cool gaze. "I'm sure you have lots of important work to do for Wolff Enterprises, right? You won't miss me at all."

Sam swooped in smoothly to close the deal. "I'd be happy to drive Gillian up the mountain when we're done."

Devlyn smiled genially. "I hate to break up the party, but I really need Gillian this afternoon. Part of what we've hired her to do is deal with paperwork…and there's a mountain of it. Sorry, Sam. Maybe the three of us can get together another time."

Sam took his dismissal with good grace. "Too bad. But I'll take a rain check." After shaking both Gillian's hand and Devlyn's, he strode back to his car, got in and disappeared down the road.

Gillian was so mad her chest was tight. "That was the most appalling show of chest-beating I've seen in a long time. How dare you bully me like that? And in front of such a nice man."

Devlyn narrowed his eyes. "I did not bully you. I merely pointed out that we're not paying you to have long lunches with guys you've just met. You're my employee. If you want to date handsome architects, you can do it on your own time. And for your information, the jury's still out on whether or not Sam Ely is a nice guy. He has a reputation for enjoying the ladies."

"You're the last person I'd take dating advice from."

"I thought it was a business lunch. Now you're *dating* the man?"

She got up in his face. "Don't twist my words."

"Don't try to make me jealous." His yell echoed across the open space.

Gillian's jaw dropped. "I wasn't…" But was she lying to herself? Had she seen Sam as an easy shot at Devlyn?

He groaned, taking her by the hand and dragging her along behind him. "I want to show you something."

It petrified her how much she enjoyed holding hands with Devlyn Wolff. Such a simple thing, and yet so powerful.

"Slow down," she said. "The grass is all wet. I don't want to break my ankle."

He relented only slightly. She was breathless by the time they reached the back of the property. The fall of the land was not as steep on this side, and the grassy field gave way to a grove of hardwood trees. The vibrantly colored leaves overhead and underfoot—combined with the foggy, misty day—created a mystical place of beauty.

Devlyn halted eventually beside a tiny, wet-weather stream. He released her hand and squatted to remove a clump of leaves from a formation of smooth, moss-covered rocks.

"What is it?" she asked.

He cupped his hands, filling them with clear liquid and standing to face her. "Spring water. From a subterranean source. As clean and pure as the first day it was created. Taste."

He held it out, unsmiling. Gillian had the odd notion that they were enacting some kind of primitive ritual. She bent her head and sipped from his curved palms. The water was cold and tart, making her throat sting at the same time that it quenched her thirst.

Inevitably, her lips brushed his skin. The intimacy of his offering tapped something deep inside her. A sensual yearning to give herself to this man.

She took a second drink and lifted her head. "Thank you," she whispered, not daring to break the protective layer of quiet that cocooned them.

Before he could squat on his haunches for a second time and drink for himself, she crouched, giving not a thought to her nice outfit. Hands trembling, she gathered water, rose and offered it to him. "For you," she said, mentally urging him to let go of whatever chains held him back.

For long seconds she thought he was going to refuse. Giving her a dark, reluctant stare, he dipped his head and sucked up a great mouthful of spring water. His teeth grazed the sensitive pad beneath her thumb. The feel of his lips on her cold skin turned her inside out.

She wanted him dreadfully, and yet she knew the danger. Was she totally naive to think she could play with fire and walk away unscathed?

Water dripped from her hands when he thrust his tongue between her fingers, one at a time. Her knees literally went weak. "Devlyn…"

"Gillian." He mocked her gently.

"I can't do this on-again, off-again thing. It hurts too much. I don't expect you to commit to anything beyond this moment, but I have to know you need me as much as I need you."

"I don't," he said flatly, gathering her into his arms. "I need you more."

The last word was muffled as he moved his mouth over hers. Every time they were together she learned something new about him. Today it was the taste of kisses that combined remorse with promises. First gentle, then demanding, he staked a claim.

His tongue probed between her teeth, tangling with hers. She heard him moan. The sound of his hunger shuddered through her like hot honey. They were pressed so closely together that his heartbeat mingled with hers. His sex, eager and ready, pushed urgently against her flat belly.

What they were doing was wild, impractical, without reason. They had no blanket, nothing to cover the damp ground. And although it was not especially cold, getting naked might be another story.

"Devlyn?" She winnowed her fingers through his thick hair as he suckled a sensitive spot behind her ear.

He had either gone deaf or he was choosing to ignore her. But last night's awkward parting had made her cautious. Self-preservation was a strong instinct.

"Devlyn." She said his name a second time, more urgently. "What are you doing?"

He lifted his head for a moment, eyes glittering, cheek-bones ruddy with arousal. "I'm tasting you." Beneath her jacket he stroked his hands over the slick fabric of her blouse.

Heat blossomed every place his hands touched. Running the tip of her tongue along his jawline to return the favor, she sighed. "I get that. But what about birth control?"

He went still, his expression tense. "Hell." Almost simultaneously, jubilation lit his face. "I have one," he croaked. "A condom. In my wallet." He released her and stepped back, at the same time extracting from his billfold what they needed and tucking it into his shirt pocket.

He grimaced. "You make me lose sight of everything. When I touch you, I burn. I never intended our first time to be in an October forest. But I don't think I can wait another minute to have you."

"You don't sound very happy about it," she muttered... though having a man speak as if he would die if he didn't have her was damned effective foreplay.

"Happy doesn't enter into it. You walked back into my life and it was as if I'd been struck by lightning. I can't explain it. And no...it's not the path I would have chosen. You deserve a man far better than I am. But I can't seem to resist you. If you feel for me even a fraction of what I do for you, I need you now."

"Here? Really?" She glanced around them as if a bed might magically appear.

"Trust me, Gillian. There are ways."

She had never seen such a look on a man's face. It thrilled and scared and aroused her in equal parts. The adult Devlyn was essentially a stranger to her, a man she had met less than forty-eight hours ago. Nothing about the situation was prudent or wise. But after last night, she couldn't deny him anything...didn't want to.

She had lived a lifetime of caution. But today was a new adventure. "Okay, then," she said. "Show me how."

Thirteen

Devlyn could barely hear her quiet response over the roaring in his head. He had plunged headfirst over a waterfall, tumbling wildly out of control. Was he really going to do this? Not only decide to make love to Gillian, but here? Now?

For a grown man, he was ridiculously confounded by their complicated circumstances and the lack of privacy. Gillian's mother's house was out for obvious reasons. And there were too many watchful eyes at the castle. Plus the fact that Gillian was uncomfortable being entertained there as a guest while her mother was an employee.

A Wolff, any Wolff, was too well-known to check into a local motel unnoticed. So here they were...

She stood watching him with those big, soft brown eyes. Vulnerable and brave, she wore her femininity gracefully. Too unsure of herself to take the lead, but not entirely convinced he would be good to her. That he could witness her hesitance shamed him. A woman deserved security in her lovers, a knowledge that coupling meant more than cheap sex.

If he could only express to her what he felt, the driving urge to possess her, to mark her, maybe then she would realize that this was no testosterone-driven whim.

But he couldn't explain her appeal to himself, much less to her.

She wrapped her arms around her waist.

"Are you too cold?" he asked, wincing as he heard the words. He sounded like a sixteen-year-old hoping to score behind the football stadium.

"I won't be," she said. "Not if you're holding me."

Glancing around them, he spotted a large tree stump, recently cut. The surface was rough, but mostly dry, protected in part by the canopy overhead. It would do. He picked her up, surprising a gasp from soft, pink lips. "Have you ever made love outdoors?"

She clung to him, arms around his neck. "Never."

"This will be a first for me, too." Her slender body, though not petite, was a negligible weight. He looked down at her, unsmiling, feeling twin currents of lust and tenderness converge in his chest. "We don't have to do this. I can wait. Probably." She felt so damned good in his arms…almost as if she belonged there.

Gillian laughed softly, the sexy sound making the hair on the back of his neck rise. "What would your employees in Atlanta say if they could see you now?"

He snorted. "They'd probably think I'd lost my mind. Kieran, my cousin, is the one who has no problem with sleeping on the ground and eating grubworms for breakfast. I'm more of a five-star hotel guy…soft sheets…a good bottle of wine. A beautiful woman."

"So you're zero for three and you still want to have sex with me?"

He stood her on the stump and put his hands on her hips to steady her. Looking up into the face of the woman who haunted his dreams at night, he was pained by the lack of confidence she exhibited in her desirability. His fingers dug into her flanks, itching to touch bare skin. "Don't tell me you're not beautiful," he said. "I'm the judge, and I happen to be pretty damned turned on right now in case you hadn't noticed."

"Men are like that." She gnawed her lower lip, her hands fluttering at her sides. It would take more than words to convince her.

He lifted the hem of her skirt and slid his hands up her thighs. "Pick up your foot," he commanded.

She was wearing sexy ankle-high boots with—thank God—no panty hose. Her skin was cool, but not particularly chilled. It was almost as soft as her blouse. He rubbed her thighs lightly, warming them with the friction of his caress.

Gently, teasingly, he curled his fingers in the waistband of her underwear and dragged it ever so slowly over her hips and down her legs. Gillian's eyelids fluttered shut, her lips parted. Observing nothing in her stance to indicate disagreement, he brought the silken scrap of nothing to her ankles.

Holy hell. No sexy movie star had ever looked as deliberately alluring. His hands shook and his shaft hardened to stone. "Step out of them, Gillian." His voice was firm.

She put her hands on his shoulders and obeyed, lifting one foot at a time. He tucked the undies in his hip pocket, put his hands on her waist and lifted her effortlessly, depositing her onto the ground.

Unzipping his trousers he freed himself from the knit boxers that threatened to cut off the blood flow to the part of his body that demanded attention.

"Touch me, Gillian." The guttural words were both command and plea.

She stared at him…first skimming her gaze over his face… then assessing his straining erection. Licking her lips like someone anticipating a treat, she took him in her hands and warmed his length. He could have told her it was unnecessary. The skin that was pulled so tightly over firm flesh throbbed and burned from the inside out. He braced his legs and dug his hands into her hair.

Every brush of her delicate fingertips marked him indelibly. Beneath her touch, his shaft leaped eagerly, aching to find release. His brain held sway…barely. He was determined to draw this out, to give Gillian the full measure of his attention, his hunger, his absolute focus.

But even a strong man had his limits. And Gillian brought him to the edge far too rapidly. Gently, he removed her hands and stepped away. Fumbling in his pocket, he located the single condom, ripped it open and held it out with a raised eyebrow.

She was bashful, clearly. He swallowed hard, his throat dry. "Please," he said. "I want you to." Her movements were sweetly clumsy as she did her best to position the latex over the head of his penis. A couple of false starts tested his patience. Finally, she managed to cover him from base to tip.

He sat down on the stump and held up his arms. "Come here, honey. Let me love you."

In her face he saw the battle between shock and excitement. Lucky for him, the latter won. She lifted her skirt and straddled his legs. He almost had an orgasm right then.

Finding her bare butt beneath her skirt, his hands guided her descent. "Easy, baby. Slowly. Do it slowly."

Her hands hovered and finally found a resting place on his shoulders. Gradually, a bit at a time, she sheathed him in her hot, moist passage. Groaning, barely coherent, Devlyn decided to shut up and let Gillian take the lead for the moment. The feel of her lithe body welcoming him was indescribable. She was silent, concentrating on the joining of their flesh. Soft and hard, male and female, as elemental as time itself.

When she had him fully seated, the head of his shaft nudging the entrance to her womb, she exhaled as if she had been holding her breath. "Oh, lordy…"

Gillian winced inwardly, embarrassed to let him see that she was in way over her head. Her few sexual experiences in the past bore no resemblance at all to what was happening at this very moment in a surprisingly sensitive spot deep within her sex.

Devlyn had his eyes closed, his head canted backward as he surged into her, flexing his hips. The strength hidden beneath his conservative clothing was astounding. He had carried her with ease. Even now, he thrust with power, filling her repeatedly.

She was on top, but that was where any semblance of domination on her part ended. Like a maestro, he played her body, slowly when it suited him…then hard and fast, making them both cry out.

His arms went around her waist, dragging her closer. The chill of the air did nothing to cool them. Skin hot and damp, he made love to her tirelessly. At moments when it was clear she was near the edge, he eased back on the rhythm, calming her frantic movements, slowing the pace.

Her skirt was rucked up to her waist, her half-naked body on display. She had never been an exhibitionist, but at the moment, modesty was the farthest thing from her mind. Desperately, she wanted to feel his mouth on her breasts, his hands on the bare skin of her back. But that would involve stopping, and she couldn't find the words to say what she felt.

Inside her, he felt enormous. She loved the sense of connection, the intimacy of their fevered coupling, the sensation of him filling her, claiming her.

Her breath caught as the inevitable climax sneaked up and

sent her reeling. "Devlyn…" Her shocked cry startled a trio of birds, who darted off into the treetops.

He held her close while she rode out the last fluttering tremors of her release. Head on his shoulder, she struggled to breathe. "I'm sorry," she muttered. "You haven't…"

He played with her hair, his big frame shuddering with un-appeased arousal. "I will. Not to worry. Give me your mouth."

It never occurred to her to protest. Their lips met, tasted, slid apart. A tiny buzz of remembered pleasure regenerated her arousal. Something about the fog and the sylvan glade enhanced her pleasure…a dreamy, unfocused, self-satisfied urge to wallow in Devlyn's passionate persuasion.

He nipped her bottom lip with his teeth. "You're going to come again."

The certainty in his ragged voice made moisture bloom in secret places she'd thought well satisfied already. *If you say so*… So intense was the vein of joy, she would have agreed to most anything.

"God," he groaned. "Where's a bed when you need one?"

She licked the whorl of his ear. "I can lie on the ground. It won't matter."

"It matters to me. You deserve to be cherished." He chuck-led raggedly, despite his obvious urgency. "I think I may have lost my mind."

Wiggling her hips experimentally, she imagined his big, masculine body on top of hers. The image brought her to the edge a second time. Panting, impatient, she ripped at the but-tons on his shirt. "Put this on the ground," she pleaded. "I want to feel you on top of me."

His face flushed dark red. Indecision painted his features. "Are you sure?"

"Yes, Devlyn. Yes."

Still buried inside her, he wriggled out of the sleeves. She undid the last button and tossed the shirt on the leaf-covered ground. "I'll go first," she said, already lifting herself from him.

His fingers dug into her hips. "Don't. Don't move."

She obeyed.

He cursed, the words choked and broken. And then it was too late. With a shout, he exploded...hard...hips pistoning wildly as he thrust, his shaft rubbing intimately at her inner flesh that was already too sensitive.

Stunned, she whimpered a sobbing cry. "Oh, oh, oh..." The second peak was more powerful than the first. Wrapped in his fierce embrace, she felt everything she thought she knew about herself incinerate...flare brightly...and fade away.

What was left behind in the aftermath was an odd sense of peace. For so long she had assumed she knew what she wanted out of life. A dependable, kind mate, a handful of children, security.

But what she had discovered instead was that she had a wild, self-destructive streak. Devlyn was dangerous...in so many ways. He was a lone Wolff, a sociable animal whose affability masked a complicated personality with enough layers to stymie a psychotherapist.

She couldn't discern his secrets, and she didn't really have the right to ask. Whatever the nature of the relationship they found themselves embroiled in, it surely didn't include the kind of permanence that merited shared confidences.

It was sex.

For some unfathomable reason, Devlyn wanted her. It wouldn't last. She knew that. But for better or for worse, she wanted him, too.

Seconds passed, perhaps entire minutes. Gradually their breathing returned to normal. And almost simultaneously Gillian felt awkwardness roll over her in a suffocating wave.

She wanted to stand up, but she wasn't sure her legs would

support her. Devlyn seemed in no hurry to move. So her hands roved with a will of their own over the smooth, taut skin of his back. Muscles flexed beneath her touch. The part of her that was feminine, vulnerable, responded to his latent power. In prehistoric times he would have been the kind of man who kept danger at bay, protecting the weak and the defenseless.

Gillian was a fully evolved woman. She had a career. Or at least she would have one again sometime. She knew how to change a tire. Was not averse to killing the occasional mouse. Balanced her own checkbook, planned for the future.

She didn't *need* a man to shield her from the world. But despite all evidence to the contrary, she craved Devlyn's unspoken strength. His personality was so unlike her own. Though she was more of an introvert, her past was an open book. Ordinary. Boring.

His silence made her uneasy. Was she supposed to say something? Do something?

In the absence of conversation or even the unmistakable sounds of lovemaking, the woods teemed with sound…a whip-poor-will's call, the rustle of small creatures scurrying through the underbrush.

Devlyn's face was buried against the side of her neck. She almost imagined that his lips moved on her skin.

Did she want tenderness from him so badly that she was willing to manufacture emotion where there was none?

For the first time since they had walked into the glen, cold seeped into her veins, chilling her from the inside out. Goose bumps erupted in places she'd rather not contemplate. At the risk of committing a sexual faux pas, she stood shakily, allowing the connection, flesh to flesh, to be broken.

Hurriedly, she smoothed her skirt. She bent and picked up Devlyn's shirt, holding it out to him. "At least we didn't ruin it."

Was that supposed to be a self-conscious attempt at humor?

If it was, Devlyn ignored it. He stood and straightened his clothing, taking the wrinkled garment from her hand without comment and putting it on.

As she watched him adjust his boxers, tuck in his shirt and zip his slacks, her stomach curled in mortification. His movements were unhurried, matter-of-fact. He must have dealt with the condom when she looked away.

Gillian was a wreck. Last night she had been hurt by his rejection. Now she was satisfied physically, but as confused as ever.

Devlyn was cool as ice.

Fourteen

The last time Devlyn remembered feeling this level of sexual agitation was the night after he lost his virginity. It disturbed him that the old wound echoed in today's encounter. But it made sense in a way. He lusted after Gillian, but he felt sleazy for having taken her, despite her compliance. Last night he had managed to walk away. Today, he had failed. Guilt and sexuality made uneasy bedfellows.

Wincing inwardly, he found her underwear in his pocket and handed it over. Gillian's face was rosy with color, her gaze downcast. She took the bikini, bent at the waist and stepped gracefully into it, ignoring his attempt to steady her. His hand dropped to his side. Undoubtedly she expected him to say something. After all, they had just indulged in wild, uninhibited, reckless sex. Or by another definition, spontaneous combustion.

She adjusted the collar of her blouse and smoothed her hair. Those simple, elegant motions dared him to dishevel her again, though he was certain she didn't mean to convey that.

He cleared his throat. "Gillian?"

She looked up at him, her expression guarded. "Yes?"

"Oh, hell." Dragging her into his embrace, he gave her a hard, heated kiss before holding her at arm's length and staring into her eyes, willing her to understand. "I'm flying blind here, honey. You've knocked me six ways to Sunday."

Suspicion etched a tiny wrinkle between her brows. "You sleep with women all the time. Everyone knows that."

"You aren't a woman."

"Excuse me?" The frown disappeared when her brows rose toward her hairline.

Good God. "You're not a *normal* woman," he clarified.

Gillian struggled free, her chest heaving in a way that threatened to distract him again. "Are you *trying* to make me regret what just happened here?"

He ground his teeth. "You know what I mean. You're different. Special."

"As in mentally unbalanced?"

"Quit putting words in my mouth, damn it." Heat washed up his neck.

"Somebody needs to. If this is your idea of pillow talk, I'm amazed you ever have a second date."

"For a female who comes across as shy and polite, you're sure loosening up." He was bemused by his utter lack of savoir faire. He'd built a reputation both in the bedroom and the boardroom as a slick operator. Yet Gillian managed to disconcert him time after time.

Prim and proper on the outside, a hot, silver flame in his arms. She didn't look at all like a woman who had just been thoroughly— Even in his own mind, he had to censor his language. Gillian made him want to be a better man.

She sighed audibly. "Can we go home now?"

Her pallor disturbed him. "Are you okay?"

She shrugged. "I don't know what I am. But I won't stay

at the castle anymore. I'll do your job. Help with the school… but this…" She waved a hand at their unorthodox trysting place. "It's really a bad idea."

"Didn't seem that way a few minutes ago." She had grit. He had to give her that. In spite of her painfully evident embarrassment, she met his gaze head-on.

"Devlyn…" She stopped and exhaled an exasperated breath. "You know how appealing you are…charming, sexual, physically close to perfect…"

"Close?"

"Focus, big guy. You have all the cards. It isn't fair. I don't know why you're slumming with the housekeeper's daughter."

His temper fired. "I've never been accused of being a snob. And damn, but it must be exhausting carrying that chip on your shoulder. I *like* you. Is that so hard to believe?"

She bit her lip. "Truthfully? Yes."

"Are you really that unsure of yourself?"

"Not as a rule. But then again, the men I've been with… and I can count them on less than one hand…they were… well…*normal*."

His lips twitched. He saw the moment she realized what she had said. "That word must have multiple meanings," he drawled. Finally, she smiled, and the knot in his gut eased a bit.

"You are incorrigible."

"There you go again…using five-syllable teacher words. It makes me hot."

"Forgive me if I point out that you're what we call *easy*."

"And you're not easy at all. Where does that leave us?"

"As the woman who recently allowed you to lift my skirt and have your way with me, I haven't a clue."

"How would you feel about moving our relationship to private territory?"

She tilted her head, frowning slightly. "You'll have to give me more than that."

"I have to go back to Atlanta after a carnival fundraiser for the school. I'd like you to return with me to Georgia."

"Why?"

"Because I'd like a chance for us to be alone together. Really alone. With no one to interfere."

"And in the meantime?"

"You were the one screaming my name a little while ago. You tell me."

"God, you're smug." But she smiled as she said it, so he figured he was okay.

"Was that a yes?"

She lifted her chin, looking down her nose at him with that prissy, disapproving, narrow-eyed gaze that made him want to kiss her senseless. "I suppose I could be persuaded to go to Atlanta with you. But in the meantime...I'm conflicted. Maybe we should abstain. It's not really practical to sneak around outside, and the thought of your family walking in on the two of us in flagrante delicto gives me hives."

"I don't even know what the heck that means, but it sounds dirty, so I like it." Her suggestion wasn't entirely unreasonable, though it might be hard to pull off. Maybe he could wait until Atlanta. It would give him time to deal with his unanswered questions about his own culpability if he let things get too serious.

She kicked at a pile of leaves with the toe of her boot. "Don't play dumb with me, Devlyn Wolff. They don't put imbeciles in charge of worldwide corporations. Earning that MBA you've got tucked in your back pocket required a lot of brain power."

He shrugged. "I'm good at math. It's no big deal."

"Not from where I stand. Overseeing an organization like Wolff Enterprises requires a complex skill set. You act as if it's a walk in the park, but I know how hard you work. Just because you make it look easy, don't assume that people take you at face value. You're a financial genius. And I know your father and your uncle are very proud."

Her quiet praise affected him in ways he couldn't explain. Gillian was *real* and honest and thoughtful. Hearing her sincere compliments humbled him.

The serious turn in the conversation was unexpected and gratifying. But he had more carnal concerns on his mind. "So we're going to try to be platonic?"

He moved toward her, grinning when she backed up and almost fell over a root.

"Stay where you are." Her cheeks were flushed again.

He held up his hands. "I was only going to kiss you."

"Look where that got us last time."

Her quick glance at the abandoned stump was enough to make him hard. Again. She didn't protest when he pulled her arms around his neck. "Kiss me," he coaxed. They were plastered together, chest to chest, but fully clothed this time.

Gillian's lips met his. He tasted her smile, her yielding, her sweet, almost innocent trust.

She tipped back her head and gazed at him, eyes filled with feminine secrets. "Are you going to wine and dine me in the big city?"

"Among other things." He'd already taken her once like a wild man. Would it be entirely out of line to try again?

He was shocked as hell when she decided to play with his zipper. Her face, shielded by a fall of dark brown hair, was hidden from him as she whispered a tempting offer. "I've always heard that to go cold turkey on something, sex, for instance, you should overindulge before you begin to deny yourself."

"Hell, yes. Smart woman. I knew there were benefits to being the teacher's pet."

She found his rigid shaft and stroked it. "Is that what you think you are?"

Her long fingers curled around him and squeezed. He groaned. "Easy there, Gillian. Have mercy." He felt like it had been days since he'd taken her...not minutes.

She released him and stepped back. "You're right. Besides, everyone knows anticipation is half the fun. Tell me again. What day are we leaving?"

He bent at the waist, his brain mush. "The carnival is to-morrow night. We'll leave first thing Saturday," he croaked. Surely she didn't intend to leave him like this.

Her smile was sunny. "I accept your invitation. I'm going to head back to the car. I'll let you finish up here." She turned and took a step in the opposite direction.

"The hell you say." He was ninety-nine percent sure she was teasing. But that one percent scared the crap out of him. Snagging her wrist in an unbreakable hold, he dragged her back. "Not nice, Gillian. You're not going anywhere."

Huge, long-lashed chocolate eyes looked at him mischie-vously. "Is there a problem?"

He took her hand and placed it over his erection. "*You're* the problem," he said, realizing that he was dead serious. What was he going to do with her?

She cupped him in both hands, going up on tiptoe to kiss him gently. "Don't worry, Mr. Wolff. I'll take it from here."

Gillian barely even recognized herself. Sexual banter? Erotically teasing and taunting a man who far outstripped her in experience of almost every kind? What had possessed her?

As she played with Devlyn's impressive shaft, she ac-knowledged that the question was not *what,* but *who.* Dev-lyn. Her lover.

He was steel sheathed in silky warm skin. Moisture oozed from the head of his erection, signaling his readiness to take her again. Understanding the full measure of how much she wanted that to happen told her she was beyond turning back.

The journey had begun. The ship cast away from its moorings. The die was cast. Any cliché she could pick. Her only hope was to enjoy Devlyn while he was hers and do her best not to beg when he was done and ready to move on.

He would try not to hurt her. That much she knew for sure. But trying was not the same as succeeding. It would be up to her to protect her heart.

Even now, seeing him at a man's most vulnerable point, her instinct was to protect him, to make him happy. The naïveté in that goal should have shamed her. Did she really want to be one in a long line of faceless women who had warmed Devlyn's bed?

But as much as she needed to be with him in the most elemental way, she also had a painful urge to save him from himself. Something in his past hung as a millstone around his neck. She knew it. And though he had shared glimpses of the events that shaped him, there was something more, something darker.

The possibilities scared her. She didn't want to rip open old wounds and have him hate her for it. But perhaps fate had brought the two of them together for a reason.

As she rubbed him with a delicate touch, he put his hand over hers. "Harder," he pleaded. "Faster."

She wanted him inside her when he reached climax. But it was an impossible situation at best. While she and Devlyn had been concentrating on each other, light rain had sneaked back into their wooded glade. It dripped from leaves overhead, filling the air with the humid, pungent scent of decaying leaves.

As Devlyn trembled in her embrace, she saw the depth of his trust. He was completely open to her, unguarded, intimately exposed.

Something cracked inside her, a wall she had tried to keep

in place to protect her heart. But it was too late. Feelings rushed in like floodwaters swamping a breach. It would be so easy to love him...and yet so terribly unwise.

Swallowing the lump in her throat, she tried to separate her messy emotions from the sensual experience at hand. Pushing aside everything but the need to pleasure him, she did as he asked. Faster. Harder. Devlyn moaned. Without words, he had allowed the balance of power to shift momentarily.

His big body warmed her, hands clenched on her shoulders, legs braced like bulwarks against the storm. When she hit a sensitive spot, he quaked and sank his teeth into her earlobe.

The sharp sting of pain made her belly quiver with hunger. Twice she had climaxed, and yet she wanted him again. To prove to herself that she still had some sort of sexual backbone, she concentrated on Devlyn. Denying her own need demonstrated that she could walk away at any time. When the situation became untenable.

She was not a victim, nor a helpless, fragile female. Choosing to be with Devlyn was a rational, eyes-wide-open decision.

He kissed her temple, his breath hot on her cheek. "I'll finish." The words were barely audible, his breath wheezing raggedly.

Leaning into him, both of her hands trapped between their bodies, she circled the head of his erection and brushed the eye. Devlyn came with a muffled curse.

When it was over, the silence was absolute but for the beat of her heart in her ears, and the faint chatter of a squirrel in a nearby tree.

Fifteen

On the way back to the car, Devlyn held Gillian's hand. She had no way of knowing, and he sure as hell wouldn't tell her...but that last bit of insanity was something he had never wanted, nor requested from any woman, ever.

It was no secret that he liked being in the driver's seat. He could tell himself that the only reason he had allowed her to pleasure him was that there was no other suitable alternative. But in truth, he had craved her touch like an addict coming off a three-day bender.

Her fingers were cold in his. He tucked her into the car and turned on the heat. They were both wet and rumpled, and God knew, it would be a good idea if they could slip into the house and change without being seen. He'd be hard-pressed to explain why they had lingered outside at the school site when the weather deteriorated.

The fact that neither of them said a word as they made their way back up the mountain didn't bother him. One of the things he liked about Gillian was her innate calm, her quiet serenity. They had talked plenty back there. The important things were said. Gillian had committed to accompany him to Atlanta.

Like a kid anticipating Christmas, Saturday couldn't arrive quickly enough to suit Devlyn.

Unfortunately for both of them, slipping into the house unnoticed was not an option. The massive front doors of the castle were flung open wide, and a trio of young men took turns unloading suitcases from a chauffeur-driven limousine.

Gillian squirmed in her seat, trying futilely to smooth the wrinkles from her damp skirt. "What's going on?" she asked.

He pulled the car to one side of the sweeping courtyard and parked. "At a guess, I'd say my sister has arrived. She's in charge of the carnival."

"That would be Annalise, right? I remember her. I was terribly jealous of her clothes and her toys. Not a very nice thing to admit, but I was just a kid."

"Annalise always loved playing dress up. And nothing has really changed."

"Do you think anyone will notice if we walk around to the back of the house?"

Devlyn shook his head, grinning as he smoothed a tendril of hair from her flushed cheek. "That ship has sailed, Gillian. Our best bet is to brazen it out."

Her smile was wry. "I'm thinking you have more experience with that kind of behavior than I do."

He kissed her softly, closing his eyes for a split second as the taste of her filled him with contentment. "Then follow my lead."

Despite his assurances, the situation went downhill as they entered the impressive front foyer. Not only was Annalise there, but also Devlyn's father, his uncle and Gillian's mother. Doreen Carlyle was holding a dustcloth and a broom.

Beside him, Gillian stiffened.

Gradually, everyone froze when he and Gillian entered, conversation dwindling, and all eyes going to the unmistakable evidence that Devlyn and Gillian had been tramping through the woods. No one could possibly know what that outing included, but Gillian's bright red face wasn't helping matters.

Annalise launched herself at him, going in for a bear hug as was her custom. He kissed her cheek. "What ill wind blew you in?"

His tall, willowy sister smacked his cheek lightly. "Be nice. I hoped you'd be glad to see me."

She turned and smiled at Gillian. "And who might this be? I thought you kept all your glittery girlfriends in Atlanta."

Devlyn bristled. Annalise had a kind heart, but a smart mouth. His surge of protectiveness warned him he was navigating new waters, but he couldn't allow Gillian to be embarrassed any more than she already was. "This is Gillian Carlyle. She's working with me on the new school project. As an educational consultant."

Doreen stepped forward, her face an older, rounder version of her only child's. "Gillian's my daughter, Miss Annalise. You probably don't remember. It's been years since she was here on the mountain."

Annalise held out her hand. "Sorry, Ms. Carlyle. If you're working with my brother, you deserve my sympathies."

"Call me Gillian, please." Gillian shook hands with Annalise and then hugged her mother. "I'd love to stay and chat, but we got caught in the rain and I'm freezing. Excuse me."

Devlyn was forced to let her escape, doomed to run interference with his relatives. Doreen excused herself as well, but disappeared down a corridor opposite from the one where her daughter was changing clothes. Devlyn spent a blissful second imagining his lover naked before he was forced to direct his attention elsewhere.

He glanced at the accumulating pile of luggage. "Are you moving in permanently?"

Annalise shrugged. "I wasn't sure what the weather would be this weekend, so I had to come prepared."

Devlyn's father, Vincent, grinned at his only daughter. "Leave her alone. I'm still hoping that one day I can keep her here for good."

Annalise pecked his weathered cheek with a kiss. "I love you, Papa."

Victor spoke up, combing through a pile of mail on a silver salver. "What did Gillian think of the property?"

"She was impressed. Sam met us there and walked off the rooms, giving her an idea of the layout."

Annalise's cheerful grin dimmed. "Sam Ely? What is Satan's offspring up to these days?"

"I've never understood why the two of you hate each other so much. After all, you work in the same building." Devlyn wasn't blind to his sister's antipathy. He just didn't understand it.

She shrugged. "Personality conflict. He doesn't have one."

The two older men chortled. Devlyn grinned wryly. "Well, Gillian was sure taken with him. He tried to whisk her away for an intimate lunch, but I nixed that."

"Because you have your eye on her?" Annalise's gimlet stare almost made him squirm. Almost.

"Because we have paperwork to get through this afternoon," he said. "Those permits won't fill out themselves."

He didn't think she was fooled, but thankfully, she dropped it. A few minutes later, Devlyn managed to escape, as well.

After showering and changing into corduroy slacks and a cashmere V-neck sweater, he tapped lightly on the connecting door to Gillian's suite. After long, agonizing seconds, she opened it.

She was wearing an outfit similar to his, only her lilac cardigan and silky ivory camisole outlined pretty breasts. Breasts Devlyn had recently tasted. He leaned in the doorframe, not trusting himself to go anywhere near her bed. "Do you feel like getting some work done?"

"Of course."

He frowned when he looked past her and realized that her packed suitcase stood ready for departure.

Her soft lips were covered in light pink lip gloss. He saw the movement of her smooth throat when she swallowed.

"Running away, Gillian?"

His sarcasm made her frown. "I told you I wouldn't stay here."

"You don't trust me," he said flatly, disturbed by how much that hurt.

"I don't trust us," she said. "This afternoon I want you to go over the paperwork with me. I have my laptop at home. I'll work from there until Saturday."

"And you'll go with me?"

"I said I would."

The sexual energy that swirled between them was almost palpable. His fingertips dug into the doorframe, holding himself in place. "Less than forty-eight hours," he groaned. "I don't know if I'll make it."

She blushed prettier than any woman he had ever met. Not that many of his female acquaintances actually blushed. He tended to date sleek, predatory versions of himself.

"Won't your father think it's odd that you hired me and I'll be leaving so soon?"

"We can work on the project in Atlanta." He straightened. "May I come in?"

She hesitated, but the flare of need in her eyes matched

the burning hunger in his belly. "We're practicing abstinence, remember?"

He held up his hands. "Only a kiss. I promise."

Gillian nodded slowly. It was no use to pretend. She wanted him. And falling in love with him would be as easy as breathing. Certain heartbreak loomed ahead like a deadly reef. But she refused to look in that direction.

Devlyn reeled her in and bent his head to trace each side of her collarbone with his tongue. He smelled divine, a combination of shower soap and a faint hint of woodsy cologne. She wrapped her arms around his neck and flexed her fingers in the soft wool of his sweater.

He mumbled something into her neck.

"I can't hear you." She tilted her head to one side as he nibbled her throat.

"Lock your door. I'll be quick."

Her knees went weak and her panties grew damp. "No." As a negative, it lacked authority.

His hand slid over her silky chemise and toyed with a beaded nipple. "Please." Even through two layers of fabric, his touch was electric.

She never had a chance to answer. A loud knock at Devlyn's outer doorway was followed by his father's booming summons. "You decent, boy? Vic and I want to talk to you about the Mexico deal."

Devlyn dropped his head to her shoulder, cursing eloquently beneath his breath. "I love my father, I love my father, I love my father…"

She giggled despite her disappointment. "Go," she said softly, allowing herself one last stroke of his hair.

With obvious pained difficulty, he straightened. "Meet me in the main dining room in an hour. We'll spread everything out and go from there."

For some reason, his words gave Gillian an image of herself, nude, spread-eagled on the table as a feast for Devlyn Wolff. Her sweater was suddenly far too hot for the temperature of the room. "I'll be there," she croaked. She shoved him away. "Go."

By the time she met him at the appointed place, she had regained control of her senses. They managed to conduct an impersonal, professional discussion about each one of the many permits and forms required for the start of a new school.

Of course, it helped that at least four different doors opened off the dining room, meaning that privacy was nonexistent. Various employees whisked in and out, readying the room for the evening's upcoming family dinner.

The architect's plans had already been tentatively approved. Once Gillian's suggestions were implemented, one more draft would be submitted and the project would be one step closer to groundbreaking.

When they had sifted through every layer of red tape, Gillian straightened the mass of paper and tucked it into a folder. "I'll spend all day on these tomorrow," she said, conscious of listening ears. "I should be able to get a good start."

"But you'll be attending the carnival, right?"

"I don't really know anything about it."

Devlyn leaned a hip on the table, laughing when one of the older maids gave him a swat on the behind. "LaVonn has known me since I was in grade school." He kissed her wrinkled cheek.

The African-American woman, surely nearing retirement, grinned. "This one was a handful. Always stealing cookies out of the kitchen."

"I was a growing boy."

"You were a menace." With a chuckle, she disappeared toward the kitchen.

Gillian was touched and confused. Who was the real Devlyn Wolff? This easygoing charmer, or the man with dark shadows in his past?

He folded his arms over his chest, snapping his fingers. "Earth to Gillian. The carnival is tomorrow night. Several members of the community wanted to have an event where they could contribute by creating a sense of local ownership in the project. Annalise offered to coordinate everything. We'll have inflatables, games, food. And all the money raised will be grassroots donations."

"That's a lovely idea."

"I'll be taking a turn in the dunking booth. How's your throwing arm?"

"I played intramural softball for four years in college. You should be very afraid."

Again, that naughty spark leaped and quivered. She cleared her throat. "My mother gets off duty in thirty minutes. If we're done here, I'll ride back down the mountain with her."

"Stay for dinner." Devlyn's eyes were dark, his expression sober. "My cousins and their wives will all be here…and Annalise. It will be fun."

"I don't want to give anyone the wrong impression of our relationship," she whispered. Even to her own ears the words sounded prissy.

Devlyn stood and straightened, a shadow of hurt in his eyes. "They know you're working here. You'll still be on the clock. I'll expect you at seven sharp."

He left the room abruptly, leaving her to hover uncertainly. She felt the oddest notion that she had injured his feelings, but that was absurd.

She went in search of her mother and found her putting away cleaning supplies in a hall closet off the kitchen wing. Gillian blurted it out. "I've been invited to eat with the family this evening."

Doreen's hands stilled. Her eyes mirrored anxiety and reluctance. "Are you sure that's wise? It's only a job, baby. We don't belong here."

"I realize that, Mama. Don't worry. I know what I'm doing."

Doreen kissed her cheek, took a garment from a hook and slipped her arms into the ten-year-old raincoat. "You're a grown woman. You don't need my permission. But I want you to be careful."

Gillian hugged her mom, inhaling the familiar scent of dusting spray. "Thank you for being concerned. But I'll be okay. I promise."

Wandering back to her temporary suite, she decided to check one more time and make sure she had retrieved all her belongings. When she opened her bedroom door, Annalise Wolff sat in a chair, slim, elegant legs crossed, her gaze unapologetic. "We need to talk."

Sixteen

Gillian's belly clenched. She put the folder on the dresser and turned to face the woman whom she had envied for many years as an adolescent. "About what? Do you have some ideas for the school?" But that made no sense, because Annalise would have gone to Devlyn directly if she had input to offer.

"About the fact that you're falling for my brother."

"Don't be absurd," Gillian said calmly, her pulse racing with anxiety. "We're working together for a brief time, that's all."

"I saw the way you looked at him when you both walked into the house."

"You're imagining things. We only recently ran into each other. He didn't even remember me at first."

"But I'm sure you took care of *that*. You've known him for years, long enough to realize that my family protects its own. If you have an angle to play, I warn you...I will do anything to make sure my brother doesn't get railroaded. He has a noble but regrettable tendency to pick up misfits and strays. And you wouldn't be the first woman to have eyes for his bank balance."

Gillian's hands fisted at her sides. "Are you always this rude, or is it me?"

"Devlyn may look as if his life is smooth sailing, but he's had some tough things to deal with over the years."

"You all have," Gillian said quietly. Annalise's plain speaking was understandable. The Wolffs stuck together for the good of the clan. "You have nothing to fear from me," she said. "I swear. My relationship with Devlyn is strictly temporary."

Either business or pleasure…the statement held true for both.

Annalise stood, tall and proud, immeasurably sophisticated. "I notice you haven't denied loving him."

"Devlyn is an admirable man. And I'm happy to be working with him. That's all."

The other woman passed her on the way to the door. "I hope for your sake that you're telling the truth. Because Devlyn will never settle down to home and hearth."

"Not that it matters to me, but why are you so sure?"

Annalise's eyes held a hint of the pain that Gillian had witnessed more than once in Devlyn's. "I just know," she said flatly. "So consider yourself forewarned."

After that, Gillian was in no mood to participate in a Wolff family dinner, but Devlyn had given her no choice. His high-handed demand left her angry and confused. Why had he insisted on her presence? She showered and washed her hair before changing into a pair of black dress slacks and a crimson silk blouse. The flattering outfit bolstered her confidence. There was a good chance that the ensemble was not dressy enough for Wolff standards, but it was her only choice.

Though she listened at the connecting door from time to

time, she was unable to hear any sounds at all from Devlyn's side. So at a quarter till seven she made her way to the dining room. Alone.

When Gillian arrived she saw that almost everyone was already seated.

Vincent Wolff stood politely. "Welcome, Ms. Carlyle. I think you know most of us. But we have new additions, I'm proud to report. Gracie, there in the pink, is Gareth's wife, and this sweet young thing to my left is Victor's granddaughter, Cammie, and her mother, Olivia, Kieran's wife."

Fortunately for Gillian, Jacob and his bride were still traveling, and Devlyn and Annalise's brother, Larkin, was not present, either. She didn't think she could have borne the scrutiny of the whole lot of them.

It was bad enough as it was. The feeling of being an outsider was keen and unsettling. Devlyn didn't help matters. He acted as if what had happened that morning in the rain was not even on his radar. And wasn't that the way she wanted it?

If Devlyn had been in a flirtatious mood, she might have embarrassed herself by mooning over him. Instead, she concentrated on chatting with the only other two people at the table who might understand how she felt.

Blue-eyed Gracie, the redhead, was sweet, but quiet. Olivia, on the other hand, was gorgeous, with long brunette hair, a curvaceous figure and flashing dark eyes that sparkled when she laughed.

Gillian exchanged small talk with them and did her best to ignore Devlyn.

Annalise stirred the pot. "So, Gillian, how did my brother come to hire you? I wasn't aware that he had even begun interviews."

All eyes turned to Gillian. Her hands, hidden beneath the table, clenched in her lap. Keeping her words even and matter-of-fact, she answered the pointedly barbed question. "I had a car accident near the bottom of the mountain recently. Devlyn was kind enough to help me when I was stranded. During our conversation I told him that I had lost my teaching job because of budget cutbacks. He realized that I could help out with the new school."

Annalise studied her for long, painful seconds. "How fortunate for you," she drawled, the expression on her face impossible to read.

Devlyn frowned, looking at his sister with irritation. "Knock it off, Annalise. Gillian is a highly qualified teacher and a resident of Burton. She's perfect for the job."

The rest of the table had fallen silent, sensing drama in the making. The two siblings scowled at each other. Annalise seemed unaffected by her brother's ill humor. She turned and smiled at Gillian, a seemingly warm, genuine smile. "Forgive my bad manners. Devlyn and I are in the habit of needling each other. But I usually don't allow collateral damage. I'm glad you'll be working with us."

Gillian was ready to crawl under the table when salvation arrived in the form of Devlyn's taciturn cousin Gareth. The other man stood, putting a hand on his wife's shoulder. "At the risk of sounding unconcerned about the new school, I'd like to get personal for a moment."

He glanced down at his pink-cheeked wife. "We had hoped to say this with everyone present, but that's starting to look like Christmas at the soonest, and some things can't wait." He paused and swallowed, his face radiating quiet joy. "Gracie's pregnant."

Pandemonium erupted. Cammie jumped out of her seat. Victor and Vincent both tried to pretend they weren't wiping away tears. Olivia beamed and Kieran smiled broadly.

No one seemed to notice Devlyn. No one but Gillian. His face froze, every nuance of expression wiped away. For a split second, anguish filled his eyes, a hurt so deep and bitter that

Gillian almost gasped aloud. She started to stand, driven to touch him, to offer comfort.

But in an instant, the grief vanished. In its place was the man with the lazy smile, the affable, bright-eyed life of the party. Devlyn got to his feet, his hands white-knuckled on the back of his chair. "To Gracie," he said, lifting his wine-glass. "To Gareth, who won't know what hit him. And to the newest baby Wolff."

Victor glanced at his brother, his beaming grin smug. "That will be two for me. You'd better find someone for those kids of yours, Vincent. You aren't getting any younger."

Vincent took the teasing in good stride, but to Gillian's assessing gaze, his soul was troubled.

Devlyn patted his father's back. "Dad knows the busi-ness is my baby. I guess you'd better count on Annalise for grandchildren. She has men hanging all over her. Surely one of them can be hog-tied before they discover what a pain in the butt she is."

Suddenly insults and good-natured teasing flew back and forth across the table in rapid-fire succession. Gillian sat back and watched the interplay, wistfully wishing she had at least one sibling with whom to trade such wicked repartee.

The Wolffs were a warm, tightly knit family.

She caught Devlyn's eye and pointed to her watch. He gath-ered the crowd's attention for a second time. "I promised Gil-lian that I would have her home early. Save some dessert for me. I'll expect my piece of pie when I get back."

Beneath a barrage of hoots and catcalls, Devlyn and Gil-lian said their goodbyes and finally made it out of the room. "I need to get my suitcase and purse," she said.

He barely looked at her. "I'll bring the car around," he said. "Meet me out front in ten minutes."

Despite the distance to her room, she was able to make it there and back quickly. Devlyn tossed her bag in the backseat and slid behind the wheel. Gillian joined him, wincing when he swung out of the portico, causing the tires to slip and spin on the damp pavement.

The rain had moved out. The night was dark, with low clouds obscuring both stars and moon.

Silence lay thick and suffocating inside the small vehicle. Gillian stared out the window, wishing she could disappear. "I'm sorry if I offended you about not wanting to stay for dinner," she said. "But I think my point was well taken. Gareth and Gracie didn't need a stranger present for their big news."

"Clearly, they would be happy for the whole world to know. Forget it."

The darkness made it easier for her to speak her mind. "You're not happy for them."

A heartbeat of hushed shock. "Of course I am."

"I saw your face. Everyone else was looking at Gracie and Gareth. But I was watching you."

"You're imagining things."

In the dark, in the quiet, she was brave. Placing one hand on his hard, muscular thigh, she sighed. "I don't expect anything from you, Devlyn, other than the here and now. But I deserve your honesty. Is that too much to ask before I sneak off to Atlanta with you?"

His hesitation was eons longer this time. "Is that an ultimatum?"

She rubbed his leg. "Of course not. But I can see how much tonight hurt you. And I want to know why."

One mile passed. Two. She sat back in her seat, no longer touching him. If he chose to retreat behind a wall of stony silence, there was nothing she could do about it.

Up ahead, her mother's small house came into view. It was tucked away in a small copse of maples that Gillian's father had planted when Gillian was small. The porch light was on, but the windows were dark. The car rolled to a stop. Devlyn cut the engine.

Gillian fumbled in her purse and found her keys. "I'm sure my mother is asleep. She was up early this morning."

"That's why you didn't want to stay, isn't it? You didn't honestly think anyone would comment on our relationship. You were embarrassed that your mother was cleaning the house while you were a guest."

Gillian knew enough psychology to recognize what was going on. She'd had to take classes as part of her teacher training. Devlyn was trying to shift the onus on to her.

"Yes," she said baldly. "I was embarrassed. It's weird."

"Only in your head. A job is a job. Your mother is a valuable member of the Wolff staff...just as you are now."

She couldn't tell if he was trying to reassure her or put her in her place. "We seem to be blurring the lines," she said. "Maybe if you decide what you want from me, it would be easier."

"Can't I have both? The teacher *and* the woman?"

"God, you're stubborn. I suppose always getting what you want will do that to a man."

He leaned across the console and slid a hand beneath her hair. "I want *you*," he said, the words gruff. "But since I'm a little too old to be screwing in the backseat of a car in my date's driveway, I suppose I'm doomed to disappointment." He pulled her close and kissed her gently. "Don't analyze this, Gillian. Just live in the moment."

It wasn't her style. It wasn't her preference. But when he touched her breast and lightly rubbed her aching nipple, she allowed herself to be persuaded. "I'll try." She tangled her tongue with his, experiencing the slow, sweet slide into arousal.

Devlyn broke away at long last, breathing hard. "Damned carnival," he muttered.

She smiled in the darkness. "I'll meet you there. My mother will want to come, I'm sure."

"And then Saturday morning, first thing, we're out of here. We'll take the jet." His hoarse words were a vow. "I'll have you in my bed before lunch."

She stiffened instinctively, and he realized what he had said.

Devlyn groaned. "Oh, hell. You won't get on the jet, will you? We'll have to drive. A whole damn day. Maybe we'll go to D.C. instead. It's closer."

She ran her fingers through his hair, dragging his mouth back to hers. "Think of it as foreplay," she whispered. "I'm sure we could get creative if we tried."

Seventeen

Devlyn's mind raced ahead, already imagining Gillian's nimble fingers pleasuring him as they traversed the interstate. Good God.

He pushed her away, breathing heavily. A few more seconds of that and he'd be tumbling her into the backseat. "Go inside," he begged. "Please."

Her soft laugh had the same effect as an electric shock. All the hair on his body stood up, and his heart stopped... beat sluggishly...and finally started again.

She opened her door and squeezed his hand. "I'll bring plenty of cash for the dunking booth," she said. "I like the thought of having you at my mercy."

He shoved her out of the car. It was either that or let her drive him insane with lust. "Good night," he called out through his open window.

As he drove away, he watched her in the rearview mirror, standing guard, tracking his progress as he rolled out of sight.

He took his time getting home. The open road called, offering the oblivion of unknown destinations and endless flight. The prospect of meandering for an hour held a distinct attraction. But his family would be expecting him, and after all they had collectively suffered, he would never deliberately cause them to worry.

The staff was gone for the night when he returned…at least the ones who didn't live on-site. He parked himself in the enormous garage and went outside to look up. Clouds still cloaked the mountaintop. Dampness seeped into his bones.

"I thought you weren't coming back."

His sister's voice startled him. He spun around and spotted a pale figure in the mist. "Still a night owl, I see."

"You expected me to change?"

Now that his eyes had adjusted to the dark, he could make out Annalise perched on a wall, her legs swinging. He shrugged. "None of us ever do, I suppose."

She hopped down. "You want to walk?"

He nodded. Once upon a time this had been their ritual, along with their brother, Larkin. The three of them would slip out late at night and prowl the mountain like a band of wild coyotes.

Annalise put her arm around his waist, rubbing her cheek on his shoulder. "I think *you* may have changed, Devvie. I've never seen you with a woman like Gillian. She's not exactly a looker."

"She's beautiful," he said, disturbed that Annalise couldn't see it. "Like a lush, quiet meadow beneath a hot summer sun."

"My big brother waxing poetic. Will wonders never cease."

He wrapped an arm around her narrow shoulders, tucking her close to his side. "I still maintain that you're a brat."

"Is this serious?"

He swallowed. "No. You know I don't do serious."

"There's always a first time."

"Not for me."

"Have you talked to her?"

"No. It's not important. She and I are enjoying a mutual attraction."

"And when she falls in love with you or vice versa?"

"I won't. And I haven't spun her any promises."

"You're my brother and I love you, but sometimes you're an idiot."

He sighed and turned their steps in the direction of the house. "Takes one to know one."

The following day crawled by. Knowing Gillian, she was up to her ears in the paperwork they had gone over, crossing *t*s and dotting *i*s and making sure not a single detail fell through the cracks. Devlyn wanted badly to call her. The impulse was so strong, he forced himself to ignore it. Her probing the night before, along with the lecture from Annalise, had left him unsettled.

Nothing had changed. *He* hadn't changed. Annalise's worries were unfounded. He had everything under control.

But when he thought about the possibility of opening his heart to Gillian, a tiny glimmer of hope flickered to life inside his chest.

Midmorning he and Annalise drove down to the school site to meet the company that was supplying the inflatable play equipment and the tents for the carnival games. In an hour, volunteers began to arrive, armed with enthusiasm and strong backs.

Annalise was in her element, cheerfully barking out orders and organizing her minions. The day was hot already. Though in Burton they occasionally had snow as early as Halloween, it also wasn't unusual to get a wave of autumn heat that brought out one last hurrah for summer.

Fortunately, this was one of those days.

During a lull in the action when Devlyn's skills and muscle weren't needed, he made his way to the back of the property, disappearing into the woods where he and Gillian had spent time alone yesterday morning.

Simply standing there, near the stump, caused his heart to slug in his chest and his erection to grow rigid with longing. He was a highly sexed man, and he understood the mechanics of male arousal. What he couldn't fathom was the way his chaotic emotions seemed to be taking precedence over his physical need at the moment.

It would be hours before he could take her again. And yet, he was excited at the thought of simply being with her. Eating greasy funnel cakes, winning a gaudy stuffed animal for her at the dart table, holding her hand.

Incredulous at his sappy anticipation, he stared deep into his heart and wondered if Annalise was right. *Was* he changing? Could he?

Shaking off the impossible notion, he strode back to the melee, his chest tight with confusion. All he wanted from Gillian was sex. And that was nothing new for him, not at all.

By four o'clock, it was time for him and his wilting sister to head up the mountain for a shower and a change of clothes. Despite her exhaustion, Annalise chattered the entire way home. She thrived on a challenge, and the day's activities had energized her mentally.

There was an awkward moment when Devlyn insisted on driving his own car down the mountain to the carnival. The rest of the family loaded up without comment, but Annalise gave him a pointed look that said she knew what he was up to.

When they all arrived at the site of the future school, a small crowd began to converge on the once-barren field. First a dozen, then two, then more and more until the place was packed with families out for an evening's entertainment.

It took him thirty minutes to find Gillian. At last he located her in the kissing booth. A husky farmer in overalls handed over a five-dollar bill and planted an enthusiastic smack on Gillian's laughing lips. The line was too long for Devlyn's liking.

He strode to the front without apology, smacked down a twenty, and putting both hands beneath Gillian's hair, kissed her long and slow until the crowd of cheering males demanded their turn.

Ignoring the impatient row of testosterone behind him, he whispered in her ear, "Come find me when you're done."

Her hair was tied up in a ponytail in deference to the heat. It made her look about sixteen. "Sure," she said, her voice breathless. "It won't be long."

He walked away, his barely leashed hunger unable to bear the sight, even in fun, of other men touching her. It was impossible for a Wolff, any one of them, to wander unnoticed. People stopped him time and again to say hello, to offer thanks for the new school to come.

Devlyn felt as if he were watching himself from a distance. He smiled and shook hands and chatted with strangers, all the while impatiently counting the seconds until Gillian arrived at his side.

Little Cammie distracted him for fifteen minutes by enlisting him to challenge her beloved daddy to a game of water pistols. It was the kind of game where each contestant pummeled a small opening and tried to pop a balloon. Kieran had already trounced Gareth and was riding high on his victory.

Devlyn stepped up beside his cousin. "I hate to disappoint your cute-as-a-button daughter, but you're going down."

Kieran flexed both hands and grasped the trigger of his neon-orange plastic revolver. "Bring it on."

The air horn sounded, and both men fired. Devlyn was cool and focused. In his peripheral vision, he could see Kieran grinning as he shot a stream of water in a calculated arc.

Six other men flanked them, but Devlyn knew his cousin was his only competition.

All across the arcade, colorful balloons rose and fattened. It was close, so close. Suddenly, Devlyn felt a small, cool hand touch his left arm. "You're doing great," Gillian cried. "Don't let him win."

Devlyn's trigger finger relaxed for half a second, his attention riveted on her laughing face. Though he immediately returned to the challenge, it was too late. Kieran's balloon popped with a loud report, and Devlyn was forced to eat crow.

He holstered the gun and slung an arm around her shoulders. "Did he bribe you to distract me?" he asked, inhaling her scent, feeling a zing of joy bounce through his chest.

Gillian's gaze met Kieran's. They both grinned.

"I'll never tell," she said, laughing in delight.

Moments later, Devlyn glanced at his watch and realized that his shift at the dunking booth was about to start. Dragging Gillian in his wake, he worked his way to the far side of the field where a metal tank stood, painted in red, white and blue stripes.

He handed her his watch and billfold and started stripping off his clothes. Her eyes widened in shock until she saw that he wore black swim trunks beneath his pants. "Get your money ready," he said.

The line for the dunking booth wound in an arc and doubled back on itself. The teenage boy who preceded Devlyn in the hot seat was a popular quarterback at the consolidated high school. His teammates were ruthless, dunking their friend time and again. The skinny kid was visibly grateful when Devlyn climbed up to relieve him.

Gillian pulled a small, folded stack of ones from her jeans pocket and waited her turn. Devlyn charmed the crowd, entertaining his would-be attackers with hilarious wisecracks.

His broad chest gleamed in the sun, his shoulders wide and sculpted with muscle. When he smiled, Gillian felt the day grow brighter.

Devlyn had been dunked only twice by the time Gillian made it to the front of the line. She took the softball handed to her by the volunteer and eyed her target. The metal circle was about twelve inches in diameter and about fifteen feet away.

Her lover watched, momentarily silent, as she tossed the ball in her hand. Up and down, up and down. Devlyn was shivering, the brisk breeze chilling his skin despite the warm afternoon. His hair was wet. He shoved it back from his forehead with a quick hand, betraying for a split second his impatience.

She smiled. "Here we go."

At a dollar a try, she had enough for twenty shots. But she was out of practice and had trouble finding her rhythm. The first seven dollars she handed over were wasted.

Devlyn sat, arms folded across his chest…cocky, laughing. "Nice try, little girl. Why don't you admit defeat? You'll never do it."

Gillian's temper flickered. Devlyn Wolff might best her in any number of ways, but not this. Not today.

She wound up a pitch and let fly, this one hitting the tank with a thud that made the steel vibrate with a dull *thunk*.

Devlyn hooted. The crowd shouted encouragement.

Gillian took a deep breath, grabbed another ball and steadied herself. This time she hit the target, but it was a glancing blow, not hard enough to engage the mechanism.

Five minutes later she was down to her last dollar, and Devlyn Wolff had become an infuriating, testosterone-driven heckler. Sweat beaded Gillian's forehead. Her hand was slippery. Drying her palms on her jeans, she reached for her final shot.

The ball felt heavy. Her arm ached. Gritting her teeth, she

refused to look at Devlyn this time. Focusing her attention on that small metal target, she reared back, took a deep breath and heaved the softball with all her might.

It hit the circle dead-on and Devlyn yelled in shock as he plunged into the icy water. The crowd went wild. Immediately, he was on his feet, waist-deep in the tank, his hot gaze trapping Gillian's across the heads of children and adults who thronged to hug her and congratulate her.

She smiled at him tauntingly, exulted at her successful attempt to bring him down. But in the pit of her stomach, tiny butterflies were born at the knowledge that retribution would come.

To say the day was a success was an understatement. The crowds stayed late. The weather was perfect. The money rolled in.

But by ten-thirty that night, even the diehards were beginning to call it an evening. Devlyn had kept Gillian by his side for hours, feeding her cotton candy, teasing her about her penchant for Skee-Ball, and being introduced to her neighbors, many of whom had grown up in the valley and stayed as adults.

He was more than ready to tuck her into the car and find some privacy when a red-faced, heavyset woman dashed across the grass intent on intercepting them. "Mr. Wolff, Mr. Wolff," she said. "This is my four-year-old grandson. If construction stays on schedule, he'll be in the first class to go all the way through the new school." She shoved the sleepy-eyed kid into Devlyn's arms. "I want to get a picture of the two of you."

Gillian stepped out of the way, charmed to see the über-masculine Devlyn holding a chubby little boy.

The woman pulled out her camera and held it up. "Smile for Granny."

The little boy managed a grin, but Gillian's amusement faded when she saw Devlyn's face. Instead of staring at the camera, he was looking down at the child in his arms. The expression on his face was terrible to witness.

She blinked, and the moment was gone, almost as if she had conjured it up in her imagination.

Devlyn set the boy on his feet and smiled at the grandma. "Thanks for coming today."

As the woman and her little one wandered off, Gillian linked her arm through Devlyn's, disturbed, but unable to put her finger on any exact cause.

He nuzzled her neck. "Only a few more hours," he said, "and I'll have you all to myself."

"I have good news."

"I'm all ears."

"I went to the walk-in clinic today and got a prescription for motion sickness. The doctor swears by it. So if you're still willing, I'd like to take the jet."

Eighteen

Devlyn sighed. "Thank goodness. All those hours locked up in a car with you would have tested my control."

She linked her fingers with his. "Am I that irresistible?"

"You have no idea." He glanced around, assessing the level of privacy. He and Gillian were a good hundred yards from the nearest carnival enthusiast, but that was still too crowded for what he had in mind. "Follow me," he said, tugging on her hand.

She cooperated without protest. Which boded well for the weekend's plans. A compliant woman made a man imagine all sorts of scenarios. He stopped in front of the first-aid tent and looked casually over his shoulder. No one was paying any attention. Holding back the flap, he ushered Gillian inside and ducked beneath the canvas. "Alone at last."

All the medical supplies had already been cleared out, but a cot remained. In the dark, he could hear Gillian breathe. "We are *not* going to do this," she said firmly.

"Do what?"

"You know what I mean."

He tracked her by feel, running his hands over her shoulders and pulling her close. "I can't wait till Atlanta. I tried. But I can't."

"We're going there in the morning."

"Seems like forever." He kissed her forehead. But his hands were busy, too. Her breasts fit his palms perfectly. She was wearing a simple, thin T-shirt, and he could feel the firm thrust of her nipples against his fingertips.

"Devlyn…" Her voice came as a soft sigh in the darkness. Wrapping her arms around his neck, she found his mouth with hers, both of them hungry…impatient.

He ripped her T-shirt up and off, shoving the bra aside to taste sweet curves, the soft flesh crowned with rigid, berrylike nubs. Gillian trembled in his arms. She was slender, delicate, so sweet.

"Wait." He dragged himself away from her and peered outside the tent. The field was empty and quiet now save for the various booths and tents that would be dismantled in the morning. All the cars were gone. Thank God.

Gillian had definitely lost her shyness with him. Her slim, strong fingers wrapped around his wrist and pulled. "Hurry," she said.

He knelt in front of her and dragged her jeans and panties down her legs. Gillian kicked them aside and pressed herself, naked as the day she was born, to his chest. *Sweet Lord.*

He scooped her into his arms and carried her four steps to the cot. Depositing her gently, he disposed of his own clothes and came down on top of her, using his hands to spread her thighs. The makeshift bed was narrow. Devlyn was big and desperate.

Canvas and metal creaked and popped as he fit himself to Gillian's warm, welcoming center. When the head of his shaft slid inside, his brain shut down. He had a faint sensation that something was not right, but he ignored it like brushing away a pesky fly. The only thing left was sensation. Wet silk wrapped around an erection that was as hard as ones he'd sported as a callow teen.

He wanted to say things to her...needed her to know what this meant to him. But his body betrayed him. Need was a razor-sharp enemy, tying him in knots, urging him to take... take...take. Thrusting firmly, he buried himself all the way to her core.

Gillian's legs wrapped around his waist.

"Am I crushing you?" He could barely push the words from his dry throat.

"No," she whispered. "You're perfect."

Her response made him flinch inwardly, but there was no time for self-analysis. Beneath him, she was soft and welcoming...intensely feminine. He moved in her, feeling something beyond the connection of body to body. Without words, she offered healing where he had asked for none.

He loved her slowly, drawing every moment into a million shattered sparkles of bliss. Something shifted inside him, a momentous fault line grinding open to reveal weakness he had never allowed anyone to see.

Even now, he couldn't share it. Not with her. Not with pure, decent Gillian. But he acknowledged its existence. Faced it down. Stood strong.

He would not be broken. Not with so much at stake.

Gillian's inner muscles clenched his shaft as she cried out. The extra stimulation was more than he could bear. He shouted as he climaxed, shuddering, helpless, spent and dazed in her arms.

Gillian stirred, wondering if she had dozed off. "Devlyn. I have to go home."

His rough tongue found her nipple and sent ripples of re-membered pleasure skating through her veins.

She shoved at his chest. "Seriously. Let me up."

He mumbled a protest but finally levered himself to his feet. Darkness was Gillian's salvation, enabling her to dress without his slumberous eyes luring her into another round of insanity.

Muttering an imprecation when his head bumped a tent pole, Devlyn dressed, as well. She could barely see him. "What time is it?" she asked.

He hit a button and illuminated the dial of his watch. "After midnight."

"Good grief."

"Don't worry," he said, a smile in his voice. "I'll let you sleep in. Be ready at ten. We'll be in Atlanta for a late lunch."

Her heart skipped a beat. Was she deliberately going to accompany this virile, amazing man to his luxurious home in Georgia for the sole purpose of having sex over and over again?

God help her, she was. Because she was infatuated with him. It was pointless to deny it or to pretend that he wasn't going to break her heart. The knowledge hurt. Badly. And her reckless avoidance of dealing with reality was blatantly uncharacteristic.

But she would have Devlyn all to herself. And for the moment, that was enough.

He held her hand as they walked back across the grass to the car. With the sun long gone, the air was chilled, the night shadowy and still. Though Devlyn was not a man for pretty speeches, she believed he cared about her.

But was that a lie she had invented to pave the way for her upcoming foolishness, or was it true? Did he see her as anything other than a convenient bed partner?

Troubled and unsettled, she allowed him to tuck her into the car. Her mother's house was only a few miles away. They completed the trip in silence, each lost in thought.

Though she protested, he insisted on walking her to the door. As before, the house was dark, the porch light left on for late arrivals.

They faced each other on the top step. She cleared her throat. "I'll be ready in the morning."

His sexy smile was nowhere to be seen. The expression on his face could best be described as somber. "Tell me you understand this is not a permanent liaison."

Agony ripped through her chest, stealing her soul, her breath. "Has Annalise been warning you about me? Don't worry, Devlyn. I'm under no illusions."

His thumbs brushed her cheeks with butterfly caresses. "If it were anybody, it would be you." They were so close she could inhale the scent of lovemaking on his skin.

"Don't," she said curtly, rigid in his embrace...unable to bear tenderness in the midst of cold, hard reality. "I don't need anything from you but your body. I'm a temporarily employed elementary schoolteacher with my life mapped out in front of me. For once, I'm planning to stray from the straight and narrow. Your conscience can remain clear."

The muscles in his throat moved. "I may be condemned to hell for this."

"For what?"

"Taking what you're offering and giving nothing in return."

"Sex for barter is prostitution. And I won't let that happen. Mutual pleasure, Devlyn. That's what this is. Now go home and I'll see you in a few hours."

A sudden noise behind her startled her badly. She whirled around in time to see a small boy scuttle from behind the porch swing. His cheekbone was bloody and bruised, his eyes huge with apprehension. "Ms. Gillian. I wanted to go to the carnival, but I couldn't. Did you bring any cotton candy home with you?"

Gillian glanced at Devlyn, whispering sotto voce. "It's Jamie. My mother takes him to Sunday school on the weekends. He lives on a farm down the road." A wretched, rundown place with wrecked cars in the yard and a roof missing shingles.

The boy was somewhere between four and five years of age. But he was small and thin and had the look of malnutrition.

She crouched in front of him. "I'm sorry, Jamie. There wasn't any cotton candy left over. Why couldn't you come tonight?"

He rubbed his unhurt eye. "My daddy needed me to work."

"To work?"

"I have to help feed the animals."

Something didn't ring true. "What happened to your face? Did you fall down?"

Big eyes looked up at her, their gaze oddly adult. "Yeah. That was it."

He was lying. She knew it as well as she knew her name. "Who hurt you, Jamie?" she asked softly, putting a hand on his arm.

He flinched and backed away, breaking the contact. "No one."

Gillian expected Devlyn to step in any moment and help her, but he stood silent and unmoving. Trying to keep her voice reassuring, she asked again, "Who hit your face, Jamie? You can trust me. I won't let them do it again."

Hope. Painful, flickering hope spread over his face. Those wary, cagey eyes darted to Devlyn and back to Gillian. "He said I deserved it."

Oh, God. "Who, Jamie? Your dad?"

Huge, silent tears welled in his eyes and made tracks down his dirty cheeks. He nodded, unable to say the words.

"Where is he now?"

"Asleep. I can count," he said with tragic pride. "When I see five bottles I know he won't wake up. That's why I ran away."

Gillian stood and turned to Devlyn. "Help me get him into the house," she said, speaking quietly so the boy couldn't hear. "He may need stitches."

Devlyn didn't move. "No." In the pale, yellowish light from the single bulb by the door, his features were a mask, totally devoid of emotion. Even his eyes were dull and lifeless. "Call the police. They have procedures to deal with these situations. Social services."

Everything inside her congealed with horrified disbelief. He wasn't going to lift a finger for either her or for the boy. "I know you don't like children," she whispered furiously, "but damn it, Devlyn, this is low. Are you really such a cold-hearted bastard?"

Her heart broke as her dreams shattered. She beseeched him with her eyes and her sheer will. "Tell me you'll stay and help me deal with whatever has to happen."

He shrugged. "I have things to do. It's late. Call 911 and they'll pick him up." Turning his back on her, he walked down the steps calmly.

Everything inside her throbbed with a pain so intense, she felt faint. "Devlyn," she shouted at him, torn by anger and desperation and incredulity.

He stopped, hesitated, turned. "What?" Without the light to illuminate his face, he was nothing more than a shape in the dark.

"If you walk away right now, don't bother to come for me in the morning."

She didn't mean to say it. She wanted to snatch back the words as soon as they left her mouth. It was a test. An ultimatum. Perhaps he couldn't, wouldn't, give her the possibility of something real. But surely she hadn't misjudged him this badly. Surely he was an honorable, decent man.

Across the distance of several feet that might as well have been the chasm of the Grand Canyon, they stared at each other. His hands were in his pockets. One large shoulder lifted and fell in a shrug that indicated nothing more than a fillip of regret. "It's probably for the best, Gillian. Good night."

Nineteen

The next hours passed in a blur of exhaustion. Gillian coaxed Jamie into the house, woke her mother, and between the two of them, they fed him and cleaned his cheek and the rest of his small body. With the blood wiped away, the cut was less worrisome. They covered it with antiseptic cream and a small Band-Aid.

The sheriff who arrived less than thirty minutes later was a gentle, soft-spoken man who got down on his knees and eyed Jamie face-to-face. "You see this badge, son?"

Jamie nodded, his little eyes heavy with sleep.

The man picked him up gently. "This badge means I'm going to keep you safe, no matter what."

"Am I gonna stay with Ms. Gillian?"

"No. But somewhere just as good. I know a family that loves little boys like you. They'll feed you and laugh with you and play games and take care of you while the grown-ups make some decisions."

Jamie yawned, his head coming to rest on a shoulder covered in a uniform shirt. "Okay. But do you think *they* might have some cotton candy?"

At 2:00 a.m. Doreen Carlyle looked at her daughter with concern. "Go to bed, honey. Don't worry about Jamie. You did the right thing. He'll be fine."

Gillian bowed her head. Locked up inside her was a torrent of hurt and desolation waiting to pour out. She loved her mother. And the two of them were very close.

But some things were too painful for words. "I know, Mama. But it's still hard." She stood up, feeling shattered... lost. "Good night. I'm sorry I had to wake you."

Doreen followed her down the hall, pausing in her bedroom doorway. "I can go in late. They'll understand." She stopped suddenly, her expression arrested. "How did you get home tonight? Didn't Devlyn bring you? Did he see Jamie?"

Gillian lied, unable to admit to her own mother that the man she had fallen in love with was a spineless, uncaring jerk. "Devlyn had already driven away. He didn't know Jamie was there."

Turning away, she entered her bedroom, shut the door, climbed into bed and cried herself to sleep.

As the hours passed, she mourned. How could she have been so wrong about Devlyn? Evidently the old maxim was true. Love made you blind.

She told herself she hadn't really fallen in love with him. How could she? How was it possible to have any tender feelings at all for a man who was soulless...lacking in compassion, utterly hard and self-centered?

The sex they had shared was nothing but carnal lust. Remembering the feel of his sure hands on her body was a mistake. Because even knowing what she knew now, she still craved his touch.

* * *

Gradually, sanity returned, overriding the huge blanket of self-pity under which she wallowed. Perhaps she was painfully self-deceptive…engulfed in circuitous rationalizations, but she began to be convinced that something was terribly wrong with her assessment of what had happened the night of the carnival.

She *knew* Devlyn, she really did. First as a child and a young adult from a distance, and now as a grown man with strengths and failings just like every other human being. He had helped her when she needed it…he had helped other women in his past, even those who didn't deserve his generosity.

Devlyn was kind and decent and caring. He was not a man who turned his back on those who suffered. So why Jamie? It didn't make sense. Because of that conundrum, on Tuesday morning, she dragged herself out of the doldrums, dressed in a simple long-sleeve jersey wrap dress in forest green and drove up to the castle.

Annalise opened the front door, clearly prepared to leave the premises. Her suitcases were stacked in a pile, ready to be loaded into a car. "What are you doing here?" she asked, her expression less than welcoming.

"I need to see Devlyn. I've finished all the paperwork he gave me, but it has to be signed." She clutched the pile of folders to her chest. "Will you please tell me how to find him?"

Annalise frowned. "I thought you went with him to Atlanta."

"No."

The two women stared at each other. Annalise frowned. "He told me at the carnival Friday night that he was taking you home with him for a romantic getaway. I said it was a bad idea."

"Well, goody for you. Obviously he listened." Gillian felt

the hot sting of tears and the urge to run. But something held her feet in place. Some inexplicable certainty that Devlyn was in crisis. Friday night, standing on her front porch, he had seemed like a walking dead man. And she didn't know why. "Did you actually see him Saturday morning before he left?"

"He was gone before any of us woke up. What happened? What did you do to him?" Now Annalise was alarmed, which made no sense, because clearly a man like Devlyn was not a fragile flower in need of protection, especially from his sister.

"Nothing."

"That's a lie. He wouldn't have left without saying goodbye to all of us unless he was deep into *I've-got-a-new-woman-to-sleep-with* mode."

"So he does this often?"

"What do you think? He's one of the richest men in the world. He's handsome and charming and sexy as hell. I think you know the answer to that."

The confirmation hurt. "Things are different now," Gillian said, trying to make herself believe it. "Something happened. We had a fight. And I don't have time to explain, but I think Devlyn needs me. Please, Annalise." The tears spilled over. "I care about him. And that may not make any difference to you or to him, but at least let me make sure he's okay. He was upset when he left. Not angry, or pissed off…more like frozen, wounded. You know he shuts people out."

Annalise stared at her. "God, I hope you're telling me the truth. 'Cause if not, he'll never forgive me for what I'm about to do."

Gillian placed the folders on a side table and ran her hands up and down her arms, trying to still the shivers of dread. "What do you mean?"

"I'm going to take you to him. On the jet, since Devlyn drove. And you'd better fix whatever's wrong, or I'll make your life hell."

Oddly, Annalise's scowling threat made Gillian want to smile. Devlyn's sister was a tigress, a fierce protector of those she loved. "If he doesn't want me there, I'll go home," Gillian said calmly, lying through her teeth. The only way she would leave Atlanta was if Devlyn made her believe, beyond the shadow of a doubt, that he was perfectly okay and that he had no feelings for her at all.

His cold, irrational reaction to Jamie had to be a symptom of something deeper, darker. And whatever that *something* was, it had caused him to give up the possibility of having a wife and a family. Gillian was willing to stake her pride and her future on it.

It was possible he would throw her out. Or worse, look at her with pity. It *could* play out that way. In which case, Gillian was setting herself up for more heartache. But some things were worth fighting for, and Devlyn Wolff was at the top of Gillian's list, even if he could never give her the family she wanted.

Annalise exhibited single-minded determination once she was convinced about a course of action. After a quick stop at the foot of the mountain for Gillian to throw a few things in a suitcase, they were off. The Wolff family jet sat on a narrow runway at a tiny regional airport. In Annalise's wake, Gillian boarded, feeling as if she was going to her doom… in more ways than one.

The luxury and comfort of the flight couldn't outweigh her distress, even with medication. Nerves and anxiety reduced her to a panicked mess. She barely held herself together. At last, she slept.

Annalise woke her up when they landed in Atlanta. "We're here. The limo is waiting. After I drop you off, I'm headed back to Charlottesville."

Gillian sat up and fumbled in her purse for a comb. "How

do I get in?" They were both making the silent assumption that her assault on Devlyn had to be surreptitious.

As they made the move from the jet to the car, Annalise handed her two items. "The key card is for the penthouse elevator. The actual key opens Devlyn's door. I stay here with him occasionally. I'll introduce you to the doorman when we get there so he won't give you any trouble."

Gillian sat back, mind numb, and surveyed the streets of Atlanta as the chauffeur whisked his passengers along, their tired bodies cradled in soft leather seats. She had never been to the sprawling city, and she fell in love with its tree-lined charm and spectacular skyline. Annalise was silent as well, brooding, her eyes fixed on the scenery.

Devlyn's home sat atop a sleek, super-sophisticated building in the heart of Buckhead, one of Atlanta's premier districts. High-end stores and specialty shops jostled cheek by jowl with unique restaurants and art galleries. Any other time, Gillian would have felt the urge to explore. Today all she could think about was whether she had made a terrible mistake.

Annalise was true to her word. After a brief conversation with a uniformed attendant, she eyed Gillian steadily. "I love my brother," she said. Her chin wobbled. "Don't give up on him."

For a moment, it seemed as if the two women might hug. But Gillian was too frazzled and Annalise too prickly. "I'll do my best."

Then Annalise was gone, and it was all up to Gillian. She crossed the swanky atrium and stopped in front of the nearest gold-door elevator. Thankfully, it was empty. She stepped inside, her knees shaky, and inserted the key card. The rapid *whoosh* as the small, mirrored box rose upward was not at all helpful to the state of her stomach.

With a quiet *ding* she reached her destination. In the hushed, empty foyer, Devlyn's was the only door.

She took out the key, and her hand froze, hovering over the doorknob. What if he had a woman inside? What if he was entertaining? Was she about to humiliate herself beyond reason?

Some invisible force urged her forward, despite her misgivings. Sliding the key into the keyhole, she turned the knob. It opened easily. She slipped inside and closed the door behind her.

For a long moment, she simply took stock. Immediately in front of her sat an elegant narrow table against a wall. On it, a pot of mauve orchids bloomed gracefully. Devlyn's keys lay beside the flowers, tossed carelessly on the polished surface. Gillian recognized the keychain. It was sterling silver, fashioned in the head of a wolf…which meant that, theoretically, the Wolff was home. Setting her purse and suitcase beneath the table, she went in search of the man she had come to confront.

The condo had to be at least several thousand square feet in size. As she rounded the wall, she sucked in a breath of appreciation. Opposite her, across a sea of plush, sand-colored carpet, an entire expanse of glass provided a magnificent view out over the heart of the city.

The elegant space, clearly meant for entertaining, was furnished with an array of sofas and armchairs. But the room was empty.

With a wing of the apartment to the left and right, Gillian was stymied. She listened intently, but could hear no sound from any corner. Her first guess turned out to be wrong. She discovered an amazing kitchen and a trio of guest rooms, each with its own bathroom. But no Devlyn.

As she reversed her steps and headed toward what must be his private quarters on the other side, her heart beat faster. The first door she came to in the hallway was open. She glanced inside and saw a neatly made bed. But on the night-stand was a phone that looked like Devlyn's. Over a chair in the corner was the shirt he had worn to the carnival. But still no sign of him.

Feeling worry mount with every step, she walked on, coming to a stop in the doorway of a large man-cave. A Schwarzenegger movie flickered silently on the far wall. The enormous flat-screen TV dominated the room. But it couldn't hold Gillian's attention. Because stretched out on a long leather sofa, dead to the world, lay Devlyn Wolff.

He was sleeping on his back. At first glance, she saw that he hadn't shaved since he left her standing on her mother's porch. His hair was wet, indicating a recent shower. He was naked but for a white towel tied loosely around his narrow hips. His sex made a noticeable mound beneath the cloth.

The sight of him paradoxically soothed and alarmed her. He was a beautiful man. His head, arms and torso were per-fectly proportioned, his big, hair-dusted thighs made to cra-dle a woman's body. She approached him quietly, her shoes making no sound at all on the carpet that matched the floor-ing in the living room. It wouldn't have mattered in any case. Devlyn slept deeply, his heavy slumber aided no doubt by the contents of the many liquor bottles strewn over the surface of the coffee table.

A trio of empty pizza boxes on the floor was the only sign that his uncharacteristic bender had at least included food. Had he simply gone to ground, hiding out from humanity? Did the office in Atlanta think he was on Wolff Mountain? The reverse had certainly been true according to Annalise. Nudging aside the pile of cardboard with her foot, Gillian sat down on the table.

Praying that she was doing the right thing, she put her hand on his knee. "Wake up, Devlyn."

Twenty

Devlyn groaned, wondering why in the hell the pizza boy was bothering him. Devlyn had left a fifty on the table in the entranceway. That was a damned good tip.

"Devlyn. Look at me."

Opening his eyes was a mistake. The light pierced his skull with agonizing precision. Lord in heaven. He squinted, trying to clear his vision. There, not two feet away, sat the woman who was responsible for his current condition. Or maybe she was a dream. He'd had plenty of those in the last few days. A few of them the kind that left him spent and mentally aching for something beyond his grasp.

"Go away," he muttered. "You're not real." He closed his eyes.

Those same cool fingers nudged his kneecap, making the hair on his legs rise with gooseflesh. "I've come a long way to see you, Devlyn. I need you to sit up."

Most of the time her strict schoolmarm voice turned him

on. Today it was just aggravating. "No one invited you. If you're real, get out."

He put his hands on the sides of his head, groaning. Getting drunk was a stupid stunt, one he'd not indulged in since he was a kid in college. And getting drunk over a *woman* was even dumber. Even if the woman did have big brown eyes and a mouth that could tempt a saint.

When he thought he could bear it, he opened his eyes again. Gillian was still there. She stared at him unblinking. "You want to talk about it?"

"There's nothing to say. If you're not going to leave, I'm going to have sex with you."

She blinked once. "Okay."

Her calm acceptance caught him off guard. "I'm serious," he said, not sure he could walk across the room, much less perform sexually.

"I'll do whatever you want, Devlyn," she said quietly. "But I won't leave."

He sat up, fighting nausea. He must have looked like hell, because she took pity on him. "Get dressed," she said. "I'll go make coffee."

"Whatever." He felt no compunction about his boorish behavior. No one asked her to barge in.

She was gone for fifteen minutes. When she came back bearing a tray with a carafe and two mugs, the smell alone almost made him cry uncle. But not quite. He hadn't shown weakness to a woman in years, and he wouldn't start now.

Gillian paused in the doorway, assessing the fact that he was still wearing a towel. "Aren't you cold?"

"No." God, no. Not with Gillian approaching him wearing a dress that made the most of her modest curves. He stood, determined to face her like a man. Beneath the towel, his sex flexed and lengthened.

She noticed. And almost bobbled the glassware as she set

down the tray. When she straightened, he made himself wait five seconds to grab a cup of the steaming, fragrant lifeline. As he sipped it, he stared at her over the rim. "I see you're still here."

"Yes. I was worried about you."

He shrugged, burning his throat with the speed at which he gulped the hot liquid. "As you can see, I'm fine."

"Are you, Devlyn? Are you really? Because from where I'm standing, you don't look fine at all."

He finished the coffee, set the cup on the table and removed the towel with a flick of his wrist. "Sofa or bedroom. You pick." The silent compassion in her gaze raked his soul like a thousand razor blades. He hadn't asked her to care...didn't want her to. "So you're just going to let me screw you?" he said. "After I distinctly heard you say not to ever come back."

"I didn't understand."

"And now you do?"

"Not really...no. But I realize that something in your past has hurt you deeply. And I want you to know that I'm sorry. Sorry for telling you not to come back. Sorry I didn't try to see things from your perspective."

"Jesus, Gillian. What kind of woman lets a man treat her like crap and comes back for more?" He heard the words leave his mouth and was appalled. But she was ripping away at layers of armor he had honed by fire over the years, and her empathy was starkly, agonizingly painful.

"The kind of woman who might be in love with you." A single tear trickled down her pale cheek, increasing his pain. Her gaze was wounded, but steady.

Fury erupted, refusing to acknowledge that his heart was bleeding. "Take off your dress." If he pushed her hard enough, surely she would leave.

She stared at him for long seconds. Then, after stepping out of her low-heeled pumps, she lifted the dress over her head and tossed it on the nearest chair. Without panty hose or a slip, the only things left were her modest bra and underpants.

Her arms hung at her sides. Though he had known her to blush on more than one occasion, at the moment, she appeared completely self-assured. Which pissed him off even more.

He was acting like a jerk. Couldn't she see that?

"You're not done." He infused the words with determination. "I want you naked."

The brief seconds that passed while watching her slide the bra down her arms and unhook it were torture. When she pushed her simple cotton briefs down her legs and stepped out of them, a groan escaped him.

Since his feet appeared to be nailed to the floor, Gillian walked to where he stood. She held out her arms, embraced him and cradled his head on her shoulder. "I could love you, Devlyn, very easily." Soft fingers feathered through his hair.

He felt himself shudder inside, a huge quaking rift that he couldn't acknowledge, dared not examine. Thirty seconds passed. Then thirty more. With her smooth, soft body pressed to his—her tenderness wrapped around him like a cloud—he almost cracked.

But the consequences were too terrible to contemplate. He jerked out of her arms, blind with a befuddled rage. "I don't want you to," he said. A piercing headache squeezed his temples. He bent and swiped his arm across the coffee table, sending heavy glass bottles flying.

Gillian watched him, arms wrapped around her waist, her eyes tragic.

He took her wrist, drawing her forward. "Last chance."

Any second now, she would slap his face...run out of the room.

But she didn't. Instead, she lay down gracefully on the sofa, her hand outstretched. "It's okay, Devlyn. Everything's okay. I'm here."

The pain in his head had escaped and now filled his entire body. Seeing her like this was more than he could bear. With a roar of confusion, he moved on top of her, fit himself to her core and pushed. Gillian gasped softly, but otherwise was silent. Her legs wrapped around his waist, and she held him tightly as he lunged into her once…twice…three times. He moaned a curse, filling her with his seed.

In the aftermath, he felt tears sting his eyes.

His stomach curled in revulsion. What had he done? Raining kisses of apology over her face and throat, he waited for her to reject him, to curse him.

Instead, she kissed him back, wrapping her fists in his hair and pulling him closer to her. Chest to chest. Breath to breath.

Aching remorse and regret flailed him. It wasn't her fault the situation was untenable. Breaking the kiss suddenly, he lifted himself off her and scooped her into his arms. His bedroom, mere steps away, seemed impossibly far. But he made it somehow.

Striding to the huge bed, he flung back the covers with one hand and laid her gently on the black silk sheets. He slid in beside her. "I'm sorry, Gillian. I'm so sorry."

She put a hand on his chin, forcing him to look into her eyes, eyes that were huge and troubled, but not condemnatory. "Make love to me," she pleaded. "Let me have all of you."

What she asked was dangerous and almost impossible. But he wanted to try. The yearning to drown in her forgiveness was unbearable. "Close your eyes," he muttered.

Gillian obeyed, wondering if he was capable of giving her what she needed…what they *both* needed. Total honesty. Complete intimacy. His trust.

She flinched when she felt the slightly rough stroke of his tongue on her nipples. He loved them one at a time, licking and sucking and pulling each one between his teeth and biting gently.

The erotic punishment filled her belly with a million butterflies and made her legs part restlessly, her body aching for that part of him that could offer her release.

Her fingernails scored his back involuntarily as fire shot though her pelvis and made her moan. It was too much and not enough.

"I want *you*," she begged. "Please. I can't wait."

He pushed her higher and higher, past the point of insanity, drawing out each teasing caress until she was desperate for the climax that hovered just out of reach. She fought wildly, trying to force him into her. But he was heavy and heartbreakingly tender.

When she knew that she was absolutely going to explode in frustration, he entered her. A smooth, determined, thorough penetration. Her breath lodged in her throat. Her heart stopped. Every cell in her body trembled on the cusp of a terrible, wonderful, unprecedented orgasm.

"Devlyn…" It was a whisper, a plea, a prayer.

He answered her instantly, gruffly. "Now, baby." Withdrawing completely, he slammed into her with a forceful thrust that smashed through some unseen barrier and sent her careening into bliss.

His big, hard body trembled violently as he shouted her name, pistoning his hips in his own out-of-control, shuddering release.

Gillian tried to pin down a single emotion but could not. Joy. Fear. Worry. Momentary contentment.

What was he thinking? Still on top of her, his sweat-dampened body was a deadweight. The time of reckoning had come.

"Please tell me, Devlyn. Why did you run away from Jamie?"

He didn't challenge her description of his actions. But he rolled to his back and slung an arm over his eyes. "He was me," he muttered.

She frowned, drawing the sheet up to her throat and holding it in a death grip. "I don't know what you mean." But the sick feeling in her stomach told her that she did.

Devlyn's chest heaved. Still he didn't look at her. "When I was Jamie's age, my mother had been slapping me around for a couple of years."

The flat, almost desolate intonation in his voice hurt something in Gillian's chest. Though she couldn't think of a single response to his horrific statement, he kept talking.

"When she drank, she liked to hit. No broken bones, no weapon but the back of her hand. I was the oldest, and I had to protect Larkin and Annalise. In truth, I don't know if she would have gone after them anyway. I seemed to inspire her fury."

He rolled out of bed suddenly and paced. "She would scream at me and back me into a corner. My father never knew, or so he says. He was working long hours away from the house."

"Oh, God, Devlyn." He didn't seem to hear her.

"Sometimes she used lit cigarettes on me. That was the worst." Unconsciously, it seemed, he rubbed a series of tiny, almost unnoticeable scars at his hip. "I never cried out. I didn't want my brother and sister to come running."

Gillian sat up, shaking uncontrollably. The fact that Devlyn was naked made his terrible monotone even worse. She had forced him to tell her this awful secret. She had stripped him bare.

She didn't want to hear any more, but it was too late to staunch the flow of ragged, hoarse words.

His hands fisted at his hips. The cords in his neck stood out in relief. "It all happened before Wolff Mountain. Dad and Uncle Vic were close, even then. Built houses side by side in a ritzy neighborhood in Charlottesville. Sometimes if it got too bad, I would run next door to Aunt Laura. She would tend to me, cry over me. I didn't understand then or later why she didn't try to stop it. But she was young…maybe scared. I don't know."

"And Annalise and Larkin?"

"Sometimes late at night they would climb into my bed and curl up against me. They felt helpless…like I did."

She swallowed. "So that day in the cave when you said you hated her and you were glad she was gone, you meant it."

For the first time, his gaze locked with hers, his eyes burning dark in an ashen face. "I did. And you looked at me like I was a monster. I didn't blame you. What kind of kid wants his mother to die?"

"Devlyn, I—"

He held up a hand, cutting her off. "I know what I am, Gillian. I'm damaged goods. And someone like you deserves a whole man, the kind of man who can make promises to you and keep them."

"Nothing that happened was your fault. Surely you know that."

He shrugged. "I saw a counselor…in college. All the Wolff kids studied under assumed names, because Dad and Uncle Vic were afraid we'd be kidnapped like our mothers had been. Since no one knew who I really was, there was no risk of anyone finding out about the Wolff family's dirty secrets."

"What did the counselor say?"

"That I had turned into a fine young man, and that I needed to put the past behind me."

Gillian said a word that she had never used out loud in her life. "That's criminal. You can't pretend abuse never happened."

"A lot of people do that. They literally block it out. It's a coping mechanism."

"But you couldn't do that."

"Maybe if she hadn't died. Maybe if I hadn't wished her dead a million times."

"Devlyn, you were a baby. And she hurt you. A mother's sacred duty is to protect her children, but she failed you."

"Who knows why she did what she did. But the counselor was right in a way. I *did* have to put it behind me and move on. And I have."

"How? How can you say that, when I see you standing in front of me bleeding and hurt…after all these years?"

His bleak smile chilled her soul. "I'm lucky. My scars are mostly on the inside. And I had a solid family to help me get through the aftermath of the kidnappings. That kid, Jamie? He's got nothing but poverty and a long road to nowhere."

Gillian got out of bed clumsily, the sheet wrapped toga-style around her. Devlyn didn't move as she approached him. Like a stone statue, he was rigid, immovable.

She stood toe-to-toe with him, searching his face. "That's not all, is it? Why can't you let me into your life for more than a casual fling? I think you care about me, somehow… at some level. But why is that so threatening?"

Even the flame of suffering in his eyes flickered out. Now he was nothing but a weary shell of a man. "You're the kind of woman who needs a home and a family. I can only break your heart, because I don't have one. I don't want to have one. After I lost my virginity—after I was so scared that I had gotten a married woman pregnant—it dawned on me that a vindictive husband would have been the least of my worries."

"How?"

"Child abuse is cyclical in nature. I'd cut off my arm before I would allow any child of mine to run that risk. So you're wasting your time, Gillian. Don't love me. Because I can't love you back."

"Can't? Or won't?"

He stared down at her, perhaps unaware of the longing etched on his face. "Doesn't really matter, does it?"

"I think it does. Wake up, Devlyn. Smell the coffee. You just made love to me twice. Without protection."

He went white. And for the first time she understood that the man whose home she'd invaded had been so traumatized by his confrontation with Jamie, that he had literally been defenseless when she forced a showdown.

Oh, Lordy. She straightened her shoulders. "If I am pregnant, I expect you to marry me." She said it calmly, though her emotions were anything but. Did she really have the guts to blackmail a Wolff?

Hell, yes. She was fighting for their future.

The muscles in his throat worked, betraying his agitation. "That monster is still inside me," he croaked. "I wanted my mother to die. Don't you understand that?"

Here it was. The final truth. "I do, Devlyn. I do. But I also believe that you loved her anyway…didn't you?"

Silence fell, an enormous raw void filled only by two sets of thundering hearts.

Wolffs didn't show weakness. And they surely didn't cry. Not as adult men. But when Devlyn broke at last and grabbed her, he held her as if she were the only steady footing in his universe.

Devlyn felt at peace, and marveled at the sensation. The tentative acceptance of healing humbled him. This brave, selfless woman standing clasped in his arms had accomplished the impossible. For one final painful moment he allowed himself to remember his mother's face. Who knew what demons tormented her? Who knew why no one stepped in to protect a little boy?

He would never know. But it was okay.

Feeling like he'd survived a war, he stroked Gillian's silky hair, her soft back, the curve of her ass. "I didn't do it on purpose," he said, his eyes damp.

"Do what?"

Somehow, he'd had the good fortune to dispense with the sheet between them. He'd never felt anything more wonderful than Gillian's naked body against his. "I didn't forget the condoms on purpose, I swear."

She rubbed the small of his back, soothing him, arousing him.

"I believe you."

"Unless my subconscious is a devious son of a bitch."

She chuckled. "Would you mind terribly? If we made a baby today?"

Hearing her say it aloud constricted his throat almost beyond speech. Imagining Gillian, her belly round with his daughter...or son... Dear God. "I wouldn't mind." There was so much more he wanted to say, but the words wouldn't come.

Gillian seemed to understand, her heart more nimble than his, more generous.

Still, he owed her more than cowardice. "I won't let you down, I swear. But you'll call my hand? If you ever see me start to do something to our child..." He stumbled to a halt, the notion unbearable.

She pinched his butt. She actually pinched his butt.

"Don't be ridiculous," she said. "You would never use your strength to harm anyone, especially a child." She took his face in her two hands. "I don't think that, Devlyn. I *know* it."

He saw the absolute confidence in her eyes and nodded, struggling to accept the truth that had eluded him for so long. "I've fallen in love with you, Gillian. In every way there is to love a woman. I didn't know that I could, but you burrowed your way into my life and my heart so quickly I never saw it coming."

Seeing the hesitance on her face was his well-deserved punishment. He had put it there, and it would be up to him to make sure she never doubted him again.

She wrinkled her nose. "You don't have to say that. I know you've been through a lot. But I can wait until you're sure."

He put his hand on her flat abdomen, stepping back to look at her from head to toe. "You're going to be a gorgeous pregnant woman," he said, mentally opening up to the fierce joy that swelled in his chest. "And I can prove that I love you." He picked her up and carried her to the bed, cradling her like infinitely precious treasure.

"How?" Her uncertainty dragged at his heart.

Dropping her unceremoniously and standing back to enjoy the view, he put his hands on his hips. "You're the only woman I've ever had sex with in this condo. And I've lived here a long, long time."

Her eyes narrowed. "You expect me to believe that?"

He lifted one shoulder. "I have intimacy issues. When I slept with women at their houses, I could leave when I wanted to. You're the first girlfriend I ever had who wouldn't take no for an answer."

She turned bright red, looking adorably guilty. "I should probably apologize for that."

He sat on the edge of the bed and put his hand on her ankle, running his hand all the way up to the top of her thigh. Her skin was hot to the touch. "Don't you dare apologize, my feisty little schoolmarm. You saved my life."

Her lashes fluttered closed as he brushed the sensitive folds between her legs. "You were drunk, that's all."

He scooted down in the bed, lifting her ankles to his shoulders, opening her up to his explorations. When he slid two fingers into her moist passage and stroked upward with his thumb, her hips came off the bed. "Devlyn!"

Laughing wickedly, he kissed the place where she glistened, wet and ready for him. "Do you think you're pregnant, Gillian?"

She gasped as he tasted her. "I don't know."

Moving up and over her, he pressed the head of his shaft to the place that was rapidly beginning to feel like home. "Well then, my love, let's hope the third time's a charm."

She sighed, a long, low voluptuous purr that hardened him to the point of pain. "You'll have to give my mother a retirement pension. It would be too weird if she kept working at the castle."

He winced, pausing to glare at her. "Can we please not talk about your mother? Or my father. Or anyone who might happen to be related to either of us? It's putting me off my game."

She dragged down his head for a kiss that was surprisingly erotic for a prim and proper schoolteacher. "Whatever you want, my dear Wolff. Did I ever tell you that triplets run in my family?"

All the air escaped from his lungs in a shell-shocked groan. "Don't even think about it."

Sharp teeth nipped his chin. "All I want to think about is you."

He heard the little gasp that signaled her ultimate pleasure. "Then pay attention, Gillian, because I plan on staying right where I am for the rest of the day."

"Not the night?"

He closed his eyes, thrusting wildly as he climaxed. "That, too," he groaned. "That, too."

* * * * *

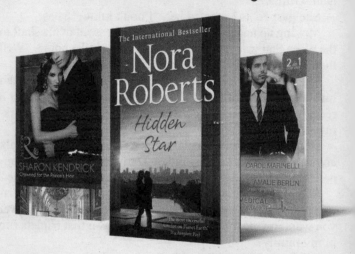

Join Britain's BIGGEST Romance Book Club

50% OFF your first parcel

- **EXCLUSIVE offers** every month
- **FREE delivery direct** to your door
- **NEVER MISS a title**
- **EARN Bonus Book** points

Call Customer Services
0844 844 1358*

or visit
millsandboon.co.uk/subscriptions

* This call will cost you 7 pence per minute plus your phone company's price per minute access charge.

KCB3